MC #1

COMPANY OF SINNERS MC

BAD COMPANY

LISA J HOBMAN

Bad Company
Lisa J Hobman
Copyright Lissa Jay/Lisa J Hobman 2015
First Published by Private Moments Publishing 2015

Second edition published by Lisa J Hobman 2018

Cover art: The Graphics Shed

First Edition/First Printing April 2015 Printed U.S.A.
Second Edition/Second Printing November 2018
Lisa J Hobman

To my very own bearded, tattooed bad boy.

They say matching tattoos are a sign of true love.

So we're sorted chicken pie ;-)

CHAPTER ONE

KELLY

I watched him sleeping.

I'd been doing the same thing for the past week since he was brought in. And with each passing day, my oh-so-unprofessional want for him grew more familiar. His natural, musky, masculine scent infiltrated my senses and I inhaled it deeply, closing my eyes and pulling it in. Memorising it. I opened my eyes and trailed my gaze over his features yet again. Such a handsome face. Dark brown, tousled hair and more than a week's worth of beard growth. I wondered if he was usually clean shaven— although he really did suit the stubble. What would it feel like to run my tongue along his angular jaw line? Trembling, I shook my head to dislodge the erotic thought.

Annie, one of his ICU nurses, had told me that he had the brightest blue eyes she'd ever seen. She only knew that from the times she'd checked his pupils.

Sadly, he hadn't opened his eyes of his own accord yet.

All I knew about him on a personal level was that his name was possibly Cameron Iss. And that was only if the note they'd found with him was actually written *by* him. My job—when he eventually awoke from his coma—was to find out why he'd tried to take his own life. As a woman, I ached to think of the torment he may have gone through to end up in my care. As a newly qualified psychologist, I was looking forward, in a macabre way, to getting inside his head. He would be my first suicide-attempt case. I glanced down to the panic alarm hooked onto my waist-band to ensure it was still there. It was one of the things I'd been informed I should keep with me at all times for my own protec-tion—some patients were known to get a little out of hand. Not that I needed it at that precise moment, but it was always better to be prepared.

The machines around my patient flashed and bleeped. But he lay still. After observing the scar on his forehead, I allowed my gaze to journey to where his long lashes fanned out on his pale, bruised features. Continuing to map his face, I made myself study the NG feeding tube with its medical tape holding it in place on his cheek and then settled my attention on his full mouth. He had those kissable, full lips... well, they would've been if they weren't distorted by the ventilator tube hanging from them.

Good grief, I was being *so* unprofessional. He deserved better.

But he was probably the most handsome—no... handsome just didn't cut it—he was the most stunning, sexy, and sculpted man I could ever recall encountering in all my adult years. Fine lines caused an indentation between his strong brows, indicating to me that he was someone who frowned a lot. Perhaps he was uber serious. Stern. Harsh even. The thought excited me and sent shivers of electricity down my spine. He was dangerous, that much I could tell. The epitome of masculinity. Let's get to the point here, he was the most gorgeous guy I'd ever laid eyes on. I chewed on my lip. As a jolt of sensation throbbed at my clit, I inhaled sharply. Just thinking about what he might be like had me pulsating and needy. But it was wrong and I knew it. Bloody typical—he was in a coma and unattainable thanks to my professional code of ethics.

I sat there a little longer, tablet in hand. I hadn't really focused on the patient record on the screen, and the tablet had gone into sleep mode—just like Cameron. Despite my state of heightened sexual awareness, exhaustion—both mental and physical—was taking its toll on me too. I could've just sat in my office, but the view wasn't quite as good in there. Don't get me wrong, the view from my office in the North Kessock hospital window overlooked the beautiful Kessock Bridge with Inverness in the distance. And although I couldn't see it from my south-facing view, I knew the Black Isle unfolded behind me, and I loved that place. From my office window I could see the sun glinting on the Beauly Firth and watch the boats as they tootled by on the calm estuary waters heading out to sea. But... well, Mr Iss was heart meltingly gorgeous and was rapidly becoming my favourite thing to look at.

The many tattoos covering his arms offered enigmatic clues into his life—possibly. I'd examined them for hours, wondering what they all meant, if anything. Maybe he was just one of those guys who liked ink. But maybe there was some deeper meaning to the numbers, words, and pictures beautifully marking the man's otherwise perfect olive skin.

One in particular grabbed my attention. It was the word Cosmic in ornate script on his forearm. Strange choice. The word was surrounded by stars, and a sultry woman with green eyes and long auburn hair, not unlike my own, was draped across it as if it were a bed. Some tattoos I'd seen before depicted women as slutty, half naked and big breasted, mere objects to be ogled, but this one was very tasteful. Yet it was out of character with the dark, foreboding images that covered his arms. There were some intricate tribal tattoos too that were really quite beautiful if you liked that kind of thing—which I never had... until I started imagining the bold ripple of ink over his muscles as he pushed himself into my flesh.

Judging by the numerous markings he carried on these relatively small areas of visible skin, I was pretty sure he had more ink on the rest of his body. Annie—lucky thing—had the job of bathing him, but it would be completely unprofessional of me to ask such questions about a patient, and so I continued to use my vivid imagination. It's a good thing that my superiors were only psychiatrists and not mind readers, or I'd be fired on the spot.

I was clearly sex starved.

At twenty-six years old I was beginning to wonder if I would ever meet someone who could make me *really feel*. I wanted someone lucid to affect me in the way the oblivious man before me was affecting me. Someone intense, fierce, dangerous, carnal. Someone who would take control of my body as well as my heart. My last so-called relationship had been with my university boyfriend, Dermott, but he was never going to be *the one*. The thing between us had ended on quite good terms, considering they had, in fact, ended. We met at med school and no one understood the pressure I was under more than he did. Ironic that it just didn't work out between us, really. We'd kept in touch and occasionally went out for drinks and ended up in bed together at the end of the night. Call us what you will... friends with benefits... fuck buddies... stupid; I've called myself a lot worse. The point is, whatever we may be isn't distracting me from what's important.

The last few years had been taken up with studying, placements, exams, and more studying. All work and no play certainly made Kelly Marie Darrow a dull girl. But I hadn't got to where I was by slacking off.

And for once, I was determined to succeed for *me*. No longer were my efforts a vain attempt to impress a father who'd left and a mother who slept around. This was my career. My life. My independence.

I put down my tablet and jotted a few professional observations in Mr Iss's paper file. There was nothing to report, really. He was still away in dreamland, and my *actual* thoughts and observations wouldn't help his case in any way whatsoever. Deciding I'd wasted enough time in his room, I walked over to his bedside and glanced down at the unconscious man. I wondered how he would feel when he awoke to find he was still alive. Would he be angry? Would he be relieved? What was it about him that touched me on such a personal level? Sighing heavily, I stroked the soft, dark strands of hair back from his forehead; his skin was warm and silky to my tentative fingertips. An overwhelming urge to kiss where I had touched him tugged at my insides and I bent forward, inhaling that familiar scent again. My heart skipped at the mere thought of my lips connecting with him, and the tingle of desire began to tighten my core. I closed my eyes briefly and managed to rein myself in at the last second. Stupid, *stupid* Kelly. What were you thinking?

"Wake up soon... please, Cameron," I whispered before turning and leaving the room. As I closed the door behind me I placed my palm over my thumping heart and wondered what the hell was wrong with me for me to behave in such a way. But there was no doubt about it. Even in his unconscious state he had some kind of hold over me. Knowing that fact both terrified and excited me beyond anything I had ever experienced.

Later that night I arrived back home at my little house on the outskirts of Inverness and wondered how the hell I'd got there. The fact that I didn't remember walking home was a little disconcerting. After clicking on the kettle, I shrugged out of my coat and kicked off my ridiculously uncomfortable shoes.

It had been a strange day to say the least.

The appointments I'd had were a mixed bag—nothing too complex, but I was exhausted nonetheless. Cases of anxiety and OCD were so very interesting, and I relished the thought of helping the people I worked with. Still, the stress of taking on board someone else's troubles was an occupational hazard, and although I was trained to remain impartial, I couldn't help but think outside of work about some of the people I encountered. My mind refused to switch off, and I hoped that this was only a new-doctor issue. But I somehow doubted that.

My eyes were heavy, and every muscle in my body ached as if I'd done a workout with ten-kilo kettle bells. Once my camomile tea was made, I picked up the steaming mug of calmness and slumped onto the sofa. Placing my drink on the coffee table, I rubbed at my tired, sore feet and mentally chastised myself—why I'd chosen three-inch heels today was beyond me. Many hours after that rash decision, and my feet were protesting vehemently. No woman in her right mind would wear such inappropriate footwear when she spent a good deal of time standing and walking around a sprawling hospital. Thinking back to the morning when I'd dressed, I realised I must've done so in a daze —or more to the point, a kind of Cameron-fuelled fog of lusty thoughts.

I reached over and flicked on my iPod. I didn't bother to look for a track I wanted to hear and instead settled for random play. There were so many songs on there that I had no clue what to expect. The intro to "Breathe You In" by Stabbing Westward floated from the speakers and as I leaned back on the sofa my thoughts travelled back to Cameron Iss. His case was so very intriguing. He'd been found near Ben Nevis by a group of walkers and was wearing jeans, black T-shirt, and a sleeveless black leather biker's waistcoat that looked like a jacket with the sleeves removed. He was slumped by a tree on a well-known walker's trail. But he certainly wasn't dressed for walking, considering the October temperature. All that was found with him was a suicide note and an iPod loaded full of what I presumed to be his favourite songs, although I was yet to listen to it. It was all rather peculiar and mysterious to say the least.

The note was another conundrum. I'd read it so many times,

looking for clues as to the guy's true identity, that I'd memorised it...

To whoever finds my body.

I'm sorry to do this to you. To cause you this upset. If I'd had any other way, believe me I would've gone down that road.

But it's all too much. I can't go on like this anymore. There comes a point in life where you just have to admit defeat. Admit that you've done all you can. But that there are some things you just can't make amends for. I'm done trying now. Done with the pain. Done with the bad memories.

Please tell Rosa I'm sorry but I had no other choice. It's my time, that's all.

Cameron Iss

I was willing him to wake up. I wanted to find out what had driven him to this. What situation had occurred that made him feel he had 'no other choice'?

And who was Rosa?

The phone rang. Ugh! I just want to be left alone. Grabbing the receiver, I answered without enthusiasm. "Hello?"

"Kelly? Kelly it's me. Look... I was wondering if you'd like to meet up for a drink maybe?"

Dermott Irons—my dirty little secret.

Handsome. *Very* handsome. To describe him in one sentence... Well spoken, English, around six two, clean shaven, dirty blond hair, and green eyes. He'd become a surgeon and, at twenty-seven, was already doing very well for himself. The sex between us had always been good, which is why I stayed in touch with him. I loved the release that sex gave me and knew that I could trust Dermott with my body *and* my safety. Neither of us had the time or inclination to invest in a relationship, which made us quite compatible in a bizarre sort of way. But we both knew where the arbitrary line in the sand was and we knew neither of us would choose to cross it.

Not again.

"Hi, Dermott. Sorry, I'm a little pushed out schedule-wise right now. Maybe some other time."

"Come on, Kelly. Surely you've got time for an old friend in between your crazies?"

Anger spiked within me at his choice of words. No one, but no one insulted my patients.

"*Don't* call them that, Dermott. I mean it. There's no need to be such a fucking prick."

"Ah, there she is. My feisty sex kitten. I was only winding you up, you know. I knew you'd bite. Come on, it was a bit of fun, that's all. What do you say about that drink?"

"Arsehole," I mumbled down the line as I examined my shabby fingernails. "Like I said, I'm busy."

"You're not busy right now. I'm down the street at Johnny Foxes. Come for one drink. Just one? *Please*?"

I could tell he was pouting and my resolve weakened. I couldn't help but smile. The fact that I hadn't been out for such a long time and that deep down I knew it'd probably do me good niggled at me. But I had to work the following day too.

Sighing heavily, I rolled my eyes. "One drink. Just *one*."

"Great. See you in ten."

I hung up and finished my tea. There was no way I'd be seeing him in ten—I needed to shower and change. Dragging myself from the comfort of my old couch, I trudged to the bathroom. The shower temperature was permanently turned up as high as I could stand it, and I switched it to the on position. Stripping out of my clothes, I caught sight of myself in the bathroom mirror before the steam distorted the image. I looked tired. The dark circles under my eyes were becoming a bit of a trademark. Maybe I was overdue a facial and some pampering. My nails were definitely in need of some TLC.

I decided that a call to my best friend, Esme, at some point soon was in order. She and I had talked about trying out the new beauty salon in the town centre, and boy did I need it.

Once I was showered and dried, I picked out a pair of dark jeans and a pretty teal-coloured top with spaghetti straps. I quickly blasted my long auburn tresses with the hair dryer and decided on a shaggy, can't-be-arsed look. It was only Dermott after all. He needed no encouragement where I was concerned. But crazy as it sounds, he was a decent human being when he wasn't trying to get in my knickers.

We sat in the pub and one drink led to another... and then another. I should've known this of old. My resolve was weak and I always gave in. Eventually, when I was feeling rather tipsy and giggling like a teenager, we made our way back to my house. As soon as we got through the front door, he pulled me into his body with one arm and slipped the other hand inside the front of my jeans.

"I know it's late and you have work, but hell, I want to fuck you," he mumbled as he nuzzled at my neck.

For a moment I remembered Cameron Iss and almost backed away. But the code of ethics kicked in and said Dermott was *exactly* what I needed in order to drive these unprofessional thoughts from my mind. So I pulled Dermott closer.

Shivers travelled down my spine, spiking at the junction of my thighs, and I moaned as he continued his delicious assault; his fingers alternately circling my clit and dipping into my entrance, making me wet. I tugged at his long sleeved T-shirt and he released me long enough to let me remove it and discard it on the floor. Smoothing my hands down his toned, muscular chest, my fingers found the buttons on his jeans and I began to release them one by one. All inhibitions had gone and I was in a desire-fuelled fog.

He slipped his hands inside my top and freed my breasts from their lace covering, toying with the sensitive flesh where it peaked, making me moan again at the sensations taking over my body.

Stepping back, I released myself from his grip and gazed into his lust-filled green eyes. "Come with me," I whispered as I took his hand and led him along the hallway and up the stairs to my bedroom. Once inside I pulled off the teal top I was wearing and watched as he slipped his jeans down his thick, strong thighs and stepped out of them. He licked his lips and watched as I slipped my jeans and panties from my body and unclasped my bra. He was devouring me with his gaze and I felt the dampness increase between my legs. I kicked my clothing aside and we stood there in silence observing each other. Only the sound of our ragged breathing could be heard. Anticipation hung heavily in the air.

Keeping my eyes on his, I stepped backwards until my thighs hit the softness of my fake fur throw. I lowered my body to the bed and lay on my back propped up on my elbows and parted my thighs in a brazen invitation to him. His rigid cock flinched as he prowled across the room and loomed over me. He dropped his knees to the bed and his mouth found mine in an aggressive exchange that drew the breath from my body, and as he entered me in one deep thrust, my head rolled back. He began to move, and my eyes drifted closed as I relished the sensations he created. It wasn't long before the tension inside my pussy was building and I moved my hips in perfect rhythm with his to find the friction I desperately needed.

Slipping my hands down his smooth skin, I grasped his tight arse and imagined the tattoos on his bulky, muscular arms. His deep thrusts driving me toward my delicious release. I trailed my nails down his back and tried to imagine the tattoos there too. He sucked on my neck, and my nipples grazed against his chest, making me moan and dig my nails into his firm flesh. Keeping my eyes closed, I could picture his blue eyes peering down at me as he drove his cock deeper; his shaggy dark hair falling forward as he ground his pubic bone into my clit.

I gasped and my eyes sprang open as I realised what I was doing. I was imagining Cameron Iss. Oh shit! In my mind, it was Cameron fucking me towards ecstasy, *not* Dermott.

I fixed my eyes on Dermott in a bid to push the errant fantasy away, but as the pleasure built, I could no longer fight the need and my eyelids fluttered closed. His mouth closed around my nipple and he bit down lightly, causing the vivid images to catch alight in me again. And as soon as that happened, it was Cameron Iss above me and inside me once again. In my mind's eye I watched Cameron's jaw tick as he clenched it, apparently fighting his own climax, ensuring my release happened first.

One final thrust hit my clit head-on, triggering the most wonderful shock waves throughout my whole body. I cried out incoherently as I clung on to the shoulders of the man inside of me, my pussy clenching around him in the most delicious way. He growled his own orgasm and the thing that brought me back down to earth was the cry of "Fucking sweetness!" Dermott's usual orgasm induced endearment. After a few moments of resting his weight on top of me and catching his breath, he withdrew and left the room. I heard water running in the bathroom as I sat, pulled the covers up over me and drew my knees up to my chest. The inappropriateness of my heady fantasy seeped into my bones.

Breathing heavily, Dermott returned and sat beside me. He reached out and stroked my cheek. "Kelly... is everything okay? Did I hurt you?"

I shook my head. "No, no, nothing like that. I think... I think I'm just tired," I lied.

"Are you sure? I mean, I would never force you—"

I reached out and placed my fingers over his lips as guilt spiked in my stomach. "No, honestly, I'm fine. You did nothing wrong. I think I'm just worn out. I'm finding it hard to... you know... concentrate. I'm so sorry."

He pulled me into an embrace. "Hey, don't apologise, darling. I totally understand. No one understands the pressures of your job more than me, eh?"

I needed to be alone with my thoughts. "Sure. Look, I know

this is really shitty of me but... would you mind if we called it a night? I think maybe I just need to sleep."

He nodded and stood to retrieve his clothing; his erection had lost its rigidity. Laughing lightly, he said, "Yeah, I know when I've been used for sex and I'm no longer needed."

I dropped my head, covered my face with my hand and groaned. "Oh, Dermott, I'm sorry. I'm such a fucking mess."

He stood and pulled his clothes on as even more guilt began to weigh me down. Once fully dressed again, he sat on the bed and squeezed my knee through the duvet. I lifted my head and was greeted by his warm smile. "I'm only messing with you. I prefer my own bed anyway. And I might just help myself to round two when I'm there. I've got a good imagination." He raised his eyebrows and I giggled, much to my chagrin.

I hated giggly women.

He kissed the top of my head. "Nighty night, sexy. Sleep well and don't work too hard."

"Bye, Dermott," I replied, feeling relieved. He let himself out and I flopped back on my bed with my hands covering my face.

What the hell was wrong with me?

CHAPTER TWO

CAMERON

The light in the room hurt my eyes as they blinked open. *Fuck me, it's bright in here.* I tried to look around but my head seemed fixed in place. *Wait a minute... am I dead?* Panic washed over me. I felt my heart thudding rapidly at my ribs and my breathing quicken. A bleeping sound mirrored the speed of my heart, but I couldn't figure out what the significance was. The most ridiculous scenarios rampaged around my brain.

1) I was dead and in some kind of holding room.

2) I was alive and being experimented on by aliens.

3) I was dreaming and I'd wake up any minute now...

I tried to speak but a strange gurgling noise was all that I managed to utter. My throat was so dry and sore. A middle-aged woman appeared in my line of sight.

"H-hi... am I... am I *dead*?" I eventually croaked at her. She was wearing all white. Some kind of uniform?

"Hello, handsome. It's good to see you." She hovered over me, doing something with her hands I couldn't see. "No, you're very much alive, and I'm Annie. I'm the nurse who's been looking after you. I'll get the doctor to come and have a word with you in a wee while. Don't you worry though. You're being well cared for."

Slowly I moved my head through the stiffness of my neck and watched as she began to tidy up a piece of machinery to the side of me that had a tube attached to it. She must have noticed my bewildered expression as she smiled and patted my arm. "Oh, don't worry about this, hon. It's just the ventilator. We disconnected it earlier when you began to show signs of regaining consciousness. You're certainly looking better now than when you were brought in. Your throat may be a little tender for a while, but give it time."

Confusion washed over me. The woman's accent wasn't what I expected. She sounded... *Scottish*. And what did she mean 'when you were brought in?' Brought in *where*, exactly? I wanted to ask but I heard the door close and I was alone again, left with the throbbing in my head and the fog in my mind.

I must've drifted back to sleep, as I found myself waking up again to find a dark-haired man standing over me. He shone a light in my eyes and I flinched.

"Sorry about that, young man. It's a necessary evil. Good to see you awake. How are you feeling? Do you know where you are? Do you have pain anywhere?"

Hmm, another Scot. Weird. And what's with all the fucking questions? "Um... no... no, I feel okay, I think," I rasped with difficulty. Annie had been right about my throat being damn sore.

"Good, good," he muttered as he walked out of view. I heard a scratchy noise which, with its rhythmical sound, I decided must have been a pen on paper. "Feel free to sleep whenever the need takes you. You're going to be weak for a while after your ordeal. You're in the best place, so please don't be concerned at all. The medication in your system will keep taking you under, but it's quite normal."

I heard a door close and the room fell silent. Despite fighting the slumber that threatened, my eyes drifted closed again.

Another period of time must've passed—but I had no idea how long—and I opened my eyes again to find another woman standing over me. This one was stunning. *Seriously fucking stunning.* Long auburn waves pulled back in a ponytail that hung over one shoulder, dark-rimmed glasses, and the most beautiful green eyes I'd ever seen. Fucking *vivid* green. My dick hardened despite my obvious less-than-well state.

There was something eerily familiar about her, but I couldn't place what it was. I didn't think I knew her as such, but it was as if my body did. A series of images of her and I together ran through my mind like a movie on fast-forward. I briefly closed my eyes, trying to grip the images with my mind to see if I *did* know her after all. But almost as soon as the memories appeared, they faded, leaving me feeling more than a little confused.

She smiled down at me. "How are you feeling?" she asked. *Huh? Another Scottish accent.* What was with all the Scots in the US these days?

"Um... I... I'm not sure. W-why am I in here?"

Her brow scrunched. "Well, sir... you were... found unconscious over by Ben Nevis with nothing but a note and an iPod in your pocket.

"Huh?" *What the fuck?* "C-can I have some water? My throat..." I coughed and swallowed past the gravelly sensation.

"Oh, yes, of course." She disappeared for a moment and while she was gone I contemplated what she'd said. *Fucking hearing must be going. I could've sworn she said Ben Nevis.*

The sexy woman returned and pressed a button that tilted my bed up. I glanced around the room, trying to figure out where in the hell I was and why she seemed familiar to me when I didn't recall having any Scottish people in my life. My eyes fell on her again and I watched as she made notes on a file. She wore a black fitted skirt that hugged her hips and the curve of her ass perfectly. The grey blouse she wore was tucked into the waist-band showing off her small waist. *Gorgeous.* My cock throbbed. Whatever the hell's wrong with me, it certainly ain't my libido.

Once I'd gulped down a full cup of water, I asked, "Sorry... I know this is crazy, but... I thought you said I was found by *Ben Nevis.* I'm sure I got that wrong, 'cause that's in Scotland and I'm pretty sure I'm American. So... w-where am I *exactly?*"

She frowned and perched herself on the edge of the bed. As she did, her tight skirt rode up, revealing more of her long, lean legs. "You heard right. You're in hospital in North Kessock at the moment."

Okay, someone is fucking with me here. That's the only reasonable explanation. I raised my head and rubbed my face. "But... I..."

She smiled and cocked her head to the side. "I can tell that this has come as a bit of a shock to you. To be honest, your *accent* has come as a bit of a shock to *me.* You're... as you quite rightly pointed out... American. I wasn't expecting that. Can you tell me your name?"

She wasn't expecting *my* accent? "My name... my name... is... um..." My heart began to race and my palms became clammy. The bleeping of the machine beside me got faster as panic washed over me again and I scrambled around my head trying to acquire that one piece of vital information. *What the fuck is my name? I know I'm an American citizen. But... who the fuck am I?*

She must've seen the fear flashing in my eyes as her brow creased and she briefly pulled her lips in. I could have sworn she closed her eyes for longer than a normal blink. "Please don't worry. You're body has been through quite a trauma. Your memory may come back in time. We just need to be patient."

I met her gaze and widened my eyes until they felt like they may fall out of the sockets. "M-*may* come back? What the fuck? What do you mean it *may* come back?"

She held up her hands. "Please calm down, sir. It won't help you to get worked up." Her voice was soothing and silky, and the more I heard her accent, the more I decided it was incredibly sexy like the rest of her. But I didn't reply. I was too busy wondering what the fuck had happened to make me forget who I was and to wind up in a whole other fucking country.

She broke the silence that hung in the air between us. "Now that you're awake, we'll start working towards finding out who you are and *why* you were found in those particular circumstances. I need to ask you a few questions when you're feeling stronger, is that okay?" I nodded and she proceeded "For now, can I just ask... Do you have any memory at all, however small or insignificant it may seem, of how you got here?"

"To Scotland? None... none at all." That simple fact disturbed me greatly.

She nodded. "Okay. As I said, it may just be the result of the trauma you've experienced. We'll try to get to the bottom of it starting tomorrow. Now... I'm sure you're still tired. The medication you're on will do that to you. But that's fine. Get some rest and I'll be back tomorrow."

"Sure," I muttered as my heart continued to try to make its escape through my ridiculously flimsy hospital gown. I didn't want her to go. I wanted her to lean over me and brush that soft, luscious mouth over my lips, my stomach, my cock.

She smiled at me, slowly, as though she had read my thoughts. And then she walked toward the door. Just before opening it, she turned to me again. "Try not to worry, okay? I'll do my best to help you."

————

Sleep must have come easily to me once again. But I was plagued with bizarre dreams. People's faces that I didn't recognise; violence; blood on my hands; shouting. I awoke with a start to find Nurse Annie at the end of my bed, writing on a chart.

"Good morning, handsome. Your colour's improving and the bruises are fading nicely. Doctor Clayton will be by to see you again soon. He's the gentleman that checked on you yesterday."

Yesterday? Fuck, how long have I been sleeping?

She pressed the button that tilted my bed up again. "Would you like some food? I'm guessing you must feel starved. The nasal gastric feeding tube will only do so much for a strapping laddie like you, and so you really need to start eating." I reached up and touched my nose but couldn't feel anything there. "Oh it's okay, deary, we removed it as you slept." Annie was clearly a kind-hearted soul, and something niggling inside me told me I didn't deserve her kindness.

Why would I feel that way?

As I dropped my hand, I noticed the drip attached to the back of it—and I caught sight of the tribal tattoo sleeve that made its way up my arm from my wrist. A flashback had me remembering being in a black leather chair as a blonde woman with piercings leaned over me, needle gun poised as she worked on the ink. I closed my eyes trying to grip the memory with my mind. I could see the top of the blonde's black lace bra as she worked on me. But that's all I could focus on.

Fuck, I'm some kind of sex-crazed maniac!

I felt heat rise in my cheeks and opened my eyes to meet with Nurse Annie's expectant gaze. "Oh, sure. Food... food would be good. Thank you."

"Scrambled eggs and toast? Haggis, maybe?"

"Just the eggs and toast, thank you, ma'am. I have no clue what haggis even is."

She chuckled at me and shook her head. "Coming right up, handsome." She gave me a little wink as she turned and left my room.

Glancing around, I looked at the other piece of machinery I had been attached to the day before. The ventilator had gone, but the blood pressure contraption with the cuff was still there.

The only equipment I was attached to now was a heart monitor and the drip in my arm. I guessed the contents of the drip was the sleep-inducing drug that had been mentioned a couple times.

A little while later and Annie was back. She removed the drip from my arm and stuck a white Band-Aid over the tender area on the back of my hand. Sliding a table up over my legs, she handed me a plastic fork. The plate of eggs and toast looked like manna from heaven and I damn near wolfed the whole lot down in seconds as Annie sat in a chair in the corner of the room watching. I felt like a fucking museum exhibit and wondered why the hell she felt it necessary to observe my every move. Silently I finished off with a glass of fresh orange juice. The acidity and tang made me squirm a little and Annie laughed.

"Well, you've clearly not lost your appetite, young man. That's very good to see. Doctor Clayton will be with you shortly. And after that, Doctor Darrow will be in too."

My face must've shown the confusion I was feeling at the unfamiliar name.

"Sorry, Doctor Darrow is the psychologist who came to see you yesterday, hon."

"Psychologist? The sex—uh, the... woman with glasses?" *Shit.*

She smirked and raised her eyebrows. "That'll be the one, Kelly is her name, yes. I'll leave you to it, but use the buzzer if you need anything." She left the room again; taking all remnants of my breakfast with her and wheeling the drip stand out too.

God, I was bored. And scared. The fact that all the memories I could muster were weird dreams or maybe flashbacks was frightening. Who was I? Why didn't I know the answer to what should be a simple question?

The door to my room opened and the stern-faced male doctor from the day before walked in. "Good afternoon. How are you feeling today? Any pain?" Either I was experiencing déjà vu or this guy only had one set of fucking questions.

"I'm okay. Apart from the fact that I have no clue who the hell I am or *why* I'm here."

He nodded and continued to the thumb through the chart he'd brought in with him.

"Your blood results are improving. You're making a remarkably fast recovery. Quite astonishing, actually. You'll be moved to the psychiatry ward later today. You'll have your own private room, but they have the appropriately trained staff to deal with someone... in *your* situation."

"My situation? I'm sorry... I'm not crazy. I just have... what do they call it? Memory loss... or amnesia or what the fuck ever."

His face became serious. Apparently my abrasive use of language wasn't to his liking, but I didn't give a fuck. He cleared his throat. "I'm well aware of that, sir, but the circumstances surrounding your arrival here lead us to believe that there's more to your story. It's just a precaution. Doctor Darrow will be able to keep a better watch on you there. The police will also be popping in to see you. We had to notify them of your arrival thanks to the suspicious circumstances. They will have questions for you too, no doubt."

The hairs on the back of my neck stood to attention and my jaw tensed. Okay, so Doctor Sexy would be looking after me. I'd deal with that. But the police? Fuck, why did the mention of them have me on edge? I muttered expletives under my breath and Doctor Clayton responded in a similar way, but I couldn't make out his words. No doubt more complaints about my language. And then he thankfully left the room.

I drifted in and out of sleep for a while until my door opened again and in came two male orderlies. They began to gather up my charts and various other bits of hospital paraphernalia. One of the guys came to the head of my bed.

"Hi there, pal. We're movin' you up to psych. I'll help you into the wheelchair and you get comfy. We'll get you there in a jiffy." I'm pretty sure that's what he said. His accent was the strongest one I'd come across so far. He helped me clamber down from the bed, and I flopped ungracefully into the chair. My legs were so damned weak; I stood there trembling like Bambi on ice. Something tugged at my dick, and I winced. I felt around discreetly and found a catheter.

Fuck!

The orderly threw a pale blue blanket over my legs and stood behind the chair in readiness. The other guy, the quiet one, held the door open as we passed him. He walked beside us as we made our way down the corridor and into the elevator. Once the doors closed, I watched as the numbers flicked up two floors higher than where we'd been before and braced myself for the car to come to a halt. When it did, the doors opened and I was wheeled down a corridor and through some keypad-entry double doors with a sign over them that said Department of Mental Health. Finally we arrived in a side room and the guys helped me into the bed and arranged my blankets around me before leaving me to rest.

The small amount of exercise had completely exhausted me and I barely had time to wonder when I'd see Doc McSexy before my head hit the pillow and my eyes closed.

CHAPTER THREE

KELLY

I was staring into space for around the hundredth time that day when someone knocked on my door.

"Come!" I shouted. Alex Clayton walked in and perched himself on the edge of my desk as he always did when he stopped by. He was my manager and mentor and I had the utmost respect for the man, but his intensity could be a little overwhelming. He was around fifteen years my senior and had a real air of superiority about him, and I had yet to see him smile. It was clear today was not going to be the day he chose to break that mould.

"Your latest patient is now in situ on your ward, Kelly. I trust that you'll wish to see him."

I leaned back in my chair and linked my fingers together. *Oh Alex, you have no idea how much I want to see him... and that's definitely not a good thing.* "Thanks, Alex. How did he seem?" *Apart from incredibly hot, dangerous, and masculine...* I shook my head in case my train of thought escaped through my mouth.

Folding his arms across his chest, he took a deep breath in

through his flared nostrils. "Well, in my opinion I see some aggression there. He likes his colourful language," he said whilst scrunching his nose as if noticing an acrid odour.

I nodded. "Hmm, I see. Has he asked any questions? Made any comments?" *For example, "Is it ethical to take my doctor out on a date?"*

"Only that he doesn't know why he's here or who he is. But I'm guessing you knew that already."

"Yes. That's nothing new. I'll need to spend some time with him trying to discover who he is. And I'm guessing the police will have a million questions too."

"Speaking of which, my secretary contacted the police again. She gave them what information we have, and they ran the name though the UK missing persons databases and nothing came up. They've contacted the FBI in the US since he awoke and we heard his accent. The Scottish police have been in contact with them too and they ran the name by them, but again... nothing. He's clearly not missed, which is strange considering the mention of *Rosa* in the note he had in his possession."

I sighed, trying to allow the frustration to vacate my body. "It begs the question 'Is he all that he seems?' I'll pop my head in before I go home." As I said this, my heart did a funny little skip in my chest. *Oh no... not good.*

Alex stood and made his way to the door. "Okay. But... Kelly, just be careful. There's something about him. I... can't quite put my finger on it, and maybe I'm being overly judgemental—I never did like tattoos—but be careful, okay? Don't spend time alone with him unless absolutely necessary, and make sure you have your personal alarm with you at all times and use it if necessary."

I smiled and nodded my silent agreement. But his warning words sent a cold chill down my spine. For the past few days— since the incident with Dermott—all I'd wanted to do was be alone with Cameron.

Like my subconscious told me before, not good.

Sooo not good.

———

I locked my filing cabinets, grabbed my coat and bag and placed my hand at my waist to feel the alarm was still in place. I chewed on my lip for a moment, toying with the idea of taking Alex's advice; but I never left the building with my alarm and it seemed silly to do so today as I was only popping in briefly on my way out. Deciding that I would simply keep my distance from him and stay by the door, I removed the device and placed it in my desk drawer before locking it. I left my office, closing the door behind me, and with a mixture of excitement and trepidation, I began to walk down the corridor toward Cameron's room. The closer I got to his room, the more my pulse began to race; I considered going back to retrieve the device. My heart thundered in my chest and I had to breathe slowly to calm my jangling nerves. I decided I was being ridiculous and so I knocked lightly on the door and waited to hear his panties-melting voice.

"Yeah, come in," he called in that deliciously deep, gravelly, American intonation. Taking one last long breath, I pushed open the door and stepped inside.

"Hello. How're you feeling today?" I asked with a polite smile.

His mouth curved up at one side slightly and a dimple appeared in his cheek. "I think I'm gonna make a recording of my answer to that damn question... save my energy." His voice had dropped to a sultry whisper and I swear I felt the vibrations of it travel right down my spine and pulse at my clit. His narrowed eyes locked on me with an intense smoulder and for a moment I was unable to speak. I watched as his gaze left mine, travelled down to my chest and back up. My nipples stood to attention and when his eyes were on mine again his mouth curved up into a full-blown, heart-squeezing, pant-inducing smile. He clearly knew he was affecting me and I felt the heat of arousal rise in my cheeks.

I blinked rapidly and cleared my throat. "Sorry, I'm sure you get asked that hourly."

Raising his eyebrows, he laughed lightly. "Ya think?"

I began to relax and thoughts of my alarm became a fuzzy ball at the back of mind as I stepped closer. "So, any more memories coming back to you?" He tilted his head to one side and observed my face intently and I involuntarily reached up and touched my hair. After a few silent moments he rubbed at the stubble on his chin and it made a soft scratching noise that I wanted to replicate with my own fingers. I knotted my hands in front of me as butterflies skittered around inside of me. My question hung in the air between us for what felt like ages, and I found myself stepping towards him again. I was standing close beside his bed now, my gaze fixed on his, like a moth drawn to a glowing light. The lack of alarm at my waist heightened my senses; yet any sense of danger I had was of a purely sexual nature.

"Nope." He eventually huffed sulkily.

After remembering what it was I had asked, I nodded, skimming my gaze over his lips and feeling mine part. "I see. Okay, well, I'm just about to go home for the day, so I'll pop in and see you tomorrow. Get some rest."

He grabbed my arm, and I yelped as he yanked me down so that my face was inches from his. Suddenly the fact that my alarm was sitting in my desk drawer was a huge issue. My breathing became fast and ragged in a fight-or-flight manner, my heart leapt, and I swallowed hard. Anxiety spiked within me and I made another strange little squeak of fear. In the back of my mind I was aware that I was making no attempts to pull away. Strangely the only thought on a loop at that moment was that I liked the fact his fingers could circle my wrist completely and that the slight hint of pain would be so easily soothed by his tongue and lips. *What the hell is wrong with me? I should be screaming, not squeezing my thighs together for friction. This is crazy. This is not me. Or... or is it?*

He growled through clenched teeth, "I'm done resting. I want out of here, sweetheart. You hear me? I need to get out and find out what the fuck is going on. This shit is freaking me out." His stare penetrated me and I suddenly felt naked as his eyes travelled down to my cleavage. The position I was in gave him a great view. He licked his lips and I tried to breathe steadily.

As calmly as I could I told him, "I suggest you let go of my arm, sir. Or I'll be forced to call for security." Damn my voice for coming out so breathy and lustful. *This isn't a game, Kelly.*

He slipped his other hand up to my hip and tingles followed in the wake of his touch. He grunted. "Funny, I don't see that little alarm thing you had yesterday." He must have noticed my eyes widen as he continued with an evil smirk. "I'm guessing that's what it is seeing as you're always checking it's there. And now it's not. You know, I could really take advantage of that fact, now couldn't I?" He gave a dark chuckle and leaned closer still. Closing his eyes for a moment, he inhaled through his nose. Another shiver travelled down my spine as I watched him. I found it strangely erotic that he was inhaling my perfume—and the eager wetness in my panties was equally as disturbing as his actions.

He opened his eyes and whispered, "Fuck, you smell good. I could eat you right up."

I twisted and pulled my wrist, freeing myself from his grip. "I think you should keep those sorts of opinions and comments to yourself, *John Doe,*" I replied with a sneer, feeling slightly guilty for the threat implied in using the name given to unidentified dead bodies. But I needed to distance myself from him emotionally. It was insane to allow the thoughts and urges that had been rampaging through me since I met him.

He laughed in that husky gravel of his. "Ouch, so now I'm John Doe, huh?" He shook his head as his expression changed. Regret replaced the malice that had been there only seconds before. "Look, I'm sorry, okay? I really don't know who the fuck I am." He rubbed his hands over his bearded face and leaned his head back. When he turned to face me, his features had softened. "Forgive me?" he whispered.

Even though my head was screaming at me to not be so utterly stupid and unprofessional, my insides had turned to jelly either through arousal or fear... or maybe a little of both. I nodded. "Forgiven," I breathed.

He closed his eyes again. "Thank you. See you tomorrow, Kelly."

I inhaled sharply. I'd kill Annie for telling him my bloody name.

———

All through my walk home, the image of his face so close to mine and the masculine scent of his skin whirred around my brain. The vividness of his blue irises shot with the slightest hint of silver that I noticed due to being in such close proximity to him. A mixture of anger and arousal crawled through me, and I shuddered against the cold night air. I should have reported the incident immediately. It was so incredibly reckless of me not to go straight to Alex and confirm that his suspicions were, in fact, correct. But what good would it do my patient? Of course Cameron was angry. I'd feel the same if I awoke in hospital in a foreign country thousands of miles from wherever home was. No... he hadn't actually *harmed* me, and as a mental health professional, I recognised that his remorse was genuine; monitoring the situation was the best thing to do. I'd give him the benefit of the doubt... this time.

Once home and through my door, feeling dirty for my misguided fantasies, I rushed to the bathroom, stripped out of my clothes, and turned on the shower. I needed to wash this feeling away. I would have to seriously consider handing him over to another doctor if this continued. My job and potentially my *life* were on the line, judging by his earlier display of aggressive dominance.

After pulling the tie from my hair, I climbed under the cascade of hot water. Grabbing the shower gel—the fragrance of which my patient was so taken by—I squeezed a generous blob onto my palm and began to wash my tense, aching muscles, kneading as I lathered my skin.

As I rubbed the soap over my body, I thought about the intensity of Cameron's piercing blue eyes again. The closeness of his face and the way in which he'd grabbed my wrist. As I closed my eyes and grazed my nipples with my palms, desire began to coil deep within me and my hand began to move lower... lower... lower, until my fingers found my dampness and swollen clit. I sighed as I began to tease the flesh there and my breathing rate increased. The more my arousal took over, the faster my fingers worked as images of Cameron's muscular, tattooed arms sprang into my mind. His large hand around my slender wrist; his jaw clenched and brow furrowed. I tugged at my nipple, imagining it to be his rough fingers, and I was transported back to his room again. Only this time I was underneath him on the bed and he was grasping me with one hand, tugging my sensitive, erect nipple with his lips, swirling his tongue around the taut flesh, and teasing my clit with the other hand as he pushed my thighs apart with the thickness of his own and stared down at me.

Pulling away, he spoke through perfect, white, gritted teeth. "Fuck, you smell good. I could eat you up. But for now I'll settle for making you come... *hard*."

My subconscious had added the last part, but oh my word did it do the job and I cried out as a fierce orgasm ripped through my tightly strung body. Pleasure rocketed throughout every nerve fibre as each muscle clenched and unclenched, pulsating with overwhelming ecstasy.

My legs buckled and I sank to the floor of the shower enclosure.

As I floated back down to earth—back to *reality*—I removed my fingers, letting the hot water run down between my legs as I rested my head against the cool surface of the tiles. I closed my eyes and was suddenly overcome with professional anger. *What the hell is wrong with me? I'm losing my grip.* Tears of self-loathing stung at my eyes and I really did begin to question my own sanity.

Cameron was the dangerous unknown and I usually *hated* the unknown, let alone the element of danger. In fact I feared the unknown with every fibre of my prissy being. Hence the reason that the only person I'd had sex with since uni. was Dermott... *from* uni! He was safe and I didn't have to feel emotion. I could just enjoy the release. So why the fuck was I thinking so intimately about this complete stranger who'd apparently tried to take his own life and had intimidated me so easily? This man that I knew nothing about, other than he had an unstable state of mind and a penchant for tattoos and aggression towards women. Hell, even *he* didn't know who he was! *Stupid, stupid woman.*

Once I was dried and dressed in my pyjamas, I opened a bottle of red wine and sat in silence as I drank the deep, blood-red liquid in the hope that it would help me to sleep without any unwanted dreams.

Sadly, the alcohol only seemed to intensify my lust.

Once again I was beneath Cameron in a large bed. His broad, powerful frame loomed over me, but in a strange way I felt safe with him. Adored even. I stared up into those intense but crystal-clear, blue eyes. The most wonderful sensations bloomed from where we were joined and travelled right to the ends of my fingers and toes. His gaze was lust filled and I reached up to touch his cheek. He tilted his face, closed his eyes and sucked my thumb into the warm wetness of his mouth. When his eyes met mine again, there was something more there. It wasn't only lust I saw. He moved his cock deep within me as his thick, toned arms held his body aloft, caging me in. My nipples brushed the hard planes of his tattooed chest and he bent to suck one into his mouth. He bit down, causing a split second of pain followed by intense pleasure as he soothed me with the tip of his tongue, stroking and teasing the tightened peak. I lifted my legs and locked them around his back as he slid his rigid length in and out of my body with delicious ease, teasing my sensitive, swollen clit until I felt myself tightening around him. He clenched his jaw and made a guttural sound as he began to thrust deeper and harder. I was so aroused and filled with need for him.

Only him.

No words were spoken as the tightening in my core grew more and more intense. I was so close to release...

I sat suddenly. Alone in my own bed. Another damn dream.

My chest was heaving and a sheen of glistening sweat covered my body. The throbbing pulse between my thighs was almost painful, and I squeezed my thighs together in the hope it would subside. Rubbing my hands over my face, I tried to calm my ragged breathing. This was getting ridiculous now. I was clearly becoming obsessed.

There was nothing else for it. I needed to speak to Clara.

Clara was my own therapist. It may sound ridiculous that I should need one, but believe me, even mental health professionals need someone to talk to sometimes. I had been seeing Clara for many years after suffering anxiety in my late teens—it subsequently turned out to be abandonment issues... well, the fact that my dad had fucked off when I was a kid. I went through a very long phase of being unable to trust. In fact, the phase was still hanging around in the background of our conversations. She was a newly qualified therapist back then and she had really helped me. If I trusted anyone, it was her. It seemed only natural to stay in touch with her, considering my chosen profession.

Luckily I had her home number and knew she was a night owl, so I called immediately and made arrangements to see her the following day. Thankfully she was very understanding.

I just had to decide how honest I was going to be.

————

The following day I walked into Clara's plush office and plopped down onto the comfy couch. She handed me a coffee and sat opposite me. As always she was impeccably dressed with her ash-blonde hair in a neat chignon. For a woman in her late forties, she looked a lot younger.

"So, Kelly. What was so important that you had to telephone me at half eleven in the evening to make an appointment?" The question was simply inquisitive. She was direct and I liked that I knew where I stood with her. No pretence.

I sighed and shook my head. "I'm so sorry about that, Clara. Really I am."

She held up her hands. "No apology needed. What I'm trying to get at is that something *clearly* has you on the run. This isn't like you, Kelly. So... come on... spill it."

"Okay... there's this man..."

"Ah." She raised her eyebrows and gave me a knowing look.

"It's not Dermott, before you say anything."

She held up her hands. "Hey, I'm not here to judge. You know my thoughts on your relationship with him."

"Hmm. You certainly don't keep that a secret."

With a smile, she continued, "So... this man?"

"Yes... this man... There's this... how can I put it? There's this *attraction* between us. Well, at least I get the distinct feeling it's not entirely one sided. But... It's not a relationship I can pursue."

Linking her fingers in her lap, she asked, "Why would that be? Are you putting up barriers again?"

I shook my head and pulled my brows in. "No, it's not like that this time. It's..." Trying to explain without explaining *too* much created a flood of sensation from last night that made me squeeze my thighs together. "Let's just say it wouldn't be right."

"It's someone from work."

I knew she meant a colleague, and a lie by omission wasn't going to help me—but technically it wasn't a *big* lie. He *was* at my place of work, after all. I nodded but couldn't meet her gaze. She'd see right through me if I did.

"The thing is, I can't stop thinking about him. I'm even dreaming about him." *Mm, the way he thrust into my welcoming flesh just hours before... in my mind, anyway*. I cleared my throat as I felt heat rush to my cheeks. "Quite explicit dreams too."

She nodded. "And you're feeling guilty?"

She knew me so well. "Very."

"Well, Kelly. You're a healthy, sexual being with certain emotional as well as physical needs. If you're attracted to this man, maybe it'd be possible to pursue a relationship outside of work but keep things professional inside of work?"

I laughed at her audacity and the future consequences of what, unbeknownst to her, she was suggesting. "Clara! You're not supposed to encourage such things!"

She raised her hands again in surrender. "Look, I'm saying this as a *friend*, not your therapist. You're an intelligent woman, Kelly. I know you could keep your head on straight at work. And if this man makes your sweet button hum, then maybe you need to see where it goes? Like I said, you have *needs*, hon. We *all* do."

My mind flicked back to what my *thoughts* had done to my 'sweet button' the night before, and I shuddered. "It's... it's not that simple. And what's with the *sweet button* crap? Ugh! Cringe-worthy, Clara." We both burst into laughter.

"Kelly, I've known you for years. I do consider you a friend more than a client—which could be seen as incredibly unprofessional of me—" *Oh the irony*... "But I have to say I'm in favour of anything that draws you from the unhealthy relationship you have with Dermott. It's almost as if you're with him because you're scared to allow yourself to *feel*. As if you're scared to even try with anyone outside of this little comfort zone you've created with your fuck buddy. If that's the case, we really need to address that... or I can refer you on if you wouldn't feel comfortable chatting to me about it." I loved the fact that she could be so blunt with me. I wouldn't have that with anyone else. Being referred was totally out of the question.

"No... no it's fine. I think... I think maybe you're right. I... I watched my parents rip each other apart emotionally whilst I was growing up and... the more my mother tried to make it work..." A lump lodged in my tightening throat. "The more my father pulled away. His cheating and leaving just compounded my worries of getting too close to people, I suppose." I felt tears escape my eyes and trickle down my cheeks. This was not a subject I readily talked about. Not even with Clara.

"Oh, Kelly, honey... I think we have our answer right there." Her voice was soft and her eyes filled with concern. "Look... I'm taking off my therapist's hat again for a moment. Listen to me when I tell you this from *personal* experience. You can't go through life comparing every man to your father. Some men stick around and *are* worth the risk. Try to remember that. And someday you'll meet someone who isn't unattainable, and you'll let yourself fall in love. I just wish you would allow yourself to take the risk whilst you're still young."

Of course she was right, but my memories of being a ten-year-old girl watching as my dad walked out the door without looking back, never to be seen again, had left me scarred emotionally. I had major trust issues. It was true. So why the hell was I drawn to someone who could potentially test my boundaries to the *nth* degree? I had no idea.

After spending an hour there, I left Clara's office with a smile on my face. Hearing myself explain the situation—even though I wasn't *exactly* honest—made me realise how stupid I was being. A weight had been lifted from my shoulders, and I walked into work humming to myself and ready to face whatever the day threw at me with renewed vigour.

The infatuation I had been feeling was just that. *Infatuation.* And as someone qualified in such matters, I knew that obsessing about things or people simply led to heartache and trouble. In that moment I was determined to push my feelings aside. I was his *doctor* and he needed me. And despite the way he acted around me and the intense sexuality oozing from his every pore, I would resist. *I have to. I really, really have to.* As I repeated those words like a mantra, I mused as to why something in the back of my mind told me I was trying a little too hard to convince myself.

CHAPTER FOUR

Cameron

A pretty young woman with dark hair and blue eyes sobbed and screamed, "No!" as a faceless someone in black behind her restrained her by the arms. She was flailing but her efforts were futile. Her petite frame was no match for the hulk holding her captive. Someone else struck me over and over with rock-hard fists. Jabbing jagged knuckles into every available patch of skin. I couldn't see their faces. Only hers. It broke my heart to see her in so much distress. How could they let her see this? Why would they *do* this to her? She didn't deserve this. She shouldn't even be involved. Nausea crept over me in a wave as pain racked my body. Blow after unforgiving blow jarred me and rendered me speechless. I wanted to shout at them to let her go. To get her out of there. But the air had left my lungs and the words wouldn't come...

And so began another day in my new version of hell. It followed another night of disturbing dreams. It was becoming the norm to wake and find a concerned middle-aged woman standing over me. Patty had replaced Annie as my nurse in the psych ward and I was rapidly growing fond of her. She was a sweet woman. Kind of motherly. I liked that about her. It was as if I hadn't experienced anything like that in a very long time.

"That was some nightmare you were having, hon. I was on the verge of getting the doctor to come and sedate you again."

I closed my eyes briefly but as soon as I did, I saw the young, dark-haired woman's tearstained face so I immediately opened them again. "That bad, huh?"

Patty nodded. "Yes, that bad, love. Can you remember anything of the nightmare?"

I shook my head. She wasn't the person I needed to share it with. Doctor Darrow was no doubt conversant in the subconscious meanings of dreams. I'd wait and tell *her* when I saw her.

"Do you think you might be up to a little walk today?" Patty asked. "You really need to start getting up and about."

I scrunched my brow. "Where would we be going?"

"You need to have your meeting with Doctor Darrow."

Bingo. Doctor McSexy. My day was set to improve. "Okay. Yeah, I guess I could manage that. Will you be with me?"

"Of course, love. Wouldn't leave you in case you fell. I'll collect you afterwards too."

"Great. Thank you."

"Your clothes have been laundered and I've placed them on the chair for you. Your catheter was removed as you slept. No man likes to experience *that* event when conscious. Are you up to washing yourself?"

My cheeks heated at the thought of a sponge bath by the nurse who was old enough to be my mom. "Yeah, I think I'll manage, thanks." The images were suddenly replaced by those of a certain sexy Scottish doctor leaning over me, half naked, cleavage glistening with droplets of water as she soaped up my chest and abs with a soaking-wet cloth. She dragged her nails over my nipples, and my dick hardened as I was filled with a need to lick the drips from her skin.

I was brought back to earth with a severe thud as the nurse's voice broke through my erotic fantasy—one I would save for later use—as she said, "Great. I'll bring you something to eat whilst you wash and get dressed, and then I'll take you to see her once you've eaten. Take it steady though, okay? Push the red emergency button if you get into any difficulty. I'll be just out here when I come back."

Patty left the room, and I stood on weak limbs to go and wash myself in the adjacent bathroom. I looked for the door lock but strangely there wasn't one. Dizziness came over me and as I waited for it to pass, I stood clutching the sink, looking in the mirror at my vaguely familiar reflection. I examined my tattoos closely. They were a mixture of text and pictures. Some of the symbols looked like some kind of foreign language and I had no clue what they said. The intricacy of some of the detail told me that I must have been in the artist's chair for *hours*. Some were brightly coloured and depicted people. The word *Cosmic* with a woman draped over it in a sultry pose had me running my fingers over the lettering. Who *was* she? Someone significant? Or just some random busty woman put there for my titillation?

The hollowed eyes of a skull stared out at me from my shoulder, and its menacing, skinless grin held my attention for a few moments as I searched around my mind for something... *anything*—but none brought to mind anything that cleared up who I was. I concentrated on my features. Shaggy hair, almost collar length, that clearly hadn't been cut in a while... thick stubble around my jaw... blue eyes that looked a little sunken and were surrounded by dark circles. My shoulders were broad and there wasn't much flesh on my muscular torso that wasn't covered in ink. I stared into the eyes of my reflection, desperately trying to bring my name to mind. But the only name that came to me was... *Rosa*. And that sure as hell wasn't *my* name, so who the fuck was Rosa and why was that the only name I could recall? Was she the girl in my dream? Who the hell knew? Not me.

Once I was freshened up, I dressed in the clothes that were on the chair. They smelled of fresh laundry detergent and fit me, but I didn't recognise them. Dark jeans with no goddamn belt and a plain black T-shirt.

Very understated.

When I stepped out of the bathroom, I noticed a breakfast tray by the bed and Patty sitting in the corner smiling. I devoured the omelette like it was my last meal. The coffee wasn't great, bitter and poor quality; but the fruit juice tasted good.

Patty walked over and gestured to the tray as if to ask if I was done. I grabbed the napkin and nodded. She removed the tray and placed it on the chair by the door. "You're looking a little brighter. I would've brought you a razor but... well... it's against policy. The risk and everything." She cringed.

I scrunched my face for what felt like the millionth time. "Risk? What *risk*?"

Patty's face turned carefully blank, but then she smiled warmly in what I guessed was reassurance. "Let me take you to Doctor Darrow. From tomorrow you'll be okay to eat with the others. That'll be better for you." I got the feeling she was purposefully avoiding answering any of my questions.

I stood and shuffled toward the door, wiping my mouth on the paper napkin that came with my food, and then dropped it onto the tray before I gripped Patty's offered arm of support. We slowly walked down the hospital corridor and she gestured for me to sit on a chair outside a blue office door. It was closed, with a silver plaque that read Dr K. M. Darrow.

Patty knocked on the door and stepped inside. I heard her mumble something to Doctor Darrow before she came out and gestured for me to enter. Walking into the room, I looked out the window and got my first glimpse of the world beyond the hospital walls. The view of a vast bridge and the town and scenery beyond was impressive but not at all familiar.

"Hello there. Please... have a seat," The sexy auburn-haired

woman said from a couch at the far side of the large, multipurpose room. I slowly and shakily walked over. I must've looked as
if I was approaching a deadly creature, but the truth was, my legs
felt as if they may give way at any minute. I slumped onto the
couch opposite her.

"Hi... Doctor Darrow, isn't it?" I smiled, hoping that *she'd*
acquired amnesia over my behaviour the last time we met.

"That's correct." She exuded professionalism; gone was the
friendly bedside manner from before. Perhaps she was building a
wall so that I couldn't intimidate her again. I couldn't blame her
really. She reached for a notepad and pen and placed them on
her lap. Today it was grey slacks and a fitted cream blouse that
hugged her shapely tits. Her hair was pinned up on her head and
her glasses were perched on her nose. Every bit the stereotypical
sultry shrink. My mind began to torture me with erotic, fabricated mental images of her and me together. I swallowed hard.

CHAPTER FIVE

KELLY

Patient McHandsome—as Annie had nicknamed the mysterious man from room 4 in ICU—sat before me on the two-seater leather couch. His thick thighs naturally parted in a masculine wide stance. I reached down and touched my alarm—mostly to remind myself of my decision to respect my code of ethics and keep my hands *off* him—and a sense of relief washed over me. I watched as he fiddled with his nails and glanced nervously around the room. He was a far cry from the intimidating man of the day before, and so I relaxed a little more.

"So... Have you remembered any further details about the reason for your presence here?" I asked him. His eyes flicked up to meet mine and I inhaled sharply, immediately feeling the heat rise in my cheeks. Yesterday when I'd had that intense encounter with him, I'd seen a totally different glint in his eyes. Now sitting before me, looking a little afraid, his eyes were the most vivid, electric shade; almost cerulean. They didn't look real. I was taken aback by them.

Lost in them even.

What could I do to make myself stop wanting him?

He broke eye contact and smiled down at his hands. "Not a damn thing, ma'am."

Shit... has he just read my mind? My heart picked up its pace and a flush of blood heated my cheeks. *Oh... hang on... it's okay, he was answering my question.* Fighting an audible sigh of relief, I cleared my throat. "Okay. Firstly I need to assess your emotional and mental well-being. This is done by the use of a questionnaire. I need you to be completely honest and not to think about the answers too much. If I'm going to be able to help you, I need you to trust me. And then I need to discuss a couple of matters with you. It may be a little disturbing to hear what I have to tell you, but... I need to talk to you about these issues all the same."

He took a deep breath and seemed to brace himself for what I had to say. Leaning back a little, I tilted my head to one side. Despite my promise, I couldn't help but notice how ruggedly masculine he was, viewed from any angle. I squeezed my thighs together, mentally reprimanded myself, and began to reel off question after question. "Would you say that since you gained consciousness you have had any feelings of hopelessness?" I gave him the list of answers to choose from:

a) not at all

b) some of the time

c) most of the time

d) all of the time

He nodded and began to answer with a firm determination as I bombarded him with one question after another. His answers were surprisingly positive, considering the circumstances in which he had been found; and the more I listened to him talk, the more I felt that there was a great chance that he had *not* attempted to take his own life.

And if that was the case, then that meant someone had tried to *kill* him.

I shuddered at the thought as the whole plot thickened before me.

Once he had completed my questions satisfactorily, I allowed him to have a drink of water before continuing on. "Okay, Cameron... I must inform you that the police will be needing to speak with you in the near future. They may go over some of the ground we have covered, and I apologise if this is frustrating for you, but it's necessary to ascertain your identity and the reasons for your presence here. We've been putting them off, but the mystery surrounding your appearance in Scotland needs to be solved, and so they will no doubt have plenty of questions for you. There will be the matter of DNA checks too. They can do this with a sample of hair, saliva, or blood, but you need to consent to this. That's why it hasn't been done before. Human rights, etcetera. Once we have the sample, we can match it to databases here and in the USA."

His nostrils flared and it was clear he was uneasy at the thought of having his DNA checked. "But... won't I only show up on the databases if I'm some kind of *criminal?*"

"There are a variety of reasons that DNA samples are logged, Mr. Iss. And yes, one of them would be if you had been involved in any previous criminal activity."

Why it bothered him so much was just as big a mystery to me as his very presence here in North Kessock. But the fact that it *did* bother him led me to believe he knew more than he was letting on. I tried to ignore the unease prickling my skin. "I must ask you again, has anything... however small... come back to you about your life? Any memories that may assist us in figuring out who you are and why you're here?"

He frowned. "Last night... I had this vivid dream. It was filled with,"—he swallowed and I watched his Adam's apple move; my hand started to rise as though to stroke it, and I made myself lower it and pay attention to his words—"*violence.* I... I was being beaten. There was this young woman... dark hair...

blue eyes... beautiful... she was sobbing and screaming, 'No!' Then... earlier today... when I was in the bathroom... a name... not *my* name... at least I'm pretty *sure* it's not my name..."

His words trailed off and he dropped his gaze.

A sudden spike of intrigue made me lean forwards as his crumpled expression told of his concern for this woman... whoever she was. I urged him on. "A name? That's good. Go on."

He brought his pained gaze back up to meet mine, and for a brief moment he was caught in some kind of trance, just staring at me. A shiver shot down my spine and goose bumps prickled at my skin. Was he feeling it too? This strange pull?

He blinked rapidly and the spell was broken. "Rosa. The name that came to me was Rosa. I don't know who Rosa is or *why* that name is so significant but... it's all I have." He lifted his hands briefly and dropped them in his lap again. It was the gesture of a defeated man. He slumped back into the couch and rubbed his hands over his face. A distinct urge to comfort him— to just touch him—fought to surface from deep within me, but I squashed it down and gripped my pen so tightly I was sure it would snap clean in two.

Focusing on him once again, I watched as a deep sadness washed over his beautifully chiselled features, and my heart ached for the loss he must've been feeling, the shared pain of sympathy intertwining with illicit desire inside of me. I nodded and made a note of his breakthrough.

Then it hit me.

Rosa was the name on his suicide note.

I sat in silent contemplation for a few moments, wondering how best to approach the matter of the note. I felt his stare and met his gaze. "Okay... Now I have something to tell you, and as I said... it may be difficult to hear. But please know that you are going to be cared for and given all the necessary help."

His brow furrowed and he nodded. I watched as he swallowed hard again and knotted his hands in his lap.

Experiencing more sorrow for this man than I ever had for a patient before, I took a deep breath. "When you were found... you were in a bit of a state to say the least. As I told you before, all you had in your possession was a tatty leather jacket, an iPod and a note. It... it was evidently a *suicide* note."

His eyes widened and he stood a little too quickly. The colour drained from his face and his hands were visibly shaking as he ran them over his head then rubbed at his face again. "So *that's* what she fucking meant. The *risk*. The *razor*. You all thought I was going to *kill* myself."

First Annie, and now Patty and her big mouth strike again. "Well... you can understand our trepidation. You had a large amount of sedatives, alcohol, and other prescription medication in your bloodstream. You should've been *dead*, Cameron. How the hell you survived that with so little internal damage is something that *none* of the doctors can figure out. You must have an ironclad constitution, that's for sure." I immediately clamped my mouth shut. What the hell was wrong with me blabbing on like I *knew* the man? Hell, he didn't even know himself!

He flopped onto the couch again and dropped his head into his hands. "But... I don't..."

"Look, I apologise. That was very blunt and it must be difficult to have such information offloaded on you like that."

His blue gaze met mine again. "No, no it's fine. I get the feeling I'm a straight-up kind of guy. I'm glad you told me. So... am I allowed to know what the note said *exactly*?"

I hesitated and dropped my focus to the file at my side. The letter was in there. It was against my better judgement to show him the note at this point. I wanted his memory to return so that he could tell me why the attempt to take his own life had occurred—if indeed he had written the note. His surprise at the mention of suicide confused the issue. As if moving of their own accord, my fingers slipped into the file and pulled out the letter. I inhaled nervously through my nose as I held it toward him.

As he leaned forward, I caught the clean, fresh scent of body wash. A manly fragranced body wash—it wasn't the hospital's standard issue stock—and I wondered if it was something that someone had given him especially or if it was just the usual stuff and it just smelled so much more manly because it was mingled with his own unique scent. He reached and took the paper from my hands, brushing his fingers over mine. As our skin made contact, his eyes travelled rapidly up to meet mine as if I'd given him an electric shock. He stared at me for what felt like minutes, but eventually the spell was once again broken and he turned his attention to the letter.

A myriad of emotions flashed across his face, and his lips moved as he read. Those kissable lips that had been distorted by the ventilator only a matter of days ago. Those lips that had been so close to mine as he intimidated me and turned me on all at once. I watched him closely for any indication that he knew the note was written in his hand, but all I saw was confusion.

After what seemed like an age he lifted his gaze. "C-Cameron Iss... is... is that me?"

My heart broke at the lost look that had taken over his sculpted face. "I really don't know. We've searched records and contacted the US embassy since you gained consciousness, but no one by that name has been reported missing. If the DNA results don't bring anything up, we may have to wait until you regain more of your memory before we can determine your identity for sure. In the meantime you'll need to stay in the hospital so that we know you're safe."

"But... I'd rather go back to the USA and try to figure this shit out. Can't I, I don't know, be transferred or something?"

I shook my head. "I'm afraid it's not that simple. You have no passport. Perhaps the reason no one in the US has reported you missing is because you actually reside here... In Scotland. Cameron is a very Scottish name, after all. Or perhaps Cameron Iss isn't your name. Iss is very unusual and certainly not Scottish.

In fact the name is very uncommon and found mostly around New York."

He exhaled a long, loud breath and ran his hands through his dark, scruffy hair again. "So... what happens now?"

"Well, we wait. You appear to be dreaming about scenarios that could actually be flashbacks. We need to meet regularly in order to figure out if that's the case. They may become more vivid and more frequent." My mind involuntarily flashed back to my own vivid dreams. Images of him looming over me as he drove into me, pushing me toward ecstasy, appeared in my frontal cortex and I felt that familiar throb between my legs. My nipples pushed forward at the lace of my bra and I swallowed hard, trying to dislodge the ill-timed fantasy.

He nodded and then fixed his gaze on me again. He stood and skirted around the wooden coffee table that sat between us and closed the remaining distance. Taking the space beside me, he sat on my couch. My heart responded immediately with a faster rhythm.

He lifted my hand and brought it to his lips, placing a gentle kiss there. "I'm so sorry for what happened yesterday, Kelly. I... I don't know what came over me. I just seemed to... snap I guess. I'm a little scared that that's who I am. Some dickweed who intimidates women. I... I don't want to be that person. I hope you can forgive me."

My heart pounded in my chest and butterflies set about dancing in my stomach. My free hand rested in my personal alarm and with an unsteady voice I replied, "I already said I'd forgiven you."

A crease appeared on his forehead and he looked anguished. "But you're afraid of me. I can see it in your eyes." He stopped speaking for a moment as he stared at me... through me... into me. "You have the most beautiful green eyes I've ever seen, do you know that?"

It wasn't fear he saw in my eyes. Trying to remain profes-

sional and emotionally distant, I moved back slightly. "Mr Iss...
seeing as that's what we'll have to call you for now... I most
certainly do not know that I have the most beautiful green eyes
you've ever seen. Seeing as I don't know you, how would I be
party to such personal information?"

A smile played on his lips as he leaned further in toward me
and inhaled through his nose. My breath quickened and I could
feel the warmth radiating from his body. "I love it when you get
all feisty like that. God, I can't help myself. You really do smell
good." His eyes fluttered closed briefly just like the day before.
When he opened them again his pupils were dilated. He still
gripped my hand in his and I sat frozen to the spot. Unable to
move. Mesmerised by him.

Heat flooded my bloodstream and I swallowed. A wry smirk
appeared on his full lips. "What I wouldn't give for just a little
taste," he whispered, his lips perilously close to mine. My head
told me to call for security or activate my alarm, but the heat of
his breath so close to my mouth left me incapacitated.

I cleared my throat. "Okay, Mr Iss. That will be all for today.
It's best to keep our sessions brief for now to ensure we don't tire
you out too much. You can return to your room now." I tried to
project my voice in a way that exuded confidence but instead it
came out husky and sultry.

I was under his spell. And I liked it.

He stood steadily. "Just in case you're wondering, I have no
desire to off myself. I do, however, have other desires. Shame I'm
so weak right now. I have a feeling I could rock your world." He
covered the pronounced ridge in his jeans with the hand that had
been clutching mine only moments before, pulled his bottom lip
through his teeth and smiled. It wasn't an arrogant smile though.
It was a smile that told me he was messing with me, in spite of
the inappropriate hand positioning. "Sorry, ma'am. Right now,
that's pretty much all I know about myself."

I suspected he wasn't sorry in the least. I pursed my lips and stifled the smile trying to break through.

I stood and smoothed my slacks down my legs as I stepped away from him. I needed the distance—especially since now I was imagining him running his hands along my thighs. "That's good to know. Thank you. Goodbye, Mr Iss." I bent to gather my papers and could feel his stare on my behind as I moved. I turned to face him once again, and with my gaze fixed firmly on his I called, "Patty, you can escort Mr Iss back now!"

The psychiatric nurse burst through the door as if she'd been listening at the keyhole—and I wouldn't have put that past her.

Holding her arm out to Cameron, she said, "Come on, hon. Let's get you back to bed."

He smirked at her. "I bet you say that to all the mysterious, handsome yanks." He winked over at me, and I couldn't help but smile. Patty tapped his arm playfully and muttered something about his being young enough to be her son, but the blush on her cheeks gave her away. It apparently wasn't just me that he had that effect on.

CHAPTER SIX

Kelly

I had to get inside the man's head. He couldn't remember who he was and that intrigued me like no other case I had worked on. He was unique. In more ways than one. Something drew me to him and that scared me. He had the kind of eyes that hypnotised. I was having to avoid eye contact for fear of turning into a damp-pantied, needy mess in his presence.

At the end of the day I took his iPod from the filing cabinet. The police had dusted it for prints already and listened to the contents therein but had reported the results as inconclusive. They had handed it back in case I needed it for my work with him, and I was glad that they had. Perhaps it would give me a little insight into what made Cameron tick.

I was a great believer in being able to learn a hell of a lot about someone from his musical taste. I hoped I wasn't wrong.

Once at home, I showered and dressed in my pj's and slipped the iPod into my own docking station. Just as I was about to hit play, the phone rang. *Bloody great timing.*

"Hello?"

"Hey, Kel. It's just me," my best friend, Esme, said. "I wondered if we're doing dinner at the weekend. I feel like I haven't seen you for ages." Esme was right. We had texted back and forth, but I hadn't been out with her for around four weeks. And it was four weeks too long.

"Oh, hi, Ez. Yeah, that'd be good. We could try that new Italian maybe?"

"Orrr, we could just walk down to Johnny Foxes and have a bite there?" Esme was a creature of habit. But I loved that I always knew where I was with her.

"I suppose we could. But where's your sense of adventure?"

"I think I left it at Johnny Foxes and that's why I need to go back." She giggled and I joined in.

The rest of the conversation was filled with ridiculous talk about Internet dating and her setting me up with friends of hers. I'd been stung by that situation before and had vowed never to go down that road again. I knew she meant well, and a date with another man would be a good way to get Cameron Iss out of my mind—or maybe not, since fucking Dermott hadn't helped in the least—but most of her male friends actually fancied her and only went out with me as a way to get closer to her.

No thanks.

No more.

Once the call had ended, I poured myself a glass of red wine and hit play on the iPod. I braced myself for what was to come. The intro to the first track was soft and melodic, and I began to wonder why I had expected the contrary. However, as the lyrics came in I realised that maybe my first instincts weren't so far from the mark.

The track, highlighted on the screen as "The Noose" by A Perfect Circle, talked of someone's heinous deeds being hidden and lied about, and I wondered what on earth someone had done to him to make him listen to such a song. And who was it that had wronged him to spark such bitterness?

The second track sent shivers down my spine. Images of a heartbroken man sitting alone with tears streaming down his face assaulted my mind. My own tears spilled over. From the lyrics I imagined he had lost someone he loved dearly. But perhaps he just enjoyed melancholy music. I guess these were questions I would only find answers to once his memory began to return.

I just hoped that it would begin to return.

The song, "Set Fire to the Third Bar" by Snow Patrol had me reading between invisible lines and coming to conclusions that I had no basis for. But if my gut feeling was right, this man was heartbroken. And once more I realised that this song told me things about Cameron that I couldn't ascertain.

Next came "Hurt" by Nine Inch Nails. Wow. The picture building in my mind was one filled with regret, hate, and loss. I began to wonder if perhaps his amnesia was some kind of self-preservation/self-defence mechanism. A way to wipe the pain from his mind. If the songs told a true story, then the man was broken. I just hoped I could help him to rebuild and repair.

I closed my eyes and drifted off to the shoreline at Rosemarkie.

The sun was setting and I turned to my right side to look toward Chanonry Point, but he was there blocking my view and creating something all the more worth looking at. His eyes were filled with pain, and the descending sun caught on the damp trails tracing down his cheeks, making them glisten. I reached up to wipe one away, but he grasped my wrist and pulled me firmly into his hard, muscular chest.

I winced as his other hand fisted in my hair and he crushed his lips into mine with a frustrated aggression that both scared and excited me. The pained noise rippling from his chest as he thrust his tongue into my mouth made my heart clench. Unable to resist, I gripped his shirt and let him lay me down in the warm sand.

"I need you, Kelly. Only you can help me," came as a hoarse, emotion-filled whisper as I felt him harden against me. The wetness of his tears mingled with my own as my will crumbled completely. In that moment I would have done anything to help heal his fractured heart and damaged soul.

A strange noise yanked me from my trance-like state, and when I lifted my hand to my cheek, I felt the tears that I had unknowingly shed for Cameron and realised the noise had been a sob leaving my body. Unable to continue, I hit the off button and climbed the stairs to my room. I was emotionally drained. And even though he hadn't directly told me in our meetings, the songs on the iPod were a deep insight into the broken man I was growing to desire above any ethics that provided an obstacle. My heart ached for the mysterious man enlisted to my care, and I wondered if perhaps I had bitten off more than I could chew.

———

CAMERON

I hated the fact that the days were passing so slowly. I was hounded by night terrors and had to be sedated on several occasions. Most nights were the same. The pain of someone's fist connecting with the already tender and bruised parts of my body was far too real. Hearing the blood-curdling sound of laughter as they inflicted pain upon me and the sickening, desperate screams of a female who was witnessing the whole thing had me thrashing around and fighting with the bed sheets as if they were in on the conspiracy. Or there would be the dreams where I was the one inflicting the agony, and these were somehow even harder to bear. The knot in my stomach told me that I didn't want to carry out such heinous acts; something was driving to do it regardless.

Following these kinds of episodes, I'd awaken to find everything moving in slow motion. The nurse's voice would sound

slurry and deep. A slight move of my head felt like it took an age
—all because of the sedatives. I hated the weakness associated
with the drugs when they coursed through my veins. Someone
could've walked right in and aimed at loaded pistol at my temple,
and I would have been powerless to stop my own murder.

And that seemed to be the expectation on waking in a drug-
fogged state. That someone was out to get me. That the people
from my dreams would suddenly materialise and finish what
they'd started. It was a living hell. And that was putting it mildly.

The police forensics had been and taken samples for DNA
checks and had shown me the old leather jacket that I had been
wearing when I was found. It was black and the sleeves had been
cut off, making into more of a vest. The back was scratched and
marked, and it looked like some patches or something had been
removed at some point. Looking at the jacket didn't spark
anything in me except for images of the blue-eyed girl from my
nightmares.

My only saving grace was that I knew I'd get to see Doc
McSexy, and for a little while at least I could forget that I'd been
beaten to within an inch of my fucking life—well, that is until
she started with her incessant questioning. In the back of my
mind I was thinking that maybe even if I did remember who the
fuck I was, I might just play dumb so that I'd have longer with
her. There was just something about her that got to me. She
affected me and I had no fucking clue why. I didn't know what
kind of guy I'd been before, but judging by the dreams I was
having, I'd say I'd been the 'love 'em and leave 'em' kind. Inter-
spersed with the violence there had been tons of erotic dreams,
or maybe flashbacks, in which I'd been fucking a different female
each time. But the best erotic dreams I had were about Kelly.

They were different.

Although I usually awoke from them feeling a sick and
empty pit of sadness inside, I never felt regret.

I'd been in the hospital around three weeks, and my strength was increasing every day. There was a lot going on behind the scenes, I was told, to try and ascertain my identity; but as far as I was aware, they were drawing blanks. I'd gotten into a kind of routine and although I was bored, it could've been worse. Judging by the terrible dreams I'd been having—more often than the erotic ones—and if they were flashbacks, I'd been messed up in all kinds of violent shit. Being here in Scotland, I felt kinda safe.

Judging by the other people in the Mental Health Unit, I wasn't their typical kind of patient. Many of them were frequent flyers and had racked up their suicide attempt air miles, and after chatting to some of those guys, I felt sorta lucky to have no fucking clue what had brought me here. At least ignorance meant I didn't have to face up to whatever demons had made me try to take my own life. If that's what had actually happened.

I was beginning to think my amnesia was a kind of self-defence mechanism. Maybe my brain had purposefully shut down to stop me from reliving that shit. All I knew was that the other people in this place needed to be here more than I did. The awful things some of those people had gone through. My God. They say that suicide attempts are mostly a cry for help. And something inside of me really wanted to do something positive. If I had tried to take my own life—and it was a big if—then I decided that once I'd figured it all out, I wanted to do something good. My brain was telling me that this way of thinking was something alien to me. And again, thinking about the dreams I'd been having, I hadn't been a very nice guy in my former life. Or at least I hadn't mixed with very nice guys.

In an effort to be the kind of guy I could at least somewhat respect, I'd been sharing books and magazines with some of the other patients, and although I really didn't want to be there, I made the best of a shitty situation.

My appointments with Kelly kept me going. We rummaged through the details of every nightmare, looking for clues. And I became increasingly frustrated at the absence of a breakthrough. The only positive was that she was there for me.

I could talk to her. Make her laugh even. I knew she was being paid to spend time with me, but it felt like she was actually interested in me as a person. The way she locked eyes with me... I knew there was a connection in spite of my bad behaviour. I could feel it in my bones... and my boner.

I awoke to a dull morning in November, and after washing and dressing, I stood at the window to my private room. The view was hazy due to a low-hanging mist—something I was becoming familiar with, since Scotland in winter can have crazy extremes of weather. I'm talking short sleeves one minute and the next waterproof coats and woolly hats. I was beginning to think I must be from a warmer climate, as I was feeling the cold all too easily, even here in my glass prison.

Things between Kelly and me were... strange to say the least. I caught her looking at me sometimes but couldn't decipher her expression. It was like she was trying to figure me out in a way that didn't involve her job. Like she was trying to find the me hidden underneath all the mystery to see if she liked what she found. But no sooner did the look appear than it vanished in the blink of an eye.

I was pretty sure I was affecting her. On many occasions a blush would start at her chest and slowly creep up her body to her cheeks. I could follow the heat as it rose. It was damn cute and I couldn't help smiling, but I really wanted to know what was going on behind those verdant eyes of hers. She was desperately trying to hide from me and remain professional. But I could see from her body language that she was struggling not to straddle me and take the full length of my cock inside herself. And God knows I was fighting this thing between us too. The last thing she needed was to be dragged into the shit pit that my life was turning out to be. But I still had this feeling deep down that I knew her even though the notion was ridiculous. It was like our fucking souls were intertwined or something. Not that I believed in that shit. Well, actually... I didn't know what I believed because I couldn't remember much. And no matter how I tried to figure it out, my stupid mind wouldn't give anything up. And in spite of the fact that she appeared so professional, I could tell that she was drawn to me too.

The signs were there. She fidgeted around in her seat and couldn't keep eye contact for very long. Her nipples made more than one appearance—not completely, you understand, but protruding through the flimsy silk blouses she wore when I locked my gaze on hers for too long. All telltale signs of attraction as far as I was concerned. And in all honesty it was more than reciprocated on my part.

I wanted her.

Badly.

Fucking desperately.

That one thing I knew for certain.

Although it was becoming more than that. I didn't just want her. I needed her. I needed a physical connection to her that would prove my emotional connection wasn't just a fallacy. It was taking over my mind and stopping me from concentrating on the shit I really should have been dealing with.

I walked down to my appointment with Kelly and knocked on her door. She called for me to go in. Once inside I took a good long look at her. Tight, black skirt and red blouse. Her auburn hair was loose around her shoulders. My blood rushed south and my dick hardened at just this sight of her standing behind her desk, peering down at some notes.

"Mornin'." I smiled widely as her eyes connected with mine and she blushed.

"Good morning, Cameron. Sleep well?"

Aww fuck, that accent got me every time. "Um... I had another horrific nightmare but it was short this time."

"Good. That's good. Take a seat and we'll get started."

I walked over and took my usual spot on the couch. She followed and sat opposite me, demurely crossing her legs to the side.

"I wanted to ask you about the iPod that was found with you. Would you mind listening to something to see if it sparks any memories for you?

I shook my head and shrugged, unsure what good it would do. "Yeah, why not? I'll try anything at this point." She passed me the iPod and I stuck in the ear buds.

She scrolled through the tracks and hit play. "Great. Okay. Close your eyes, please, and relax."

I did as she asked and the opening bars of a song began to play. A haunting piano and guitar with voices I didn't really recognise to begin with. But as I sat there, eyes closed, the lyrics began to talk about being unable to find peace, and for some reason that resonated deep within me. I couldn't explain the sudden ache in my chest, and I clenched my fists as my jaw tightened and a ball of emotion lodged in my throat. As the chorus kicked in, my heart skipped in my chest and a cold shiver traversed my spine. I was overwhelmed with deep sadness and images of Kelly and me holding hands and smiling as we held each other, but no sooner had the image arrived than it was replaced by me sitting in a desert. The lyrics spoke of being far apart from someone and finding it hard to accept the fact. The image in my mind was of me watching the sun go down, an orange glow cast around me. I was all alone and my face was damp. Anger welled up inside of me, and I couldn't take the oppressive loneliness anymore.

My eyes sprang open and Kelly was watching me. I pulled out the ear buds. The music was faint now, but still it was too much. "Please... turn it off. I... I don't want to listen to it anymore." My voice cracked as I spoke and I realised the dampness on my face wasn't just in my imagination.

She tilted her head to one side inquisitively. "Are you okay,

Cameron? Did it spark memories for you?" I sat there in silence, clenching and unclenching my jaw, trying to figure out why the song'd had such a profound effect on me and what the hell Kelly had to do with any of this. I stared down at my hands and didn't answer and she pushed again. "Would you like to share anything with me, Cameron?"

I forced a laugh. "No. Nothing came to me," I lied. "It's just a fucking buzz kill of a song. Don't you have anything a little more light-hearted?" I wiped my hands over my face as I tried to make a joke of the situation.

"Okay. We don't have to listen to any more for now. Do you need a break?"

"Nope. I'm fine," I lied again. I was getting good at deception. Or maybe I always had been. "What the fuck was the song anyway?"

"It's a song by Snow Patrol. 'Set Fire to the Third Bar'. Does that ring any bells with you?"

I huffed like a teenage kid. "Nah. Someone should set fire to the fucking CD, man. Fuck."

"Are you sure there's nothing you want to discuss after listening to the track?"

Anger spiked within me at her insistence and my fists clenched. "I said no."

She raised her eyebrows and nodded. After a brief pause where she appeared to be doing that analysing shit on me, she finally seemed to accept my vague answers and dropped it. "Okay... so your dream last night. Can you tell me about it?"

"Actually, there was more than one."

Without making eye contact, she began to make notes. "Okay, fine. Start at the beginning."

"Uh... Okay... So, I was in a dark room. There was a guy tied to chair and I was... I think I was... I don't know... interrogating him about some shit or other. I... I hit him a few times and he was crying out for me to stop." I swallowed hard. Shame crept up my spine like an ice-cold finger, and I twisted my hands into knots.

"It seems that you're finding it difficult to talk about this. Why do you think that could be?"

"I don't know. Maybe I'm feeling guilt? If this is how I was before... Well, I can't say I'm exactly experiencing a whole lot of pride right now over my behaviour. The poor guy was distraught. When I think of his expression and the way he begged for mercy..." I dropped my head into my hands as the scenes from my dream played over again in my mind like a horror movie. The spatters of blood, the sound of crunching bones as my fist made contact with various parts of his face.

I shuddered and a wave of nausea rolled over me.

I heard her inhale deeply. "Okay. That's fine. It's clearly distressing you so, let's move on."

Relief swept through me at the opportunity to stop thinking about the awful scene. "There's been a new addition to my dreams... a bike. Motorcycle, that is. Sometimes I'm just riding at high speed, feeling the wind in my face, and I... I feel calm. Kind of serene, you know? But then... then I'm being chased by other bikers. I can never see who's chasing me. I just... I feel it. Fear... panic... adrenaline. I try to look over my shoulder and my bike skids out from underneath me, and I wake just before I hit the ground."

"Bike... okay... interesting. This is a recurring dream?"

I nodded my head. "Yeah... it's happened a couple times now, and it usually wakes me, but then I drift off into another nightmare soon after. Or... or some other kind of dream. That's what happened last night."

She nodded and made more notes. "I see. So... tell me about the subsequent dream."

I lifted my gaze and stared into those beautiful green eyes, shaking my head. "Oh... I don't think you'll wanna hear the next one, sweetheart," I told her in a warning tone.

Tilting her head to one side in that sexy way she had, she said, "Mr. Iss, I'm your doctor, not your sweetheart, and we won't get anywhere unless you tell me everything. You need to trust me. No matter what the content of your nightmares is, they could hold the key to your identity. So... try me." The defiance in her voice made my dick harden. Oh, baby, I would love to try you.

I raised my eyebrows as if to say, 'All right, you asked for it.' And keeping my gaze locked on hers, I began. "You were involved. I was in here... in your office... for my session with you. You were sitting on your desk this time and you were staring at me... You had on this little grey skirt, not as tight as the ones you usually wear. Kind of... I don't... flippy, floaty fabric. You ... began to unbutton your blouse, but you kept your eyes locked on mine. I couldn't take my eyes off of you. You opened up the blouse and exposed your lace-covered breasts to me and touched yourself. You were chewing your lip and caressing your nipples." I paused for a moment, expecting her to tell me to stop... But instead she was listening intently. Her lips parted slightly and her tongue slipped out to wet them.

"Then... you slipped your skirt up farther and spread your thighs... You... you... weren't wearing any panties." I swallowed hard as I recalled the eroticism of the dream and my dick began to throb. "You crooked your finger for me to come to you, and when I obliged, you slipped your hand into my pants and gripped my... gripped me. I shoved my pants down and you leaned back on your desk. Before I knew it I was fu—"

She cleared her throat and blinked, looking away as if coming out of a trance. She held up one hand. "Okay, stop. I get the picture. You know, it's not exactly unheard of for a patient to become attached to or infatuated with a care professional in some way. It's a kind of... a safety blanket thing," she told me without making eye contact. It was as though she was trying to convince herself that it was just infatuation. She began to flick through her notebook.

I tried not to smile and pulled my lips between my teeth for a second. "Oh... okay. I—I didn't mean to embarrass you." But honestly, deep down, I think I did intend that all along. I wanted to see how she'd react. See if she'd become aroused at my words. I'd felt the sexual tension between us and I was sure she had too. The difference was that *I* was okay admitting to it. A pink glow had spread up her chest to her cheeks, and her nipples were pushing at the fabric of her shirt. If I didn't know better, I'd say they were definite signs of arousal. But hell, I couldn't remember my own name, so what the fuck did I know?

She stood from the couch suddenly, and a look of confusion came over her pretty features. "I think we can call it a day. I have an urgent meeting to prepare for, and so it's probably best." Her voice was terse, and an air of annoyance had come over her.

What the fuck? She'd asked and I'd told, so what was the fucking problem? She made her way to the door and I followed.

"Hey, you did ask. So why do I feel like I've done something wrong here? It's not like I told you the damn dream to turn you on," I lied. "You said you needed to know. Why are you being like this?"

She turned toward me but there was still no eye contact. "Like I said, Mr Iss, I have a meeting."

"Like hell you *do*. Come on, what's wrong? We won't get anywhere with finding out who the fuck I am if you do this shit. I need to know who I am, dammit." Anger washed over me and I backed her to the wall. Clearly a former character trait rearing its head. "You're not being fair. This is my rehabilitation, and you're just cutting me off." I was aware that my tone was coming off as aggressive, and so I made an effort to soften it. "I... I need you, Kelly." There were never truer words spoken. And as the words fell from my lips, I realised the weight of them. I did need her for my rehabilitation, but there was more to it. My attachment to her was growing. And not just in a sexual way. Part of me suspected the sex stuff was the tip of the iceberg. I knew there was something so much deeper—and that scared the crap out of me.

Her chest began to rise and fall rapidly, and I was so close, I could smell her perfume. She always smelled so damn good. Like a field full of the sweetest roses.

"Cameron, that particular dream did nothing but tell me that you are subconsciously sexually attracted to me and feeling rather horny. There's no point dwelling on it further. Now I think you need to back off..." One of her hands hovered by her waist. The other came to my chest to push me away, but my strength was back and her attempt to lever me away was futile.

My eyes widened as I stared into hers. The scent of her body did strange things to me, something sprang to life within me. A hidden part of me that liked to play some kind of cat-and-mouse game. And right now I was very much a lion toying with its prey. I caged her in with my arms and leaned in closer, rubbing my nose down her cheek. "What perfume do you wear? I need to get some so I can think of you when I you're not around and I wanna come."

She gasped. "Cameron... This is... Your behaviour is... inappropriate." Her voice was a whispered breath that caressed my cheek, making my dick stand to attention until it ached. She fumbled around at her waist as a panicked expression took over her beautiful face. I guessed the little black alarm she usually carried wasn't where it should be.

Using this to my advantage, I touched my nose to her neck and inhaled her rosy scent again. My chest pressed into hers and an involuntary groan erupted from the back of my throat. "You're so soft." Without thinking, I licked a slow trail from her collarbone up to her ear. Then I suckled her neck and placed kisses along her quivering flesh back around to her throat.

She shivered and goose bumps appeared on her skin. Her

hand reached out for the door handle, but it was just out of her reach.

She could've shouted for help. I'd have stopped if she did. But she raised her lips toward mine and pushed her breasts more fully against my chest.

Removing one of my hands from the wall I slipped it into her hair and covered her mouth with my own. My God, it felt so good to kiss her. Deep and wet and it tasted so good. I'd dreamt about doing it so many times, but the reality was so much better. Her hands gripped my T-shirt and she seemed to be fighting the urge to kiss me back, but after a few moments she relented and opened her mouth, granting entry to my tongue. Her lips were soft and yielding but her kiss was urgent. I pressed my whole body into hers, my hard cock grazed her belly, and she moaned into my mouth.

Taking that as my cue, I slipped my other hand down her chest and caressed her nipple where it peaked under the satin of her blouse. She gripped my shirt tighter and deepened the kiss. I wanted to throw her down and take her right there on her office floor. I guessed it was quite some time since I'd fucked anyone, and this felt so damn good. But I was trying real hard not to handle this whole thing wrong.

Whatever the fuck this whole thing was.

And let's be real here… I had already over stepped some major fucking roadblocks with what I was doing. Why the hell give up now?

Pulling away, I gazed into her hooded green eyes. "Tell me to stop."

"W-what?" she breathed as a look of confusion appeared on her beautiful face. I glanced down at her plump lips, swollen from my passionate onslaught. I wanted to taste her again.

"Kelly, if you want me to stop then you have to tell me. I won't force you to do anything. I don't want to be that kind of guy, regardless of what I was like before."

Her nostrils flared and she pulled her bottom lip into her mouth as if she was toying with what to do. The angel and the devil, so to speak. I could see it in her eyes the moment the devil won out. Releasing her lip, she said, "No... I won't tell you to stop."

Fuck! Gliding my hand down the curves of her body, I hiked up her skirt and squeezed her tight, little round ass, still with my gaze fixed on hers. I guess I was looking for permission, but she didn't speak. She just gasped again. I moved my hand around to the front and caressed her pussy through the lace of her damp panties. I could smell her arousal mixed with the heady scent of her perfume and even though I couldn't recall much from my past, I was sure it was the best thing I'd ever smelled.

She slid her arms around my shoulders as if she needed the support and I took her mouth again. Sliding my tongue in, I tangled it with hers. So fucking good. Once my fingers were inside the lace, I found her wet for me. She wanted me. I began to tease her clit, adding pressure when she ground herself into my hand.

CHAPTER SEVEN

My mind was screaming at me to stop him. But I really didn't want to. The way he held me against the wall with his hard body and kissed me with a sense of urgency made my insides turn to jelly. I'd never been kissed that way before—with such desperation—and so my mind was fogged with desire for him and all rational thought flew out of the window.

He was possessive and dominant.

And I liked it.

I never knew that I wanted to be treated that way until he happened.

He clearly knew how to handle a woman's body, and I was simply relishing the sheer pleasure radiating from where his fingers caressed me—roughly then calmly and then roughly again—throughout every nerve ending. He slipped two fingers inside of me, and I inhaled sharply at the intrusion as he continued to circle my swollen clit with his thumb. I moaned and fought to keep my eyes on him. His dilated pupils told me he was just as turned on. That and the erection digging into my hip.

He mumbled against my mouth in a deep, lust-filled rasp that sent shivers down my spine, "Kelly, you feel so fucking good. I wish it was my cock inside you right now. I want to feel you around me while I make you come."

His crude words shocked me but spiked my desire simultaneously, and I wanted to take him up on his fantasy. It was my fantasy too, after all. But instead I just stared into his eyes wordlessly; needing that connection. I was startled at what I saw there. Gone was the aggressive stare from earlier as he'd backed me up against the wall, and it had been replaced with a look of awe. He watched my every expression intently as if witnessing a woman in the throes of passion for the first time.

The sensations his fingers were creating were intensifying, and I ground myself into his hand as I pulled him to me and thrust my tongue into his mouth. My hands fisted in the long, shaggy strands of his unkempt hair. His fingers slipped and slid in my wetness, and suddenly he touched a part of me inside in such a way that the pleasure skyrocketed. It was so intense that I could see stars. He dropped his head to my breast and pulled my stiffened peak into his mouth, teasing it with his teeth through the fabric of my blouse. Gasping for air, I felt my muscles tighten and clench around his fingers as my orgasm shot me into outer space. I dropped my head forward and leaned into him for support, biting down on his shoulder to stifle the cry I was desperate to make, and a growl erupted from his throat. I released his skin and his lips returned to mine once more. The kiss was rough again and I was shocked at how I let go and thrust my tongue into his mouth. I was never this wanton. A second orgasmic wave almost floored me, and he swallowed my cries. I was grateful for that as the walls of the hospital were far too thin for this type of encounter to go unnoticed. Anyone could have walked into the room at any time thanks to the no-locks policy. But that just heightened the excitement even more.

I began to float back to earth and opened my eyes. When I

did, I realised his were fixed on me once again, and he was smiling a sexy, lopsided smile.

He had watched and felt the whole thing.

My breathing was ragged and his fingers were still caressing me, drawing out the most amazing sensations for as long as he could while I tried to make sense of what had just happened.

"My God, you're beautiful when you let go like that," he whispered. He leaned in again and kissed me with an uncharacteristic tenderness, like I was his lover and this had all been normal, but I suddenly felt ashamed at what I'd allowed to happen and I covered my face with my hands.

Removing his fingers from my vagina, he gripped my hands and pulled them away, our skin sliding together in a sensual, intimate way. "Hey... hey, don't do that. Don't cover your face. I want to look at you. You have no clue how amazing it is to watch you come. I could look at you all damn day, Kelly. You're so fucking beautiful."

I felt the heat of my cheeks increase and I couldn't meet his eyes. "Don't... please." My voice was hardly recognisable as my own.

"Don't what? Don't give you a compliment? Don't tell you the truth?"

"I... we... That shouldn't have happened. I can't believe—"

He stopped my words with his mouth as he pulled me into his body. His erection was still strong and proud and straining at his jeans as he pressed himself into me. I wanted him so badly.

When the kiss ended, he pulled away slightly. "Well, I for one don't regret what just happened. The only thing I do regret is that we're in your fucking office and I can't be inside of you right now."

"I wouldn't sleep with you, Cameron. It wouldn't be right. This was a mistake as it is." I tried to sound calm but failed miserably.

He chuckled, but the smile on his face was a little menacing.

He slipped his fingers into his mouth and sucked my juices from them. Turned on beyond measure yet horrified by my inability to control myself sexually, I gasped and opened my mouth to protest at his vulgarity; but what could I say after what I'd allowed him to do to me?

Once he had devoured my arousal from his fingers, he sneered at me. "You want me to fuck you, Kelly. It's written all over your face. And the signs are visible all over your body. And remember *I* know how wet you are. *I* did that. You want me inside of you. Why don't you just admit it? Huh? You've been attracted to me from the beginning."

I snorted at his attitude. Even if his words rang true, I wouldn't admit it. "My God, you're so arrogant."

He dragged his tongue across his lower lip as he stared into me. "This isn't arrogance, sweetheart. I know what I felt. And what I saw in your eyes."

I began to panic. "It's unethical. I could lose my job. It's, it's—"

"Fuck ethics, Kelly. Don't be so fucking straight laced all the time. Live a little."

I pushed on his chest and this time he moved back. I straightened my clothes and glanced down to find a damp patch on the silk over my left breast. Oh shitty shit. I was grateful that I'd brought a jacket to work with me.

Amusement came over me at my train of thought. I'd just had a sexual encounter with a bloody patient in my office and here I was worrying about how I looked? Crazy. Definitely crazy. There was no other logical explanation. I'd obviously been studying and working in my field for so long that the lines were becoming blurred.

I realised that Cameron was still standing before me with an expectant expression on his face. I smoothed my hair before I told him, "This... this can't happen again, Cameron. And it won't. It was wrong. I could get fired. It was stupid of me. We... I overstepped the mark here. It's entirely my fault. You're my patient and I've acted like some... some tart. I've abused my position of trust. That's just not me. It's not who I am or how I behave. I... I apologise." My words came out in panicked rush and my eyes began to sting as the weight of what I'd done really weighed heavy.

He stepped toward me and reached out to touch my cheek. His brow furrowed. "Excuse me for pointing out the obvious here but you don't hear me complaining do you? And believe me when I tell you I don't feel abused. Not in the slightest. And you are in no way a... a what did you call yourself? A tart?"

His warm smile did nothing to reassure me. What had I been thinking? I shook my head. "That's not the point Cameron. I—"

He reached up and tucked a stray strand of hair behind my ear, suddenly tender again. I was getting whiplash from his changing mood. "Then what is the point? You can't tell me that you haven't felt the sexual tension between us. We just acted on how we felt."

He was right, of course, but I couldn't admit to it. I wouldn't admit to it and it didn't change the fact that it was wrong. So wrong. "You're quite an intimidating man. And whilst I do find you attractive it is my job to help you figure out who you are and why you're here. It's not my job to use you for sexual gratification."

His mouth turned up at one side. "Says the woman with the damp panties and the just pleasured glow. Look... you don't need to worry. I've decided I'm not a guy who kisses and tells. That's the beauty of amnesia I guess. You get to rebuild yourself into the kind of person you wish you were. No one will find anything out from me. I'm just a little sad that we won't get to do this again. Watching you fall apart for me was... beautiful. Just so you know." He adjusted himself in his jeans, stepped away from me and pressed on the door handle pulling it open a little. I was still leaning on the wall for support as my legs had turned to jelly. I turned my head toward him and he smiled. "Relax, Kelly. Please?" His voice was soft and I was thankful for the wall at my back.

When he had gone I slid down until my bottom hit the floor. I rested my head in my hands and began to sob. What the hell was I playing at? What the hell was I doing? Those two questions were being screamed at me by my subconscious over and over.

But I couldn't answer them.

I had nothing except tears of self-loathing.

CHAPTER EIGHT

CAMERON

I returned to my room and slumped into the chair by the window. I could still smell her on me, and my dick was reluctant to relax just like the rest of my tensed-up body. Running my fingers through my hair, I closed my eyes and replayed the events that had taken place only minutes before. The way her eyes drifted half closed as her arousal took over. The way she dug her fingers into my shoulders and bit me and the feel of her pussy tightening around my fingers. Fuck, what I wouldn't give to do it all over again but this time with my cock. What a shame it wouldn't be happening anytime soon.

She'd made that very clear.

The fear in her eyes when she came back to earth told me that there was a good chance I'd be seeing a different doctor from that moment on. I had to get used to the fact that there was no fucking way she would face me again. And shit if that didn't piss me off.

Hell, I was beginning to regret pushing her so far. She clearly wanted me, but... maybe I could've handled things differently.

Taken things slower maybe. The problem was that I couldn't hide my attraction to her and I'd acted instinctively. That fact alone scared the crap out of me. Who the hell was I, and why would I act in such a sexually aggressive way toward a woman who was clearly out of reach?

Was that it?

Was it the challenge?

My mind scoured the recent memories of dreams I'd been having and the erotic nature of many of them. The women who'd featured in my unconscious encounters were faceless—that is, apart from Kelly. What made her different? Maybe it was just the fact that she was the one I was thinking about at the time. She was real. The others were either figments of my lurid imagination or memories of lays past. Either way, they didn't help me to identify myself.

Feeling more tense and aroused than I cared to be, I walked into my bathroom and leaned against the door in the hope that my weight would act as a deterrent for any of the well-meaning nursing staff intent on bursting in. I unbuttoned my fly, shoved my jeans down a ways, and gripped my cock firmly. Closing my eyes, I called to mind the way Kelly's body felt and smelled; every teasing memory played in my head as I moved my hand up and down, squeezing my shaft and driving myself towards the release I wished I could've had with her... in her. Fuck I wanted to be inside her. Feeling her pussy tighten around me as her soft tits rubbed against my bare chest. Thrusting hard into her until she cried out my name and I marked her as my own.

I let my head fall back against the door as my breathing accelerated and I remembered the noises she'd made as I fucked her with my fingers. A grunt left my chest and I chewed on my bottom lip as deep, intense pleasure radiated from where I slipped my fist along my rigid cock. Suddenly my mind was pulled in another direction. My imagination was running wild and in my mind's eye I glanced down to see Kelly naked on her knees before me as she pulled the full length of my erection into the wet cave of her mouth. Fuck, my fantasies were definitely improving. Her breasts bounced as she stared up at me and increased the speed of her sucking. If it were real, I would have grabbed a handful of her silky auburn curls —not to hurt her but just to control her pace. I wanted this to last as long as possible, but the images of her flashing through my mind were enough to send any guy over the edge. My grip tightened and once more I was inside her, feeling her sliding her body down on mine, and I could hold back no longer. I gritted my teeth and fought the roar trying to escape my body as I came hard.

Once my body had calmed enough for me to take a walk, I cleaned myself up and went to the nurse's station to check if the library cart was due to come around. The old volunteer, Charlie, was around seventy and more or less the hospital grandpa. He'd recommended some fantastic books for me to read, the last being "The Catcher in the Rye" by J. D. Salinger. I identified with Holden Caulfield in a way that made me once again question who I had been before I lost my memory.

As I stood chatting to Patty at the nurse's station, I heard the clicking of heels on the tiled floor to my left. I looked towards the sound and smiled. Kelly was walking toward me with her head down. She was reading a pile of papers as she walked and her brow was furrowed. She stopped and lifted her head, meeting my eyes as she did so. My gaze trailed down her body and landed on the jacket she was wearing to hide the evidence of our earlier encounter.

"Erm... Cameron... I... I need to speak with you.... It's a matter of urgency."

"Okay, let's go to my room." I gestured across the corridor.

"No... no... let's go to my office." She turned to walk away, not giving me a chance to reply.

"Hell yeah," I muttered under my breath—or so I thought—

but she stopped dead and turned around, fixing me with a hard, cold stare.

"Hurry along now, Mister Iss," she hissed. Okay, so there wasn't going to be an imminent repeat of our last meeting. Fuck.

"Okay, okay keep your panties on." I chuckled. But again my sense of humour was far from appreciated. Her responding pursed-lipped death stare almost burned holes in my head and told me I'd better keep my jokes to myself in future.

I followed her until we reached her office. She stepped inside and held the door open for me and I kept my gaze fixed on hers as I walked into the room. But once she had closed the door, she looked away and went to sit behind her desk. Oh... so we're behaving all professional now, are we?

"Please take a seat." She gestured to the chair opposite which afforded her a large wooden barrier between us. I reluctantly sat.

With what I hoped to be an innocent smile, I tilted my head to one side, trying to look cute. "I'm guessing you didn't invite me in here for an encore, huh?"

She sighed and removed her glasses, placed them on her desk, and rubbed at the bridge of her nose. "I did inform you that what happened was a mistake. There will be no repeats. And most certainly not after what has been discovered."

Huh? Suddenly I was all ears. "What do you mean 'after what's been discovered'?"

"Your DNA seems to match that of a known criminal in California."

Her words were like a blow to my solar plexus. "Oh, fuck... no way." My worst fears had been realised. I really was a badass piece of work. I had hoped my gut feelings had been misplaced, but I was so wrong.

"The police will want to speak with you again. There are no warrants out for your arrest at present, but it seems there is a history of offences that go *way* back. Most of them related to..." She swallowed as if she was about to throw up. "To violence."

"So... is this definitely me? I mean... this criminal is definitely who I am?" My voice was weak and croaky as the reality of the whole situation weighed on my shoulders, pushing me down.

Kelly carried on, ignoring my question. "Your true name is Cain Somers. The name on the suicide note, Cameron Iss, appears to be an anagram of your real name. And... there are connections in your past to a motorcycle club responsible for robberies, gang wars, and money laundering. The details of this are a little sketchy at the moment, but I'm sure the police will find out more."

A heavy weight pressed down on my chest and suddenly I couldn't breathe. I tugged at the round neck on my T-shirt knowing full-well that it wouldn't help the sensation of asphyxiation. I pushed my seat away from the desk and lowered my head to my hands, trying to pull air into my lungs and calm myself down. Cain Somers? I repeated it over and over in my head. Why did the name not sound familiar to me? And who would give me an alias that was a fucking anagram? Or... or did I give myself the alias? I felt like I was on some dumb episode of fucking Scooby Doo and someone's mask was about to be removed. The only trouble was, it was mine.

Suddenly remembering one of my very vivid dreams of a blue-eyed, dark-haired girl. "So... so who is Rosa?"

She linked her fingers and leaned forward on her desk. Concern flashed in her eyes. "It transpires that Rosa... was... is your seventeen-year-old sister." The concern transformed into sadness.

My stomach plummeted like I was on some giant roller coaster. "Was? Was my sister? Do you mean she's... she's dead?"

She sighed heavily and briefly closed her eyes, and I knew then that I wasn't going to like what was coming. A line appeared between her eyebrows, and her voice came out in a husky whisper. "Rosa Somers is currently logged as a missing person. She hasn't been seen since before you were discovered over by Ben Nevis."

A cold shiver ran the full length of my spine, and my mouth suddenly dried out. I could almost feel the colour drain from my face as I fixed my stare on Kelly and let what she had said sink in.

Her earlier words about the police wanting to speak to me rolled around my mind. I suddenly sat up straight as dread washed over me. I held up my hands. "Wait... wait a minute. Do they think I have something to do with her disappearance? Is that what all this is about?"

It made total sense now. The fact that our little indiscretion wouldn't be happening again. Of course now she knew I was a fucking criminal. Now she had figured out what I already knew. That I was no fucking good for her. Unless I was finger fucking her and giving the best fucking orgasm she'd had in her prissy fucking life. But I clearly wasn't even good enough to make her come now. I balled my fists as anger rose along with bile in my throat and I inwardly began shrinking to a pile of nothing before her. Because evidently that's what I was to her. Nothing. Nothing but a fucking violent criminal.

Her eyes widened slightly as if she were reading my mind, and I could swear I saw panic appear there for a split second. "Honestly, I don't know. But it seems that Rosa was your only remaining family member. There is no trace of anyone else related to you still living, I'm afraid."

Fuck.

In the space of ten minutes I'd discovered I was a known criminal, I had a sister but she was nowhere to be found, and all my other relatives were dead. Fuck. I stood and began to pace the room as the reality of the situation hit me. I could end up in prison for something I couldn't even remember having any involvement in. And what kind of fucking person was I anyway? Who in their right mind would be instrumental in the disappearance of their fucking kid sister?

My heart drummed heavily at my ribcage and I suddenly felt lightheaded. I could hear Kelly speaking, but her words were more like an echo in the distance. I turned to look over at her and saw her rushing to the door and shouting for help. The whole thing seemed to happen in slow motion, and I found myself on my knees, struggling to breathe. I gripped my chest and fell forward into blackness.

CHAPTER NINE

KELLY

The huge hulk of a man falling to the floor was not something I had expected to witness. The way I'd handled things had been very presumptuous and a tad unprofessional. In some small way I think I was subconsciously punishing him for making me want him. It was ridiculous, unprofessional, and unfair of me. I had just figured he would take on board what I had to tell him and would handle it like the strong, arrogant arse he appeared to be.

Clearly I had been very much mistaken.

And this had been a huge learning curve.

I was beginning to wonder if I was actually cut out for my chosen career. After all, if I had fallen so easily for the first attractive patient that came under my care, what did that say about me? And although I wanted to blame the sexy American who had become the centre of my albeit small and confusing world, I knew beyond any shadow of a doubt that this was my fault. My issue. I was the one in the wrong here. When I added to all of that the very small fact that I was still struggling to figure him out, there was no real wonder why I was consumed with doubt about my capability as a psychologist.

As soon as I saw the colour drain from his face and his knees began to buckle, I ran to the door and shouted into the corridor for help. Mack and Dennis, the two orderlies from the ward, came dashing in, and I was so grateful that they had been close by. Dennis collected a wheelchair and they managed to get Cameron/Cain back to his room. After a panicked phone call confession about my harsh delivery of the trauma-inducing news to my patient, Doctor Alex Clayton came down and checked him over, but Cameron's... Cain's pulse and blood pressure were thankfully returning to normal and he began to come around.

His eyelids fluttered open and he glanced nervously around the room. "What the fuck happened? Where am I?"

Alex tried to reassure him. "It's okay, you're in the hospital. You banged your head when you fell. You may feel a little disorientated for a while but... well you had just received a barrage of sensitive information in a less than sensitive manner, so it's understandable." Alex glanced at me with a disapproving raise of his eyebrows.

Cam... Cain's brow scrunched and he closed his eyes for a moment, and I mentally chastised myself for not only my earlier lack of sensitivity but also for continuously muddling up my patient's name in my head. It would take some getting used to. When he opened them again, they were wide and stark with fear. "R-Rosa? Where's Rosa? Fuck, I need to find Rosa." He tried to sit up, but both Alex and I jumped forward.

"Whoa... whoa... just stay calm, okay? You've had a blow to the head. You can't go rushing around," Alex informed him.

"But you don't understand! They're going to kill her!"

A cold shiver travelled the length of my spine, and my heart leapt. "Who... who is going to kill Rosa, Cain?"

"The fucking Company. They'll kill her!" He shouted and fought against Alex, who tried to hold him down. Cain was much more muscular and heavily built, and so Alex's attempts were futile. Mack and Dennis rushed forward to help too. Alex stepped away and returned moments later with a syringe which he jabbed into Cain's arm as my distressed patient hurled expletives into the room. As the sedative took effect, his angry cries became sorrowful whispers of him repeating his sister's name over and over.

My heart broke for him.

Tears stung at my eyes as I watched the giant of a man succumb to the chemicals racing through his bloodstream. Desperation to help him tightened at my stomach. The heaviness of guilt weighed me down too. Our bizarre relationship, whilst purely sexual in actuality, had had a deep, resounding effect on me regardless of what it might have meant to Cain. They say you should never confuse sex with love, but every single line I had ever drawn in the metaphorical sand was now blurred or completely wiped out. What the hell did I know anymore about right and wrong? I'd allowed a confused, scared American man with no real identity to finger fuck me to the most intense orgasm I'd ever experienced. But the tenderness in his eyes afterwards and the way he had tried to reassure me had confused me. Why the hell couldn't I just let it go as sex? The realisation that my need to help him on a more personal level meant that my feelings were developing despite the necessity to fight them. I wanted to help and that was that. End of. I needed to find out more. What the hell was *the Company*? And why would they kill his kid sister? What had happened to cause such conflict that would endanger the lives of those he loved? The only conclusion I could glean was that it must have been something drastic.

————

CAIN

The room was dark and the foul metallic stench of blood hung in the air. My skin was damp with sweat and my chest heaved as I tried to pull cleaner air into my lungs. The problem was that there was no fucking cleaner air. Rosa was somewhere in there. I just had to find her. They couldn't do this to her. Not my baby sister. She had nothing to do with this fucking shit. What kind of fucking barbaric bastards was I dealing with here? These people were supposed to have my back. We were like family. So why the fuck had they turned on me now?

In the distance I heard screaming. It was her. It was my Rosa. Nausea and anger knotted inside me in equal measures and I clenched my jaw, fighting with myself not to call to her and give myself away. I'd let her down. The kid I'd looked after since my stepmom and Dad were killed by a rival club thanks to a drug deal gone wrong. I had been seventeen at the time and that poor little kid had only been six. And here I was fighting for her fucking life. Fighting with people who knew me. Who supposedly loved me. Who loved her. I'd failed her. How the fuck would she ever trust me again? If she even survived this hell. We had to get out. We had to make a break for it. And as soon as I found her, I'd make it my fucking mission to get her to a safer place.

When I awoke, the room was dimly lit and the door was ajar. I went to sit up but my head whooshed as if I had done a 360-degree spin. The nurse that had been there when the doctor injected me appeared in the doorway.

"Hey, there. Good to have you back with us. I'll let Doctor Darrow and Doctor Clayton know that you're awake."

"Wait!"

She stopped and turned to face me. "Yes?"

"Look... I need to get out of here. Can... can you help me? Please?"

She began to back away with pity in her eyes. "I'm so sorry, love, but no. You need to be here right now." And with that she disappeared.

I slammed my fist into the mattress and shouted, "Fuck!" into the empty room.

Doctor Darrow entered a few moments later, closely followed by Doctor Clayton and a huge fucking giant of a guy in a security uniform.

Doctor Clayton approached me with caution. "Mr Somers. How are you feeling?"

"How the fuck do you think I'm feeling? I'm stuck in fucking Scotland while my kid sister is being held against her will by fucking maniacs. So, yeah, peachy. Just fucking peachy."

"Look, Mr. Somers, your aggressive nature is in no way helping the situation. We have informed the police that your memory appears to be returning, and they are going to attend the hospital to meet with you. They will be able to help you, I'm sure of that. But until we can substantiate these dreams as factual flashbacks, you will have to remain here where you can be cared for. It's for your own good, believe me."

I closed my eyes and laid my head back as the doc checked my blood pressure. Rifling through my scattered thoughts I tried desperately to make sense of things. To piece the fractured jigsaw together. To try and discover what else I could remember. But I drew a blank. I knew that there was Rosa... and that the Company had taken her. But... I couldn't remember who the Company were exactly. I knew that they must know me and I them. And that something big had gone down. And that Rosa was in danger... But why? What the fuck had happened? Why couldn't I remember?

That night I was restless. Not surprising, really. I was plagued by more dreams, but this time they weren't quite as horrific...

Rosa was skipping toward me with her motorcycle helmet hooked over her arm. I shook my head and smiled. I couldn't help myself. She was so damn cute, and just seeing her made my day. Tall and lean with long, stringy legs that didn't seem to belong. Her dark, almost black hair was tied in long braids. The vivid blue streak in the front matched the colour of her eyes. Her peers were standing, just staring as she slung her backpack on and secured the chin strap on her helmet before kicking her leg over and slipping her arms around my waist.

"Hey, big bro. How's it going?" She squeezed me and I patted her small hands with mine.

"All the better for seeing you, kiddo. Good day?" I asked over my shoulder.

"Meh... you know... it's high school."

She wasn't a huge fan of the whole academic thing, but she was incredibly bright. Sadly she wasn't one of the cool, popular kids. In fact, many of the kids her age avoided her on account of her big brother and the bad company he kept. I was always assuring her that what they thought didn't matter, but I know that her lack of friends affected her.

"Hey, your patch is coming off your cut again. Remind me when we get home, and I'll take a look and sew it back on for you. Can't have you representing the club looking all messed up, huh?" That was Rosa for you. Always looking out for me even though I was supposed to be the adult. I was more than capable of sewing my own patches on, but I would let her do it anyhow. She always said she liked to feel useful.

I didn't need to reply. Instead I nodded my head once and turned the key in the bike's ignition, and the beast roared to life. We pulled away at speed down the road toward home...

CHAPTER TEN

KELLY

My nerves jangled as I waited for Cameron... or should I say Cain, to arrive. Dammit, I needed to get used to this change in name. And to be honest, the name Cain seemed to suit him better. Cameron was a Scottish name, and he was very much an American. I repeated his name over and over in my mind in a bid to acquaint myself with it, but all it did was produce images in my mind of my American in a kilt, bare chested and staring at me with that blue-eyed smoulder. My nipples stood to attention just at the thought. I had a major thing for a man in traditional Scottish dress anyway, but Cain, the all-American bad boy in all his tattooed glory, kitted out in this way made my breasts feel heavy with lust and set my needy clit tingling.

There was a knock at the door and it snapped me back from my latest inappropriate fantasy. I inhaled a long, deep breath and shook my hands in front of me like a boxer warming up for a fight. "Come in."

He walked into the room and I instinctively gravitated toward him by several steps; and as I did so I noticed that he did the same. Warmth flooded my veins and I smiled in a way that I hoped would be reassuring, considering our last encounter and the information I had imparted. His responding smile was curt and I watched as he raised his arms toward me briefly. But he suddenly clenched his fists and then slipped his hands into his jeans pockets. I wasn't sure what he'd been about to do, but that one small action caused the ache of lust to turn to one of deep longing. I wanted to wrap my arms around him and tell him that everything would be okay. He looked so lost but so very handsome at the same time. Patty, his nurse, had brought him some clothes. They had belonged to her son, who had emigrated to Australia, and they almost fit him. But the lack of a belt around his waist meant the blue jeans hung low on his hips. Belts were not allowed on the ward for reasons of suicide risk.

With his vivid blue gaze fixed on mine, Cain once again walked slowly toward me. He wore a pale blue button-up T-shirt with the first two buttons unfastened. The sleeves were rolled up to the elbows, revealing the tattoos on his muscular forearms.

Needing to release myself from his magnetic draw, I turned and walked over to sit on one of the couches where I usually conducted my therapy sessions. I cleared my throat. "Hi, Cain. Have a seat." I gestured to the couch opposite, and he sat.

Resting his elbows on his knees, he steepled his fingers. "So... have you found any more skeletons in my closet?" he asked, tilting his head to one side and piercing me with his intense cerulean stare.

The sensuality that emanated from that very simple head movement sent another rush of blood to my sex. I looked away for a moment to gather myself and break the spell that he seemed to cast over me whenever we made eye contact. "No. I was hoping you may have had some more flashbacks."

He rubbed his hands over his face and fell silent for a moment. "Just dreams. I think I used to pick up Rosa from high school on my motorbike. And..."

"And?" I shifted in my seat as images of Cain straddling a shining hunk of power exacerbated my desire.

"And she mentioned something about a patch coming loose on my cut. In the dream I was wearing a leather vest or... or the police called it a waistcoat when they showed me, and I think *that* was what she was referring to. I... think the connections to the motorcycle club that you mentioned were significant. I... I think I was a member."

I dropped my gaze again. Shit. So he was—or *is*—a member of a club that rains down violence and crime on a poor neigh-bourhood somewhere in the United States. This can't be good. So why am I not put off? Why do I not care that he has poten-tially harmed other human beings? What does that say about me? Why does it not matter to me in the slightest what he's done in his past? When I lifted my head and met his eyes again, I saw regret; and something that felt like relief rapidly swept through me. If he regrets his past actions, then that means he's not all bad. "You seem... you seem unhappy about that," I observed.

"Yeah, well, it was you who told me that I'm connected to violent crime. Fuck! How am I supposed to feel?" He ran his hands through his hair, and I watched as the strands fell back to caress his skin. But his devastation was almost palpable.

I needed to reassure him, and the urge to hold him almost overpowered me again. "Look, we don't know for sure that you held responsibility for any crime, Cain."

He stood and began pacing. "Oh, come on, Kelly. Don't try to fucking sugar-coat *shit* here. I'm a fucking criminal. I have a record. And now my sister is paying for my mistakes. Someone *has* her, and I can't fucking help her if I'm here trying to figure out who the hell I am!" His deep, gravelly voice bellowed out and the veins in his neck protruded. My heart palpitated in my chest and I blinked rapidly at his outburst. Suddenly the door felt too far away.

My eyes flicked from the door to Cain. "Cain, please calm

down." He began to stalk toward me and I stood, ready to bolt. I held up my hands. "Please sit down. We will get to the bottom of this, and we will try and figure out where your sister is—"

He stopped right in front of me and gripped my arms. "And what if we're too late, huh?" His eyes flashed with anger.

I began to shake as the cold dread of fear washed over me. If he *was* the criminal it seemed he had turned out to be, I had to be careful. I had no clue what he was capable of.

He pleaded at me with his stare. "Kelly, I know my memory is sketchy, but from the dreams I've been having, I know that I love that kid with all my heart. I'm responsible for her, but I wasn't involved in her disappearance, that much I know. I think I pissed someone off and *they* took her as revenge. How could I live with myself if they harm her because of something *I* did?" His voice had softened and wavered as he spoke. "I need to go to her, Kelly."

The pain in his eyes made my heart ache for him. I raised my hands and gripped his elbows as compassion overtook my fear, pushing aside the knowledge that this depth of caring for him overstepped my professional boundaries by miles. "I want to help you, Cain. I really do. But I don't know how we could get you out of here and on a plane to the USA when you have no passport. And let's face the facts as they are. You don't *actually* know where she is or where you're from exactly. You'd be going there blind, and America is a huge place to be lost in."

He clenched his jaw and closed his eyes. "I feel so fucking useless, Kelly. Why is my memory not coming back quicker? How can I make it happen faster?" He opened his eyes again and locked them on mine. His anguish was almost palpable. My eyes began to sting and my throat tightened. I wanted more than anything to comfort him and ease his worry. I could only imagine what this was like for him, and *that* was bad enough.

"Cain, I'm so sorry," I whispered, wishing it could be different between us. "There's nothing you can do to make things happen quicker. You have to let the healing occur at a natural pace. The brain is such a complex organ to deal with, and to be quite honest you're lucky to be alive as it is. You can't force it. We can encourage it, of course. That's why we have these sessions. But there's no magic elixir that will make your memory return at the flick of a switch."

He closed his eyes once again and let his head drop forward. "I'd do anything. *Anything* to be able to help Rosa. I'd give my *life* just to know she was safe again."

Those words were my undoing and I pulled him into my arms as he broke down. His violent sobs vibrated through me and I managed to guide him back to the couch. I sat and he immediately crumpled into me and rested his head in my lap, clinging to my hips and pouring out the anguish he was feeling. He wasn't alone in feeling useless. I wanted so much to take this pain away and give him what he needed but there was nothing more I could do.

Once he had calmed and the sobs had subsided he raised his body again, rubbed his hands over his face and exhaled a ragged breath. "Fuck, I'm sorry Kelly. I... I don't know what came over me. You must think I'm a total fucking pussy."

I handed him a box of tissues. "I think nothing of the sort. You're going through an incredibly traumatic time. There's no need to apologise for getting emotional. It's a wonder it hasn't happened before." My God, could there be any more layers to this man? His endearing vulnerability at that precise moment almost had me a quivering mess, melting to a puddle on the floor. He was both dominant and soft-hearted. Such a heady combination sent images racing through my mind of what he would be like making love to me. Arrgh. Focus, Kelly. Focus.

"Look... Is there any chance that I could maybe get out of here for a break? You know, some fresh air that doesn't involve the hospital grounds? I hear the Black Isle is beautiful. I'd like to maybe go there."

"Oh... I don't think—"

"Oh, come on, Kelly. As my doctor you could make it part of my rehab. Couldn't you?"

Oh God, those eyes... that face. I think it was safe to say I would have done anything for him right then. A voice in the back of my mind was screaming at me, telling me how unprofessional I was being... had been... but the part of my brain that made decisions chose to ignore the voice.

"I'll see what I can do."

A grin spread across his handsome features.

Oh, great. "Don't get excited. You won't be allowed to go alone."

His smile disappeared and he leaned toward me. I froze and swallowed as he reached out and engulfed my hand in his. "Maybe *you* could accompany me? Give me a tour."

He gently squeezed my fingers and ran his thumb over my knuckles. Not a particularly sexy gesture, but it seemed anything he did was sexy to me and my body reacted accordingly. Shivers graced my skin at the casual yet somehow intimate contact.

He stared at my lips and licked his own. A pulsing throb began at the junction of my thighs, and my nipples stood to attention. I really needed to listen to the voice in the back of my head, but my heart was pounding so hard that it was drowned out.

"One of these days, Kelly, I'm gonna find out how good it feels to be inside you. To fuck you and have you call my name when you come."

I gasped at his coarse language and I clenched my core muscles, trying in vain to fight the spike of desire and the dampening of my underwear as my body betrayed me. "You... you really need to stop talking to me like that, Cain," I stuttered. "It's... I don't like it. It's highly inappropriate and—"

He chuckled darkly and interrupted my protestations. "You forget that I know how wet you get for me. The effect I have on you. You affect me too. Do you know how hard you make me? It'd be a shame to waste that. Don't you think?"

His face was perilously close to mine and his breath teased my lips. The more I leaned back, the more he leaned toward me until I was almost on my back. How the hell he had gone from crying about his kid sister to seducing me was a mystery. Although I was very much aware that amnesia patients did sometimes exhibit irrational behaviour, this felt different. And I would have been a fool to give in.

But who was I kidding? I was a fool.

His hand slipped up my inner thigh and I pressed my knees together, trying again to contradict my body's desires, but it didn't stop him. His mission continued and I felt my barriers falling as he fixed me with a penetrating gaze that could have melted my panties right off. I relaxed my thighs, and his fingers brushed lightly over my sex.

"I can feel the effect I have on you." He slipped his body closer to me and gripped my hand. He manoeuvred me so that I could feel the thick, hard ridge of his cock through his jeans. "And now you can feel the effect you have on me, Kelly. You'd better be thankful for my current state of unpreparedness. If I had a condom, I'd take you, right here, right now on this couch."

A voice in my head was screaming yes, just do it, take me, and my body was a willing associate. Another countering voice in my head was trying desperately to make me see sense, but the first voice chose that precise moment to remind me that I had condoms in my purse from my last encounter with Dermott.

"We... we can't. Someone could walk in. We can't keep doing this. This is not me. I'm *not* a slut." Although I spoke the words out loud, I was talking to myself. Trying to remind myself that I had only ever trusted Dermott with my body. But the excitement that this illicit exchange with this dangerous man was provoking in me was like nothing I had ever experienced before.

"I don't think you're a slut. Far from it," he growled deeply, and that alone almost had me falling into the abyss. "I think you're a beautiful, sexy woman who needs to loosen up and go with the flow a little more. You don't know what pleasures you're missing out on. I could show you. I could make you feel so good. If I can do this to you with just my fingers, imagine how good it would be with my tongue... my cock."

He began to tease my sensitive flesh through the cotton fabric of my panties, and against my better judgement, I squeezed at the ridge in his jeans, wishing for a split second that we were somewhere private so that I could give in.

He buried his face in my cleavage and mumbled, "God you smell so good. You always. Smell. So. Fucking. Good." His fingers slipped past the barrier before them and I gasped as they entered me.

Suddenly there was a knock on the door and I was snatched back to reality with a resounding thud that matched the one made by heart.

Back down to Earth.

To sanity.

"Shit, shit what am I doing?" I spoke in an angry whisper and shoved him off of me before I stood quickly to straighten my clothing. He sighed heavily and adjusted himself. Then stared at me and licked his fingers. Bastard! "Erm... come in!" I called.

Patty appeared around the door. "Hi, Dr Darrow. I'm sorry to interrupt, but... your next appointment is waiting."

Oh my God, what the hell was wrong with me? Insanity was taking over. That was the only explanation. I turned to face Cain. "That will be all for today, Mr. Somers."

He nodded with an appearance of defeat. His shoulders slumped. With a sharp raise of his eyebrows he said, "Okay... and what about the thing we talked about?"

Shit! He's not going to hint at our sexual exchange in front of Patty? "The thing?"

"Yeah... the thing about me going out for some fresh air?"

Phew! Thank goodness. "Oh... oh, yes, that thing. Leave it with me and I'll see what I can do." Now get out, get out, get out!

His brow scrunched and he appeared less than convinced at my words. He eyed me closely and suspiciously as he passed me to leave the office. Patty held the door open for him and closed it once he had exited.

"Kelly, is everything okay, dear?"

"Yes, Patty. W-why do you ask?"

"I don't know... I just get a strange vibe from that young man. He looks at you as though he could devour you, and that worries me."

Oh, Patty, you have no idea. "Not at all. He's just struggling to come to terms with his situation. I think maybe he needs to get out of here for a couple of hours. Have a change of scenery."

"But... he couldn't go out alone, so who would take him?"

Okay... time to plant the seed. "Well... I'm off tomorrow. I could escort him for a while."

She frowned. "That's not really part of your job description, Doctor, babysitting patients. And I'm not sure that being alone with him is such a good idea. I mean, we don't know—"

"Patty, if I need advice on how to deal with my cases from a registered mental health nurse, I will be sure to come and find you," I snapped.

She clamped her mouth shut and widened her eyes at me as a blush rose from her neck to her cheeks. "I'm sorry, Doctor. I didn't mean to interfere."

"Then don't," I hissed in a less-than-civilised manner. She rapidly turned and left the room. When I was sure she had gone, I walked over to my desk, slumped into my chair, and exhaled a long, shaking breath. "I'm going stark raving mad."

CHAPTER ELEVEN

Cᴀɪɴ

I presumed from the way our "meeting" ended that there was no way I was being let out of my fucking prison anytime soon. But it didn't stop me from hoping. I was trapped somewhere thousands of miles away from the one person who needed me, and it was literally driving me crazy. If I didn't have a reason for being in this fucking hospital to begin with, the fact that I was here would soon give me one. Each time I looked at the view beyond the glass of my window, anger rose inside of me. I was definitely the type of person that thrived outdoors, and the sooner I could get there the better. But I was reliant on a woman who couldn't fucking make up her mind what she wanted in her own life, so how was she going to be any help in mine?

As soon as Kelly popped into my head again, I realised I couldn't get the sexy smell of her out of my mind and wanted nothing more than to relive the encounter over and over. I had a nice memory to take into the shower with me later that day, and as I let the hot water slide down my chest and over my stomach, I imagined her mouth on me. Licking and sucking her way down my abs until she reached my favourite body part. I gripped my hard shaft in one soapy hand and pinched my nipple with the other, but my forceful stroking was a poor replacement for her mouth; and as I let my thumb roll around the smooth skin at the tip, I realised that my imagination was in no way good enough to create the sensation of what her tongue would feel like swirling at the head of my cock, but it was all I had and so I made the most of it.

As images of Kelly's wide-eyed stare turning into half-lidded bliss rampaged through my mind, I remembered the way her pussy tensed around my fingers as pleasure overtook her. My movements became faster. Harder. Fuck, I needed to be inside her. And then it hit me. I needed to be inside her. And need was a hell of a lot deeper than want. Why the fuck was she getting to me so much? I decided to close out every single negative thought and concentrate on working my cock as I imagined Kelly, soft and naked beneath me. Me pounding hard inside her slick clenching body, and I came with a deep, sated growl.

Once my latest Kelly fantasy had come to an end—pardon the pun there—I dried myself off and I sat by the window with my latest book. It was another classic, but my head wasn't in it right then. The scenery through the glass mocked me as the early evening sun highlighted the distant mountains and bounced off the water as it descended. I placed my book down and watched the sky change from pale blue to orange then red and finally a deep, dark blue dotted with tiny specks of silver. Fucking beautiful. I wanted so much to be out there breathing in the chill of the evening. As I watched the stars appearing, I wondered if Rosa was out there looking up at those same stars somewhere. Was she missing me? Was she wondering why the hell I'd abandoned her? Suddenly the need to be outside, to escape from my confines, was almost overpowering. I stood and leaned on the window ledge, closed my eyes and hung my head.

"Hang in there, kiddo. I'll figure it out. I promise." A lump lodged in my throat, and I hated that my emotions were getting the better of me again. I had to figure a way of at least getting outside. The air inside was stifling, and doing nothing was more tiring than I had expected. I crawled into bed just after sundown with a heaviness in my heart and worry about my little sister niggling at my brain. I was determined to browbeat Kelly or Dr Clayton until one of them agreed to me getting some fresh Scottish air. Escorted or not, I didn't care. So long as I was outside.

Eventually, as I lay in bed with my eyes closed, my traitorous mind began to taunt me again. Worry about my kid sister was replaced by more images of Kelly... naked. Then it was Kelly in sexy underwear. Lace-top stockings with garters, no panties, and a bra that pushed her lush breasts up for my greedy gaze to devour. If only the images were real. Fuck... now there was a sight I would give my right arm to see.

Did she dress like that? I wanted to know more about her. I knew very little. In fact when I actually put my mind to thinking I knew nothing. Did she have a boyfriend? I didn't see a ring on her finger, so I guessed there was no husband. Nah... she didn't seem the type to be unfaithful. But then again, she didn't seem the type to get hot and heavy with a patient. Just goes to show you can't judge a book and all that crap.

I began to imagine the type of guy she could be with, and my stomach knotted. Why the fuck did it bother me so much to picture her with another guy? I guessed any guy worthy of her would be smart... another doctor maybe. He'd be all clean-cut and free from tattoos. He wouldn't cuss, nor would he be so bold as to push her up against a wall and stick his hands inside her underwear. Yeah... he'd be the total fucking opposite of me.

And he'd deserve her.

Why the hell my train of thought was taking me down the woe-is-me track I honestly don't know, but when I drifted off to sleep it was with an uneasy feeling in the pit of my stomach...

The road ahead of me was long and there were red-tinged

rugged mountains on either side of it. My heart was beating so fast and the sense of urgency was at an all-time high. What if they had harmed her? I would never forgive myself. I guess they didn't take my news too kindly. But after what happened on the weekend, there was no way I could be involved anymore. No, that was just a step too fucking far. And now this. If anything was going to confirm that I needed out, this would be it.

My grip on the handlebars of the Harley tightened as my mind tortured me with images of my kid sister being harmed by those vicious bastards. I knew they were monsters because I had been one of them. They had taunted me in the message they had left on my bathroom mirror in what looked like blood. I hadn't waited around to check if I was right. After running through the house calling her name to make sure it wasn't some sick, fucked-up joke and she was nowhere to be found, panic set in.

They hadn't taken her to the clubhouse. They wouldn't be so obvious, but I still made that my first port of call. The place was rarely empty, but I found it locked up. No, they were making me work for it. And so here I was, ten miles out of town on my way to a fucking derelict water tower and warehouse. Talk about fucking cliché. My only hope was that I arrived before they hurt her. Well... that and the fact that I hoped I could convince them to let her go...

———

Kelly

I had an unusual spring to my step on the way into work in spite of the fact that it was actually my day off—and these were few and far between. Goodness knows how I was so chipper, when the events of the last few weeks had taken me on a roller coaster ride that I never anticipated. I had decided I was going to conduct an extracurricular meeting with Cain today but out in the open as he had requested it. There was a park that lay equidistant between my home and the hospital that we would be going to. It wasn't exactly what he had requested, but he really had to be crazy if he thought I was willing to accompany a volatile and potentially dangerous man—who was almost twice my size—to a place out in the middle of nowhere where anything could happen.

I had decided that this session would really be about relaxing and breathing in some fresh Scottish winter air. We couldn't exactly discuss his case in public, and so today I would simply grant his wish to be outdoors.

Patty had reluctantly agreed to bring a coat of her son's from home that would fit Cain and had texted to say she would leave it at the nurse's station. She was evidently disapproving of my plans. This had been obvious the day before, judging by the way she shook her head as she walked away from me following my request for the outdoor attire. In all honesty I couldn't blame her. It was a stupid plan. But despite the unsettling facts that had been unearthed about his past, the less tangible aspects of his personality I'd come to know during our sessions told me that he wouldn't hurt me.

Once I'd made myself a coffee and chatted to some of the nursing staff briefly about their excitement over plans for a night out—well, it was my day off and I didn't take those lightly—I found Cain sitting in the communal day room with the other patients. The large, brightly lit and clinical room was multipurpose, acting as a dining space at one end and a leisure area at the other. He had his nose in a book, and I have to admit that I found that very attractive. I walked toward him, but he was so engrossed that he didn't even look up. Clearly Moby Dick was an enthralling story. After a few seconds of standing there, I cleared my throat and his attention was finally on me.

"Oh... hi, Kel... um... I mean Doctor Darrow. Sorry... great book." He nodded toward the thick paperback in his grasp.

I smiled and shook my head. "No worries at all. I'm glad you're finding something to occupy your time. Look... speaking of occupation... I thought we could... maybe go for a walk."

His face lit up, and the grin that spread wide across his features almost made my heart stop. How could one man be so gorgeous? Surely he had the fair share of looks belonging to at least five other men. Somewhere in the world, there were five poor guys who were seriously lacking in the X-factor due to Cain being overloaded.

He sat up straight and placed his book down on the table beside him. "Yeah? Seriously?"

I nodded. "Seriously. Come on, let's get out of here for a wee while."

He leapt to his feet and followed me to the nurses' station. I was relieved to find the area empty this time and I collected the beige, fleece-lined jacket from behind the desk. Bless her. Patty had even brought a scarf. I told myself I would thank her later with flowers or Highland toffee, her favourite sweet treat.

Once we were inside my office to collect my own coat, doubt set in. I turned to Cain with a very serious expression. "Can... can I trust you, Cain?"

A line appeared between his brows. "What do you mean?"

"Look... I'll be honest... I'm having second thoughts about this. What if you... what if...?"

He stepped toward me and placed his large hands on my shoulders, squeezing gently. "Kelly, if you're worried I'll bolt when we get out of here, don't be. I wouldn't do that to you. I wouldn't jeopardise your career by disappearing on you when you've helped me so much. Okay?"

The fact that he had me all figured out was both disconcerting and impressive. I was beginning to wonder which of us was the shrink. But reassured at his sweet and calm reaction, I swallowed hard and nodded. "Okay. I can't believe I'm doing this. But technically you're not a danger to yourself... or to anyone else from what we know. You're not wanted for criminal activity at the moment and—" I stared at the floor as I tried to convince myself I hadn't made a monumentally bad decision.

He stared hungrily out the window then placed a finger under my chin and lifted my face. "Look, if you don't think we should go, then that's fine. I don't want to put you through this. It's not worth it for a little fresh air."

Even now, even here, he put the needs of others before his own. His consideration made my heart melt, and my mind was made up.

CHAPTER TWELVE

Cᴀɪɴ

I walked with Kelly down the road, and for the first bit all I could do was just breathe. Outside smelled so good; clean and fresh and I was lost for words. Knowing the person I was shaping up to be I guessed that this wasn't something that usually happened to me. Determined to break the silence I decided to make conversation as we walked.

"So... I was wondering if there are any... I don't know... mind exercises that I can do to help me figure out where Rosa's being held? Or maybe you can hypnotise me." Who the fuck was I kidding? She already did that without trying. "I'd do anything to make my memory return faster. I know it's a lot to hope for all at once, but—"

She stopped and grabbed my arm, turning me to face her. "Cain, you need to stop stressing about that and let it happen naturally. You know that phrase 'a watched pot never boils'? Well this is one of those kinds of situations. I totally understand your desperation to find Rosa, I really do, but honestly the best thing to do is relax. Forcing things may have a detrimental effect. Our sessions and your dreams are giving us a hell of a lot to go on. Believe me, you're doing really well."

For a moment I got lost in the green of her eyes until I realised I was staring. Heat rushed to my face, and I nodded rapidly before turning to continue our walk.

We ended up at this inner city green area called Beechwood Park. It was a huge green space lined with trees, and there was a kids' play area at the opposite end. A little confused, I followed Kelly over to a bench just inside the entrance.

"I thought we were going to see the sights not to play on the swings."

She sat down on the bench and smiled up at me. "Yeah, well, I'm not sure we have time to go hiking in the Highlands today. Let's make do with a sit down and a chat in the fresh air, eh?"

I shrugged and took a seat beside her. The park was clearly popular. People walked their dogs or pushed strollers along the pathways that criss-crossed the area. I guessed she had chosen this spot so she wouldn't have to be alone with me outside the comfort zone of her hospital office. I kind of understood, but it didn't stop me from feeling a little disappointed.

We sat in silence for a while and I caught her watching me. I wished I knew what was going through her mind.

After what felt like forever I decided to break the silence. "So... we just going to sit here and not talk?"

She tilted her head to the side. "Well, today is my day off, so for once I don't want to talk shop. What do you want to talk about?"

I chuckled. Even her regular questions sounded full of inquisitiveness. "Why do I always feel like you're assessing me?"

Her smile was warm and sweet. "Maybe because I am. It is my job, after all."

"Well... as it's your day off, I'm gonna turn the tables." My mind raced with a thousand questions I wanted to ask. Most of them totally inappropriate. Things like where did she grow up and what was her favourite colour sat alongside questions like what colour underwear was her favourite, did she prefer satin or lace, and did she wear thongs or sexy panties under her skirts? I stretched my arm across the bench behind her, making myself comfortable. She glanced at my arm and then back at me. But I carried on with nonchalance. "Tell me what a girl like you finds romantic. What makes you all warm and fuzzy inside?"

She smiled and shook her head. "Of all the questions you could have asked."

"Yeah, but I get the feeling if I ask anything more in-depth, you'll tell me to fuck off. So... come on, what do you find romantic?"

She tried to stifle a grin. "Well... I'd like to be surprised. Not that it's ever actually happened. Dermott, my..." She stopped and it was clear she was hesitant about sharing personal information. No doubt she was usually very guarded about such things. She glanced at me again, and I nodded and raised my eyebrows in encouragement. "Dermott, my only real boyfriend, isn't really the romantic type. And I guess... Well, I guess I'd like for someone to make me compilation CDs of tracks they know I'd love."

Hearing her say that she had a boyfriend set my jaw clenching. But I was fucking dumb if I expected anything else. She was gorgeous and compassionate, and any guy would be lucky to have her. I hoped that this Dermott prick knew just how lucky he was.

Forcing the negativity down, I laughed. "Seriously? Isn't that a little cheesy? Damn, I forgot to bring the crackers."

She slapped my leg playfully. "Hey! You asked, so don't take the piss."

I held a hand up in surrender. "I apologise. Go on. I promise not to judge."

She narrowed her eyes at me and pursed her lips. "Hmmm."

"I promise." I made a cross sign over my heart.

"Okay... Well, I think flowers for no reason would be nice. You know, just because a guy thought it'd be nice to get me some."

"Compilation CDs and flowers, huh? You're easy to please." As the words fell from my lips, I imagined her being easy to please with my fingers and tongue. My cock flinched and I adjusted my position on the bench in the hope she wouldn't see the evidence.

She shrugged. "Yeah, I guess so. I'm not impressed by status symbols. You know, flash cars, expensive jewellery, and stuff like that just don't do it for me. I want someone who cares about me, not my outfit or how much money I make."

"I agree. I'd rather have someone real. Hey, get us agreeing on stuff." We both laughed a little. Thinking that she had begun to relax, I decided to delve a little deeper. "Tell me about your life... You know, the general stuff, family, friends..."

She laughed lightly. "Erm... no I don't think that's—"

I held my hand up to halt her. "Okay, no specifics. You can leave out the names and places if it makes you feel better. But... I just want to know a little bit about you. Surely that's only fair?"

She sighed and pursed her lips to fight the smile there. I seemed to amuse her plenty. "Well... okay, then... I grew up in a little village called Ballaschulish up near Glencoe. My mum was a teacher there."

"And your dad?"

She stared up at the sky for a while and I wondered if I'd overstepped a line. "He left."

"Aw shit, I'm sorry."

"Yeah, well, he was an arsehole and he's had to live with his decision for sixteen years."

Oh, fuck. Trust me to put my foot in my big mouth. "You haven't seen him since he left? Since you were a kid?"

"Nope. Not interested. He could turn up on my doorstep, and I'd tell him to get lost."

Her voice wavered in spite of her strong words, and I felt like a total dick. I reached over and squeezed her hand, but she snatched it away. "I'm fine. I didn't need him growing up, and you can't miss what you haven't had."

I decided that we needed a change of topic. And after her mention earlier of a boyfriend, there was something niggling at me that I simply had to clarify. "So... you mentioned this Dermott guy, but it sounded kind of past tense... Is there... is there someone special in your life now? Some... significant other?"

She snorted and turned to face me. "Oh, yeah... I'm married with three kids, clearly that's why I let you fondle me in my office." The venom in her voice took me off guard.

Shit, I'd hit a raw nerve. "Whoa, hey, jeez, I'm sorry." I rubbed my hands over my face before taking a deep breath and daring to continue. "Look, I know this isn't something that you usually do. It's obvious that you're... I don't know... fairly *innocent*."

She gasped incredulously. "What? You think I'm a virgin?"

Fuck, can I say anything right here? "That's not what I said. What I said was innocent."

"Oh, so because I didn't do anything for you in return, I'm crap, am I?"

I laughed at the unsaid words she'd somehow heard. "I never said that either. My God, uptight much?"

"Well, if you must know, I've only ever slept with one man, and he was Dermott, my university boyfriend. And we... we did stuff, so I'm not as innocent as you might think. But... Urgh! Why am I telling you this anyway? It's got absolutely nothing to bloody do with you."

She looked away from me.

I leaned forward and touched her chin to turn her back around so I could connect with her, eye to eye. "Hey, why are you getting so defensive? I haven't said anything bad." My voice was soft, and I noticed that her pupils dilated when I spoke this way. Fuck, she wanted me. Once again my cock wanted in on the action, but I tried to ignore the fact and focused my attention on her reaction to me. I made a mental note to keep testing the theory of what my voice did to her. "I think it's amazing that you've only slept with one guy, and it's pretty damned obvious that I want you, Kelly. You know what you do to me. And this... this fucking situation is driving me crazy. All I want is to be somewhere alone with you so you can relax and let go. Without the risk of someone walking in on us." I traced her bottom lip with my thumb. "And I think you want that too if you're honest."

Her nostrils flared and her chest began to rise and fall rapidly. Her brow furrowed and she pleaded at me with her eyes. "But... but I don't want to be some conquest, Cain. I'm not like that. There's a reason I've only ever had sex with one man. I don't trust easily. I don't commit to relationships because I've never met anyone I felt safe with. And you of all people can't give me that."

I clenched my jaw and exhaled a long breath. She had a point. "You think I see you as a conquest?"

"Well what else am I? I'm supposedly an unattainable woman who is breaking every ethical rule by even having this conversation with you. We've yet to fully figure out who you are, and once we know that, you'll disappear off to the States and I'll be left here to get on with my life and deal with the conse-quences of my actions. To be quite honest with you, I neither need nor want another fuck buddy."

Hearing her refer to me as another fuck buddy twisted my insides until the pain was almost unbearable. I clenched my fists as I thought of the other fuck buddy she hinted at. No doubt the fucking asshole Dermott. I wanted to fucking shred the bastard.

My heart began to pound at the inside of my ribs and the desire to claim her as my own was overwhelming. What the fuck did she take me for? Couldn't she see what she did to me? I had no clue why it mattered so much and why my gut reaction was so irrational.

I slid myself closer to her on the bench as I fought to calm my erratic breathing. "I want you. Now. I want to be inside you, Kelly." My voice wavered as I spoke and was softer than I expected. I began to relax as I continued. "And yeah, the more you protest, the more I want you. But not because you're a conquest. I think... I think I like feisty women." I smiled. "I can't explain what the fuck it is, but there is something here... between us. I know you feel it too. Is there anything I can say to convince you to take me home right now?"

She frowned and dropped her gaze. It was evident from her confused expression that there was an inner battle going on. Her job and career were on the line. If she agreed to this affair, then she was overstepping more than one line. But I wasn't about to go telling anyone.

Her silence was deafening until she eventually spoke. "I... can't, Cain. I have no clue what's going on in my head. I hate that you're all I think about at the moment. I fantasise about you. I dream about you. It's... it's not right. You're my patient and I hardly know you. Shit, you hardly know you. This is so, so... wrong. The way I'm attracted to you is just plain wrong. What the hell is wrong with me?" From the number of times she said wrong, I began to get the impression she was trying to convince herself again. She suddenly turned, and the anguish inside of her burned in her vivid green eyes.

"Hey, there is nothing... and I repeat... nothing wrong with you, Kelly." I shrugged. "The heart kind of makes up its own mind sometimes. And so does the body. Take me home. Let's just explore this some more, huh?"

As we sat there in silence I reached out and stroked my hand down her cheek. God, I wanted her so much. I somehow had the distinct feeling that nothing but Kelly could ease the ache inside of me. But I was asking a lot of her. Too much in fact. There were so many valid reasons she should say no. But I hoped beyond all hope that she didn't.

CHAPTER THIRTEEN

KELLY

I played the whole scenario over and over in my mind. Why the hell was I even considering this? I'd studied for so long to get where I was, and I was considering doing something so reckless that I could risk everything. But I was considering it. No matter how much I fought it, my feelings for this mysterious, dangerous man were growing exponentially with my desire for him. And my inherent curiosity as to why this had all occurred needled me from deep inside my psyche.

It was completely ridiculous. I knew this and reiterated the point over and over inwardly.

I figured maybe I just needed to sleep with him once to get him out of my system. Taste the forbidden fruit, so to speak. Once would surely be possible without being caught. But then I reminded myself of what happened to Eve in the Garden of Eden after taking only one bite.

She was doomed for eternity.

And I wondered if that would be me.

So be it.

I turned to face him once again. "Maybe we just need this once? Clear our heads. Find out why we're so intrigued by each other." I looked to him for a response. He slipped his hand to the back of my neck and pulled me to him. His lips crushed mine and his erratic breathing told me that he was desperate for me too. Me. Why? Our tongues battled for dominance, but of course he won. Forcing me into submission as I imagined he would in every other way.

I began to throb at the apex of my thighs and I pulled away from his mouth. "Come with me." I told him in a lust-filled whisper as I stood and began walking toward the gates of the park and then down Drumsmittal Road toward my home.

———

Cain

Fuck, she's really going to go through with this. My brain was in some kind of meltdown, and it was hard to walk with the raging hard-on in my boxers. I hoped she didn't live too far away from the goddamn park, as I didn't think I'd make it.

Although she thought this would be a one-time thing—some way to figure out how she really felt—I knew different. I knew that once I had a taste of her sweetness, there would be no going back. I'd be addicted. If she told me that was the end of it after the first time, I wasn't sure how I would handle it. But right then I ignored the sinking feeling in my gut and focused on getting to her place.

We walked up a road of houses that were painted white, and I followed her through a metal gate and up to the red door of a house that had two pointed-apex windows in the roof. She glanced up and down the road and then fumbled with the keys and dropped them. I picked them up from the floor and unlocked the house for her as she watched my fingers working. I wondered at that point if she was as turned on about this as I was. If she was desperate to feel my fingers on her, in her, as I was eager to feel hers on me.

Once in the small hallway, I closed and locked the door behind us. "Do you share this place with anyone?"

She shook her head no and chewed on her lip. Taking that as a cue, I shoved her against the wall and crushed my lips into hers as my hands fisted in her hair. She whimpered and clutched at me, pushing the winter jacket from my shoulders. I obliged and released her so that I could shrug the damn thing off. I needed there to be no barriers between us. She discarded her coat too, and the bundles of scrunched winter cloth lay at our feet.

I pulled the sweater from my body and dropped it to the floor with the coats as her gaze trailed up my chest and her fingernails dragged down my ink. I hissed in through my teeth as shivers travelled the length of my spine. No words were spoken but the heaviness of desire hung thickly in the air between us, palpable as an entity in its own right.

I turned my head and glanced up the stairs that ascended from the other end of the entrance hall. When I returned my focus to her, she simply nodded her head. I gripped her hand and she followed me as I walked up to the next level of the house, taking the stair two at a time. She lifted a finger and pointed to the door to the right at the top of the stairs, and I pushed it open.

Her bedroom smelled so damned familiar because it smelled of her and I took a lungful of the sexy fragrance as I stepped inside. She gazed up at me with an unreadable expression and I slipped my hand into her silky, soft hair. "Are you sure about this?"

Nodding silently again she lifted her hands and began to unbutton her silk blouse. Her hands were shaking and it was taking too long. Pulling her hands out of the way, I yanked at the fabric and buttons went flying across the room. I threw the blouse, not caring where it landed, pulled her into my chest, and took her mouth in a hot, wet, needy kiss that told her exactly what I wanted from her. My tongue slipped in and out of her mouth as she reached up and tugged at my hair.

If I wasn't already turned on...

I pulled away and dragged the black lace bra cups down, which forced her plump, pert breasts up toward me. God, they were beautiful. I squeezed one firm mound of flesh and devoured a pink, peaked nipple, swirling my tongue over the end as she made that little whimpering sound again and her nails dug into my scalp.

"Fuck, you have the most amazing tits." As soon as the words fell from my mouth, I realised how crass I sounded. But she didn't seem to care as her mouth fell open and she panted, head back, eyes closed. Reaching around, I popped the button on her skirt and pushed it down past the curve of her round ass until it slipped to the floor, leaving her standing before me in matching black lace underwear. "I have to taste you. I have to," I told her before I dropped to my knees and hooked my thumbs into her panties, pulling them down and allowing her step out of the flimsy fabric. She staggered back and leaned on the wall.

Pushing her thighs apart so she widened her stance a little, I sunk my face into the soft line of hairs covering her sex and inhaled the feminine scent of her arousal. With my hands firmly gripping her hips, I slipped my tongue into her dampness and dragged it forward. Her nectar tasted sweet and so I did it again, this time circling my tongue around the little nub, making her cry out.

Yep... I was addicted already.

I continued to do this, licking and sucking at her sensitive flesh as she dug her nails into my shoulders and I felt her shaking. I lifted one of her long, smooth, lean legs and dropped it over my shoulder as I slipped a finger inside of her. The noises emanating from her throat had me even harder and throbbing for her.

But I wanted more of this. My cock would have to wait.

Pulling away, I gazed up at her as I worked her into a frenzy with my fingers. Her eyes had glazed over and kept on drifting closed.

"Come for me, Kelly, I want to taste you as you come for me." I returned my tongue to her clit as she exploded around me. I gazed up and watched as she revelled in the pleasure I'd given her. Her cries were the most erotic sound and the sight of her tugging at her nipples almost made me shoot my load there and then. She looked and sounded so much better than I ever imagined she would when she really let go.

Her legs began to buckle and I gripped her tighter with one hand. "It's okay, baby, I got you, just let go." She released her nipples and dragged her hands against the wall as if feeling for support but finding none. As I leaned in again and continued to suck at her clit, another orgasm hit and she crumpled into me.

I set her leg down and stood. Her sated and relaxed body sunk into my waiting arms and I scooped her up to carry her to the bed.

CHAPTER FOURTEEN

KELLY

He laid me back on the bed and completely removed my bra from my body this time. The sated glow that had taken over me was beginning to subside, and I watched him as he removed his jeans and boxers, letting his impressive cock spring free. He turned to throw his remaining clothes onto the chair in the corner of my room which afforded me an opportunity to take in the sight of him naked in all his masculine, tattooed glory.

His thick erection stood ready and waiting to take me, and I was becoming a desperate aching mess for him all over again. I couldn't remember ever being so turned on and wet with anticipation and need. He turned and glanced around the room, and as I had suspected, his back was covered in tattoos as well as his arms and chest. Some kind of crest with a winged skull, flames, and a broken halo and the words Company of Sinners in black writing covered most of his back.

He really was quite spectacular.

Dangerous looking but so incredibly sexual.

"Condoms?" The husky simplicity of that one-word question

snapped me from my ogling, and I lifted my gaze to meet his eyes. His lopsided smile made my stomach flip, and it was clear that he knew I'd been gawking at him.

"Erm... top drawer... nightstand."

He stepped over to the small chest of drawers beside my bed and pulled the handle. The view of his tight, muscular arse had me squeezing my thighs together again. I wanted to dig my nails in him, scratch him, bite him even.

Shit, stop that, Kelly! Who the hell are you right now?

He rummaged around and pulled out something with a chuckle. I heard a buzzing sound and my cheeks began to burn with embarrassment. Oh my goodness... beam me up, Scotty... I was now aware that the bright pink vibrator didn't match him for size, and he turned to show me it with a raise of his brows and a sexy smile. "Hmm... we might have a little fun with this next time." He grinned.

Next time? Uh-oh... I'm done for...

Once he had found what he was looking for, he turned. The muscles of his chest rippled as he moved toward me once again and his rigid cock bobbed and flinched, the head glistening and ready. I wanted to taste him there as he had tasted me, but I was too mesmerised to even speak, let alone move. He knelt on the edge of the bed, and it dipped under his weight as he began crawling up my body. He leaned and placed wet kisses along my thighs before trailing his tongue in circles along my tingling, over-sensitive skin until he reached my breasts. As he pulled one nipple into the wet heat of his mouth, I let a moan of delight fall from my lips. His fingers caressed my other nipple, tugging and squeezing, sending jolts of pleasure direct to my sex.

I was so ready for him again.

He braced himself on his elbows and pushed my thighs apart with his so that he could rest his pelvis against mine. The ridge of his cock lay against my clit, and I gasped at the sensation as my nerve endings sprang to life once more.

He sucked at my neck and fondled my breast again as he rolled his hips. He was driving me mad with pleasure, but I needed more.

"Cain..." I breathed, not really knowing what to say. The thought of voicing my desires to this... to all intents and purposes... *stranger* had me feeling silly, inexperienced and—as he had quite rightly pointed out—innocent. But then again, I'd let him get *this far*. Stupid, stupid, Kelly. You need to stop this right now. Pushing the voice of reason to the back of mind, I moaned his name again. "Cain..."

He pulled away and gazed down at me as he smoothed his hand down my body and slipped his fingers into my sex again. The scent of my arousal drifted from where he played and I clenched my muscles around his fingers, relishing the sensation of him touching me so intimately. I knew what I needed but couldn't find the words. Keeping his eyes locked on mine, he removed his fingers from my body and ran their glistening tips along my bottom lip. Such an erotic act. I sucked his fingers into the heat of my mouth and groaned.

"What do you need, baby? How do you want me to make you come this time?" His eyes were dark and his voice a throaty growl.

"I need to feel you... I need..."

He smiled sexily. "You want to feel my cock inside of you, don't you?" I nodded and chewed on my lip. "All you have to do is ask, baby. Just ask. Ask for what you want."

"Cain... I... I can't..." Overcome with some ridiculous, misplaced shyness all of a sudden, I turned my face away, not daring to meet his eyes.

"Hey, don't ever be scared to tell me what you need. I want to make you feel good. And this is just between you and me, okay? No one else needs to know. It's just for us, so relax."

He pulled back and rested his arse on his thighs. I heard the ripping of a packet and turned to watch as he stretched the latex sheath down the length of his proud erection.

Why can't I say the words out loud?

He returned his weight to my body once again and covered my mouth with his. This kiss was more tender, his lips soft and undemanding, and our tongues tangled together just like our limbs. His thick manhood rested at my entrance, waiting for my permission.

The overwhelming need to have him inside of me. To connect with him on such an intense and intimate level tugged at my insides, and I ached with desperation for him between my legs. Nothing else existed in that moment. Nothing but need and want. Desire and lust hanging between us. I was ready to beg.

Come on, Kelly, just ask.

Taking a deep breath for courage, I moved my mouth to his ear. "Make love to me, Cain. I need to feel you inside of me. Make me come again." The words sounded wanton and alien, but they had the desired effect on him—he pulled back and thrust forward, sinking himself in to my wet, waiting core with a deep, gravelly moan.

"Awww, Kelly, you feel so good around my cock. I knew you'd feel good, but *fuck*... you're so ready for me. I knew you wanted this too. And it feels... so... fucking... good. So right."

His words had me clenching my muscles, which in turn made his pleasured groans come again. He began to move his length in and out of me at a slow, delicious pace, and my hips moved in perfect synchronisation with his, creating the friction I needed. His lips found mine again and the hand that wasn't holding him up found my breast. I slipped my hands down the taut skin of his back and dug my nails into the firm mounds of his arse.

"Fuck, I could stay inside you all day," he mumbled against my lips as his kiss became more urgent. And at that moment it was all I wanted too. The sensation of his thrusts against my sensitive bud was pushing me higher once again. He moved and closed his mouth around my nipple, and I ran my hands back up his body until my fingers were tugging at the shaggy strands of his hair. Oh my God, the pleasure, the tightness, his weight on me... So, so good.

"Fuck, Kelly I can't get enough of this. I can't get enough of you, but I can't hold back any longer."

I found my voice again. "Don't hold back. Just let go... please... I need it too."

———

Cain

The feel of her tight pussy clenching around my cock stirred up all kinds of desperate feelings within me. Although I couldn't actually remember, I felt sure that I had never felt this good. How could anything ever have been this good?

I was meant to be with her.

She was mine.

When she told me to let go, I buried my face in the crook of her neck and picked up my pace. She lifted her legs and wrapped them around me, making my thrusts deeper still. The intensity of the adrenaline rushing through my body like a drug had me clenching my jaw and trying to hold off for as long as I could.

I didn't want it to end.

I pulled away and fixed my gaze on hers as she clung to me, gasping and moaning. The look of sheer bliss in her eyes pulled at my heart, and raw emotion flooded me. My God, what she did to me. I was struggling to hold back, and when she cried out and clenched hard around me I let go, joining her in a mind-melting orgasm that ripped through my nerves like electricity. My cock throbbed inside of her as I emptied myself and slowed my thrusts, drawing out the pleasure for as long as I possibly could.

I lay there for a long while, covering her body with my own and stroking my fingers across her silky skin. I listened to her breathing and felt her heart beating against my chest. I wanted to stay. To forget the shit that was going on outside these four walls and just make love to her over and over. But reality wouldn't allow it.

Reluctantly I rolled to the side and pulled her into my chest, kissing the top of her head as her arms came around my waist. "Wow... that was... wow... fucking amazing."

She began to shudder and I felt damp trickles down my skin. Fuck, she's crying. I wriggled myself down so that our faces were level, but her eyes were closed and tears were leaving glistening trails down her cheeks and soaking into her hair.

"Hey... hey, Kelly look at me. Baby, what's wrong?"

"Stop calling me baby. I'm not yours, okay? I'm nothing to you. And this... Oh my God, what the hell have I done?" she growled angrily.

Her sobs vibrated through me, and my stomach knotted.

She tried to pull away from me but I gripped her tighter. "Stop this. Just look at me, Kelly, please."

She began to pound her fists into my chest. "I've ruined everything. How could I have been so stupid? I'll lose my job... my career will be over. And all for what? For a few mind-blowing orgasms? I'm a stupid, idiotic bitch!"

"Whoa, come on now. Calm down. There's no reason to have a goddamn meltdown."

Her eyes widened and she shoved me away before sitting up and glaring down at me. "There's every reason to fucking melt down, Cain. I just slept with a sodding patient!"

Anger began to bubble up from somewhere deep inside me. My nostrils flared and I gritted my teeth. "Um... yeah I was there when it happened." I sat and swung my legs over the bed turning my back toward her. "Don't worry, we don't have to do it again," I bit out.

"You think?" I clenched my jaw at the derision in her voice.

I gathered my jeans and boxers from the chair in the corner of the room and disposed of the condom in the little garbage pail underneath it before I pulled on my clothes.

"Well, I'm glad I rocked your fucking world." Sarcasm dripped from my tongue and I was suddenly filled with self-loathing. Why had I pushed her so far? Why had I insisted on this? It was too fucking soon. Dumb fucking prick. I began to walk toward the bedroom door.

She reached out and grabbed my arm, and I swung around to face her. I took a long look at her naked form standing before me, figuring it was probably the last time. Her hair cascaded down her back, leaving her perfect breasts exposed to my hungry gaze. And fuck if I wasn't getting hard again. So fucking beautiful. Why does she have to be so damn beautiful?

"Cain, please." When I locked eyes with her again hers were sparkling with unshed tears and all I wanted to do was fucking hold her. I hated that. Hated that I was so drawn to her. Like I knew her already. Like I needed her. It was dumb and clearly not reciprocated. I had to get the hell out of Dodge.

"Please what, Kelly? Huh?" I was trying hard to keep my temper in check when all I wanted to do was holler in her face and tell her how damned frustrating she was. My attention was drawn to her breasts again. "Put some fucking clothes on, would you, before I take your mind off all this shit."

She grabbed a robe from her closet and pulled it on, securing it around her waist. "Cain, I'm begging you, please don't tell anyone what happened here." Her lower lip trembled and for a split second I wanted to turn and walk out of there.

I shook my head as something akin to hurt squeezed at my insides. "I can't fucking believe you're even saying that. Did I not already tell you that what happens between us stays between us? Does nothing I say get through to you?"

"I'm just so scared. This is one colossal bloody mistake I've made. And I keep compounding it. It has to stop."

I stepped toward her, closing the space between us. "Yeah, I get it. Fucking me was a mistake. I'm not good enough for you, I already knew that. Not only am I your patient, but I'm a criminal with tattoos who doesn't even know who the fuck he is. Well, you have nothing to worry about, Kelly. You can forget this ever happened. But excuse me if I don't." After taking one last look into her eyes I turned and left the room.

CHAPTER FIFTEEN

KELLY

I dashed around my room, grabbing fresh underwear and a blouse to replace the ruined one—I just hoped no one had been taking notice of my attire this morning when I called in to collect Cain, or this could be the end of my career—and hurried into the bathroom to clean myself up. I was terrified he would do a runner. My heart pounded at my ribs and I kept bursting into tears. The shitty thing was that he had the wrong end of the stick completely. I was terrified that the way he had made me feel when he was making love to me was just that... I felt loved. The way he worshipped my body as if I meant something to him and he meant something to me. The intensity of my desire for him went beyond lust. How could I possibly have felt so connected to the man? It was utterly, ridiculously, effing crazy. You don't fall for someone so quickly. I know they do in romance novels but this was real life.

I needed to get a grip.

My career was on the line here. And love wasn't as important as that... was it? Especially when the so-called feelings were one-sided. He was clearly a player. The way he handled my body didn't ring true as someone who believed in monogamy. Nor did it ring true as someone who couldn't remember his own life. I began to question how genuine he was being. And that was wrong of me. This was my fault... my guilt making these thoughts occur. If I hadn't let things get so far, I wouldn't even be thinking this way.

Once I was dressed, I ran down the stairs as quick as I could and found him sitting on my couch. His head was hanging down and he looked a little lost. Was I wrong about him? A tiny spark of hope lit up inside of me. He must have heard me come in because he stood and turned. His face was a mask of seriousness.

I forced a weak smile. "Hey. Thanks for not running away."

He snorted derisively. "What am I, eight?"

"I just meant—"

"Yeah, I know what you meant, Kelly. I wouldn't want to ruin your fucking life would I? Oh wait... I already did that." The bitterness in his voice made nausea rise up my throat.

I stepped toward him. "Please don't be angry with me, Cain."

He held him arms out wide. "Angry? Why would I be angry, huh? I got what I wanted. It's all good, baby."

Okay, I'm going to throw up. He can't mean that. But then again, how could I blame him if he did?

"Okay... okay." My eyes began to sting once more and I nodded but couldn't bring myself to look in his eyes. I didn't want to see what was there. I doubted that it would be good. "I just thought that it was... I don't know... more to you."

He laughed without humour. "Ha, I can't believe you actually thought I wanted something other than a quick fuck. Man, talk about gullible."

I closed my eyes as tears came once again. It served me right.

But it hurt like hellfire.

The walk back to the hospital felt like the longest journey I'd ever taken. He walked a couple of steps in front of me and didn't speak. I was clueless at that point as to how he would handle returning to the place he considered a prison. I just hoped that he would be decent about things and not make the situation any worse than it already felt.

Once we arrived back at the ward, Patty was waiting at the nurses' station and she visibly relaxed as we walked toward her.

"So, did you enjoy your taste of Scotland, Cain?"

He glanced at me briefly before answering. "Oh yeah, it tasted amazing. Shame it couldn't last." The double meaning wasn't lost on me.

"Well, maybe Doctor Darrow will take you again soon." I cringed at her choice of words.

"Nah, I doubt that. She has better people... erm... *things* to *do* with her time."

Ouch.

"Well as long as you enjoyed your wee taste of freedom, eh?" Patty was relentless.

"Oh yeah. I really enjoyed it. It was fun while it lasted." He glanced at me again. "Well, excuse me, ladies, but I think I've had enough exercise for one day. I'm going to go play some cards with the guys." He turned and walked away.

"Is everything okay, dear? You look like you've been crying. Did something happen?" The look of concern in Patty's eyes had me on the verge of tears again.

I shook my head. "No, I'm fine. It's just the wind out there is quite strong, and I think I may be coming down with a cold."

"See, I always tell you that you work too hard, Kelly. You maybe need some time off."

"Yeah, maybe you're right, Patty."

She laughed. "Well, it had to happen sometime, I guess."

Bless her. After the way I had snapped at her lately, I really didn't deserve her friendship. But I was more than grateful for it. I smiled and turned away to make the short journey to my office, feeling more than a little grateful that she hadn't noticed my change of clothing.

Although it was my day off, and I could've gone home, but I was afraid I'd burst out sobbing before I made it to the hospital's lobby. My office was the closest safe spot I could think of. Once I was behind my desk again, I rested my head on my arms and let the tears flow. If only time machines had been invented. I would climb right in there and go back to life before Cain Somers or Cameron Iss or whatever the hell his name was.

There was a knock on the door, and Alex walked in before I had time to wipe away the evidence of my pity party. I peered up at him angrily. "Isn't it customary to wait until you're invited in, Alex?"

He scrunched his brow. "I'm a doctor not a vampire, Kelly." Huh? "Anyway, aren't you supposed to be off today?" Without waiting for my answer, he continued. "Word on the Patty-vine has it that you're feeling under the weather."

Good grief, talk about word travelling fast. "Oh, yeah, just a little tired, that's all."

"Well, I've been investigating, and you haven't taken any holiday time this year yet. What's that all about? Even today, on your day off, here you are. Don't you have any friends?"

"Excuse me?"

"Friends? You know? Those people who put up with us when no one else will? The ones who encourage us to get drunk and let our hair down."

"Alex, I know what a friend is, and of course I have friends."

"Well, good. As of now you're on annual leave."

What? "You can't force me to take leave. That's preposterous."

"No, Kelly. What's preposterous is the fact that you never stop working. Today is a prime example of that. You go home and work on cases. You do the same on weekends. You never switch your brain off. As your immediate manager, I'm telling you to take some time."

"I can't just up and leave my patients."

"Yes, you can. We have a member of staff on secondment whilst his department goes through some changes. He can step in. Magnus Reilly. I think you know him already. Anyway, you're so efficient at your note keeping, he can slip right in for a couple of weeks."

I shook my head. This wasn't right. "But... but Cain Somers... we're close to a breakthrough there—"

"Yes, and Magnus has dealt with amnesia patients before. Don't sweat it. It's time you took a break."

I swallowed, trying to dislodge the ball of emotion tightening my throat. I wanted to be at home in all honesty. But I was scared of what may come to light when I wasn't here. Would I have a job to return to?

"Do I get a say in all this?"

Alex smiled—it was a first—and shook his head. "Nope. Doctor's orders."

I nodded and my lip began to tremble.

"Hey, you're not being suspended. I'm just concerned about you. Crying at work isn't something you ever do. It just proves to me that you need some time out. That's all. Okay?"

Once again I nodded, unable to speak in case I began to sob and told him everything. I grabbed my bag and slipped on my coat again. Suddenly a wave of tiredness washed over me. No wonder, considering the antics of the day.

With a small, feeble smile, I stopped beside Alex. "Thank you. And... I'm sorry if I've let you down."

"Not in the slightest. Don't go thinking that. Just take a couple of weeks, go away somewhere warm. Chill out."

Going away somewhere warm sounded like just the thing I needed. Perhaps I would do just that. As I left the building, I pulled out my phone and hit dial.

"Hi, Kelly. How are you doing?" Clara's friendly and concerned voice was my undoing and I broke down.

"Oh, Clara... everything is going wrong," I sobbed.

Without hesitation she replied, "I'm free right now. Come on over."

I agreed and hung up as I inhaled a deep calming breath. I wanted to feel relief, but I didn't because as much as I wanted to confide completely in someone, in Clara, I knew I couldn't. Once again I would have to lie, and that thought broke me yet again.

I left the hospital with a heaviness in my heart and made my way to see my therapist for another session where I would play 'hide the truth'.

CHAPTER SIXTEEN

C<small>AIN</small>

I'd made the decision to stay out of Kelly's way for the rest of the day. I'd said some pretty fucked-up shit. None of which I meant. But that's male pride for you. It was my intention to apologise at our appointment the next day. I was relieved that, since my memory was returning in pieces, the frequency of my appointments with Dr Darrow had been increased.

As it got to bedtime, regret was niggling at my brain and I wished there was some way I could contact her and apologise for my asshole behaviour. But alas, I would have to wait. After showering, I crawled into bed and switched the light off immediately. I had no interest in reading even though it was fairly early. I closed my eyes and it wasn't long before sleep took me...

I let my eyes flutter open and turned my head to the side. She was smiling at me. Her beautiful green eyes full of life and vitality. Her deep red hair fell in curls and waves knotted with sleep around her pillow. My heart was filled with an intense love for the woman and I immediately pulled her into my arms. Her soft tits pressed against my bare chest and I slipped my hands down to cup her ass. I liked to wake and find her naked beside me. I leaned in and kissed her with a tenderness that I hoped she would read as my undying devotion to her. All the others before her... and there had been many... paled into insignificance when I looked at her. She made me a better man.

She reached out and cupped my face and I covered her hand with my own. "Have I told you how much I love you today?"

She smiled and shook her head no. "But then you have only just woken up, so I think I can forgive you."

I pulled her and manoeuvred so that she was beneath me and placed a hand at either side of her head before I bent to kiss her full, luscious lips. She slipped her arms around me and played with my hair as I kissed the soft skin of her neck and trailed my tongue down to the ink on her shoulder. The tattooed roses and vines intertwined around her slender arm with our initials at the centre were the most beautiful way for her to affirm our love. Who needed a fucking wedding ring? I didn't give a fuck that the rest of the crew ribbed me for being pussy whipped. They could stick with their fuck-'em-and-leave-'em lifestyle, but give me my woman and her smokin'-hot, curvaceous body any day of the fucking week.

"I want you, Cain. Make love to me."

Her sweet voice made my spine tingle and my cock spring to life. There was nothing I wouldn't do for this woman. The love in my heart for her was overwhelming, and as she wrapped her legs around me and I sunk myself inside her welcoming body, I felt the tension in my shoulders melt away. "God, I love you so much, Melody, so, so much."

"Unh, Cain, I love you too..." Her softness beneath me felt so right. I was *meant* to be with her.

She was *mine*.

I sat up with a pounding heart and glanced to my side. Of course I was alone and in a fucking hospital bed in Scotland, covered in sweat.

What the fuck?

Melody?

Oh my God, that was it!

The reason I was drawn to Kelly. It must be that she reminded me of my girlfriend back home who must be called Melody. And now I'd been fucking unfaithful to her with my doctor. Bastard fucking shit! From the way my heart pounded for her in the dream it was clear that she was my true love. I clutched to the dream with both hands as I searched for something, anything to write on. But of course there was nothing in my room thanks to fucking security.

I dashed out the door and over to the nurses' station. Glancing at the clock, I realised it was almost nine thirty, and my appointment with Kelly was at ten. Patty was behind the desk on the phone, and I drummed my fingers on its shiny surface, impatiently waiting for her to finish. Finally she hung up the call.

"Patty, please... do you have a pen and paper I can use? It's... it's urgent."

Concern washed over her ageing features. "Cain, is everything okay, hon?"

"Yeah, yeah, fine, but I need to write some stuff down as soon as possible, please." My words fell from my mouth in a rush as my heart continued to pound. She scrambled around her work station and pulled up some paper and a pencil and thrust them at me. I grabbed them and began scribbling illegibly and frantically, every piece of the dream I had managed to recall. My chest heaved like I was running a marathon, and Patty looked on with worry still etched on her face.

Once I was satisfied that I had documented every part of the dream I could remember, I made my way down the corridor and sat on the seat outside Kelly's office. I had to explain. I had to apologise. I needed to find Melody as well as Rosa. And I needed to make Kelly see that I hadn't intended to hurt her. That the reason I was so drawn to her was that she felt familiar to me and surely that was a good thing. Another piece of the puzzle clicked.

I bounced my knee and chewed on my nail. Why the fuck was time passing so slowly? I needed to speak to Kelly, and I was on the verge of barging into to her office and demanding that she speak to me when her door opened and some old dude stepped out. Must be another patient. He wore a pair of brown slacks and a cream shirt with a blazer. He looked a little too smart to be a patient, and I didn't recognise him as one of the inmates.

"Cain Somers, I presume?" he asked, staring straight at me.

I scrunched my brow. "What's it to you?"

"I'm Doctor Magnus Reilly. I'm replacing Doctor Darrow for—"

I stood quickly. "What the fuck? Replacing her why?"

He smiled warmly and held his hands up as he shook his head. "No, no, Mister Somers, you misunderstand me." His voice was soft and he had a kindly nature, but that meant nothing at that precise moment. He continued, "It's temporary. I'm just stepping in whilst Doctor Darrow takes some well-earned rest."

I shook my head and clenched my fists. "Well, there's no fucking way I'm talking to you, dude. She never told me she was going on vacation. Why would she do that? I mean... we were making progress. I don't get it." Anger rose within me, and I had to rein myself in before I punched the fucking wall.

"I understand your trepidation, Cain, but in all honesty I'm just as qualified to deal with your case as Doctor Darrow so—"

I stepped forward and pointed in his face. "Yeah? Well you don't know me and I can't trust you. So we'll just forget it until Kelly gets back." I turned and stomped down the corridor and back into my room, slamming the door almost off its hinges.

How the fuck dare she do this to me? And of all times she could do it, she fucking abandons me now when I need her the most.

I needed to see her. I needed to talk to her. But the only way that could happen would be for me to break out of the fucking prison I was being kept in.

I had to think fast.

————

KELLY

Esme and I sat enjoying the plush dining room of the Kingsmill Hotel. We'd had a wonderful afternoon of last-minute pampering following my eviction from work and were now eating a posh dinner in romantic surroundings that should have been experienced with a lover and not a best friend. Esme, my oldest and dearest friend, had been plugging me for information all day. But so far I had managed to avoid her questions and change the subject. She was staying over at mine, where she had parked her car, so I knew the Spanish Inquisition was set to continue into the night.

The problem was that she could read me like a book. The way she looked at me told me that she had drawn her own conclusions, and I knew I'd have to come clean at some point. We sat in ponderous silence, savouring a delicious meal, and I could feel her eyes on me.

I huffed and placed my cutlery down. "Okay... what do you want to know?"

Esme placed her wine glass down and clapped her hands like a giddy schoolgirl, making her blonde curls bounce. "Thank goodness! I thought you were going to keep this up all bloody night! Okay... so what's his name? What does he look like? Have you fucked him? If so, was he good?" Her eyes were wide and her grin even wider. I couldn't help but laugh. Sadly, the laughter was short-lived.

"Oh, Ez. As much as I really want to I... I can't tell you. I would be putting you in a very awkward position, and that's just not fair." My lip began to tremble, and a look of grave concern replaced the excitement on my best friend's face.

She reached across the table and squeezed my arm. In a just audible voice she asked, "Kel, how long have you known me?"

I shrugged. "I've know you most of my life."

"And have I ever broken your trust in that time? Have I *ever* judged you? Have I ever given you a reason to not trust me?"

I shook my head as I dabbed my eyes with my free hand. "No, no and no."

"Then whatever it is you can tell me. Okay?"

"Remember Clara, my therapist? I saw her today and she said I need to tell someone because I couldn't tell her either."

Esme's worried gaze burned into me. "But you usually tell me everything. And I know how much you trust Clara. So this must be something big. Look, I promise I will listen with an open mind. Like I said, I won't judge you."

I swallowed to try and dislodge the ball of emotion that was tightening my throat. "But... this may be the one time you do judge me. And you'd have every right."

"Kel, you're worrying me, honey."

I took a deep breath. "I... I kind of met someone. But... oh God, Esme what have I done?" My stomach knotted and my appetite was gone.

She scooted her chair around to me and took my hand firmly. "Go on."

"He's... he's a patient." I waited for the gasp and the look of horror to descend.

But her face stayed impassive, completely non-judgemental, and in that moment I loved her deeply for that. She nodded. "Okay. Tell me more."

"He came in under suspicious circumstances. Unconscious, and we discovered he had overdosed. There was a suicide note. But... it's stupid... I felt drawn to him immediately. Couldn't stop thinking about him... still can't. When he gained consciousness, he turned out to be American but was suffering amnesia. I've been working with him to figure things out, but he's struggling to regain his memory. There have been... encounters..." Tears left wet trails down my face, and I closed my eyes as guilt and shame needled my insides, convicting me of my unethical and highly inappropriate behaviour.

"Oh, honey. Have you... have you slept with him?" I simply nodded and more tears spilled over. She scooted her chair around to my side of the table, pulled my head to her shoulder, and stroked my hair. "Kelly, do you love him? Have you fallen for him?"

I pulled away as I thought about her question. Oh my God... I wasn't falling at all... I was already plummeting into the abyss. The deed was done. My heart was given.

I stared into her concerned gaze and my face crumpled. "Yes... Yes, I have fallen for him. But... he told me that he had used me for sex. I can't blame him because I acted like I was ashamed of what I'd allowed to happen... And I was, but not because of him. I was ashamed because I'd broken so many bloody rules. But he was so cruel with the way he acted afterwards."

"Oh, sweetie, no." She folded her arms around me as I sobbed into her shoulder, and I clung to her as my anguish and self-hatred poured out.

Ten minutes later we were walking home arm in arm. I was inhaling deep lungfuls of air, trying to calm my raging heartbeat and churning stomach. Esme hadn't outwardly judged me, but I wondered how she really felt and if she would admit it to me even if she was disgusted with me.

As if she read my mind, she stopped me in my tracks and turned me to face her. "I can see those cogs turning, Kel. But I want you to know that I don't judge you. At all. Okay? So you've fallen in love with someone you shouldn't have. So what? These things happen and the heart makes up its own mind sometimes."

I gasped at hearing her say the words that Cain had also said. "But... it's got to stop. I can't treat him when I have such strong feelings for him. This has happened so fast, and that in itself tells me that it can't be real. I slept with him to get him out of my system, Ez. That's all I thought it would take. But now I know I'm a fucking idiot. Sex with him was like nothing I've ever experienced before. There was this deep connection. And despite what he said, I know he felt it too. I think his reaction afterwards was pride because I had rejected him and told him it had been a mistake."

She appeared thoughtful for a few moments. "Once he regains his memory, will he be returned to the States?"

I shrugged. "I... I guess so."

"Well, lovely, I think until then you are going to have to be strong and pass his case over. Tell Doctor Clayton you feel intimidated by him or something."

I nodded, but the thought of not seeing him every day twisted my insides and made my heart ache. Fresh tears sprang forth, and once again I was enveloped in the arms of my very best friend.

We eventually reached my home and Esme gasped. "Oh, fuck. I... I think you have a visitor."

I spun around to see a dark, shadowy figure sitting on my doorstep. I knew that Cain was locked in the ward back at the hospital, and so I presumed it was Dermott hoping for a late-night hook-up. That is until the figure stood and walked towards me.

"Kelly... I had to see you."

My eyes widened and I covered my mouth. "Cain!"

CHAPTER SEVENTEEN

CAIN

My heart began to pound as I saw the shock register on her face. She'd no doubt call the cops and have me arrested for stalking. I stepped toward her with my hands held up in surrender. "Kelly, please don't be scared. I… I just need to talk to you. They wanted me to talk to some old fucking dude who knows nothing about me. But I… I couldn't do that. You're the only one I trust. You. No one else."

She held up a hand to halt me. "Cain, you have to go back. Think of the shit storm this will cause. You can't be here."

The blonde-haired woman she was with clung to her arm. "Kelly, should I call the police?"

Kelly kept her eyes locked on me and shook her head. "No, Ez, it's okay. I'll call a cab and have him taken back. This is crazy."

"Please, Kelly. I'm not gonna fucking hurt you. I just need to talk. That's all. Just talk. I… I had another dream. It kind of shed some light on shit. I need to talk to you… to apologise… to explain."

The woman called Ez turned Kelly around, and they had a whispered conversation with manic hand gestures. But then the woman pulled out her cell and dialled.

I stepped forward, closing the gap between Kelly and me and took her hand. "Please, Kelly, I need you. Don't do this. Don't send me back without hearing me out."

She closed her eyes for a moment and inhaled a shaking breath. When she opened them again, I could see the pain and conflict reflected back at me. "Esme is calling herself a cab. She's going home so that you and I can talk."

Relief flooded my veins, and my legs almost gave way beneath me. I released her hand and ran my hands through my hair, letting the air from my lungs rush out. "Thank you. Thank you both."

We stood waiting outside the gate in silence until the cab arrived. Kelly walked Esme to the car, and they had another whispered conversation that ended in a long hug. Esme smiled over at me before she climbed in, but her expression was tinged with a mixture of worry and sadness. I guessed that Kelly had told her about us.

Once the cab had pulled away, Kelly silently walked past me without eye contact and unlocked her front door. She held it open so I could step inside and then closed it and locked it behind us.

She removed her coat and flicked on the lights in the hall-way. After assessing me with her gaze she said, "Well, you look like shit."

"Gee, thanks. I was thinking the opposite of you."

She gave me a small and brief smile and walked through into her living room. I followed and slipped off my coat. After throwing it over the couch, I slumped down against the soft cushions. And she eyed me warily.

"Okay, so what was so urgent that you had to break out of hospital?"

I peered up at her where she stood. "Aren't you going to sit down?"

She huffed. "Is it imperative to the story?"

"Well, no, but—"

"Well then, just get on with it and then you can go back."

Okay, she's not going to be all warm and welcoming. Can't say I blame her really. "Okay... I... I had another dream. I think this one was pretty significant and it kind of... explains a lot."

She folded her arms across her chest. "Go on."

"I... um... I had a woman... back home."

She snorted. "Only one?"

Ouch. "Yes, only one. Her name was Melody... and she looks a lot like..."

She slumped onto the chair opposite me. "A lot like who?" Her expression told me she already knew the answer.

"Like you." I gazed over at her. The guilt inside me squeezed at my gut, and I wanted to say so many things but just couldn't find the words.

She nodded. "I see... I see."

"I guess that explains why I was so drawn to you. And why I needed to be with you so badly."

"I guess so," she whispered, and her eyes glazed over with tears.

"Kelly, I'm so sorry. If I had known, I would've—"

She sneered at me. "You'd have what? Not wasted your time on someone as innocent as me?"

Dropping my gaze to my knotted fingers, I shook my head. "I wouldn't have hurt you with the things I said. I'm so sorry. You've got to believe me, Kelly."

She laughed humourlessly and swiped angrily at the errant tears trailing down her cheeks. "Have I? Oh well, then. Everything is hunky dory and you can go now."

Knowing how much I had hurt her made me die a little inside. She didn't deserve this. Immediately I stood and moved across the room to crouch before her. "Hey, come on. I didn't mean to do this to you. I... feel like a total bastard. Not only have I hurt you, but I've been unfaithful to someone I can't even really remember. What does that make me?"

Her face softened a little and she smiled. "A lucky guy to have so many women who want you."

I returned her smile and pulled her into my chest. I stroked her hair and kissed her head. "This is all just so confusing. When I dreamed about her... the love I felt..."

She pushed me away. "Yeah, I get it. Please don't torture me more, eh?"

"I didn't want to talk to the other guy. Only you. I only trust you." I gazed into her eyes and was immediately drawn in. Without thinking, I slipped my hand to the back of her head and kissed her. After a few seconds she pulled away, and I realised I was being stupid. "Aww, fuck. I'm sorry. It's like I can't help myself around you."

"Well, you have your woman to think about now. Although how she'd feel about being spoken of as your possession, I'm not sure." She smiled and once again I felt like an asshole.

"I wrote everything down. From the dream. I wasn't sure if you'd want to hear... as... as my doctor, I mean."

"You'd better take a seat and tell me everything, then."

I moved back to the couch and began to tell her everything I could remember about the woman who supposedly had my heart.

KELLY

I listened to Cain talk about Melody and the way he had felt about her in his dream, and I fought my threatening tears. It served me right for falling for someone so inappropriately. And so damn quickly. What could I possibly love about him when I hardly knew him? I wished I could say it was just physical, but in all honesty it wasn't. Sure there was a definite physical attraction and sex with him... wow. But there was so much more. It hurt so much that I had finally discovered what it felt like to love someone only to know that he had never really felt anything for me. It had been the woman I reminded his subconscious of that had his heart all along. In fact he loved her so much that he'd had her likeness tattooed on his skin. The reclining redhead on his forearm. A permanent reminder of his one true love. What a shame he only had shattered memories.

My mind drifted back to the difficult conversation I'd had with Clara. She had been wonderful. I'd cried and she had let me. And as I had told Esme earlier, Clara had totally figured me out. Her words rattled around my head.

"I know there is something you're not able to tell me, Kelly. But you need to talk to someone. You need to share this pain. Please talk to a friend and let someone shoulder this burden with you. You can't function and carry this alone. Whatever it is it will swallow you up if you don't talk to someone."

I was grateful to Clara for encouraging me to spill my darkest secrets to Esme. And she was right. It felt good to know that someone else knew and wasn't judging me. But what had been the point? The object of my affections now sat before me telling me how much he loved someone else. Karma is a bitch.

Focusing my attention back on my patient, I made notes of the significant things. Tattoos of their initials, the room they'd made love in. The woman's appearance. Her name—and an unusual one at that. All fairly significant memories. And I knew that as soon as I passed this information along to the authorities, they would place the final pieces of the jigsaw together and Cain would eventually go home. An email I had read before I was sent off on leave told me that they had discovered Cain's home address but that I wasn't to inform him of this until they completed their investigations and ensured he would be in no danger if he returned.

The paperwork was already being processed, and although these things took time, it wouldn't be much longer. As soon as his replacement passport was issued, there would be no reason for him to be kept here. I realised that the quicker the breakthroughs came, the sooner he would be fully aware of his past and his real home.

At least there were no warrants out for his arrest. That was one saving grace. At least when he did go home, he would be able to commence the search for his sister; the police had uncovered nothing connected to her apart from a missing persons report. The authorities were simply dotting the i's and crossing the t's. And it was my duty to pass every breakthrough on to them. And this breakthrough would go some way to confirming what they had already ascertained. After all, his identity was pretty much confirmed. And if there was someone there, a loved one, whom they could contact to confirm his identity...

Sadness flooded me at the thought that somewhere across the sea there was a woman waiting and wondering where Cain was. Worrying about him. Her heart breaking at his disappearance. I pitied her but at the same time envied her. In my breaking heart and my confused mind, I wanted so much to be the one he wanted. In an ideal world, I wouldn't be his doctor, and he wouldn't have someone waiting for him.

But an ideal world it was not.

We drank coffee and sat in an uncomfortable, tense silence. He clenched his jaw and the crease in his brow deepened.

"Are you okay, Cain?"

He shook his head. "She must be worried sick. She must wonder where the hell I am. She must think I don't love her anymore." He lifted his head, and the pain in his eyes took my breath away.

"But when you get home and explain, she'll understand. She'll welcome you back with open arms. I can guarantee that."

"But... what if *I* don't feel the same anymore when I see her? What if the feelings I had in my dream never return? What if this amnesia has changed all that?"

I smiled, but I knew it would be tinged with sadness. "I'm sure the feelings will return."

He tilted his head to one side and scrutinised me. "Are you saying that as my doctor because you know it to be true or as someone who's just too damn kind to say what she's really thinking?"

I cringed. "A little of both, I suppose."

The telephone rang and my heart leapt. We both turned toward it and gulped. Cain glanced over at me. "You haven't seen me. I haven't been here. You have no clue where I am."

I nodded and lifted the receiver. "Hello?"

"Kelly? Oh, thank God. Are you okay?"

"Hi, Alex," I answered as breezily as I could. "Yeah, I'm fine. Just chilling with a good book." I grabbed a magazine from the table and fanned my heated skin. I glanced over and caught a look of incredulity on Cain's face, and when I flipped the magazine over, I was greeted with a stern-looking man staring at me in accusation from the cover of Psychologist's Monthly. I cringed and rolled my eyes before remembering I was on the phone. "Is... is everything okay?"

"No... no, it's really not. Cain Somers has somehow managed to get out of the hospital and has absconded."

I gasped and glanced over to where Cain sat chewing his nails. "Oh, no! But how?"

"He seems to have overridden the door code."

"Oh, gosh. But what made you think I wouldn't be okay?"

"Look... please don't take this the wrong way, but... Patty thinks he's fixated on you. Apparently he went ballistic when he discovered you'd gone on leave. He refused to speak with Magnus."

"I see. I see. Well, you don't need to worry. He's not been here," I lied through my teeth.

"Just keep your doors locked and dial 999 if he turns up, okay?"

"Sure. Yes. But you know, Alex, I think he's harmless. Maybe a little stir-crazy and fed up. That's all. It's my guess he just needed some fresh air."

"I hope you're right, Kelly. Sorry to bother you on your time off. Especially at this late hour."

"No worries. Bye, Alex." I hung up and watched as Cain stood and grabbed his coat.

"Where are you going to go?"

"I'll go back. I'll apologise and tell them I needed some air like you said. Don't worry. I won't mention you."

I nodded and kept my eyes locked on his for a moment longer than necessary. He stepped toward me and pulled me into his chest, wrapping his arms around me. Being there felt so right, regardless of what I had discovered. The heat of his body seeped through my clothing and into my skin as if there were no barrier between us. Just like the time we had made love here in my home. The memory flooded my heart with a mixture of longing and pain, twisting at me and taunting me with something I could never have again.

Loosening his grip, he cupped my cheek. "Kelly, what I said before about using you. I... I didn't mean it, okay? I felt such a deep connection to you that it fucking freaked me out. I'm kind of sad that things have happened this way, and I'm angry with myself for how I treated you. You're a truly amazing woman. Damn sexy too."

He smiled, and I melted into his penetrating blue gaze. I knew what he was going to say. I knew I was his doctor, and it needed to be this way. But that didn't make it hurt any less.

"What happened between us... Now that I remember Melody, I should regret it... but... I can't. Making love to you felt... so *right*. Even though now I know it was wrong. But regardless of all that... I don't deserve you. The more I remember, the more I think I don't deserve to be loved... by *anyone*. And I know I could never give you what you need. I'm too fucking messed up. I'm not whole. I'm half a fucking man right now. And this latest memory has just thrown more crazy into the melting pot. I love someone in the US? Fuck, why can't I remember her if she's so damned important to me? It's terrifying. What the hell will she think of me when I go back? Because I *have* to go back. I have to find Rosa. How can I give anyone a part of myself when I'm not whole? I have so much to figure out... even with Melody. I have so many fears, and no one deserves to have to deal with that shit. I can't think of a future with anyone until I get my past straight in my head. But you deserve that. You deserve someone who can commit to a future with you completely. And I'm so sorry, but I can't do that. The sad thing is that even though you reminded me of someone I love... I know I really *do* love you, but... I just can't deal with all of this right now. I'm so sorry, Kelly." His voice broke and my heart squeezed as more tears spilled over from my eyes. He kissed my forehead and pressed his lips there for a few seconds before pulling away and walking toward the front door.

I didn't follow.

CHAPTER EIGHTEEN

Cain

The trouble I had caused by checking out without telling anyone became evident when I arrived back at the hospital to a crowd of cops. I was immediately escorted back to the Mental Health Unit and marched into Doctor Clayton's office. He interrogated me about where I had been and how I had managed to escape. He didn't use that exact word, but that's what he meant. Never, since being there, had I felt more like a fucking dangerous criminal. I wondered if they'd be tagging me next.

When I was eventually allowed back to my room, it was almost two in the morning and I was fucking beat. I stripped down to my boxers and went to rinse my face. As I turned to walk away I noticed the ink on my back. I hadn't taken much notice of it before, but now I was intrigued. There was a winged skull with flames and a broken halo above it. Company of Sinners? What the fuck? I guessed I wasn't the kind of person to have a rock band tattooed on his back. But who were they? Were they the people in the back of my mind when I was dreaming about Melody? Were those the guys I was thinking about when I remembered I didn't care what the fuck they thought?

The whole situation was exhausting, and I just wanted it to be over. Not the suicide kind of over. But the kind of over that meant I could just get back to my own fucking life. I climbed into bed with more questions than I'd had when I awoke.

Where the hell was she? We were both supposed to be on time. I paced up and down outside the two-storey house, waiting for her to arrive. The owner of the house was late too, damn him. But it wasn't like Melody to be late. She was so goddamn pernickety about shit like that. I glanced down at my Cosmic tattoo, and there she was smiling up at me from my forearm, all draped and sexy looking with those big green eyes that got her whatever she wanted every fucking time. But fuck it, she was my everything. Signing the lease on our first proper home together was a big fucking deal. She'd been so great about Rosa still living with us. And getting out of the trailer park was going to mean pulling further away from the Company.

It's all Melody had wanted.

Being my old lady had gotten tedious pretty damn fast. She knew what the guys were like after serving them beer at the clubhouse since she was old enough to do it. But the fact that her pa had gone meant that she had no one except me keeping her there. The fact that her mom had left as soon her pa had gotten involved in the Company and that he had died in the line of duty, so to speak, made her all the more determined that any kids we had would grow up without this crazy-ass lifestyle.

Kids... shit.

The thought of being a daddy scared the crap out of me but excited me all the same. She was only a couple months along, but knowing that a life was growing inside her belly—a life that we created together—just made me love her more. She was gonna be an amazing momma. I just knew it.

I pulled out my cell to check the time and realised I had a

text message.

Hey babe. The lease is signed. I talked to Cliff and he let me sign it by myself. Didn't need us both after all. I'm at the house waiting for you. And I may just be a little naked and horny when you arrive ;-)

I laughed and shook my head. My God, woman. You're so damned frustrating, but boy do I love you! I made my way up the path to the white front door and opened it. I pulled my bottom lip into my mouth and tried to stifle my grin. But who was I kidding? This woman got my motor running with the smallest of gestures. My excitement to see her and to celebrate almost had me running through the house. But I was trying to play it cool. Letting her have her fun.

The house was cute. A little small, but it had a proper yard and a front door that locked. It needed decorating, as the white walls were a little too clinical, but we'd get around to that eventually. The nursery was going to be the first job and then Rosa's room. I'd gotten the plans straight in my head.

I felt sure the baby would be a little boy, and against her initial fears for presuming, Melody had chosen a really nice powder blue. Rosa wanted red for her room, but Melody and I were trying to talk her out of it. She was almost eighteen now though and knew her own mind, and boy did she let us know it. Melody wanted our room to be all romantic. She had her heart set on this huge fucking four-poster bed. And right then she could have had anything she wanted.

She was taking care of my baby, after all.

When I stepped inside the house, I could smell her perfume. "Melody! Baby, I'm here. Where are you?" I called. But she was being sneaky and there was no answer. I grinned and tiptoed further in. I don't know if it was down to the hormones and whatnot, but she was insatiable. Not that I was complaining. I loved her body, and her tits had gotten a little bigger—a fact I was more than happy about.

I slowly made my way to the back of the house, where the kitchen and the stairs were, and loosened my T-shirt from my jeans as I walked. I anticipated her lying on a blanket or an air mattress or something, naked and waiting for me with that sexy look she got when she was aroused.

The sound of "Set Fire to the Third Bar" by Snow Patrol travelled through the atmosphere and sent shivers down my spine. The song always made me feel sad; but for her own sentimental reasons, Melody loved it very much. She said there was real beauty in the melancholy of the lyrics, and listening to it made her grateful that she had me with her. It was my guess she had it on repeat on her iPod. She played it everywhere ever since I'd gotten her the portable speaker.

I rounded the corner and stopped dead.

A cold shiver like an electric current ran down my spine and I dropped to my knees as the bottom fell out of my whole fucking world.

"Oh, fuck... oh, fuck no! Melody! No! Baby, no! Melody, no, don't do this. Open your eyes, baby, please."

She lay there, completely still, at the foot of the stairs. Blood oozed from her head and created a crimson halo around her, and her beautiful body was lifeless as I scooped her into my arms. As I did so, a long sigh left her lungs and for a minute I was filled false hope. I pulled her away from me. "Melody? Melody that's it, breathe for me baby, just breathe," I begged. But the stark realisation that it was simply the remaining air expelling from her lungs stabbed me in the heart, and I crumpled once more. "Noooo! No... please," I sobbed as I rocked her back and forth. I blinked the tears away from my eyes and let them trickle down my face. Her once rosy cheeks were pale and her skin cold.

"Come on, baby, wake up now, okay? We have to get you to hospital. Come on, sweetheart, come on, Melody. Don't leave me, okay? Stay with me, okay? You and this baby mean everything to me. Everything. I'm nothing without the two of you,

Melody, do you hear me? Nothing." I placed my hand over her stomach for a moment, but the cold of her skin emanated through the fabric of her flimsy sweater and I couldn't stand it.

Reluctant to give in or give up, I kissed her forehead and continued to rock her. "Please, just wake up, sweetheart. We're gonna move in here and be so happy. I swear it. You'll see. No more Cosmic. No more nothing that isn't just me and you and our little boy. I promise. I'll walk away from the club right now... right now if you wake up for me. Come on, baby, wake up for me now." Sobs racked my body as I shouted at her even though I knew it was pointless. A, painful grinding radiated through my head and my face, and I realized that in my agony I had been gritting my teeth until my jaws ached. My stomach rolled and I squeezed her limp body to my chest. I was too late. "No! No, don't you do this. Don't you fucking leave me! Don't you dare fucking leave me, Melody."

The lyrics filling the air spoke of being far away from a loved one, and my heart almost split in two as I rocked my beautiful Melody in my arms.

Her eyes remained closed, her chest remained motionless. My heart remained shattered.

She had already left me.

———

KELLY

"He's inconsolable, Kelly. We really need you to come in. He's asking for you, and he wouldn't explain to anyone else what was wrong. Please. We've had to sedate him. *Please*, love."

Patty's worried voice down the phone line gave me the shivers.

What the hell had happened that meant she had to ring me at five in the morning when I was supposed to be on leave? I fumbled around for my clothes, and after taking the quickest shower ever, I dried and dressed myself in a hurry.

As I walked faster than usual toward my place of work, the sun was just beginning to rise and there was a distinct chill to the air. I wasn't sure if it was the actual temperature or just the fact that my blood was running cold as I tried to figure out what had happened to upset Cain so much.

I signed in and dashed to the elevator, willing the car to travel faster than its cable was allowing and wishing I'd taken the stairs. When I walked through the Mental Health Department doors, Patty and Alex were waiting for me.

"How's he doing?" I asked as I removed my coat.

"He's sleeping. We had to sedate him again. He purposefully banged his head on the wall several times and said he needed to forget," Alex informed me with a cringe.

The thought of him trying to erase something from his memory scared me. Goose bumps rose on my skin, and I scrunched my eyes for a moment. "Oh, no. I wonder if his memory has returned altogether and he doesn't like what he's discovered."

Alex nodded thoughtfully. "I think that may be the case. Once he comes around, you will need to be careful. He's restrained at the moment, as we feared he would harm himself further."

Hell, it must be bad, then. I nodded and Patty took my coat from me with a worried smile. I made my way to Cain's room and stepped inside. A gash on his head had been stitched, presumably as he slept, and his eyes were sunken and very dark but rimmed with red. I pulled up a chair and took his hand. I sat there just stroking his skin and trying to hold myself together, but it broke my heart to see him like that.

I must've dozed off, as I awoke to find my head resting on his bed and my hand still clutching his. As my eyelids fluttered open, I could hear the sound of raw, broken sobbing. Lifting my head slowly, I looked up toward Cain's face. Tears cascaded from the corners of his scrunched eyes, and his lips were twisted in a mask of agony.

I stood and brushed his hair back from his forehead. "Hey... hey, Cain, it's me, Kelly."

He opened his eyes and peered up at me through the pools of saltwater. "She's... she's *dead*," he whispered.

My stomach dropped and I gripped his hand tighter. "Who? Who's dead, Cain?"

"Melody. And... and our baby."

"I... I don't understand... Please can you explain?"

"I remembered. I remembered because I was the one who found her. She's gone and our baby died with her." He closed his eyes again and let out a heart wrenching, guttural roar that made me gasp and step back in a split second of fear. I covered my mouth with my hands and watched helplessly as he fought angrily against his restraints. Eventually he relented and lay there, shaking, jaw clenched and eyes squeezed tightly shut as if doing so would erase the newly discovered truth.

All reason and protocol flew out the window along with any concerns I had about my job, and I stepped forward once more. I bent over him, wrapping my arms around him as best I could. He needed comfort, and at that precise moment, I didn't give a damn about anything but giving him what he needed. Unwelcome and inappropriate memories slipped into to my mind about how I had felt when he made love to me. My breasts pressing against his hard chest and his weight on me as he filled me. My heart ached in the knowledge that it would never happen again.

This was my own selfish grief.

I was grieving for a love that was far from perfect and wasn't ethically right but that meant *something*. I shared in his grief at that moment and wanted more than anything to turn back the clock. I wanted for this terrible sequence of tragic events never to have happened to him. I wanted him never to have suffered *once* let alone *twice*. But most of all I wanted never to have met him. Never to have known him. Never to have had such a deep sexual and emotional connection with him. Never to have been so intensely and sexually awakened.

And never to have fallen so completely and unequivocally in love with him.

As I held him, he turned his head into my neck and continued to pour out all of his pain and anguish onto my skin, and my own eyes let go of the tears I had been fighting. I just held him like that for what seemed like hours. It was wrong to want him to so desperately. I knew that. But it didn't stop me from wishing I could take his grief away with my body. To love him and show him that he wasn't alone.

Every so often he mumbled pain-filled words that twisted my insides, and I tried so hard not to sob. He needed someone to be strong for him.

And right then *I* was that someone.

"Our baby... Oh, God, our baby... Melody... Melody, no..." His voice was a strangled and unfamiliar sound. Gone were the arrogance and strength he had exuded since he gained consciousness.

What was left was a defeated and heartbroken man.

Without caring about the consequences, I reached down and unfastened the restraints at his wrists and helped him to sit up. As soon as he was upright, he grabbed for me and buried his head at my breast as his arms came around my waist, his bulk dwarfing my petite frame, and more hurt and pain overcame him. I stroked his hair and soothed him as best I could, but I knew there was nothing I could say to him that would take away the shock of the grief he was feeling for the second time. Experiencing the horrific accident at the time it had actually happened must have been bad enough, but now to be going through it all over again....

He pulled away and gazed up at me, bone-deep loss darkening his eyes. I wiped his cheeks with my thumbs, and he cleared his throat and swallowed hard. "She... she fell. We were signing a lease for our new house..." He closed his eyes. "She was trying to surprise me. She was only ten weeks pregnant, and we were so happy. We were excited about being a mommy and daddy. We were going to paint the nursery right away. She was at the house waiting for me, but I... I didn't *know*. I didn't hear my phone and I was waiting outside. I could've saved her if I'd seen her message sooner... I could've saved her, Kelly, but I *didn't*. It's all my fault. They're both gone, and it's all my fault."

Once again the inappropriate twang of jealousy tugged at me. She had been carrying his child. I had never considered having a family, but the fact that he was so excited about the prospect made my selfish pain much worse. I mentally slapped myself. This isn't about me, for God's sake. He's blaming himself for what happened, and he shouldn't. "Hey, shhh. No, no, it's not your fault, Cain. It's really not."

He lowered his head and shook it with vehement determination. "But she slipped and fell down the stairs. There was no carpet yet, and she hit her head. I found her lying there.... I want to forget again, Kelly, I can't live with this shit in my head. I can't live knowing that I killed her."

I gripped his face in my palms and forced him to meet my gaze. "You did not kill her, Cain. It was a tragic accident. But that's all it was... an accident. You didn't kill her. Please don't blame yourself."

"And now someone has Rosa. They'll kill her and it'll be my fault too. I need to go home. I *have* to go home."

I loosened my hands until I was tenderly cupping his damp face, and I asked the question which, once answered, I knew would break me. "Cain... do you remember where home is?"

He nodded. "Home... home is *Utah*."

My heart plummeted in my chest.

It really was over.

CHAPTER NINETEEN

KELLY

The following day—with my annual leave postponed—I sat at my computer, searching the Internet for anything I could find that would tell me if what Cain had dreamed and remembered was true.

Sadly, I found what I needed. A newspaper article in the Salt Lake City Mail confirmed that one year earlier, his girlfriend, Melody Johnson, had died at number 4 Rose Acres, Alpine.

Melody Simone Johnson, resident of Rose Acres since birth, died July 1st, aged 24 years, after falling down a wooden staircase at a home she had just leased with her partner, Cain Somers. Sadly, it was discovered that Miss Johnson was ten weeks pregnant at the time of her death. It is said that Mr. Somers and his sister were inconsolable at the funeral, which was attended by over three hundred motorcyclists, mainly Company of Sinners MC, where Miss Johnson and her partner were members. Whilst CoSMC (aka Cosmic), are not renowned for their peaceable relationships in the area, it is said that they handled themselves with aplomb as they bid farewell to their sister.

Cosmic... the tattoo on his arm...

I clicked on a link that accompanied the archived article, and it brought up a photograph which made me gasp and cover my mouth. The likeness between myself and the pretty, smiling, green-eyed woman looking back at me was eerie to say the least. Her hair and eyes were almost identical to my own, and I clutched at my chest as tears spilled over onto my cheeks. Realisation hitting once more.

There was a knock at the door, and I swiped the tears from my face before calling, "Come in."

Patty appeared in the doorway. "Hi, hon. I just wanted to check in on you. Are you okay? I brought you some tea." She placed the steaming mug on my desk and twisted her hands uneasily in front of her.

"Hi, Patty. Yes... I'm fine. Just been trying to confirm the memories that Cain has regained. It appears he was right. He lost his child and girlfriend just over a year ago now."

"Oh, poor wee lamb. How awful."

"I know. It's like he's experiencing it for the first time all over again."

"Are you going to take your leave, Kelly?"

"No... not right now. Cain needs me. I need to be here."

"Look, I'm going to say something, and I know you won't like it. But I've seen this happen to doctors before, and it never ends well... You are becoming personally involved in Cain's case. I know you feel some kind of responsibility, but it's not your situation to worry about, hon. You'll make yourself ill if you get so attached to your patients. It's not healthy for you."

Rather than getting angry and shouting at her, I nodded. "Thank you for your concern. I do appreciate it. But you really don't need to worry. I'll be fine."

She nodded with what seemed to be reluctance and left the

office. There was absolutely no way I was taking leave. I had to be close by in case Cain needed me. He'd said before that I was the only one he trusted. I wasn't about to let him down when he needed me the most.

But if I was honest with myself, that wasn't my only reason.

Cain was on the verge of exiting my life forever, and so every single minute with him was precious. Okay, so things wouldn't be the same as they had been. And maybe I was torturing myself by being so close, but I couldn't bear the thought of being anywhere else. I told myself that I needed the time to get used to the fact that he would be leaving, but I was kidding myself. There would be no getting used to that fact.

I was becoming a psychologist's nightmare. The fact that I was avoiding Clara's phone calls and unwilling to discuss things with Esme wasn't helping, and I knew this. But I needed to stay in my little bubble of denial.

"The sad thing is that even though you reminded me of someone I love... I know I really do love you." His words continuously rattled around my head, and I clung onto them with every fibre of my being. The thought that his feelings may have changed now he knew the truth about Melody haunted me, but I pushed the intrusive niggles to the back of my mind.

He loved me.

He'd said so.

But oh my God, did that make it harder. Knowing that what we had shared hadn't just been amazing, mind-blowing sex to him. The shattered potential of the whole situation cut me in two. And he would be leaving soon. He would go back to his life in Utah and concentrate on finding his sister whilst I remained here in the UK and faded into a distant memory.

It was too much.

———

In the days that followed, more of Cain's memory returned bit by bit and, even after much protest, he had been handed over to another doctor. I was reluctant to let this happen, but it appeared that Patty hadn't been the only one to realise I had gotten too attached to his case. Thankfully no one knew just how attached I had become. But my feelings for Cain had strengthened in vain. He was focused on getting back to the States, and I couldn't help him with that. The police were still investigating the situation over there to ensure that he would be in no immediate danger once he did return.

All he cared about was finding his sister, understandably. After lots of Internet research on my part, I had failed to uncover anything about Rosa and her disappearance. It was as if someone had managed to sweep the whole situation under the carpet.

———

It was the beginning of December and the weather had been pretty cold. After a lot of insistence on my best friend's part, Esme and I had been spending lots of time together, and she had been a wonderful support to me. It was a relief being able to talk openly about my feelings for Cain. She didn't try to tell me that everything would work out. Nor did she tell me it was a lost cause even though it felt that way.

Cain and I hadn't seen each other much at all. I had been carrying out visits to other mental health establishments and acting as a consultant too. My work was taking me away from the hospital quite a lot, and I was sure that it wasn't by accident. When I did walk the corridors, Cain was often chatting to police officers or playing cards with the other patients, and I chose not to make a point of seeing him.

I had to think of my heart.

On one of the rare days when I was actually sitting in my office going through paperwork from one of my visits, there was a knock at the door. "Come in," I called with my head down and attention focused on my work.

"Hey."

I gasped at the familiar voice, and my heart rate picked up. I removed my glasses. "Cain, h-hi. How are you?"

He slipped his hands into his pockets. "Doing really good, actually. Thanks. How are you?"

Forcing a smile, I told him, "Oh... you know... busy as ever." I twisted my fingers in my lap and felt the heat rise from my chest to my cheeks. He looked amazing. His hair was longer now, and his beard was trimmed short. He wore a long-sleeved grey T-shirt and faded black jeans. Clothes that had been donated to the department by local charities. But somehow, even in someone else's castoffs, he looked sexier than ever. The grey of his T-shirt made the blue of his eyes even more vivid, and it clung to the ridges and striations of his abdomen. The intensity of his gaze sent a surge of electricity through my body, and my nipples grazed the lace of my bra. My clit began to ache as my body remembered how he had made me feel. He still affected me, there was no doubt about that. He glanced down at my lips and licked his own before shaking his head slightly.

Once his eyes were locked back on me, he nodded. "Good... good... It's good to be busy."

Things felt so strange between us. Sexual tension hung in the air between us, but the strain of his guilt for feeling that way was palpable, and that saddened me. "So, how are things going?"

"Well..." He stepped forward, and I gestured to the seat opposite my desk, determined to keep a professional distance between us. He sat and leaned to rest his elbows on his knees. "I'm leaving the hospital."

"Oh?" My stomach dropped and my eyes widened. Why had no one mentioned this? "Are you going back home? To Utah?"

"Nah... not yet, anyways. They're giving me a place to stay.

An apartment in a kind of halfway house. They think I can manage there until it's okay for me to go home. They... they think Rosa may be dead. The police, I mean." He dropped his head forward, and my heart ached for him. All I wanted to do was to wrap my arms around him. But I couldn't. "They haven't been able to find any trace of her, Kelly."

Hearing him say my name again made my heart skip, but the sadness in his voice was audible too. "Oh... I'm sure they will keep doing everything they can to find her."

He shrugged. "Yeah... well, I'm not giving up, no matter what they say. She's my flesh and blood. She's all I have left in this world, and I owe it to her to do everything I can to get to her. To find her. She didn't deserve any of this shit."

"Oh, Cain. I know she didn't. And deep down, I... I feel that you'll find her." Against my better judgement, I stood and walked around the desk, drawn to him like a moth to a flame. I sat on the edge of the desk and reached out to pat his shoulder. Such a lame and useless gesture, but it was all I dared to offer.

He stood and stepped toward me. Reaching up, he tucked a strand of hair behind my ear and stroked my cheek with his thumb. "I miss talking to you."

I avoided eye contact and instead looked at my nails, which were in need of a fresh manicure. "Me too. But... we've been through this, Cain. It was over before it started."

Sadness emanated from his very being, and the heat from his body beckoned me toward him. Unable to stay away, I stood and slipped my hands up his arms, stopping at his muscular biceps. I slowly lifted my gaze to meet his and had to swallow down the emotion vying for escape.

He rested his forehead on mine, and his warm breath made my skin tingle. "God, I really do miss you. I miss everything about you. I miss just being around you, Kelly."

A flood of heat rushed to my sex, and I pulled away, removing my hands from his body. "No... you don't. You just think you do. It probably doesn't help that I resemble Melody so much. Once you leave here, you'll forget all about me." I laughed, trying to make light of the situation.

He shook his head. "You don't know what I feel inside. You don't live in my head, Kelly... or my heart." He leaned in and placed a tender kiss on my lips. "I'd better go. I'll come to say goodbye before I leave."

Unable to speak any more due to the tightening of my throat that trapped my voice, I just nodded. He stroked my cheek again, and after a look of deep regret, he turned and left the room.

I walked back around to my desk and slumped into my chair. Pulling out my cell phone from my bag, I scrolled through and found Esme's number. She answered after one ring.

"Ez..." I sniffed as tears finally ran freely down my face. "I need you."

———

I arrived home in a daze and unlocked the front door to my quaint little house. I frowned as I tried to recall the journey home. Things had descended into some kind of blurred reality since Cain announced that he was leaving the hospital. Once he was in the halfway house, it wouldn't be long until he left the country, and then it would really be over. Although realistically, it already was.

I removed my coat and hung it in the hallway. The living room seemed cold, and so I flicked on the gas fire and the Christmas tree lights before pouring myself a large glass of red wine. I discarded my shoes and slumped onto the couch. The silence in the room was deafening, but I didn't feel like watching TV. I knew I wouldn't be able to concentrate. I watched the white lights as they flickered on and off, highlighting the gold, red, and green ornaments on the tree for a few moments, lost in another trance-like state. It would be Christmas alone again for me. Leaning over, I switched on my iPod in its docking station and scrolled through the track list.

I hit play and closed my eyes, imagining... Cain bursting in through the front door and finding me here. He had decided not to leave and told me how desperate he was to be inside me again. Of their own volition, my hands travelled down to my breasts, where I could feel my nipples straining at the fabric of my blouse. In my head it was Cain's fingers toying and teasing me there. Making me wet with need and lust for him. Only him. I slipped my skirt up my thighs and parted my legs, remembering how good it had felt to have him rest the ridge of his cock against my clit. I slid my hand inside my panties and down into my dampness... Cain's tongue flicked at my sensitive flesh, driving me crazy as he circled my sensitive nub of nerves before inserting his tongue into me with one fluid movement. I clenched my muscles and gasped at the sensation.

As I squeezed my nipple between my thumb and forefinger, I increased the speed of my fingers where they worked my clit... Cain's long, thick fingers slipped in and out of me, spreading my arousal around and making me ready for him. And I was so ready. My belly began to tighten, and the pressure of my fingers increased until I almost soared over the edge, but I was determined to make this fantasy last. Slowing my movements, I pushed my blouse up and pulled one side of my bra down so that my breast was forced upward. I rolled my nipple around and moaned at the sheer pleasure that sparked throughout my body. Once again Cain's tongue was at my centre. Licking and sucking at my clit. Make me come, Cain. I want to come for you. Only for you. My fingers increased in speed and pressure once more as the tightening became more and more intense. The sound of my heavy breathing echoed around the room and I spread my legs wider. I needed this. Needed him. Cain... Cain... An orgasm ripped through my body like rays of light and I kept moving my fingers... Cain's tongue continued to roll and slide over my swollen clit as I repeated his name over and over and over.

The movement of my fingers began to slow... My breathing rate calmed... The throbbing of my clit decreased and once again I was lying alone on my couch as the emotion-filled voice of Lykke Li singing "Gunshot" filled the room. As she sang about how much she loved someone she had lost, my tears began to flow in earnest and my body was racked by violent sobs.

I had lost the one man I had ever felt a real emotional connection to. It was a doomed situation from the beginning. It was a love without hope and without foundation. And I doubted I would ever feel that way about anyone ever again.

CHAPTER TWENTY

CAIN

After a month or so of coming to terms with my returning memory and the loss of Melody and our baby, I had moved into a one-bedroom apartment in the city of Inverness. I no longer needed to be kept at the hospital at North Kessock and was no longer seen as a danger to myself despite my crazy outburst when I had realised all over again that Melody and our baby were gone. There was assessment after assessment. I saw many different doctors, and the cops interviewed me several times.

December in Scotland was fucking freezing. And I didn't feel particularly festive. Kelly and I had kept a professional distance, and I missed her like crazy. It wasn't the sex. It was her friendship. The fact that she genuinely cared. The way she looked at me made my heart melt. And okay, I'd only made love to her properly once, but God, I missed that closeness.

Although my memory wasn't fully restored, I did know that sex had been an important part of my life, and not having that connection with someone made me feel like half a man. Now that I was free of the hospitals constraints, I had considered going out to get laid to try to make myself feel better. But my heart wasn't in it. My heart, was in fact, pissing me off, pining for a woman I'd lost forever whilst simultaneously racked with guilt for wanting another woman I couldn't forget.

I hadn't been cleared to return to the USA because they still thought I may potentially be in some kind of danger there, but I was informed that steps were continuing to be taken to find my sister. For some reason the memories surrounding the incident that led to my being in Scotland and the disappearance of Rosa were the ones that were refusing to fucking show up. Instead I was being plagued with snippets of situations that I couldn't grasp. There was nothing tangible that I could offer as to where my sister could be.

Cosmic as a whole was denying all knowledge of me and my sister, which told me that they definitely had some fucking involvement in her disappearance. In fact, something in the back of mind was bothering me about Melody's death too. I couldn't quite put my finger on it, but something was bugging me. They were a Company of Sinners after all. They were a fucking bad company. That much I knew. But I couldn't give descriptions or names or locations. And Utah was a big-ass fucking state. It turned out there were Cosmic crews all over the goddamn place. And I didn't know anything more than that.

So there I was sitting in my little flat, as they called it, watching some show about teenage wannabes trying to get to be famous rock stars and win a recording contract. Talk about a pile of shit. I'd been advised that alcohol should be avoided on account of the meds I was still taking, but every so often I threw caution to the wind and drank a few beers.

I glanced at the clock on the wall. Eight in the evening on a Saturday. Fucking great. I know how to live. I was just contemplating eating a bag of chips I'd gotten from the local store earlier when there was a knock on the door and I scrunched my brow. Who the fuck would be checking up on me at eight on a

Saturday? I'd had my daily visit at five, and so I guessed it must be a neighbour needing to borrow milk or something. The place I was in was filled with those coming out of rehab or mental health care, and most of them kept to themselves, which was fine by me. I felt like a fucking fraud to be taking up an apartment that could have been put to better use. But I had nowhere else to go.

Dragging myself off the brown leather couch I walked to the door and opened it. What I saw... or rather who I saw had my mouth falling open in shock. The best shock I'd had in fucking months.

"Kelly? What the hell are you doing here?" Shit, way to make someone feel welcome, dickweed.

She smiled nervously. "I... I thought you might like a little Christmas tree for your flat." She held up a huge bag that was overflowing with sparkly shit.

Rubbing the back of my neck and trying not to focus on how amazing she looked and smelled, all the while trying to hide the fact that I was now sporting a huge fucking boner, I smiled. "Oh... right, yeah. That's great, thanks. C-come on in."

She cringed and bit her lower lip. "If it's a bad time... or if you don't celebrate Christmas or—"

I laughed and held the door open, gesturing for her to come in. "Why the fuck would I not celebrate Christmas, huh?"

Her smile returned, and she stepped into my living room. She glanced around and began removing the scarf from her neck. "Nice place you've got here."

"Oh yeah. Totally amaze balls." My mock teenage-girl reply was drenched in sarcasm, and she hit my arm playfully. I rubbed my arm and pouted. "Want a drink?"

She narrowed her eyes at me. "What have you got?"

I crossed my arms defensively over my chest. "Well I don't have any beer, if that's what you're wondering."

She scrunched her face suspiciously and pursed her lips for

a moment, and I thought I was busted. But then a sly smile appeared on her luscious lips. "Shame. I would've loved a beer."

"Ah, well... it just so happens I think some appeared in my fridge just now. Only on doctor's orders obviously."

"Oh, obviously." She grinned. I loved that her playful nature was coming out, and the way she cocked her head to the side just about made me throw her down and climb on top of her. God, I'd missed her so fucking much.

Once I had grabbed a couple beers from the little refrigerator in the kitchen area and adjusted my cock in my boxers, I cracked off the caps and returned to hand one to Kelly where she sat on the couch.

I sat on the chair opposite, needing to keep my distance. Being close to her would be too much, and I couldn't be sure I would be able to keep my hands to myself. "So... how've you been?" I asked her, suddenly feeling like an awkward teenage geek.

"Shouldn't it be me asking you that?"

I chuckled. "Ah, what the hell. Let's break with convention, huh?"

She laughed but her eyes remained guarded. Secretive. "I've been okay... I suppose."

That didn't sound good, and deep down I hoped it was down to the fact that she's missed me too. "You suppose?"

She placed her beer down on the small wooden coffee table and sighed heavily, her gaze locked on her bottle. "I know I maybe shouldn't say this. And that maybe you don't want to hear it but... I've missed you."

I widened my eyes. Surprised at her revelation. And so fucking relieved. The air rushed from my lungs and my dick hardened even more, to the point where it was almost painful. I tried to ignore it and concentrate on what she'd just said. "You have?"

She nodded and glanced up at me. Her pink cheeks revealed her embarrassment at admitting her feelings. "I really have."

I placed my beer down and moved to sit beside her on the couch. "But I haven't gone very far."

Her smile was small and fleeting. "No... but I don't see you every day anymore. I'd sort of got used to that. And soon you'll be gone for good."

I reached out and took her hand as my heart began to race. "Well... I'm here with you now."

She turned her face and gazed into my eyes. "You are," she whispered, and I could sense her pain.

Needing no other words, I slipped my hand into her hair and crushed my lips into hers. Her hands clutched at my sweater and our tongues melded together, reacquainting and reconnecting. The urgency of her kiss took me off guard, but I reciprocated with just as much desperation. She scrambled onto my lap, and her long skirt bunched up around her thighs as she straddled me. Her core rubbed against my erection and that fuelled my fire. Keeping my mouth on hers, I reached down and pulled off her each of her boots in turn, dropping them to the floor as she bit my lower lip and I moaned my appreciation.

I was so hard for her.

I yanked my sweater from my body and dropped it behind the couch and then tugged at the hem of the cute blue sweater she wore, and she pulled away so that I could strip it from her. My hands roamed over her soft, bare skin and cupped her satin-covered breasts as her fingers slipped into my hair, tugging desperately at the long strands. She removed her hands from my hair and scratched her nails down my chest and over my nipples as she rolled her hips, rubbing herself over my cock.

I inhaled sharply.

"I fucking need you, Kelly. I need to be inside you. Tell me I can make love to you," I growled against her lips.

She pulled her hands away from my hair and reached

around to unclasp her bra, discarding it to one side. I devoured each perfect breast, one and then the other, biting at the stiff peaks that beckoned to me. Her breathy cries told me the answer she hadn't uttered, and I tugged at the skirt she wore, pulling it up her torso and off over her head.

I wanted no barriers between me and her skin, her tits, her pussy. I needed that intimate connection with her, and right then I would have ripped every item of clothing from her body to get what I needed.

With her mouth on mine, she reached between her legs and stroked my rigid cock through my sweatpants. Desperate to be inside of her, I lifted my ass and yanked the damn things down along with my boxers so that my cock was free for her to touch. Skin to skin. And my God, it felt so good. She gripped me and began to stroke me. It was too much and not enough simultaneously.

"Stop... Kelly, stop... I don't wanna come until I'm inside you."

Wordlessly she slipped off my lap, dropped to her knees, and sucked me into her hot, wet mouth. Fuck, I'd wanted her mouth on me for so damn long. I gripped her hair, trying to stop the onslaught of pleasure. "Whoa, baby, slow down... fuuuuck... that's too good... too fucking good."

She pulled away and smiled sexily up at me. "You said you wanted to come inside me, but you didn't say where."

Oh, she was playing dirty. And I fucking loved it. She sank back down again, taking me all the way in, and I gritted my teeth, desperately trying not to come in her greedy mouth.

I gasped and scrambled around my head for words to express my need, but my brain was in meltdown. "Pussy... now... Kelly, I want to be inside you."

Freeing my erection again, she stood, hooked her thumbs into to the waistband of her black satin panties, and pouted. "All you have to do is ask, baby."

Hearing her call me baby in that sexy-as-all-hell Scottish accent nearly un-fucking-manned me right then, and knowing that she had used my own words back at me made me fall harder. Gazing up at her through half-closed eyes, I smiled and shook my head. She stood before me, naked. Her full breasts with their pretty beaded nipples begging for my mouth and her curves on display only for me. I wanted to dive right in.

I needed this.

I needed her.

CHAPTER TWENTY-ONE

KELLY

I'd missed him so much more than I should have. I was able to admit it to myself once I was with him even though I'd tried so hard to tell myself I was fine. I'd missed the intense connection that ran between us like molten lava, glowing and beautiful but so very dangerous. For days, I'd fought the decision to visit him, until Esme insisted that I did, just to prove to myself once and for all that there was nothing between us. She knew what she was doing. And she knew damn well that there was something between us.

He had been the central focus of all my fantasies. But making myself come with my vibrator or my hands was nothing compared to the feeling of being with him. I needed that connection to him like I needed air to breathe. And here I was breaking all the rules yet again. I was wet for him and wanted him so desperately. I gazed down at him where he sat with his joggers halfway down his legs, his cock thick and glistening from my mouth.

"Straddle me again, Kelly. I need to fuck you now, sweetheart."

His voice was gravelly with lust and hearing him speak increased my desire for him tenfold. I needed him inside of me too, but I'd missed his tongue and the way he made me feel when he kissed me everywhere. Stepping closer to him, I reached and slipped my finger into his mouth. He obliged and sucked on it, pulling it deep into his luscious mouth. But then I removed it and pointed to my sex. A wide, knowing smile took over his handsome face and he leaned forward, grabbing my hips and pulling me to his mouth.

Oh, wow, it felt so good to have his mouth on me again. I let my head roll back as his tongue delved into me, licking and sucking at my sensitive bud of nerves as pleasure coursed through my veins. His fingers dug into my arse cheeks and he groaned against me. The sensation was like the world's most powerful vibrator, and I gasped, gripping his shoulders.

"Oh, that's so good... so good," I moaned.

"You taste amazing... all woman," he mumbled against my clit, and the vibrations of his deep, lust-filled voice caused my core muscles to spasm. He reached to tug on my nipple, and I cried out and collapsed forward.

"Oh, God, what you do to me, Cain."

Giving me one more long, slow lick up my centre, he pulled me into his lap so that I straddled him again. He pulled me down onto his rigid flesh as I was cresting the wave of the most intense orgasm I'd ever had, and the feeling of him pounding straight into my already tensing muscles and rubbing against that sensitive place inside me brought on an even more powerful climax as he lifted me up by my hips and thrust himself into me, hard, with a carnal grunt. I couldn't get enough. I felt him tense up and when I locked my gaze on his he was clenching his jaw and making the sexiest sound over and over as he pushed into me.

"Kelly, oh fuck, Kelly... Kelly, I love you.... Oh God, Kelly, I love you so much."

His words shocked me to the heart, but the intensity of the sensations he was creating in me pushed me over the edge again. This time when I cried out, it was his name falling from my lips as my heart soared.

My greedy muscles clenched at him as my nails dug into the tattoos on his shoulders. I threw my head back as I bounced up and down on his thick, rigid cock, unwilling to give him up just yet. The orgasm rolled around my body relentlessly as he pulled me down and held me tight to him with a final libidinous growl.

Once again I collapsed into him and buried my face into the crook of his damp neck as he clung to me. His chest heaved against my sensitive nipples, creating little shock waves of pleasure that I could hardly handle.

When his breathing had calmed, he pulled away from me and nervously gazed into my eyes. "I... I'm sorry about that. I... think I got caught up in the moment."

I smoothed my hands through his overgrown shaggy hair as a sense of sadness weighed heavy on me at his apology. "It's okay. I know you didn't mean it."

His face scrunched. "Hey, I didn't say I didn't mean it. I said I was sorry because I blurted it out at the most clichéd fucking time, Kelly. But believe me when I say I do mean it. You're all I can think about. Ever since I laid eyes on you, I've known I felt something for you. And then when my memory came back and I thought it was because of your similarity in appearance to Melody, but... it's not just that. It's more. Not being around you made me realise that. I've known for a while, but... I knew there was no point in saying anything."

I swallowed hard, trying to relax my tightened throat. "You... you really love me?" Saltwater began to sting at my eyes.

He nodded and pulled me down to kiss me tenderly.

―――――

Cain

Well, it was out there. I'd admitted how I felt at the worst possible moment. I was just relieved she didn't think I was some unoriginal dumb-ass. Well, if she did think that, she wasn't admitting to it. The problem was, now that it was out there, I was terrified of the future.

I pulled her down and kissed her long and deep, and she melted into my body. She fit me like a glove, and the fact that soon I would be leaving to go home scared the shit out of me. Her life was here, and I didn't want to drag her into the shit that would no doubt be waiting for me back in Utah.

This meant one thing.

We were temporary.

She pulled away and gazed into my eyes. "Cain, what's wrong?"

"Oh... nothing." I sighed, realising that keeping things from her was futile. It was her job to delve deeper. "I just feel a little scared is all."

She cupped my face and kissed the tip of my nose. So damn sweet. "Scared of what?"

"Kelly, I'll be going home soon... back to the US. Where the hell does that leave us?"

She closed her eyes and rested her forehead on mine. "Can we... can we just not think about that now? I just want to be with you. I shouldn't even be here, Cain but... there's nowhere else I'd rather be than right here with you for now."

Her words broke my heart, and I was at a loss for what I could say in response to her, so I pulled her down and kissed her once again, slipping my fingers into the silky strands of her hair. I hardened beneath her again and shifted to lay her down on my couch.

"If we only have a short time together, I want to spend as much of it as possible making love to you. I don't know how long we have left, Kelly, but whatever happens, I want you to know that I will never forget you."

She parted her thighs and I slipped myself inside of her again, needing that intimacy with her even though it only reminded me of what I'd be missing when I left. I took my time. Slowly worshipping her body and gazing into her eyes. Without uttering a single word, I made love to the Scottish siren who had captured my heart and touched my soul.

CHAPTER TWENTY-TWO

Kelly

I awoke and glanced over at the clock on the nightstand. It was just past nine in the morning. I didn't have to be anywhere, and I was determined to relish the luxury of something Cain and I didn't have much of. Time. We had made love most of the night, and I had chosen to ignore the heartbreaking notion that soon he would leave to return to his life across the Atlantic.

We had eventually collapsed naked into his bed, wrapped around each other, at three in the morning. He had made me come every way he knew how, and I was paying for it now with the tenderness of every muscle in my body. But boy, was it worth it. I rolled onto my side and propped myself up so that I could watch him sleeping. He lay on his back with one muscular tattooed arm above his head. His face was tilted toward mine and his other arm was stretched out under my pillow.

He mumbled in his sleep, and I leaned closer to try and hear what he was saying.

"Melody... baby... love you so much... no one else."

My stomach plummeted as if I were falling, and I chewed

the inside of my cheek, hoping to halt the tears that needled my eyes. I turned to climb out of bed, but as I tried to stand I was pulled back as Cain grabbed my wrist.

"Hey, sexy. Where d'you think you're going?" His gruff morning voice turned my insides to jelly.

I sniffed and made sure to stay facing away from him. "Oh, I was just going to the bathroom."

"Yeah? Well, hurry back, okay? I have an undercover issue you might be able to help me with." He grabbed my other hand and slipped it beneath the duvet and curled my fingers around his erection with a chuckle. I forced a laugh and yanked my hand away, needing the distance from him and his distracting body. I stood once again and made my way out of the bedroom into the compact bathroom, where I sat on the toilet lid and dropped my head into my hands.

Not only would he be leaving me soon, but I would never fill his heart the way Melody had when she was alive... and still did after her death. That much was evident. I was kidding myself if I thought otherwise. Ten minutes later, and there was a bang on the bathroom door.

"Hey.... Hey, baby, are you okay?"

It irritated me when he referred to me with that supposed term of endearment. It irked me that I was jealous of a dead woman too, but the green-eyed monster was mostly definitely present, crouching there and laughing in my face, taunting me with 'I told you so'.

I cleared my throat. "Y-yeah. Be out in a sec."

"Come on, Kelly. I know there's something wrong. Please tell me what it is. Was it the undercover thing? I... I didn't meant to offend you. I... I guess I just didn't want our lovemaking to be over, that's all. And I was trying to be cute."

"No, it's fine." I quickly splashed water on my face and dabbed it dry with Cain's towel. I opened the door, and he stood there in his fitted boxers, looking all tousled and delicious. I couldn't help but smile. "How dare you look so sexy when you first wake up when I look like this?"

He tilted his head to one side. "I don't get what you mean. I see a sleep-deprived, incredibly sexy woman with a not-so-long-since-fucked hairdo and the best tits I have ever had the pleasure to devour." My smile faded rapidly. "Aww, fuck, what did I say now?"

I pushed past him and began to gather my clothes. "I really should go."

"Whoa, hey, stop. You're doing that fucking meltdown thing again, and it makes me crazy. He grabbed my arms and turned me to face him. "Tell me what's wrong. Now." Gone was the playful man I had awoken to. I gazed up into his fierce blue eyes and gulped. Sheer dominance. "I mean it, Kelly. I can read you like a fucking book. Something is off with you, and I want you to tell me the truth."

"You... you were talking in your sleep... about... about Melody."

His nostrils flared and he closed his eyes. He released my arms and stepped backwards. Once he opened his eyes again, he stared at me with a pain-filled expression. "Maybe you're right. Maybe you should go."

My lip began to tremble at his rejection, and I couldn't speak. He walked to the bed and sat, dropping his head into his hands as I finished gathering my clothes and dressed in silence. I went into the bathroom, ran my fingers through my tangled hair, and dabbed concealer under my puffy eyes. Once I was ready to leave, I left the bathroom and returned to the bedroom. But Cain was gone.

I nervously walked through to the living room to retrieve my bag and found Cain standing looking out the window. He had slipped on a pair of jeans, but his torso was bare and I was once again reminded of his former life by the tattoos gracing his back.

I cleared my throat and he turned to face me. I managed a small smile. "I'll go now."

He nodded. "Sure... Take care, Kelly, okay?"

That's it? That's all he's going to say? I was determined not to cry in front of him again and turned to leave, but anger got the better of me and I spun around to face him once more. "You know, Cain, I'm not the bad guy here. I wasn't the one telling someone else how much I loved them in my sleep. So why do I feel like I've done something wrong? Why do I feel like you've just let me go?"

His responding sad smile made my stomach clench, and I was glad at that precise moment that I hadn't eaten.

He sighed and pinched the bridge of his nose. "I'm sorry. I didn't mean to make you feel that way. I just... I just feel like I'm living with a ghost. When I'm awake I can't stop thinking about you. But then... when I'm asleep it's her haunting me. Maybe... maybe I just need to exorcise that ghost before I try to move on? I just don't know. And... and I have to leave soon. We're only going to get hurt if we carry on."

His change of direction gave me whiplash again, and I shook my head. I had no clue what to say and I scrambled around my brain, trying to process his words. "Cain, you were the one who said you loved me. Remember that."

I turned and walked out of the door before he could respond.

———

Cain

I watched her walk out the door and my stomach twisted and roiled. What the fuck was I doing? I was telling her I love her in one breath, then kicking her the fuck out in the next one? No wonder she was in tears when she left. She probably couldn't keep up with me. I was struggling to keep the hell up with myself.

I walked back through to the bedroom, stripped my clothes off, and went to turn on the shower. Once my skin was clean again, I grabbed my towel only to discover it smelled of Kelly. There really was no escape. My head was fucked, and to say I was confused was an understatement.

Once I had pulled on clean clothes, I decided to try and lose myself in daytime TV; but pretty much as soon as I switched it on, the phone rang. I stared at it for a few moments, wondering if maybe Kelly had decided to give me another bitter piece of her mind about my treatment of her. I figured if she had, then I should at least hear her out.

"Yeah?"

"Mr Somers?" I recognised the male voice immediately.

"Yeah, what's up, Doctor Clayton?"

"I have some great news. Your travel arrangements have been made, and you are cleared to return to Utah. We are recommending that you see a therapist over there to help you readjust, but we see no reason now why you can't go home."

A fucking double-edged sword.

I got to go back and try to find my sister, but that meant leaving Kelly behind. There was no point trying to convince her of a long-distance love affair. Not that she would agree to it anyway after my recent behaviour.

Realising I had fallen silent, I returned my focus to the call. "That's... that's great. Thank you. When will I be going back?"

"You have a few days whilst we finalise the arrangements. Your flight is booked for the twentieth."

Fuck! I was going home five days before Christmas? Man, that was harsh. I thanked the doc with less enthusiasm than I should have and hung up.

CHAPTER TWENTY-THREE

Cain

"You know it's not that easy, Cain. You can't just walk out on this club like it was never a part of you."

I glanced around the familiar room with its stench of tobacco and then back to the man sitting at the head of the old oak table as his words rattled around my brain.

I chose my words carefully. "Look, Colt, I'm going to be a father. I... I can't be a father who deals in illegal shit. I've gotta give this kid a chance, man. Surely you understand that?"

He slammed his fist down onto the old gnarled surface. "It's not that fucking simple!"

"Well, make it that fucking simple. I. WANT. OUT!" I bellowed.

The door opened and Colt's VP walked in. "Everything all right in here?"

"Yeah, Six, everything's fine. We're just discussing Cain's request to leave the Company."

Six's eyes widened. "What the fuck, man?"

I sighed heavily and clenched my jaw. "Melody's pregnant and I just want to give our baby the best start in life. That's all."

Six eyed me suspiciously. "So it has nothing to do with how the deal with the Legion went down?"

The deal with another club, Loki's Legion, had gone down real bad. A girl around Rosa's age—the daughter of one of the rival members—had been killed. Wrong place, wrong time, unfortunately. Thankfully Colt had the district attorney in his pocket, and so there had been no arrests and the incident had been kept out of the press. But there would be repercussions.

It was just a matter of when and how.

The Legion were notoriously violent, and they very much believed in an eye for an eye. Knowing an innocent kid had been caught in the crossfire of the soured negotiations made me all the more determined to call time on the whole MC life. Unlucky for me, it sounded like the prez and the VP weren't going to make it that easy for me.

Colt spoke again in a low, determined voice. "If I were you, Cain, I would think very carefully about this whole thing. You're better off with us than against us. We can't protect you if you're out on your own."

"Just because I want to leave doesn't mean I'm against you. Fuck, you've been my family for longer than I can remember."

"Then you need to rethink your decision. For your safety and for the safety of your unborn child and old lady."

I stood slowly and peered down into the ice-cold eyes of the man I looked up to as a father figure. "Are... are you threatening me, Colt?"

Without his face changing in expression, he kept his determined stare fixed on mine. "I am merely pointing out what would be best for all concerned, Cain."

I grimaced and shook my head. Sounded like a fucking threat to me.

I awoke with the usual sheen of sweat that accompanied

flashback nightmares. This one in particular had spooked me. In my mind, now and after reliving Colt's threat, there was no doubt that the Company were involved with Rosa's disappearance. But why? From the way I felt in the dream, I considered them family. Why would they go out of their way to fuck me over? Was it simply because I wanted to get out?

The thing that pissed me off more than anything was that the one person I wanted to speak to was the one person who no doubt would tell me to fuck off. I was determined to try regardless. After showering and dressing, I left the tiny apartment I had been calling my makeshift home and began the walk across the city to Kelly's place. I was aware that she had a couple days off and was this time determined to actually take them, so I hoped that Esme hadn't whisked her off somewhere.

After glancing around the road, I knocked on her door. No response. I waited for a few moments and then banged harder.

"All right, all right! I'm coming!" I heard her shout from inside.

The door was yanked open and I was greeted with a wide-eyed stare. She stood there in full make-up but wearing grey yoga pants and a black tank top with a hairbrush in her hand. She still looked fucking amazing. The shock of seeing me was evident as she froze to the spot before blinking and shaking herself out of a trance.

"W-what are you doing here, Cain?"

I held my hands up in surrender. "Look, I know I'm probably the last person you want to see, but I need to talk to you. Can I... Can I come in? Please?"

Her nostrils flared and she pursed her lips. "You'd better make it quick I have things to do and places to go."

"Sure. No problem." I stepped inside, and once she had closed and locked the door behind me, I followed her into the living room. I looked her up and down. Her perfume smelled fresh and recently applied, and it was clear to me that she was getting ready to go out.

"Where you off to?" I couldn't help allowing my curiosity to win out.

"I have a date," she replied with defiance.

What the fuck? Moving on fast much? "Oh... I see. A daytime date, huh? You don't know the guy all that well and you need to meet him in daylight?" It was none of my business.

"Not that it has anything to do with you... but it's Dermott."

I snorted as jealousy needled at my skin and I shivered. "Your college fuck buddy?"

She scowled. "My university boyfriend."

"Who also happens to be your fuck buddy." Anger I had no right to feel twisted inside of me, and I clenched my jaw.

Her bitter laugh didn't help my mood. "Well, let's face it, Cain, you've made it quite clear that I'm no longer wanted in your life. So I'm moving on. Now what did you want to talk to me about?" She folded her arms across her chest, but it only served to draw attention to her tits. I am a hot-blooded male after all.

Suddenly I wanted to leave. The desire to tell her about my latest breakthrough seemed insignificant and pointless. "Forget it. I'll deal with it on my own." I turned to walk away.

Her voice stopped me in my tracks. "Why are you acting like a jealous lover, Cain? Anyone would think you cared."

That was it.

I turned around.

I shrugged off my coat and flung it to the floor as I stormed toward her. Her eyes widened again and she backed away. That was fine, because the farthest she could go was against the wall.

And I liked her against the wall.

When I was pressed against her and her chest was heaving against my own, I peered into her verdant eyes. Her pupils had dilated. "Why am I acting like a jealous lover? I'll fuckin' tell you why, Kelly. He fucks you, but you mean nothing to him. You're just a way to get off for that prick. You're wasting your life on that asshole. But me? I *do* fucking care!"

She pushed against me. "Oh, and you're so different, are you? You didn't fuck me to get off at all then?"

I clenched my jaw and spoke through gritted teeth. "Yeah, Kelly. I got off. I fucking got off plenty. But the difference is *I* don't fucking call you when I'm horny and then disappear for weeks on end only to do the same thing again."

"No, you're so much better." Her voice dripped with sarcasm, and the hairs on my neck prickled. "First you fuck me and tell me it was just for fun. Then you tell me you love me and then you talk about your dead girlfriend in your sleep. But when I tell you that's why I'm upset, you reject me and tell me to go and there's no future for us! So, Cain, can you tell me how that makes you better than Dermott? At least I know where I stand with him. Plus there's the minor fact that you seem to be forgetting. You are leaving to go home, Cain. And home is thousands of miles away from me."

As she uttered that final sentence, her voice broke and so did my heart. As tears spilled down her cheeks, I crushed my lips to hers and took her face in my hands. I could taste the salt of her tears as I kissed her with all the pain, anguish, and jealousy that was running through my veins. She resisted to begin with, but then she dropped her hairbrush and reached up to gripped my T-shirt in her clenched fists. Her lips parted and her tongue began an aggressive dual with mine.

She whimpered and tugged at my shirt as I slipped my hands inside her yoga pants and squeezed her ass. Her burning, angry gaze locked on mine, and she yanked her tank top over her head, and her braless breasts grazed my chest. I reached down so that I could tug yoga pants, pulled her pants clear of her legs and throw them across the room. I roughly grabbed her naked ass and in a second her legs were around my waist. She gripped the hem of my T-shirt and I heard the fabric rip as she swiped it from my body. With my gaze still locked on her beautiful green eyes, I pulled at the buttons of my fly and she frantically shoved my jeans down, first with her hands and then the remaining distance with her feet until I could step out of them and kick them aside.

As I pushed her soft, feminine curves against the wall with the hard planes of my body, she attacked my mouth once more and grasped strands of my hair. I rolled her nipple between my thumb and finger, tugging and squeezing. The erotic groan that escaped her throat made me throb for her.

Without thinking of the consequences, I thrust myself into her wet and waiting centre, making her cry out and scratch at my back. The way she struggled at first scared me. But then I realised she was trying to pull me closer, deeper. I bent and sucked a rosy-tipped nipple into my mouth as she tugged and my hair and clawed at my skin in desperate need.

"Don't ever say I don't fucking care, Kelly. I care. I care more than you'll ever fucking know. You belong to me, Kelly. You're made for me. This is where I'm supposed to be," I mumbled as I moved inside of her with urgency.

"Don't say that, Cain, it hurts too much to hear you say that when I know I'm going to lose you," she sobbed into my shoulder. "Please don't say any more. Please."

I pulled away and was immediately trapped by the sadness in her eyes. I slowed my movements and ran my nose down hers. "Kelly... I love you."

She closed her eyes and pulled my mouth to hers. I knew it was a bid to stop me saying the words again.

———

KELLY

The intensity of this physical and emotional connection we had shattered my heart into tiny pieces as he said the words I couldn't bear to hear. I pulled him closer and thrust my tongue into his mouth, tangling with his to make him stop.

His movements were slow and punishing in the best possible way. Every deep thrust ground against my clit, driving me closer and closer to the edge of the abyss. He reached for my breast and tugged on my nipple, sending shock waves of pleasure through every single nerve ending.

"Harder, Cain, don't hold back. Harder, please." I knew I sounded desperate, but I didn't care.

He picked up speed and I clawed at his arse, pulling him closer and as deep as I could get him. But nothing was close enough. He would never be close enough. One final deep thrust from Cain accompanied by a guttural growl was my undoing, and I exploded around him in ecstasy as he buried his face in the crook of my neck and clung to me, holding me so tightly that I could hardly breathe and drawing out the pleasure for as long as he could.

When his breathing had calmed, he began to pull away and my feet once more found terra firma. He sunk to the floor, resting his elbows on his bent knees and his head in his hands.

"That's not why I came here."

I crouched beside him and stroked my fingers across his shoulders as tears stung at my eyes. "I didn't think it was."

"You were right... I was jealous and I have no right to be."

"No... you don't. You confuse the shit out of me, Cain. I get whiplash from your decision making."

He laughed lightly. "Yeah... I get why. I just..." He tilted his chin up and met my gaze. He clenched his jaw for a moment, his brow deeply furrowed. "I just can't help myself around you. I feel possessive. I don't want you fucking that prick Dermott. I know I have no right to act like I own you, but I can't help how I feel."

I glanced over at the clock on my mantel. "Oh, shit. I'm going to be late." I sat up and grabbed my clothes.

"Wait. What? You're still going to meet him?" The look on his face told me he couldn't quite believe I would go.

"I can't just stand him up, Cain. He's waiting for me at the coffee shop."

"Has nothing I've said to you made any fucking difference?" His voice rose along with my anxiety.

"Honestly? Yes. Of course it has. I won't be sleeping with him today or anytime in the near future. But I know that you're leaving soon, and I have to get used to that fact. We both do. And he's not a former patient, Cain. This... this thing between you and me is wrong. It's toxic and it shouldn't keep happening, and I shouldn't keep letting it. But I can't help myself around *you* either. But I need to move on. We both do."

He stood and yanked on his underwear and jeans angrily. "Well, you have a great fucking time with him. Say hi from me, huh?" After grabbing the rest of his clothing and dressing quickly, he stormed toward the door, leaving me open-mouthed and a little dumbstruck. I waited for the front door to slam, but then I heard him cursing. "Fucking stupid fucking asshole." And then I heard his stomping footsteps returning.

He stood in the doorway, panting. The colour had drained from his face and he nervously ran his hands through his hair.

"W-what's wrong, Cain?"

"I... I didn't use a condom, Kelly."

I smiled sadly as I hugged my arms around my body. "It's fine. I'm taking the pill. And I'm clean, I can assure you of that, so you have nothing to worry about. And although it may be unethical, I know that you're clean too. From the blood tests that were carried out at the hospital."

"Oh... Oh, okay. That's... that's good." He nodded and exhaled heavily. "I'll leave now." He turned and walked away from me once again.

It was becoming a habit.

CHAPTER TWENTY-FOUR

KELLY

My half-hearted wish to see Dermott evaporated as soon as I heard the door close behind Cain. I grabbed my cell and dropped him a text message to tell him some lie about a premenstrual headache. Knowing how squeamish men get about such things—well, how squeamish Dermott gets—I knew there would be no issue. Stupid, considering his chosen career. His response was a succinct "Maybe some other time."

After making a quick call to Esme, I set out to see her instead. I needed my best friend and the advice only she could give me. I was grateful that the walk to her apartment was short, as the weather chilled me to the bone and the dreariness of the day matched the way I felt inside.

All I wanted to do was turn around and rush to Cain. Tell him that I hadn't gone to Dermott because all I could think about was how my rugged, damaged American felt inside my body and my heart. How after all these years I finally got what people meant about toe-curling orgasms. Tell him that he had changed me beyond recognition and that I was finally completely awake.

And that when he left, there was a good chance I would drift back into my unwelcome slumber. Tell him that I wanted to go with him. Leave all this dull-as-shit stuff behind and follow him anywhere. Let him unlock more of my deep, dark desires. That I didn't want to only have the memory of his lips around my nipple, his cock buried deep within me, and his intense love inside my heart. I wanted the *reality*. With him and only him.

But part of him still loved Melody, and although he had all of me, I never would have all of him.

When I arrived at Esme's block, she buzzed me in and I climbed the stairs to the second floor. She was waiting with the door open, bless her.

"What's happened, hon?" She held her arms open wide for me, and I stepped into her embrace, trying hard not to let my emotions get the better of me.

I took a deep breath and pulled away. "Cain turned up earlier."

"Ah. Let me guess... you fucked him, didn't you?"

The muscles of my lower belly tightened at her words as I remembered the rough, carnal way he thrust himself into my willing body and the way the cold wall felt against my bare back. I swallowed hard and closed my eyes briefly as I allowed myself to be transported back in time. I'm guessing my lack of answer told her all she needed to know, as she shook her head and stepped aside for me to walk in. Esme was the most organised person I knew. Except when it came to her apartment. She was a bit of a hoarder, and her cluttered space was littered with antiques and knick-knacks. It was an OCD sufferer's nightmare.

I took off my coat and slumped onto the burgundy Chesterfield couch. "What's wrong with me, Ez? I must seriously be off my bloody rocker."

She sat beside me and grabbed my hand. "It's called being in crazy, stupid love, honey. If only it were easy to just stop ourselves feeling that way. It would be easier on the likes of you psychologists. And the suicide rate would be a hell of a lot lower."

"I was so determined to move on and let him go though. So determined."

She smiled and tilted her head to one side. With a questioning raise of her eyebrows, she asked, "Did your heart get that memo? I'm guessing not."

I growled in frustration and dropped my head back. Cain's natural dominance and my willingness to submit to him so readily had changed me. The intensity of our connection—both sexual and emotional—had brought out desires in me that I hadn't even realised were there. I had always enjoyed sex. Sex was good. Until Cain. Now sex meant so much more. Passion, spontaneity... and above all, love. And I was on the verge of losing it all. Deep down I knew that these changes were irrevocable, and it twisted me inside out.

My eyes began to sting and I hugged my arms around my body. "What the hell am I going to do? He's leaving soon. I have no idea exactly when, but I'm pretty sure after he goes, I'll never see him again. How will I cope, Ez?"

"It'll be tough, Kel. But I'll help you all I can. I promise you that. We'll get through it together. You'll see."

I swiped an escaped tear away and hugged my arms tighter around myself as the pain inside became almost too much to bear. I was on a downward stretch of the roller coaster with no way of reaching the elusive top. How could I possibly get through it? How? The whole situation was lost. I was defeated. I laughed humourlessly. "I wish I had your confidence."

———

I arrived back at work a few days later feeling less refreshed than I would have liked. My time away had been filled with thoughts of Cain and what he was doing. He never did contact me again to tell me the reason for his last visit. And so he had no idea that I had cancelled on Dermott. Not that any of it made any difference. He was going to be leaving at some point. I was just waiting for someone in the know to tell me when.

I swivelled my chair around and peered out at the Beauly Firth to the south. The recent snowfall made the still water appear black in contrast, and I was reminded that it was only six days to Christmas. My mum was living in the South of France with her new lover, a retired artist; and despite the many hints and several direct invites, I had no intention of joining them out there for the holidays.

There was a knock on the door, and as usual Alex didn't wait for me to respond. "Good morning, Doctor Darrow. Raring to go after your break?"

I swivelled back around to face my unwelcome guest. "Oh, yes. I feel great." My voice lacked the enthusiasm that the words were trying to purvey.

"Well, the good news is that our success story is returning to the USA tomorrow, so that's a positive one for the figures."

My heart jumped into my mouth. "I'm sorry, what?"

"Mr. Somers is returning *home* tomorrow," he repeated with a grin.

Shit, why am I only hearing this now? "Oh... I had no idea it was going to be so soon."

"I thought you would have been the first to hear. He has spoken very highly of your treatment of him. Says if it hadn't been for you, he has no clue where he would have ended up. I think you have yourself a fan there, Kelly."

"So it would seem." I forced a smile even though my stomach was churning and my heart was doing its best to escape through my clothing.

"Well, I'll leave you to it. Oh, and Patty has the details on the staff night out for Christmas. I hate the things personally, but it's only one night a year, so I suppose I can cope with that."

"Yes... yes, quite." I hadn't taken any notice of what he had said. My mind now racing to figure out how the hell I would get to Cain before he left. Alex walked to the door and was just about to leave. "Alex, wait!" He stopped and turned to face me. "Is Cain... Mr Somers calling in to say goodbye at all?"

"No idea. I'm guessing he just wants to get home now. Probably glad to see the back of us all." He chuckled and left my office.

I dropped my head into my hands as bile rose in my throat. This was it. He was really leaving. The downward stretch of the roller coaster ride continued and once again I was reminded that everything I had shared with the mysterious American biker was coming to an end.

Not that it ever had really begun.

My gut twisted and my throat constricted. At that moment I was glad to be alone in my misery, but I actually wanted to go home where I could curl up on my sofa and cry myself to sleep. Or drink enough wine to make me forget all this for a while. If only human beings could willingly switch off feelings and emotions. I knew I would have willingly flicked that switch.

———

Cain

It was all arranged. My flight the following day would be from Inverness and would take me almost four and half thousand miles away to Salt Lake City International Airport. Kelly would remain here in Scotland and would no doubt be cajoled back into Dermott-the-Prick's bed. Fucking bastard asshole. I hated him. And I hated the fact that he would have my Kelly all to himself as soon as I was gone. She was my Kelly and the thought of him putting his fucking hands on her made my blood boil.

Okay, so he was a fucking surgeon, probably had tons of cash and a flashy car. But it was my guess he had a fucking wiener for a dick. At least I made her come. I put her needs first. Seeing her mouth open and eyes closed in ecstasy as I drove into her was the best fucking sight I could remember. And I could remember a hell of a lot now.

The fact that he used her twisted my insides. Because that's what he did. She was no more to him than a hooker. Why couldn't she see that? Why did she let him? Because she used him too? Yeah that's what she would have you believe, but I wasn't buying that. She deserved so much more than the dick-weed could give her. Fuck, she was in my head, my heart, and my fucking soul. Whoever I was before the incident that took my memory bore no resemblance to the man I had become. The man she made me.

The reality of the situation was sinking in, and I have to admit that I was filled with trepidation. What would I find back home? Would Rosa still be alive? My stomach clenched as I thought about my kid sister being put through hell because of my desire to separate myself from the club and its criminal activity. And there it was again, the need to go home regardless of what I was leaving behind.

The few clothes I had were packed into a donated suitcase, and all my documentation was collated. There was nothing to do except wait. I couldn't understand why I hadn't heard from Kelly. I felt sure that she would at least want to say goodbye. But then again, remembering what happened the last time we met, maybe she was too pissed even to think about me now.

The telephone rang and I grasped at the handset, hoping it would be Kelly.

"Yeah?"

"Mister Somers, this is Suzanna Laing from the American Consulate in Edinburgh. It's just a call to let you know that your cab has been arranged for nine this evening, and all of your documentation has been cleared. You have to be at the airport by nine forty-five, and one of our representatives will see you there.

"Yeah, okay. Thanks." My heart sank.

"If there is anything else you need, you have my direct number."

"Yes. Yes, I do. Thank you."

"Have a safe flight home, Mister Somers."

I hung up the call and slumped back on the couch. Rubbing my hands over my face, I closed my eyes and thought back over the time I had spent in Scotland. It had been brief, but somehow I felt at home. Leaving was going to be difficult, but I had ghosts to lay to rest in the States, and I couldn't do that from Scotland. Most importantly, however, I had to find my kid sister and make sure no harm ever befell her again. Once she was back with me, I wouldn't be letting her out of my sight for a long fucking while.

My appetite had gone.

It wasn't like me to not want to eat, but my churning stomach wouldn't allow anything more than a couple slices of pizza and a soda. It was as if I was waiting for a fucking firing squad instead of a flight home.

Home.

Would it feel like home when I got there? Would anyone be there to welcome me back? Considering the Company of Sinners had disowned me, I doubted it. But it didn't matter. I only wanted to get answers from them. I was done playing nice. They were no longer my family.

Family. I laughed at my choice of words. Apart from Rosa, Kelly was the closest thing to family that I'd known in a long time. She was under my skin, like a fucking tattoo. And just as difficult to forget. Because like a tattoo she would be removed from my life but the scars would still be there. Invisible ones that only I was aware of. I knew that I had to go home. But in doing so I was leaving behind the one person who, despite all the fucking bullshit that brought me to Scotland in the first place, had made me feel complete again.

I sat staring at the congealed cheese and tomato before me, and my stomach lurched. I stood and threw the rest of the food in the trash. What the fuck do I do for two hours until they come for me? I paced the floor, watched shit on TV, and I wished I still had the iPod that I had arrived with; but Kelly still had it as far as I knew. It was a shame because maybe some of the songs I used to love would help prepare me for what was to come.

I stood gazing out the window and off to the distant snow-covered mountains. I wondered what Kelly was doing now. Would she be glad I'd soon be out of her hair for good? I wouldn't blame her. For me, leaving was like having my heart ripped from my chest, but I'd caused nothing but a shit storm of trouble for her.

I lost interest in the view and began to reminisce about how good it felt to make love to her, to feel her clench around me as she locked her stunning green eyes on me and moaned in that sexy husky way that I loved, and to call her name as I emptied myself inside of her How amazing it was to have her soft body beneath mine and her heart beating against my chest as I lovingly caressed her breasts and kissed the delicate skin of her neck. Just the thought of her made me hard, but my heart ached with a kind of emptiness that scared the shit out of me.

Suddenly, there was a knock on the door that dragged me, mentally kicking and screaming, from my reverie. Damn cab turning up too fucking early.

I opened the door and my breath caught. "Kelly."

"I... I couldn't let you leave without saying goodbye," she whispered in a wavering, small voice.

"Come on in," I croaked as I stepped aside. She smiled nervously and walked past me and into my compact living space.

She turned to face me. "I wanted to let you know that... the day I was supposed to meet Dermott, and you came around... I cancelled. I couldn't go to him. Not after what happened between us and the things you said."

"You came over just to tell me that?" I smiled and shook my head, but inside my heart leapt for joy. I stepped toward her and held out my hand. "Can I take your coat? Can I get you a drink? I think I have some soda left."

She shrugged out of her winter jacket and handed it to me. "I'm okay, thanks. Not really thirsty."

"Do you wanna sit down?" I lamely gestured to the couch, unsure of how to behave and what to say after my dumbass behaviour and how things were left the last time we were together.

She nodded and sat, eyeing me warily. "Are you all ready to go?"

I pulled my lips in between my teeth and closed my eyes as I nodded.

"That's good. I'm sure you'll be happier when you get back."

I opened my eyes and scrunched my brow. "You think?"

"It's home, Cain. It's the place you belong."

"I'm not so sure. The thing is Kelly, you won't be there. And I'm not sure I like that idea very much." My voice was quiet and to my own ears I sounded a little lost.

Her eyes became glassy, and the sadness of her smile almost broke me in two. "I don't like it either, Cain but it's for the best."

"I wish I could believe that, Kelly. But... I know I'll be leaving a piece of my heart here in Scotland... With you." Hearing my own honest words fall from my lips would have shocked me a few months before, but I had learned to be my true self with her. Well, this new version of my true self. A version I actually liked. The agonising truth was that I never could imagine being this honest and open with anyone else, ever again. I trusted this woman completely. She saw through the bullshit and the arrogance and she didn't judge. She simply loved me. I'd become this person because of her. Not only had I gained my old memories, but I had made new ones that I would never forget. Ever. No matter how far away I was from her.

She would always be tattooed on my heart.

Tears spilled over and left damp trails down her cheeks, and a sob escaped her throat as she covered her face with her hands. "I'll miss you so much. But... please... when you go, don't keep in touch, okay? I... I think it'd be too painful."

I walked over to where she sat and dropped to my knees before her. Removing her hands from her face, I spoke again. "If that's what you really want, baby, I'll do it. But it'll be one of the hardest things I've ever done. How the hell do I move on from you? I wish I knew, Kelly, I really wish I knew." I slipped my hands into her hair and crushed my lips to hers as her arms snaked up around my shoulders and she grasped at me, pulling me closer.

―――――

Kelly

Knowing that this was the last time I would see him, my heart shattered. As he kissed me, tears relentlessly fell but I was past caring. Desperation and need took over, and all worry and inhibitions melted away. I didn't care that I shouldn't be there. Didn't care that I was breaking all the rules again. All I cared about was being with him one last time. Showing him how I felt with my body when words were simply not enough.

He picked me up from the couch, his lips still connected to mine as our tongues danced a prelude of what was to come and he carried me through to his bedroom. I held onto him tight, never wanting to let him go.

Gently he laid me down and with reverence in his eyes, he began to undress me as he muttered words of love and placed kisses everywhere he touched. Once I was naked before him, he removed his own clothes and lay beside me, pulling me into his strong embrace and caressing my face, neck, and breasts. He left tingles in the wake of his touch and I ached for him. I needed him inside of me. To have this one last act of love between us. He cupped my breast and rolled his thumb over my erect nipple and I gasped as the sensation spiked at the junction of my thighs. I reached down between my legs and pressed my hand there, trying to stop the ache that only he could satisfy.

This wasn't fucking. This was really making love. The way he trailed his fingertips along my bare skin sent shivers like waves of light through my body in a way I had never experienced before. He placed his hand over mine where it rested over my sex and linked his fingers through mine. His erection pressed at my hip and I reached down to stroke him there.

Although a deep growl vibrated through his body, his kisses were no longer urgent or demanding but loving and tender. I trailed my hands from his cock up over his rippling torso and ran my fingers over his ink. I was trying to remember every detail of his body. His smell, the planes of his chest and abdomen, the sweet, gravelly noises he made as he tasted me and devoured my nipples sending intense pleasure radiating through each and every nerve ending and almost making come undone. But I fought it. I needed to savour every sensation, every touch. This was the last time I would be in his arms. The last time we would make love. And the last time I would see him.

Rearing up on his strained forearms, he nudged my thighs apart as he gazed down at me with longing and desolation in his eyes. A sob left my throat, and I clung to him as he entered me slowly. Filling me, stretching me, loving me. He lowered himself to rest his body on mine, and I tried to absorb and memorise the delicious feeling of his weight on me so that I could lock it away and keep it for those lonely moments when he had gone. His warm breath and soft lips feathered over my neck, and his heart beat a rhythm that called out to my own.

How would I ever recover? How could I carry on, knowing that he was thousands of miles away? He said he would be leaving a piece of his heart here, but in reality he was leaving with mine firmly in his grasp. I was ruined for all other men.

He rolled his large, muscular body until he was on his back and I straddled him. His gaze was filled with sadness and wonder as he smoothed his hands up my thighs, followed the curve of my waist and cupped my breasts. Once again I melted at his touch, unable to unlock my gaze from his. He gripped my hips and began to move me up and down his rigid length as I tried so hard to imprint the feeling of him deep inside me into my mind. I didn't want to forget this connection, this feeling of intimacy. I would never have it again.

I ground myself into him, my sensitive, pulsating clit rubbing against the base of his cock as he pulled up to a sitting position and teased my nipple with his tongue and teeth. I couldn't stop my eyes drifting closed as I relished the wonderful sensations he was creating.

"Kelly, baby, I want you to come. I want you to come while I'm deep inside you and I want to remember the way you feel around me, the way you sound and the way you look right now. I don't ever want to lose that memory. Ever. Come for me, Kelly."

His words and the emotion I heard in his deep, gravelly voice were all the triggers I needed as I once again locked my gaze on his and cried out his name, repeating it over and over like a prayer. My body clenched around his and he growled my name as he found his own release. The intense explosion of pleasure I felt battled with the overwhelming sadness flooding through my body and mind.

This was it.

This was the end.

CHAPTER TWENTY-FIVE

Cᴀɪɴ

I sat on the plane with my eyes closed as I replayed my last hour with Kelly over and over. Torturing myself with images I would no longer see for real. It was like looking through photographs of the best memories only to know that the people in them were gone forever.

I reached into the little bag I'd picked up at the duty-free shop and pulled out a bottle. It was the same perfume as the bottle Kelly had on her night stand. The fragrance that pulled me in every time I smelled it on her. Removing the little glass rose stopper, I held the bottle to my nose and inhaled but regretted it immediately as the ache in my heart grew. I replaced the stopper, put the bottle back in the bag, and closed my eyes. I rested my head back as the rush of take-off flipped my stomach this way and that. I wondered what she was doing. But as the images of her rampaged around my mind, my eyes began to sting and I immediately opened them and rubbed them hard, eradi-cating any outward evidence of emotion. I was surrounded by people who wouldn't understand why a fucking huge tattooed man would be crying on a plane. I didn't feel like talking to anyone to explain that I'd left my heart back on the ground with a beautiful Scottish girl called Kelly.

Oh God, Kelly. My Kelly. It was over. I was out of her life and she was out of mine. My jaw ached from clenching it so hard, and when the stewardess came around and asked me if I wanted a drink, my heart leapt and I opened my eyes, desperate to see Kelly standing by me. But of course it was another woman with a Scottish accent. A blonde. I shook my head, unable to speak in case I fell apart.

Kelly had handed me an envelope and my iPod just before she left, but she told me I wasn't to open the envelope until I was on the plane. I promised her I wouldn't. I'd been clutching at it since take off but every time I tried to open it, a lump formed in my throat and I couldn't bear to relive the goodbye that was no doubt written in the pages.

The goodbye we had shared physically and emotionally had been almost too much to bear. Holding her in my arms for the last time had been like ripping my beating heart out of my chest. The pain of her loss had battled with the intense pleasure of coming inside of her—losing myself in her one last time. And in spite of my aching heart, my cock remembered the feel of her and wanted more. So much more.

An hour into the flight, and I was still clutching the envelope. I knew it would hurt to read it, but I figured it would be the closest thing to hearing her voice that I would get, and I loved her voice. I could close my eyes and hear her saying my name like she was beside me. But she wasn't. I needed to open the letter. My heart was broken anyway and I suppose once something is broken beyond repair, breaking it a little more makes no difference. I pulled out the triangular flap with shaking hands. My heart began to pound and my eyes were already stinging.

I unfolded the paper and glanced down at it through foggy eyes. Fuck, I was welling up before I read a single word.

Cain

Knowing you has been one hell of a roller coaster. Things went way beyond what I could ever have anticipated; and although I know it was wrong, I can't regret it. I won't allow myself to do so. I've learned a lot about myself in the time you've been here, and whilst not all of it has been good, I think you have taught me not to settle for anything less than magnificent. As for sex, well, it shouldn't be just a way to release tension. It should be an expression of deep feelings that words just don't cover. I never would have expected that it would be a man like you who made me realise this—but you did, and I'm so glad that I discovered it with you.

Thank you for making me feel special, desirable, and loved. I will keep the memories of us with me forever.

I have added some tracks to the iPod. I hope you don't mind. I wanted to give you something that you could use to remember me by—if you want to remember, that is.

The first three tracks are ones I chose especially for you.

Take care and be happy, Cain. And know that whilst I couldn't say the words out loud—they were simply too painful—I do love you. And you will be forever in my heart.

Yours,

Kelly

I wiped the moisture from around my eyes and looked inside the envelope, hoping there would be a photo, but there wasn't. My heart sank. I slipped the ear buds into my ears and hit play, holding my breath.

I had never heard the first track before. It came up on the display as "Gunshot" by Lykke Li. Listening to the words, knowing they expressed Kelly's innermost feelings, squeezed at my heart. Every sentiment she was experiencing at losing me was evident there in the words ringing around my head, and I clutched my chest with one hand and the letter in the other. These were my last connections to the woman I loved beyond all sense and reason. Through the song she talked of the pain she knew I was feeling and that she was feeling it too. I'd had no idea she felt so strongly; she had never told me she loved me. But having read her letter, I now knew that it was because it was too painful. I totally understood even though it was killing me not to have heard her say the words.

The next song was slow and sultry, and the familiar voice of Alanis Morissette singing "Til You" sent shivers down my spine. She passed on the message from Kelly that her life had been some kind of a rehearsal until I arrived in it. I chewed on the inside of my cheek and my throat constricted as I fought the pain and anguish desperate for release from within me. I listened and let the tears fall unabashedly now, grateful that the seat beside me was empty. She had been drawn to me from day one and I had experienced the same pull. Like we were pieces of a puzzle that were incomplete without each other. How the hell do you move on from that? How the hell do you move on and leave a love like that behind? How do you face an uncertain future alone and without the one person who helps you make sense of the all the shit going on in your head? I guess I was about to find out, and knowing that fact knotted me up until I was leaning forward resting my head in my hands and sobbing like a fucking baby.

At the end of the song I hit pause and wiped my face on the sleeves of my sweater. I leaned my head on the window and peered out at the lights of passing cities and towns below. I could just make out the multicoloured festive lights blinking as we left mainland Scotland behind and an overwhelming sense of loss almost took me down again.

Kelly's third and final message to me came as the lyrics of "The Only Exception" by Paramore. I had learned from very early on in my relationship with Kelly that I was her only exception. She didn't trust men. She didn't sleep with patients and didn't let herself fall in love. But with me she had submitted to all three of these changes. And from the words of the song, as they brought on a fresh batch of emotion welling up from deep inside me, I would always be that one person who made her see things differently. The one who made her dare the step outside of her comfort zone. I wasn't exactly proud of some of it—enticing a doctor to be sexually intimate with a patient was not something I could put on my résumé—but knowing I'd had an impact on her life like she'd had on mine made me smile in spite of the loss I was feeling. And from my returning memories, I had discovered that she too was my only exception. I had only ever loved one other woman; and from what I remember of losing Melody, I swore that I would never go through that again. Until I met Kelly and she stole my heart, the old me had presumed I was broken beyond repair. I was no good to anyone as a lover or a friend. I didn't want to love or be loved. She changed that about me.

She was my only exception.

As the track ended, a smartly dressed woman in an air steward's uniform walked down the aisle, handing out drinks. I took a soda and paid for it with the last of my Scottish notes. Another twinge of sadness niggled at me and I had to turn away and focus on the blackness outside the window once again.

————

Over fifteen hours later, I unlocked my motel room door and stepped inside. I hadn't slept much on the flight, and I'd met with the police and other officials at the airport who had talked at me for God knows how long. I was handed a stack of documents and contact numbers along with a brand-new cell phone. If I hadn't been so fucking exhausted, I would have been grateful and impressed with how they had dealt with me. As it was, I was mainly stunned at how familiar yet oddly foreign their American accents seemed.

I fell into bed fully clothed, and sleep took me almost immediately...

"Cain, you have to get out of here. Who knows what they'll do next? We've already lost Melody."

"Rosa, I'm not going anywhere. They're not scaring me away. This is my home. My life is here. And fuck if I'm going to run scared. And Melody fell down the stairs. It was a freak accident."

The colour drained from Rosa's face. "I... I overheard Colt and Six talking..."

I sat up straight. Bile rose in my throat and my stomach roiled as if I knew what was coming. "And?"

"And... they were involved, Cain. And... and I think you're next."

My eyelids fluttered open and for a few moments I was completely disoriented. I glanced at the bedside clock. I'd somehow managed to sleep eleven hours. Fuck! I crawled out of bed and went to the tiny bathroom, where I took a quick and very cold shower. I was planning to do some of my own research and find out who the fuck had Rosa—and what the hell had happened to Melody. I had no clue how the hell to go about it, but what I lacked in know-how, I made up for in sheer fucking determination.

If my returning memory served me correctly, there was a library just along the road from the motel; it was as good a place as any to make a start. Plus if I kept busy, I wouldn't mope, wondering what Kelly was doing. Just thinking about her made my chest ache. I pictured her sitting on her office couch with her glasses on while some patient told her all about their problems. Would she be listening or would she be drifting off and thinking of me? My stomach flipped and I rubbed my hands over my face. The last thing I needed was to get lost in some pointless fucking fantasy about a Scottish girl that I couldn't have and shouldn't want.

I had to put her out of my mind and get on with picking up the shards of my life.

CHAPTER TWENTY-SIX

CAIN

With my memory almost back to what it should be, I walked down the street and decided to call into the coffee shop and grab a caffeine fix on the way to the library. There was some serious heavy metal parked directly outside, and a buzz of familiarity trilled through my veins as I examined it more closely.

I stepped through the door and immediately made eye contact with a bearded and tattooed guy in a leather vest, around my age, peering at me over his shoulder like he'd seen a ghost. Keeping his stare locked on me, he swivelled around in his stool and shook his head.

"What the fuck?" I walked to stand in front of him, and he stepped down from his perch and pulled me into a strong-armed embrace, slapping me on the back. "I knew you'd fucking come back, dude. I just knew it."

The word six jumped into my mind for some bizarre reason. "Hey, hi. I guess I know you?" Why wouldn't his name come to me? He clearly knew who I was.

He pulled away and held me at arm's length. "Know you?

You're like a fucking brother to me, man. What the fuck happened to you? You don't know me?"

I narrowed my eyes and chewed on my lip, trying to fit a name to the oh-so-familiar features. The word six rattled around my head again. "I'm sorry, man, but the only word that comes to me is the number six."

He laughed heartily and threw his head back. "Fuck, man, don't do that to me. You totally freaked the shit out of me. Thank fuck! I thought someone had been messing with your head." He pulled me into another hug and continued laughing.

Realisation hit me. "You're Six! That's your name!" The memory came flooding back and images flashed through my mind of us riding motorcycles side by side on an open road, laughing and pranking on each other.

He pulled away again. A worried frown appeared to cloud his features. "Fuck, dude. You really didn't know me?"

"I... um... I've been suffering from some kind of post-trau-matic amnesia. Things are coming back to me gradually, and I'm almost back to normal... whatever that is... But I have lots of questions. I need answers, man. I need them now."

Clenching his jaw he paused and nodded. "Can I get you a coffee? We can talk."

I nodded. "Flat white."

He turned his attention back to the young guy behind the counter and ordered my drink. Once the order was placed in front of him, he grabbed the steaming mug and nodded toward a booth at the rear of the shop. "Let's go back there. It's quieter."

I followed him and he placed my coffee down and slid into the seat and so I took the bench opposite.

"So... where the fuck have you been, man?"

How did he not know the answer to that? "I ended up in Scotland. Fuck knows how I got there. But I was found uncon-scious with a fucking suicide note."

For some reason Six didn't seem shocked by my story, which made me very suspicious.

"It's good to see you, buddy. People have missed the crap out of you."

"They have? That's nice." I had so many questions that I didn't know where to start. Had I trusted Six before? I was pretty sure I didn't right now. "Six... I need to know what the hell happened to me. And to Rosa. My memory is sketchy at best and..."

"Your memory's sketchy?"

Did he look relieved?

"Yeah... yeah, like I said, I suffered some kind of post-traumatic amnesia. Things are coming back gradually but... well, there are still blanks."

Worry glazed his eyes. "Sure there are." He glanced down at his phone and back to me. "So where were you heading off to?"

"Library. I figured I'd look at some old newspapers." I waited while he typed something onto his phone's screen and nodded. Not sure whether or not he was actually listening, I continued. "Maybe find out what the hell happened to get me to Scotland."

His phone buzzed and he was clearly distracted by it. "Yeah. Good idea. Look... I gotta run. But... how about I meet you tomorrow? Maybe I can help fill in some of the gaps."

He glanced nervously around the coffee shop and then back to his phone.

I rubbed my chin. "Is everything okay?"

"What? Oh, yeah, fine. Look... I know this may sound a little... I don't know... cloak and dagger, but... just stay out of public places until after we talk tomorrow okay?"

"Huh? Why the fuck would I want to do that?" What the hell was he playing at?

"Look, trust me, okay? Just stay in your motel after you've been to the library."

"But the library is a fucking public place, Six."

"Yeah, but... I can't explain right now, okay? Except to say the thing that concerns me won't be affected by you visiting the library."

Talk about fucking cryptic.

"Anyway, Cain, I really gotta be going. I have a... um... um... a meeting I have to get to. Should I meet you here tomorrow? Say around three?"

I got the distinct impression something was going on but I figured I hadn't got anything to lose by agreeing, considering I was still pretty much in the dark about lots of things. I shrugged. "Yeah. Okay. See you tomorrow at three."

He patted my shoulder affectionately and left me to drink my coffee. Once he had gone I decided I could no longer stomach my drink and I left too. I made my way the couple of blocks to the library. It was right where I had expected it to be, which was a relief as it meant things were becoming clearer. I walked through the red double doors and over to the desk where a young, prim, brown-haired woman was rifling through a card file. She had a long, slender neck, and there was something quite graceful about her delicate fingers as they flicked through each piece in turn.

I cleared my throat and she glanced up at me. A blush flooded her cheeks and she tucked her hair behind her ears. She almost floated as she made her way to the desk. All ballerina like. Poised and elegant. Her brow scrunched and she opened and closed her mouth a few times before eventually saying, "Oh, hi, sir. Can I help you?"

"Hi, okay, so I need to look at some old newspapers. Do you have those?"

She nodded nervously. "Um... sure. We have microfiche if that's any good? We haven't moved with the times, really. It's the best I can do." She cringed.

I was scaring her. I felt like a monster. "Okay. Can you show me how to look through it? I haven't used it before."

"Absolutely. Follow me."

The young woman took a deep breath and then led me through to a small room off to the left. The bizarre-looking contraption was perched on an old oak desk. After she had showed me the basics, the girl skittered away, leaving me to file through newspaper articles from the past several years.

After flicking through insignificant piece after even more insignificant piece, something caught my eye and almost stopped my heart dead.

Melody Simone Johnson, resident of Rose Acres since birth, died July 1st, aged 24 years, after falling down a wooden stair case at a home she had just leased with her partner Cain Somers. Sadly, it was discovered that Miss Johnson was ten weeks pregnant at the time of her death. It is said that Mr. Somers and his sister were inconsolable at the funeral which was attended by over three hundred motorcyclists, mainly Company of Sinners MC, where Miss Johnson and her partner were members. Whilst CoSMC (aka Cosmic), are not renowned for their peaceable relationships in the area it is said that they handled themselves with aplomb as they bid farewell to their sister.

The beautiful green eyes of an all-too-familiar beautiful face smiled out at me. My lip began to tremble as I read the words over and over. Flashbacks of standing in a cemetery with my arm around Rosa flicked through my mind along with the guttural roar of Harley engines.

I clutched my chest as physical pain overcame me. The article was the only one I could find relating to Melody, and it cut me to the core. It didn't explain who was responsible—in fact, it made out that the whole thing had been a tragic accident. Something inside of me told me there was more to it.

There were minor articles relating to my being arrested for disturbing the peace, assault, and other fairly minor misdemeanours; but they were all from a few years back and by the sound of it I had served my time, paid my fines, and carried out community service. More delightful shit to be proud of. Way to go, me.

I sat there until I felt a tapping on my shoulder.

The young woman startled me and I swivelled around, making her step back in alarm. "Ex-excuse me, sir? I'm so sorry, but we need to close. You can always come back tomorrow."

"Oh, shit... um... excuse my language. I apologise. I had no idea it had gotten so late."

"You seem to have been engrossed. You must be starving by now. It's five thirty and you haven't moved all afternoon." Her smile was warm. She seemed like a sweet girl.

My stomach growled at the thought of food and we both laughed. "Yeah, it sounds like you're right about that."

She stared at me for a moment. "Can I ask you something?"

I shrugged and responded with a light, "Sure."

"You look awfully familiar. Are you from around here?"

Fuck, what do I say? After what Six had said, I was unsure how my response should go. "A long time ago, but I... I moved away."

She nodded. "Ah. You must just look like someone from around here. It sounds crazy, but I knew a girl in school... Rosa... She was a couple years younger than me... maybe three actually.... You look just like her brother who used to pick her up on his huge motorcycle. His hair was shorter and he didn't have a beard, though. But your eyes are very similar."

Rosa? Fuck. "Really. Oh. Small world, huh?"

She looked thoughtful for a few moments. "Yeah. It was so sad what happened to her. She was quiet in school. Like me. I had a rough time and left as soon as I could. Rosa... um... disappeared. It was terrifying. She was involved in one of those motorcycle gangs. I wish I'd made an effort to get to know her instead of being a coward. I maybe could have helped."

Hearing her talk about my kid sister made my insides knot

and my heartbeat pick up pace. I had to get out of there. "That sucks. I hope they find her."

She shook her head and dropped her gaze to the floor. "I doubt it. It's been so long that I really can't see her being alive now."

A cold shiver travelled my spine and nausea came over me in a wave.

The girl glanced back up at me. "Hey, you've gone really pale. You should go eat. Sorry for rambling on. I just have to stay quiet for so long during the day that once I start talking, I can't seem to stop."

I swallowed, trying to combat the urge to vomit. "Ah, don't worry about it. I'll be going now."

"Will I see you tomorrow... um... mister..."

"The name's Cameron," I lied. "And yeah, maybe I'll be back for more research."

Her responding smile was wide. "Great. Bye for now."

I grabbed my jacket and made my way out to the fresh air as quickly as I could. Once outside I breathed in deep lungfuls of the early evening air and rubbed my hands over my face as I began to walk back to the motel.

The urge to speak to Kelly—just to hear her voice—was so overwhelming, it made my knees buckle. I stumbled and had to steady myself against a wall like a fucking wino while passers-by jeered at me. It was a good thing I had no cell number for her or I would have been saying to fucking hell with us being over and I would have been on a flight back to Scotland. But that would do Rosa no good. And it wouldn't give me answers, nor would it help me to piece together the puzzle that my life had become.

I called into a burger bar and ordered a take-out that I ate as I walked. Although my stomach was protesting it's emptiness I really had to force the food down. Hearing the woman at the library talking about Rosa being missing and her theories on whether she was alive or dead scared the shit out of me. I was hoping that I could sleep and then get some answers from Six.

Once I was back in the cocoon of my motel room, I stripped and showered in the hope that the hot water cascading down my tired muscles would ease some of my tension. But of course every time I closed my eyes I was plagued by visions from my nightmares of Rosa screaming no, with tears streaming down my face.

After watching crappy TV for a while I decided to at least try and sleep, although my nerves were jangling at the prospect of hearing the much-needed answers to my questions when I met with Six. Crawling under the covers, I laid flat on my back with one hand behind my head and closed my eyes.

CHAPTER TWENTY-SEVEN

Cᴀɪɴ

Melody's verdant gaze penetrated my soul as she smiled down at me. Her tearstained cheeks told me she was only smiling on the outside. As I admired the view of her breasts, visible through the taut, semi-transparent fabric of her tank top, she scooped her long auburn waves over one shoulder and bent to kiss me. God I loved those lips. I grasped at her hips, digging my fingers into the flesh of her naked ass.

"Fuck me, Cain. I want to forget all the shit and just feel good," she whispered into my ear, sending shivers through my body like electric sparks.

She stretched up and swiped the tank top from her body, revealing her creamy, pert mounds to me as they bounced free. Reaching up, I cupped the firm flesh and rolled my thumbs over the tightened pink buds of her nipples as she slipped her body down over my rigid length, eliciting a deep, pleasure-filled groan from my throat and a breathy moan from hers. God, she was tight and wet for me. I loved that about her. She was always ready. Insatiable even. And no matter how many women I'd had in the past, none compared to the feel of being enveloped by her warm, yielding flesh.

Lowering my hands once again, I lifted and lowered her, slowly thrusting myself inside her. I clenched my jaw and watched her writhe and cup her breasts as she took over and rode my cock, rolling her hips as she moved. The amazing sensation she created coiled deep in my groin and I was almost ready to explode.

"I need more, Cain. Faster, deeper." She grasped my hands, removing them from her ass and shoved them above my head. As she leaned over me, I captured a nipple between my teeth and grazed it, making her cry out, "Yes... oh God, yes! Make me come, Cain, I want to come over and over again so that it's all I can feel. Love me, please love me." There was an edge of desperation to her voice that spurred me on.

"I love you, baby. I love you so much" were the words that fell from my lips in a passionate reply.

I closed my eyes tight, fighting the desperate urge to find my own release, but when I opened them again and gazed up at her, Melody had been replaced by Kelly's writhing body driving me toward my climax. Confusion washed over me as she took what she needed from me and I from her.

On the verge of a mind-melting orgasm, I awoke covered in sweat and with a raging hard-on gripped in my hand. My stupid fucking brain was mixing up the two women I adored yet again.

The fact was that I could be with neither of them.

I angrily turned the shower knob to cold and stepped under the icy torrent. Why the fuck did my subconscious insist on torturing me with things I could never have again?

It wasn't. Fucking. Fair.

Once I was dried and dressed, I made my way out of the motel and down the road toward the coffee shop where I had bumped into Six the previous day. Pushing through the doors, I glanced around to see if anyone seemed to recognise me; but everyone was getting on with breakfast, oblivious to my presence. The smell of fresh pancakes wafted through the air, and my stomach growled in response, and so I walked over to the counter and placed my order. I took a seat on one of the high stools that Six had sat on, and an older woman came and poured aromatic coffee into a mug before me. I slipped my hands around the hot ceramic and inhaled the aroma of burnt caramel, which instantly transported me back to the morning I had drunk coffee with Kelly after I had shared the returning memory of Melody. I closed my eyes as a strange sense of homesickness washed over me.

Suddenly someone pulled me back from my daydream. "Oh, hi, Cameron." I turned my head in the direction of the familiar voice and was greeted by the pretty smile belonging to the young woman from the library.

"Hi... um..." I realised she hadn't given me her name the day before.

She blushed vivid pink, which was kind of sweet. And I trailed my gaze over her delicate features. She was slim and definitely the type of girl you could say was attractive. But she wasn't Kelly. And of course that meant I had no interest in her sexually. The realisation created a sinking feeling in my stomach. The girl tucked her hair behind her ears. "Oh, gosh, sorry, it's Chloe. How rude of me to ask your name and not give you mine."

I held a dismissive hand up. "Hey, no problem at all."

She shifted nervously from foot to foot. "So, are you coming to the library today?"

I inhaled a long breath and let it go slowly. "Oh, I don't know, Chloe. I didn't find out what I needed yesterday. I'm beginning to think I won't find what I'm looking for there."

She tilted her head inquisitively. "Oh... is there anything I can help with?"

"I don't think so. But thanks for asking. I'm meeting with my... um... friend, Six later."

"Six? Six the guy with the motorcycle and muscles?" The blush rose in her cheeks again and I smiled.

"Yeah, that would be him. Do you know him?"

She shook her head vehemently. "N-no... I mean I've seen him around... But no... no I don't know him. Not... not really," she sighed and an expression of sadness graced her eyes for a moment. "He's intimidating... menacing." Her cheeks flamed again as she turned her attention back to me.

I got the feeling she hadn't intended to say the latter part of her sentence aloud. I chuckled and shook my head. "Yeah he kinda does look a little menacing. You want me to introduce you?"

The pink blush to her cheeks increased until I could have fried an egg on her face. "Oh, gosh... no... no. Oh. Well... I'd better go open up. Have... have a great day, Cameron." She raised her hand in a little wave and hurried away.

My stack of pancakes arrived and I turned to devour them. So despite her words I had established that Six had an admirer in a cute Chloe-shaped package. Should I let him know? Or would doing so drag sweet little Chloe into a world of shit and pain? I shook my head at my train of thought. Okay, so I couldn't remember Six entirely, but from what I could remember and from the feeling I got on seeing him, I sensed he wasn't the kind of guy to hurt a woman. Yeah, I'd have fun filling him in on that little snippet of news.

Once my plate was empty and coffee cup was dry, I wondered what the hell I could do with the hours I had left before meeting with Six. I was under strict instructions—advice, anyway—to stay out of the public eye, which limited me greatly.

Once I'd paid for my meal, I left the coffee shop and made my way back to the motel. There wasn't much to do that wouldn't involve me being out in public, and so I decided I had a date with my iPod. I'd just have to be sure and skip past the songs that Kelly had put on there. I didn't need anything to remind me of her smile, her eyes, or her smell. They were emblazoned on my brain for all eternity.

I arrived back at the motel and heaved a deep, disinterested sigh. I wasn't in the mood for hiding out. I needed answers and fresh air. Neither of which were available within the four walls of the cheap, tacky place I currently was calling home.

I stuck in the ear buds and skipped to track four. The familiar music sent shivers down my spine, and the lyrics of "Duality" by Slipknot told me that I hadn't exactly been living happily prior to my arrival on a whole other continent. Well, that's if the songs had been chosen for a reason like Kelly's had. The lyrics were angry and scathing and spoke of agony and an anger that I imagine I was experiencing when Melody died. Maybe that was the story behind the whole track list. I remembered the track that Kelly had asked me to listen to, "Set Fire to the Third Bar" by Snow Patrol, and the anguish the song brought to the surface. Bringing to mind the dream of finding Melody in a pool of blood and the same song floating through the air on what should have been a wonderful day, I began to question whether I should continue to listen to the playlist.

Against my own better judgement, I didn't hit stop. The next track spoke of living in a world where nothing was as it seemed. There was an undercurrent of mistrust. And as I listened, I began to understand why that particular song had been put on there. It was how I felt about the Company. In the back of my mind, I knew that they had something to do with the death of my fiancée and the disappearance of my sister. The lyrics made a knot form in my stomach as the haunting voice of Trent Resner resonated deep within my bones. Yes, this was how I felt. These were my thoughts. I was questioning everything and everyone. Trusting no one. Not even the people I had previously considered my family. The only person I truly trusted apart from myself right then was Kelly. And she was thousands of miles away.

I closed my eyes and allowed myself the luxury of remembering her for a while. The way she pursed her lips and tried not to laugh. How she fit so perfectly around my body and in my arms. My dick clearly remembered too, stiffening in my boxers as the memory of her perfume and the smell of her arousal enveloped my senses. The way her skin felt beneath my fingertips.

For a brief moment I considered jacking off to the images in my head, but I knew the ache in my soul wouldn't be eased by a quick orgasm, and so I kept my hands clear of the bulge in my pants. I fucking hated the distance. The distance between Melody and me couldn't be overcome. But the distance between Kelly and me... Fuck, what was the point in torturing myself? I had to be in the US. But my fucking heart was back in Scotland. I could buy a plane ticket. I could go back. But then what about Rosa? Awww, fuck.

As the song ended, my head clouded with so many confusing and conflicting images and thoughts that my heart rate increased to an almost painful beat and sweat beaded on my upper lip. I was on the verge of some kind of panic attack and I needed to get out.

Regardless of what I had been "advised" to do by Six, I found myself wandering around the streets of Rose Acres. I came across a familiar-looking row of houses. One in particular stood out more than the others. It was a vacant property with a white door. I was drawn to the building, and without thinking, I found myself walking up the pathway. As I reached the property, an image of Melody lying in a pool of blood assaulted my memory. This was it. This was that house. My house. The place of Melody's death. A lump lodged in my throat, and my eyes became blurry with tears as I stared at the closed door before me. The heartbreaking lyrics of her favourite song whirred around my mind, reminding that I was never going to see her beautiful face again. And I would never hold our baby in my arms. The pain of grief almost brought me to my knees as I blinked rapidly, trying to clear my vision so that I could walk away and leave the place that would no doubt haunt me forever.

CHAPTER TWENTY-EIGHT

CAIN

At three o'clock I returned to the coffee shop to meet with Six. I ordered a coffee even though I didn't really want one and sat at a table where I could face the door and watch for his arrival.

Right on cue he pulled up to a halt on his bike and climbed off the hulk of metal. The tall, broad guy removed his helmet and ran his fingers through his shaggy, collar-length hair before making his way inside.

Vain bastard.

I stood to greet him and he pulled me into one of his rough, backslapping embraces. "Fuck, dude, I'm so glad you're still here. It's good to see you, man."

"Where was I gonna go?"

He held his hand up and gestured to the guy behind the counter, who seemed to understand what he wanted. We both sat down at opposite sides of the table and Six shrugged. "Oh, I wondered if you might get spooked and jump a flight out of Dodge."

I shook my head. The thought of leaving had crossed my

mind several times since I arrived, but I had no intention of following through on it. "Nah. I have too many questions that need answering."

He nodded with a look of deep concern. "Sure... sure you do. So... what you been doing today?"

He was clearly evading my need for information, so I thought I'd play along... for a while. I glimpsed the library across the street and smiled. "Hearing about an admirer you may have."

His brow crumpled. "Me? I've got an admirer? Come on, Cain, who is she? It is a she, right? If it's a dude, I'm not interested, bro."

Raising my eyebrows at this suggestion I may have been a bit of a prankster, I told him, "Oh, she is most definitely female."

He glanced around the room with a grin as if trying to figure out if she was in the coffee shop. "Spill it, dude."

"You by any chance know a girl called Chloe? Pretty, around twenty years old, works in the library?"

He scrunched his face and laughed at the same time. "Are you yanking my chain?"

"Nope. She went all doe-eyed when she found out I knew you."

"You're talking about sweet Chloe? Chloe with the big hazel eyes and chocolate brown hair? The one who used to pole dance over at The Fox Hub?"

Huh? I sat up straight. "Wait, what? She used to do what?"

"That's where I first met her. You must remember her, dude. She was the best fucking dancer they had. But then... well, something happened, I don't know what, and she left. Disappeared for a while. When she came back, she got a job in the library, and I haven't seen her much since."

Well, you definitely learned something new every day around Rose Acres. So Chloe was a dancer? Wow. I thought back to her demeanour and her clothing. Dowdy was the word that sprang to mind. Pretty, yes, but I couldn't imagine her gyrating around a pole in skimpy undies. I felt sure he had her mixed up with someone else.

"It can't be the same Chloe. Chloe from the library is so... demure."

"Hang on." Six fumbled through his pocket and pulled out his phone. "Look." He handed the device to me and I watched, open-mouthed as the video played of the same Chloe—only her hair was mainly blonde on the screen—and she was slipping and sliding around a shiny chrome pole, wearing heavy make-up, lace panties, stiletto heels, and nothing else but a smile. I glanced up at Six and a strange but unreadable expression had taken over his features.

The music playing in the background was familiar. "What's that track?"

"You're kidding me, right? I'm showing you your little sassy library assistant cavorting, and all you can think about is the song? Queens of the Stone Age would be proud. It's their track 'I Appear Missing'." He laughed. "Fuck, man, you must have it bad for someone if you're not looking at her tits."

He didn't need to know about Kelly. "Come on, man. She seems really nice. Don't you think you're being disrespectful?"

Six's cheeks turned beet red and he grabbed the phone, hit the stop button and slipped the phone back in his pocket. "I was just trying to prove a point."

"Yeah, well, now you have. She really seems to like you."

He shook his head. "I doubt it. Let's just say that I'm not exactly the kind of guy someone like her goes for. Well not her now anyway. She wasn't working at the club long. I don't think she was right for the place. She was too... I guess... nice."

"Sounds like you might like her too." For some reason this high-school act we were putting on was a welcome distraction to the real reason for our meeting.

The server brought a mug of coffee and placed it down in front of my companion. Six rubbed the back of his neck and poured around half a ton of sugar into the mug. "Yeah, she's pretty. But... well, she's not into the whole biker thing. After Rosa went missing, there were protests in the town trying to get us evicted. They all blamed us. She was one of the protesters."

And there it was. I was back down to earth with a bang. Rosa was missing.

"Okay... while we're on that subject. You said I should meet you here and you could help me with answers?"

"I can. Let me finish my coffee and we'll get down to the nitty-gritty of the shitty."

I clenched my jaw at his jovial manner. "It's no joking matter, Six."

"I know. But it can all be explained. All of it."

I waited as he consumed the molten coffee in less than five gulps. I figured he must have some kind of high pain threshold or an asbestos lining to his mouth.

"Okay. I'm ready. I can help. I know the shit that went down. You'd better come with me." I followed Six out to his bike, and he handed me a spare helmet. "Hop on. And don't grip me too tightly, dude. I love ya but not in that way." He winked and chuckled as he flung his leg over the beast of a Harley. I followed suit and decided to grip the metal bar behind me rather than getting up close and personal with the six-foot-plus wall of muscle.

We roared along the main street of the little town of Rose Acres, heading north. People either waved in acknowledgement or turned away quickly, avoiding making any kind of eye contact. It was a strange reaction, but maybe there was more to it that I didn't fully understand yet. Or maybe it was all connected to the protests.

Being on the back of the bike was strange. I guessed that sitting in this position wasn't what I was used to. I closed my eyes as more flashbacks arrived in my mind's eye. Watching the scenery whizzing past and feeling the warm breeze against my skin. It was clearly a part of my being, my make-up, of what made me who I am. I wanted to be in control. The deep-seated need to take to the open road on my own bike twisted my gut. I shouldn't be sitting here like a pussy. I should have my hand on the throttle, opening it up and letting the engine roar. But I didn't have a bike, so for now this would have to suffice.

Not too far out of town, we pulled up onto the forecourt of an old white building with peeling paint and a faded sign over the main door that read, "Picture House". The areas to the side of the building were surrounded by ten-foot-high chain-link fencing with gates that were locked and secured with a keypad. Six brought the beast to a halt, and I rested my hand on his shoulder as I flung my leg off the bike. Once he had climbed off and our helmets were on the seat, I followed him as he walked toward the main gate.

"This place familiar to you? You used to be the only one who could break the fuck in when the code was changed and Colt forgot to tell everyone what it was. He'd go fucking AWOL with some woman and we'd be stuck the fuck outside. You always managed to get us in."

"Yeah? Well that explains a lot." Memories of the desperate need to get out of the hospital and go find Kelly—and my apparent talent at overriding security codes—sprang to mind. Kelly... fuck, I miss her. An unwelcome dull ache settled in my stomach, making me take a deep breath to try and calm the twisting and churning. The name Colt sounded so familiar, and something I couldn't quite grasp at the back of my mind told me not to trust him. That he was a man to be feared.

Six punched a code into the keypad, and the gate released. I walked through and waited as he went back for his bike, pushing it through the narrow gap and parking it alongside some similar hunks of metal.

He climbed some steps at the side of the building and pulled open the heavy metal door. The inside of the place had that familiar smell of cigarette smoke and alcohol. There were beat-up old leather couches arranged around a huge flat-screen TV mounted on the wall. Other chairs and tables were dotted around too like someone's den. At one end of the main room was a wooden staircase. To the side of that was a bar where a woman with short blonde hair, tats across her bare shoulders, and a tight-fitting pink tank top was working; her black bra was just visible through the fabric of her top. Another flash of familiarity struck. I watched her chewing gum and stacking glasses as she bobbed around to some rhythm I couldn't hear. The thin white cables were the giveaway that she was listening to an MP3 player of some kind.

"Yo! Delilah! Look who the cat dragged in!"

The girl swung her head around, slammed down the glass she was holding, and vaulted over the bar.

She ran toward me, her Daisy Dukes showing tattooed legs too. She was screaming "Ohmygodohmygodohmygod!" as she leapt into my arms. Her slim legs wrapping around my waist and her face buried into my neck. "You're alive!"

I chuckled and scrunched my face as she nuzzled me. "So it would appear."

She jumped down again and gazed up at me with her big brown eyes filled with wonder. "God, I've missed you."

"God? No, I think you have me mistaken. My name's Cain." I smirked as I held my hand out to her. She slapped me playfully before wiping tears that had sprung from her eyes.

Her lip trembled and she mumbled, "Fucking jackass. You look so different. But it's so good to see you." Before reaching up on tiptoes to kiss my cheek.

"Hey, Delilah, cut the guy some slack, huh? We gotta go see Colt. Is he in?"

"Sure. He's upstairs."

Six lead the way and as I followed I peered over my shoulder at the little blonde as she hugged her arms around herself and more tears slipped down her cheeks. Delilah... Delilah... tattoos... Delilah did my tattoos! A sense of hope zipped through me, raising my heart rate at the prospect that my memories were returning at an increasingly rapid rate. What I couldn't quite grasp was the reason for Delilah's emotional response to my return. What were we to each other? She clearly had feelings for me, but did they go deeper than friendship? Was she someone I could trust? The love in her eyes told me that I could. I gave her what I hoped was a warm smile and she beamed back at me as her eyes glistened.

CHAPTER TWENTY-NINE

C A I N

While we climbed the stairs, Six shook his head and glanced over at Delilah, whose gaze was glued to me. He laughed. "She's still got it bad, poor kid."

"Still?" The fact that he inferred her feelings had been a long-term thing made me question my relationship with her even more—and what the hell kind of shit I had walked back into. Was I going to have to watch myself around her? I wished right then that I could at least remember something so I didn't put my fucking foot in my mouth.

He stopped at the top of the stairs and turned to me. "How hard did you hit that thick head of yours, anyway?" Lowering his voice, he rubbed his chin and nodded. "Ever since you broke up with her and started out with Melody, man. You broke that chick's heart. She wanted her place on the back of your bike and felt sure you were gonna give it to her."

I scrunched my brow. "Oh... okay."

"Yeah, she wasn't the only one you pissed off. Sadie was pretty fucking angry too. But that's a whole other story. Lolita has moved on now and Cally is fucking getting married. Can you believe it?"

Delilah, Melody, Sadie, Lolita and Cally? Fuck, I was a total player. What a dick. "I was kind of popular with the ladies, huh?"

"Oh, man. You were the guy to bed. All the chicks were after you. I got so fucking sick of hearing how you were the best lay ever and the shit you could do with your dick. A guy doesn't wanna hear those things. You know?"

I shrugged. "I guess not."

I was still trying to wrap my head around it all when he became sombre. "Yeah. Everyone was shocked when you took up with Melody. Fuck, man. She must have had some... Aw man. No, no, I won't disrespect your girl. It's just that... She was different, you know? You were in love. Deep love. But not in that pussy-whipped way the guys used to bust your chops about. Nah, man. You guys were just meant to be. Can't fucking believe what happened. I'm so sorry, Cain."

Anger needled at my insides at hearing him almost admit to being involved. Why else would he have said he was sorry? "What did you fucking do to her?" I growled as I stepped into his space and fronted up to him.

His face washed over with confusion. "What? You think I... Whoa, no, no, Cain you got it all wrong, buddy. Come on." He gestured to the carved oak door at the top of the stairs and opened it.

At the head of a huge table sat a man who looked familiar from one of my dreams. His thick grey hair was tied back in a ponytail, and he had dark-rimmed glasses perched on his nose as he worked on some papers. When the door whispered shut behind us, he glanced up, paused, and then removed his spectacles.

"Well I'll be..." He stood slowly and leaned on the table. "Aren't you a sight for sore eyes?"

An uneasy twist still gripped my guts, and I glared back at the grey-bearded man as he began to make his way from his end of the table toward where I stood. He matched me in height.

When he came to a halt before me, he placed his hands on my shoulders. "Brother, we thought we'd lost you." His voice cracked and he pulled me into my second strong, male embrace of the day.

Confusion and adrenaline coursed through my veins as I pulled away to connect with his pale blue eyes.

I felt a hand on my shoulder. "He's had a rough time, Prez. Post-traumatic amnesia," Six explained. "He can't remember what happened to Mel."

Colt closed his eyes and lowered his head. "Aww, fuck."

"He needs answers."

"No damn wonder. You'd better take a seat, Cain." He gestured toward the chairs lining the table. "You won't want to be standing for this."

Six and Colt sat, and I followed suit. They shared an ominous glance, and Colt laced his fingers together on the table before him. He cleared his throat and took a deep breath.

"Now... as I don't know how much you remember, you'll have to stop me if I go too fast, okay?" I nodded and he continued. "Okay... We had a deal going down with Loki's Legion. They were trying to buy some land on the edge of town, outside of the limits but a little too close for comfort. I met with Deak, their president. We talked and everything was amicable. So it seemed. They agreed not to pursue the land purchase if we agreed to give them some of the illegal alcohol trade in return as a good will gesture."

So far I was keeping up but struggling to figure out where I fit in. "Okay. So what happened?"

"So we were keeping an eye on things. Making sure they didn't encroach. One night some of our guys—Weasel, Rapid, and Popsicle—were out patrolling the land the Legion had been trying to buy. Some of the Legion were there with their old ladies, on Company land with their bikes, and when our guys confronted them, there was a showdown. Fists were flying at first, but then things turned bitter, and shots were fired. Deak's daughter was there with one of their guys. I guess her dad had no idea she was seeing him. She tried to step in to calm things down, but she was caught in the crossfire and died. It was a bullet from your gun that killed her." My head began to swim. I had killed a girl? I'd killed Deak's fucking daughter? Oh, fuck. My stomach roiled and I was about to throw up. As if he saw the pallor of my skin and read my thoughts, Colt quickly carried on, "But you didn't fire it. Weasel had taken your gun, you know, the engraved one your dad gave you? Anyways, he claimed it after you'd told us you'd be leaving, and you handed it over, saying you didn't need it anymore. He dropped it at the scene and they were gunning for you after that." I wasn't sure whether I should be relieved that I hadn't fired the fatal shot, but my gut continued to twist. This was a whole lot to process. And the fact that the names being thrown around were only vaguely familiar didn't ease my stomach. If this guy had claimed my gun, I should know who the hell he was. But I couldn't put a face to the name.

Colt leaned toward me. "When we told them you didn't fire the shot, they didn't believe us. Thought we were just covering for you. Deak wouldn't meet with me. Anyway, they tried to get us in shit with the law when we were going across the county line to make a delivery, but we managed to sweet-talk the chief, and the paperwork got filed in the garbage. When the Legion realised they hadn't sunk us that way, they set out to fuck you over. An eye for an eye. They were at the house on the day Melody signed the lease. Two of the Legion were hiding out in the bedroom closet and jumped out, intent on kidnapping her. But she kicked one in the balls and broke the other guy's nose. She was trying to run away from them when she tripped and fell down the stairs.

"When they saw she was hurt really bad, the two guys freaked out and left her there, escaping out the back and across the fields onto the land they were trying to buy."

My heart hammered at my chest as I heard Colt recount the death of my beloved Melody. Nausea washed over me and I leaned my head in my hands. "But... but if Melody got killed, why was Rosa taken? And what the fuck happened to me?"

Colt sighed heavily. "Because, son, as soon as you found out what had happened, you took your gun back from Weasel and went and killed one of the two guys who tried to kidnap Melody. The reason things went to hell is because it turned out you killed Deak's younger brother."

My skin crawled with cold sweat and I almost lost my breakfast. I'd killed a guy after all. The relief at not being the one who killed Deak's daughter was short-lived. Who the hell was I? Who the hell am I now? Suddenly Kelly's beautiful smiling face came to mind, and my stomach plummeted once more. What the hell would she think of me? I had killed a man. I was a cold-blooded murderer. Okay, so it was some kind of revenge killing, but two wrongs never make a damn right. She would never look at me again the same. If I hadn't already lost her, this would have been the final nail in the coffin. My eyes began to sting and I was overcome with homesickness for a place that never should have been my home—but it was, because she was there. The need to crumple into Kelly's arms and have her tell me she forgave me for all the shit in my past was so overwhelming. A strangled sob left my chest as I dropped my head forward into my hands again. Could this situation get any more fucked up?

Colt laced his fingers together before himself. "Deak snapped. He'd lost his daughter and his brother, and you were the fucking devil. He wanted you dead. He blamed you for his daughter's death, and then you made shit a whole lot worse. And then I heard through Sadie that they were going to take Rosa."

My eyes snapped up to meet Colt's. "Sadie? I don't—"

"She was one of the house bunnies," Six chipped in. "You and Sadie used to fuck. She was one of many, Cain. You liked the ladies. Before you fell for Melody, that is. Sadie had it bad for you and didn't take too kindly to losing you when you chose to be faithful to Mel. When all the shit went down, she left and joined the Legion in some stupid bid to get her revenge. But she heard stuff being said and felt bad, so she came to tell me."

I turned to face Six. "Okay... So where did they take Rosa?"

Colt cleared his throat, and my head snapped back so that I could meet his gaze. "They didn't take her." Colt looked me right in the eyes as he delivered his news.

I shivered, not completely understanding but wanting to, needing to get to the bottom of things. "Then who did?"

"We did." Colt's matter-of-fact tone made the hairs on my arms stand to attention.

I stood, ready to pounce. "What the fuck?"

Six stood beside me and placed his hands on my shoulders.

I shrugged him off.

Colt held both his hands up. "Sit down, Cain. It's not how it sounds. Please... just sit."

I gulped down the knot of anger in my throat and, dropped my body heavily into the chair once again. "This had better be fucking good."

"Rosa is safe. She's somewhere the Legion won't find her. We had to take the necessary precautions, Cain. But rest assured, your sister is safe and well."

I scrambled around my brain, trying to piece together the dreams I'd had, the terror I know I'd seen her endure. "But... she was crying and shouting at the men who held me. They hit me and she saw—"

"That's why we took her. They attacked you when you were driving her home from school one night. Luckily we'd been tipped off by Sadie and we got there just before they killed you. Rosa was distraught. We took her into the Denver territory, and from there she was moved on. You... well, we had to fake your death. You were drugged and hidden on board a container ship. Jinx, one of our guys, was in charge of drugging you to start with, but he paid someone on board ship to keep you unconscious until you arrived wherever the ship was going. We thought it was better not to know. Anyways, Jinx wrote the instructions out for the guy on board ship, but when it was too late and the ship had already sailed, he realised he'd gotten the calculations wrong and that he had given you too much of the drug. Jinx was convinced you were dead. But there was nothing we could do. We didn't know where you were. And there was no way for us to find out. He didn't know the guy he'd paid off. There was no way to contact him. We were pretty sure that if the guy had found you dead, he would have thrown you over board. No one would have been any wiser. You get the picture? And anyways, if we had been able to contact the guy and we'd have tried to locate you, they would have followed. And you'd be dead regardless."

I looked down at my hands. They were shaking violently.

As if there were some divine intervention at work, the door opened and Delilah walked in sheepishly with a glass full of amber liquid. "I... I'm sorry to barge in but... I figured Cain might need a drink."

Colt glanced up and nodded, gesturing for her to come in. I turned my head and stretched my lips into something like a smile as she handed me the glass. I gripped it with a juddering hand and took a large gulp. She squeezed my shoulder and left.

I closed my eyes briefly, trying to make sense of it all and not having much success. When I opened them again, I took a large gulp from the glass; the burn that followed the swallow told me it was neat whiskey. "So... you... you didn't kill Melody? And you didn't try to kill me?"

"Fuck no!" Colt leaned across the table and gripped my arm. "*You* are family, son. You, Rosa, Melody. Family, do you hear me? We were trying to protect all of you. I know it seems like a fucking dumb-ass way to go about it, but... it seemed like it was a good plan."

"But... I remember... I had a flashback of you and me arguing about me wanting out. I thought..."

"I won't lie to you. It broke my heart that you wanted out. And I knew that this shit was going on, and I couldn't tell you what they were planning. But the Legion had already green lighted you. If I'd told you what was going down, you would have tried to sort it out yourself and gotten killed for sure. I couldn't risk that. I hope you understand. And I'm sorry that things got so fucked up. The suicide note, the additional drug to wipe your memory, and the alias were supposed to keep you out of the country. We figured that while the authorities wherever you wound up tried to figure out who you were, you'd be safe. We hoped they'd lock you up in some hospital and look after you. Well, that was the original plan, but then Jinx realized he'd fucked up big-time and we thought you were dead. We had no way of finding out."

I clenched my jaw and spoke through my gritted teeth. My knuckles turned white where I gripped the glass in my hand as I remembered the club's betrayal. "But the police in Scotland tried to contact Cosmic. No one would admit to knowing me. Is it any wonder I was suspicious?"

"I know. I know. We thought that if we welcomed you back, you'd wind up at the mercy of Loki's Legion. Fuck knows what they would have done to you if they'd gotten to you."

Anger was building inside of me. "You could've just told me from the start. You didn't have to drag me through hell."

Colt banged his hands on the table. "Be honest, Cain. What does your gut tell you that you would've done if we'd told you?"

I thought for a moment. "I would have... I..." Revengeful thoughts ran through my head as the image of Melody lying in a pool of blood assaulted my frontal lobe.

Colt held his hands up. "Exactly, Cain. You would have wound up tortured and dead and Rosa would too."

And what if somehow I'd convinced Kelly to come back here to Utah with me? The thought that I could have potentially put her in danger through my own selfish need for her made me hate myself.

My clenching jaw ticked. "I don't understand why you couldn't come up with another fucking plan."

"We had so little time. When we found you out at the Legion warehouse, you were in a bad state. Rosa was next. And fuck knows what they would have done to her, Cain."

But they hadn't done it. Because the Company had gotten us out of there.

I rubbed my hands over my face as some kind of acceptance washed over me. I was alive. Rosa was alive. My memory was coming back. I had a lot to be thankful for—all things considered.

I sighed heavily. "So... now that I'm back?"

Colt's nostrils flared and he clenched his fists before him on the table. He glanced over at Six, and when his stare met mine again, I saw a dark foreboding in his eyes. "If you want to stay alive... you can't stay here."

CHAPTER THIRTY

Kelly

Life after Cain was uneventful to begin with. But images of him haunted me. Conversations we'd had during our sessions played over and over in my mind. The sound of his voice the time we had sat in the park before I took him to my home and my bed for the first time kept replaying in my mind like the soundtrack to the most powerful and heartbreaking of all the memories.

Every single time he popped into my head, the accompanying ache knotted my insides and made my eyes sting. It had been a week. That's all. Just one week. And I was in pieces. There was no end in sight.

I was just about functioning on a day-to-day basis, but being at home, alone, was difficult. I could feel him there. I know that sounds crazy, but it was as if the place were haunted by his memory. I knew he was still alive and I know ghosts are a myth, but it's the only way I could explain how it felt to be without him.

I was desolate.

I hadn't known him that long, but that didn't matter to my heart. Nor did it minimise the vastness of the pain I felt.

Nights were the worst. I would lie in bed and close my eyes, hoping that a dreamless sleep would come and be kind to me, but of course it never happened. My dreams were so vivid. So real. I could feel his fingertips on my body. Smell his skin. Feel his weight on top of me only to wake and discover I was still alone and he was still in America.

Esme had been amazing. I have no idea how I would have got through losing Cain without her. She'd taken me on several nights out—along with lunches, dinners, and even breakfasts. I guessed she thought I wasn't eating, as she was continually trying to ply me with food. In a way I have to admit that she was right. I had very little appetite.

I threw myself into work head first. I had some very interesting cases to work with, and I was doing a lot of outreach stuff too. Patty was constantly asking if I was okay. I must have been wearing my despondency like a merit badge. I was, however, managing to convince myself that I was fine.

At least I thought I was.

Sitting at home on a Friday night was no fun. But then again, excitement was something that had been distinctly lacking in my life since Cain left. I was halfway through a bottle of red wine and a large packet of very salty crisps when the landline rang.

"Hello?" My tone was filled with disinterest.

"Hi, sexpot! Long time no fuck," came the familiar chuckle down the line.

"Urgh... Dermott, I'm not coming out if that's why you're calling."

"You're not? Shit, you sound half-pissed and grumpy as hell. I'll be right over. You need cheering up."

"No, no I'm—" The line went clunk as he hung up before I could get my sentence of protest out. Oh, shit.

I glanced down at my scratty yoga pants with a patch of off

white in a blob on one leg where I had spilled yoghurt earlier. Well, he'll just have to take me as he finds me, 'cause I'm not getting changed.

Twenty minutes later there was a knock on my door. I dragged myself off the couch and looked through the peephole. Dermott's face looked bulbous as he gurned at me through the tiny hole. I rolled my eyes and yanked the door open.

"There she—" His smile disappeared "Oh, shit, what happened to you?"

"Nothing. Just working hard, that's all."

His eyes trailed down my body and back up again. "Well, you look like shit."

"You don't have to bloody stay! Fuck off back home!" I shouted, giving him a shove for good measure.

He just laughed and grabbed me, pulling me against his chest. "Oooh, I love it when you're feisty. When was your last good shag?"

I pushed him away from me. "Good grief, Dermott, is sex all you think about?"

"Nope. I think about the state of the global economy from time to time, but that's not half as much fun."

His cheesy grin made me smile as it usually did. He meant no harm. In fact I got the feeling that sex wasn't actually the thing that was on his mind for once.

"Why are you here?" I huffed sulkily.

He flung his arm around my shoulder and rested his head on mine as we walked into the living room. "Like I said, I got the feeling that you needed cheering up." He held up the carrier bag in his other hand. "I brought Bridesmaids on DVD. It's gross in places but so bloody funny. If that doesn't cheer you up, then nothing will."

I punched his arm playfully. "Awww. Don't tell me you're going soft on me?"

"Nah. I'm hoping you'll cheer up enough for a quicky." This

time when I punched him it was a lot harder, but all he did was guffaw loudly.

The movie was a lot of fun and we almost ate our weight in popcorn and crisps; but when it was time for Dermott to leave, a sadness seeped in to kick out the temporary good mood I'd been experiencing.

Dermott hugged me as we stood at the door to say goodbye. "Are you going to tell me what's going on with you?"

I allowed my gaze to drift anywhere but at him. "No."

"Don't beat around the bush, Darrow, eh?"

"Sorry, but it's just something I have to deal with by myself."

He sighed and rested his chin on my head. "Do you want me to stay?"

"I'm not fucking you, Dermott."

He chuckled. "I kind of already gathered that. I just meant to keep you company. You don't seem yourself, and I'm worried about you."

His kind tone made my eyes sting, and I pulled away.

He tilted my chin and looked into my eyes, and I could tell he was assessing me. "Have you fallen for someone Kelly?"

Unable to reply with words, I closed my eyes and nodded my head as tears spilled over.

He pulled me into a hug. "Oh, sweetheart. I knew there was something going on. Who is he? Want me to punch him for you?"

"You can't. He's not in this country."

"Shame. If he's hurt you, I'll get on a fucking plane and go find him. What did he do?"

"Nothing. He did nothing. He just... had to leave." He stroked my hair and I was overcome with sadness. "But he didn't hurt me. Not through any fault of his own."

"This has been going on a while, hasn't it?"

I nodded again. "I need to forget about him and get on my with my life. I'm just finding it a little difficult, that's all."

He cupped my face and ran his thumbs over my cheeks to wipe away the tears. "Look... I know I've treated you like a... like a... well, like a fuck buddy, but... I care about you too, Kelly. I hate to see you so sad. The light's gone from your eyes and I want to help. If there's anything that I can do to make this easier, then just tell me, okay? And I don't mean rebound sex. I mean anything, Kelly. You're one of my dearest friends, and you're usually so full of life. Even when you're tired out, you've usually still got fight in you. But now you just look... lost. I don't like it."

I forced a smile. "I'm not too keen on feeling this way either."

"Do you want me to stay?"

I mulled over his suggestion for a few seconds. "Yes. But there won't be any sex."

"How about I sleep in your bed and just hold you? I'll keep my undies on."

He had a way of making me smile. "That would be nice, thank you."

He removed his coat, and we made our way back through to the living room. I walked to the bathroom and splashed my face with cold water, brushed my teeth, and stared at my pale face and sunken eyes in the mirror. Dermott was right. The light in my eyes was dim—if it was there at all.

When I arrived in my bedroom, Dermott was already under the duvet. He'd kept his T-shirt on and I presumed his boxers too. I climbed into bed beside him and he pulled me into his warm, comforting embrace. He held me close and stroked my hair as my tears soaked his T-shirt.

I heard him sniffling and I pulled away. "Dermott? Dermott, what's wrong?"

He cleared his throat and chuckled. "Oh, God, take no bloody notice of me. I'm feeling all sentimental."

I reached up and wiped his damp cheek. "Sentimental? You? Why?"

"Oh, I don't know. A mixture of things, I guess. I think I

always expected that you and I would end up together, which I know is crazy. But... This is the end of you and me and any chance there was for us, and that's kind of sad. But... I hate to see you hurting like this. I love you, Kelly. And you deserve to be happy. You deserve someone who can make you smile, not cry. I just hope... I just hope he realises what a sweet, wonderful woman he has left behind and comes back to make things right." His voice cracked, and his words caused more of my own tears to fall. The tenderness he was showing was so out of character, but I loved him for it. I just couldn't bring myself to tell him that Cain wasn't coming back. Ever.

I nuzzled into Dermott's chest once more, and for the first time ever, I felt that he understood my silence. There was no need for more words. This was the end of the Dermott and me from before. We were entering brand-new territory. As he held me close, I drifted to sleep properly for the first time since Cain had left.

CHAPTER THIRTY-ONE

Cain

After only a couple of nights in the dive of a motel, I moved into the Company of Sinners clubhouse. The top floor was dotted with various rooms, a couple of which were kitted out with beds in case the "mood" took anyone at the many parties and gatherings held in the place. The room I was using was run-down but clean and a massive improvement on the motel. At least here there were people to talk to. Colt had convinced me that this was the safest place for me to stay temporarily in case Loki's Legion had gotten word that I was back but that I would have to move on and soon. Maybe I should have been afraid, but I wasn't.

My main concern was getting to Rosa and making sure she was okay. Colt assured me that he was trying to arrange for me to go see her but that it could take time; things had to be put in place to divert the Legion's attention away from what we were doing. How the fuck did they get so damned powerful?

I was lying in bed staring at the ceiling as images of Kelly rolled through my mind—they always did when I was alone. I reached for the bottle of perfume that smelled like her and took a long inhale of the familiar fragrance. God, I miss her. When the hell will I stop feeling this way? Someone knocked on my door, snatching me back to reality.

Reluctantly I placed the bottle back in the drawer. "Yeah, what do you want?" I shouted. The feeling of being trapped inside this crumbling old building wasn't encouraging a good mood in me, and I was deliberately making sure everyone knew it. The door opened and someone belched loudly as he poked his head around it.

I lifted my head and met Six's wide, stupid grin. I shook my head. "God, you're disgusting."

He acted all coy. "Aww, shucks, you're just saying that." He bounded across the room like a puppy and flopped down on the edge of the bed. "Come on, dude. I got something for you."

I sighed and rubbed my hands over my face, wondering what the fuck was so exciting. "What is it?"

"Nah. You gotta come see. Not telling."

"How old are you, six?" Right then he was living up to his name.

He laughed and bounced the mattress up and down. "Come on, come on, come on."

I rolled my eyes as I climbed up off the bed. "Well, seeing as you won't let me catch a fucking break, you'd better show me. And it'd better be fucking good."

He slapped me on the back and dashed out of the door with me following sulkily behind. We walked down the stairs, out the side door, and across the gravel to a garage at the back of the lot.

Six stopped and rubbed his hands together. "Man, you are gonna love me."

He pulled open the metal door and walked over to a tarp in the middle of the dimly lit space. Yanking off the sheeting with a flourish, he yelled, "Ta daaaa!"

And I came face-to-face with a motorcycle.

My motorcycle.

Shiny black paint work with my name and the Cosmic logo emblazoned across the tank in silver. Memories came flooding back to me all at once like a massive physical impact and I staggered back. Images of speeding along open roads with a grin pulling at my face. Watching rocky mountain ranges whiz past me as I accelerated without fear, adrenaline pumping through my veins. Standing over the bike, cloth in hand, as I polished it lovingly with immense pride. A sense of freedom like nothing I could remember experiencing since all this shit happened. I wanted it all back. I wanted to feel that way again. I wanted to feel normal again.

Fuck me.

I just wanted to feel.

An overwhelming mixture of emotions gripped me and a sob left my throat. I covered my mouth with embarrassment twisting my insides. Sadness, elation, anger, and regret bubbled to the surface all at once as I dropped to my knees before the one thing that represented good things in my life. It was an unexpected reaction to an inanimate object, and as I knelt there and closed my eyes, I was overtaken by the urge to get on the bike and get away. Far away. Since the majority of my memory had returned, I'd discovered that I had far too many ghosts in my past and way too many misdemeanours to answer for; I was sure I'd never find any peace. But if I could just get on my bike...

Six gripped my shoulder. "Hey, Cain. I'm sorry, buddy. I... I thought it'd make you happy. I never imagined it'd damn near kill you to see your bike again. Are you okay?"

I sniffed and wiped my eyes roughly. "Yeah... yeah, I'm fine. Fuck... just a little overwhelmed, I guess. It's been a long time." Once I had gathered myself, I stood and straddled the metal body of the bike. It was as if the beast had been built just for me. It was a strange feeling to be *so* connected to the hunk of black metal, but apart from Kelly, it was the only thing that made me feel human again. I glanced at Six with a grin turning up my lips.

He cringed. "The problem is you can't really take the bike out. Not yet. But... when Colt takes you to Rosa, you can ride it then."

I nodded. "That's okay. I can deal with that." The Legion was some bad shit. I didn't have to like it, but I got it. "So long as I get to ride eventually and I get to see Rosa."

"Colt will make it happen, my friend. Trust him. He just wants to protect you."

Six left me alone to get reacquainted with my bike and I spent the rest of day working on it. I polished it, changed the oil, stripped the carb, cleaned it up, and put it all back together again. It was somehow cathartic and the afternoon flew by. I hadn't been hounded by thoughts of Kelly or memories of Melody at all, and I managed to convince myself that it wasn't denial. It was just me moving on.

Well, I convinced myself for a short while at least.

I was washing up in the kitchen behind the bar and drifting off into a daydream about Kelly. I imagined her sitting in her office looking out the window. Would she be wondering about me too? Every time she entered my mind, I got a sinking feeling in the pit of stomach. I shook my head, determined to set the daydream loose, when Delilah appeared beside me. I turned to find her watching me closely, her head leaning on the door frame and a small smile playing on her lips.

"Hey, Delilah. What's up?"

She blinked as if coming out of a trance. "Oh... nothing. I was just wondering if you were going to stick around for the party tonight."

I shrugged. "What party?"

"Colt invited some of the other Cosmic charters here with their old ladies. The men are going to discuss the shit with the Legion and come up with a way forward, and then we're having a cookout."

Old ladies. An image of Kelly wearing Daisy Dukes and

thigh-high boots entered my head and made me smile. She'd never wear shit like that. I chuckled to myself, forgetting I wasn't alone. I glanced over at Delilah, whose gaze was still fixed on me. "Sounds good. I'll be there."

She chewed on her lip and smiled, her eyes bright and her cheeks pink. "Great. I was hoping you'd say that. I was worried you'd be hanging out in your room."

I smiled and gave her a wink. "Nah. I'll be there. Can't stay cooped up in there forever, huh?"

"Cool." She paused as if she was going to say more but then skipped out of the room, leaving me to finish up.

CHAPTER THIRTY-TWO

KELLY

Days became weeks, and for the first time in what felt like forever, I was dealing with an interesting case again. A young woman called Gina. I had been assigned to help Gina after she had refused to work with a male psychologist, Magnus, one of my peers with whom, incidentally, Cain also had refused to work. But the cloud of paranoia hanging over her made her mistrust everyone—including those who were trying get the bottom of her problems.

Especially men.

Our sessions were emotionally fraught as she tried to deal with the demons in her mind whilst adjusting to life in hospital. A place she didn't want to be and didn't feel would help her. She was a very closed person, and I was struggling to get to her to open up to me. Eventually we had our first breakthrough. She finally had begun to look me in the eyes and smile. She told me that I was easy to talk to and that I didn't come across as judgy even though it was partly my job to be so. We even laughed a little. But it was the day after our breakthrough that would change my life forever.

It was around two months after Cain had gone and I was still going through the phase of relating everything in time to accumulative hours, days and weeks since he had departed for the USA. And yes, I suppose I *was* in some kind of grieving process but the only person I could confide in was Esme.

I was due in to one of my sessions with Gina and I was refreshing my memory by reading the notes from our last session. She had confided in me about some of her darkest nightmares where people were conspiring against her, but I had drifted off to a conversation Esme and I had been having the night before. I'll admit that it was unprofessional of me to bring my personal thoughts into work continuously, but let's face it, it was far from the worst thing I'd done at work in connection with Cain.

"So you haven't heard anything at all from Cain?" Esme asked before taking a gulp of her red wine. We were in Johnny Foxes eating dinner, and I had been staring at my plate.

I shook my head as I wondered where he was and what he was doing. Had he moved onto the next woman? I hoped not. But hope was a waste of time.

"I bet he'll get in touch after he sorts things out over there, honey." She was trying to reassure me, but nothing was really helping to fill the Cain-shaped hole inside of me.

"I doubt it. Why would he get in touch?" I lifted my gaze, hoping to see anything but pity in my friend's eyes. But like I said, hope was a waste of time.

Her eyes were filled with pity. "He loved you, Kelly. You loved him. Surely that counts for something?"

I laughed without the faintest hint of humour. "It means nothing, Ez. He and I were never meant to be. We were doomed from the start. It's just as well that he left or I could have lost everything."

She placed her cutlery down and glared at me disbelievingly. "Oh, and you haven't lost everything anyway?"

Someone hammered on my office door, making me jump and dragging me back to reality. I placed Gina's notes down and went to open the door. Gina stood there, wild-eyed, staring at me.

I smiled, trying to make her feel at ease. "Oh, hi, Gina. You're a little early."

"I need to speak to you now." Her voice was calm and unwavering despite her appearance.

I nodded. "Okay. Come on in. We can start now." I turned and began to walk over to my couch. The door slammed and before I could turn, I felt a thud on the back on my head, the force of which knocked me to my knees. A searing throb vibrated from the point of impact all the way down my spine, and I was overcome with nausea.

I cried out in agony.

Her voice bellowed out as a hoarse banshee screech. "It was you! You told them! You bitch!" She began to hit me again with whatever it was that she held in her hand, and I fell forward, covering the back of my head with one hand and trying to reach for my personal alarm with the other.

Where the hell is everyone?

My vision became blurry as I tried to make sense of what she was shouting at me. But the pain shooting down my neck was far too intense. I tried to scream for help but instead a sob fell from my mouth as another blow came and I felt the bones in my fingers crunch.

"G-Gina stop... please... stop." My voice came out as a weak and mousy croak.

Although petite, she loomed over me where I cowered, wielding what looked to be a large document stapler. "No! You bitch! You deserve to die! I knew you were just like them! You're on their side!"

Another blow, this time to the side of my face. I cried out again as a sharp, head-splitting sting shot through my cheekbone and up the side of my skull.

Another thwack followed by a stabbing pain, and I tasted the metallic tang of blood.

Finally managing to grip my personal alarm, I pushed the button with every ounce of determination to survive that I could muster.

She hit me again. And again.

Then nothing.

———

Cain

Later on after I had showered and changed, I could hear lots of voices down in the main room, and I made my way there to check on what was happening. As I descended the stairs, I could see men of all ages laughing and drinking beer with their women draped all over them or around them.

"Here he is!" Colt's voice boomed out louder than the ACDC track playing in the background.

A loud cheer rang out around the room, and when I hit the last step, I was engulfed in a group hug. People slapped me on the back and told me how much they'd missed me. Some looked familiar but others were people I was sure I'd never even met. It was a strange feeling supposedly to have been missed by people I couldn't yet put names to, and I tried to ignore the unease in my gut.

"Cain, I don't know how many of these folks you will remember, but these are the members of your extended family. This is the main man from the Denver charter. Cain, Ike here has been looking out for Rosa since she was moved out of here."

Ike grabbed my hand firmly and shook it. So this guy knows

the whereabouts of my kid sister, huh? My heart rate increased and the moisture in my mouth suddenly evaporated. "Where is she? Is she okay?"

"Don't be panicking, son. Rosa is very safe. She's not in Denver right now. But you have nothing to worry about. She's with people who can protect her."

Why was no one willing to tell me anything? I couldn't shake the feeling that these people who called themselves my family were hiding way too much from me. I narrowed my eyes and felt my nostrils flare. "And where is that exactly?"

Ike chuckled and I wanted to punch him. "Safe is all you need to know, son."

I matched the man in height and I got closer until my nose was almost touching his. My jaw was clenched. "I'm not your fucking son, old man. Now tell me where the hell my sister is!"

Ike glanced angrily over at Colt, who laughed and gripped my shoulder a little too tightly. "He's been through a lot, Ike. Don't mind him. He means no harm."

Ike responded through gritted teeth. "Well you'd better get him out of my fucking face before I mean him some harm."

Six appeared at the front of the gathered group and yanked me away. "Come on, bro. Let's go get you some beer and pussy, huh?" I allowed him to put his arm around my shoulders and lead me away. When we were out of ear shot he whispered, "You can't talk to Ike that way, man."

I stopped to face my closest ally. "He has Rosa, and I want to know where the fuck she is. She's my sister. Why won't anyone tell me?"

He pulled me toward the bar and shoved me against a stool. I reluctantly sat as Six ordered me a neat whiskey from Delilah.

He turned back to me with a look of concern. "Look, Cain. The reason he's not telling you is to protect you from yourself. He knows that if he tells you, you'll go shooting off up there to get her, and by doing that, you'll alert the Legion to where she is and that you're back. You'd be putting us all in danger. We told them you're dead. If they find out we lied, there'll be all-out war."

Delilah placed the glass full of amber liquid before me, and I grabbed it and downed it in one gulp. "Fuck. I can't rest, Six. I need to see her. The flashbacks are scaring the shit out of me, and I'm terrified she's suffering some kind of physical abuse or mental trauma or... or what the fuck ever. My head is torturing me with visions of her screaming and crying. And I've missed her eighteenth fucking birthday." That particular realisation hit me like a ten-ton truck and I dropped my head into my hands. "Awww fuck, shit fuck!"

"Look, she was given a great celebration. Don't worry. And seeing you will be all the gift she needs."

I lowered my voice. "Does... does she know I'm okay?"

Six shook his head. "No, man. It was decided that it was best not to tell her. Not until you go up there anyway." Shit. So she's somewhere with strangers and she doesn't even know I'm alive? Fuck. She could be grieving my death without any need. The poor kid. My heart broke a little more.

I heaved a deep sigh and glanced into the centre of the room where the party had kicked up a notch. Scantily clad women I didn't know gyrated around rubbing their tits in the men's faces as Alice in Chains' "Them Bones" blared from the wall mounted speakers.

"There's something more going on here, isn't there, buddy?" Six's eyes were filled with concern.

I shook my head. "Nothing I can do anything about."

"Come on, man. Me and you... we were partners in crime. Told each other everything before you left. Well... almost everything. I mean I'm a guy and I don't do all that advice shit, but... well... you know... if you got something going on, maybe you should get it off your chest, huh?"

I sighed long and deep. "I met someone. In Scotland."

"No shit, really?"

I glanced to my left and Delilah was behind the bar but hovering around us like a puppy waiting for scraps. I turned my attention back to my friend. "Yeah. Before I remembered about Melody. The funny thing was it turns out she looks just like Melody. Long auburn hair, same soulful green eyes, and fucking curves to die for. I... Awww fuck, Six, I fell for her. Hard. I'm fucking in love with her and she's thousands of miles away. And do you know what really fucking gets to me? I would've married her. I've never felt that way about anyone. Not even Melody. I loved Melody, I remember that feeling. But with Kelly..."

His eyes narrowed. "Didn't she wanna come back here with you?"

I smiled at the impossible thought. "She couldn't. The shit would've really hit the fan."

Six nodded knowingly. "Married?"

I took a long pull of my drink. "Kelly was my psychologist."

His eyes widened so much I thought they were going to pop clean out of his head. "No fucking way. Oh, man. Did you... you know..." He leaned in conspiratorially and grinned. "Did you fuck her?"

Although I knew he meant no harm by it, I had to rein myself in when I heard him talk about her like that. Instead of punching him I closed my eyes briefly and willed my temper to calm. "Six, I loved her. I love her. So... we didn't just fuck, okay?"

The grin disappeared from his face and he nodded. "Shit, man. I'm sorry. That must've been hard. You know, leaving her behind and all."

My gaze drifted over once again to Delilah as she bit her lip and cocked her head to one side. Six gripped my shoulder and drew my attention back to him. "Look, maybe you just need to move the fuck on, dude. Huh? Go pick a woman and get your rocks off. I'm sure Delilah would be game for that. And you'd feel a whole lot better."

"How old is she anyway? I guess I've fucked her before from what you've said."

"Don't worry, man. She's twenty-three. And smokin' hot, in case you haven't noticed. And look at those tits, bro. Don't you just wanna... you know..."

I discreetly trailed my gaze down to her pert breasts. They were smaller than Kelly's. Kelly had the most amazing tits and fuck, I missed her. Another whiskey appeared before me, and I closed my eyes and gulped it down just like the first one, the alcohol making a beeline for my head and slightly numbing my senses. I opened my eyes and glanced over at Delilah again, who was smiling at me longingly. Maybe a really good fuck is what I need?

Six chucked his chin at the pretty blonde. "Hey, Delilah, why don't you take Cain up to his room and... you know... help him to relax a little?"

Delilah hadn't moved her gaze from my face. "Sure thing. Come on, Cain."

She walked out from behind the bar and took my hand. I followed her up the stairs, but in the back of my mind a seed of guilt sprang to life and began to grow.

Once we were inside the room where I'd been sleeping Delilah, pushed me back onto the bed. "Just lie still and relax, Cain. I'll take your mind off of everything," she breathed.

I lay back and felt her tugging at the buttons on the front of my jeans. Next thing I knew my pants were halfway down my thighs and I closed my eyes, hoping to lose myself in what was to come—no pun intended.

Delilah moaned as she drew my rigid flesh into her mouth. I clenched my fists and fought against the fabricated images my brain had conjured up of Kelly performing this very act on me. I had to forget about her. Deciding I needed to keep my focus on the girl I was with and not the girl I couldn't have, I pulled myself up a little and rested on my elbows as Delilah worked my cock with her hand and mouth. She gazed up at me as she licked the full length of my erection, and I inhaled sharply as she circled her tongue around the sensitive tip. Pleasure, like some kind of drug, seeped through to every nerve ending in my body, and I growled my appreciation. She was good. But she wasn't Kelly. I pushed myself all the way to a sitting position and looked down at her where she knelt before me. I wished so hard that the blonde head bobbing up and down on me and devouring my favourite body part was covered in long auburn waves belonging to a certain Scottish beauty.

I closed my eyes again as I reached down and cupped her breasts, toying with her nipples through the fabric of her top. She released me from her mouth and moaned again, lost in her arousal as a pink flush crept up her slender neck. Pushing herself off of me, she stood and with her gaze locked on mine, she pulled her tank top from her body to reveal her petite braless tits to me. She must have been wearing a padded bra before.

"I'm yours, Cain. You can do anything you want to me. Anything at all. I'll fulfil all your fantasies if you'll let me." She slipped her jeans shorts down her legs—revealing that she wasn't wearing panties—and stood there before me naked. A fine line of blonde hair covered the middle of her pussy. Her hips were narrow, and suddenly it hit me how completely different from Kelly she was.

I didn't like it.

I didn't want her.

She stepped forward and straddled me, grinding herself into me as she kissed my neck. Nausea crept up on me, and I didn't know if it was the whiskey or just the fact that I felt like I was being unfaithful.

"Kelly... Oh, fuck, I mean Delilah... Delilah, stop. Please. I... I can't do this." I lifted her from my lap and placed her on her feet. When I glanced up at her, she was twisting her hands together and her eyes were glistening.

I felt like shit.

"What did I do wrong, Cain? All I ever wanted was to belong to you. I've loved you for so long. I didn't care if you needed other women, but *I* wanted to be yours. Only yours. Why don't you want me? What's wrong with me? Why don't you love me back?" The brimming tears overflowed and trickled down her cheeks.

I pulled my boxers and jeans back up as I stood. Dragging the blanket from the end of the bed, I wrapped it around her. "You've done nothing wrong, okay? I just... My head is fucked right now. So much has happened. Melody is—"

She held up her hands. "I get it. I understand. I'm sorry. I know you're still getting over Melody. I'm such an idiot. Please forgive me." But she really didn't get it. Yes, I'd mentioned Melody, but she didn't know about Kelly and she hadn't picked up on what I'd said before. What she didn't know was that I was missing the Scottish girl with all my heart and any sexual act with another would feel like betrayal. Regardless of the fact that Kelly was thousands of miles away.

"Hey, no. There's nothing to forgive." I pulled her into my arms and kissed the top of her head. "You're a beautiful, sweet girl and you deserve better."

She laughed humourlessly. "I'm not as sweet as you think. And all I want is you. You're plenty good enough. You always have been no matter what's in your past."

I stroked her cheek. "I'm sorry, okay?" She nodded and wiped her face with the blanket. "I'll... um... leave you to get dressed." I tipped her nose with my finger and left the room. Once the door was closed behind me, I leaned against it and inhaled a deep breath as I chewed on the inside of my cheek. The pain of losing Melody and Kelly hit me all over again, and I figured whiskey was the only thing that would help me to numb the pain.

Back down in the bar, Six spied me and waved me over. "Feeling better?" He winked and punched my arm.

"Oh yeah, much," I lied.

"I knew Delilah would help you out. She gives the best blow... I mean... she's... she's a sweet woman." His cheeks must have been bright red at slipping up like that when he thought I might've made Delilah my old lady, but I couldn't tell thanks to the dim light.

"There you are, Cain." Colt appeared behind me with Ike. "We've been talking and we feel it would be best if you left and headed up to Canada for a while."

I scrunched my face. "Canada? Fuck, are you kidding me?"

"This situation is no joke, *son*." Ike over pronounced the word son, and I guessed he was trying to show me who was boss. I couldn't be bothered to argue with him. "Believe me when I tell you that Canada is the safest place for you and for Rosa."

Hang on, so I'm supposed to take Rosa away from her home too? Again? Hasn't she been through enough upheaval? I shook my head. "No way. I have my family around me right here. You said so yourself, Colt. I'll stick around. Rosa can come back and we'll be fine. I'm going nowhere."

Colt clenched his jaw and narrowed his eyes. "You have no fucking idea what you're saying. You staying will cause all-out—"

"War, yeah I get it. But what if I'm not prepared to run anymore? What if I want to be here where I belong, huh?"

"You got balls, kid. I'll tell you that much. But my boys and me won't be defending your ass if the shit hits the fan. Just so you know." Colt growled in exasperation and stormed away with clenched fists, a string of expletives falling from his tight lips.

―――――

I finally retreated to my room, seething with anger. Delilah had disappeared and I was relieved of that. I flung myself on my bed, grabbed my iPod, stuck in the ear buds, and hit play. The first track that hit me was American Head Charge's "Just So You Know", and I laughed darkly to myself. I guessed the song was one I had chosen originally because of Melody, but as I listened to the lyrics, it was images of Kelly that sprang to my mind. And despite the anger in the deliverance of the words, the soft melody of the chorus made my insides churn with emotion and loneliness.

CHAPTER THIRTY-THREE

KELLY

I awoke to bright lights being shined in my eyes. I was lying on a bed in a white room and could hear the familiar husk of Alex's voice. "She's coming around, Officer Bower."

"Al... ex?" I croaked. "Wh-what happened?"

I gazed up into concerned hazel eyes, and he smiled. "It's okay. You're safe. Can you tell me your name?"

"Yes... yes, of course, it's... K-Kelly Darrow."

"And can you remember anything of what happened to you?" He checked my pulse.

I closed my eyes and images of a wild-haired girl assaulted my frontal lobe. "Yes... Gina... Gina... erm... hit me." I opened my eyes once again as they welled with tears.

"That's right. But I want you to know that you are perfectly safe now. Gina has been taken away from here. She can't hurt you again." His large hand stroked my head, but I winced as its soreness became evident.

Being assaulted at work was something that had been high-lighted in university as a possibility, and we were coached in how to avoid situations where it could happen and how to deal with such incidents should they arise. But despite my preparedness, I never imagined I would be a victim. No amount of classroom training could have readied me for the intense and heartbreaking emotional scarring I would experience following the attack I had suffered. It shook me to the core and made me question every-thing I had worked for. The fact that I had been attacked by a woman somehow made it worse. Gina apparently had been dragged off me, kicking and screaming accusations that I was trying to kill her. She was sedated and removed from my office and subsequently taken to a more secure unit. The whole situa-tion was horrific and terrifying and I was quickly ushered off on compassionate leave.

Taking time out from work was wasn't something I ever did lightly, but going up to the Isle of Skye with Esme had definitely been the medicine I needed. The little cottage she had booked was just over the Skye Bridge at Kyleakin and it overlooked Loch Alsh. It was a small but very sweet little house, painted white and hunkered low against the elements.

The two bedrooms had been squeezed into the eaves and afforded occupants a magnificent view of the imposing bridge and the boats sailing by on the calm waters beneath.

Esme had packed plenty of DVD movies—mainly comedies —to keep us occupied, but there were board games in the cupboard by the fireplace too. The weather was bright but cold and I had made sure to pack plenty of sweaters, scarves, and hats.

My fractured left hand was encased in plaster, and the itching skin there was driving me mad; but my face and head were healing nicely, and I was thankful that I hadn't needed stitches. The glue had matted my hair, however, and I was self-conscious about it. Hence the assortment of hats.

We sat eating breakfast at the kitchen table one morning

when Esme announced the plans for the day. "We're going to see the Old Man of Storr today. There's a cute little café on the way, so we're sorted for cake and coffee later. It's in a centre for the elderly that I discovered when I was researching the area. The cafe is actually run by the lovely old dears too. And... well... They've... they've got a vacancy actually."

I scrunched my brow. "Are you thinking of a career change? This is news. Although I can't imagine you with a blue rinse serving cake. Although the old guys would probably love you. You'd have to watch yourself there." I giggled at the thought.

She chewed her lip and knotted her fingers. "I was actually thinking of you, honey. The vacancy is for a clinical psychologist."

Confusion washed over me. "Me? But... I have a job."

"I know. But after what happened, I thought maybe a change of scenery and a fresh start might do you good. You know, working with people who are less likely to attack you with a blunt instrument."

The thought that I was in the wrong job had crossed my mind on more than one occasion since I had met Cain—and especially since the assault. "What's the job?"

"It's a counselling role. Working with people at the centre who are adjusting to life in residential care. They do some amazing work, Kel. I think you should check out the job description. They're... Look, this is going to sound terrible, but I sent your CV in and they want to meet with you."

My eyes widened and I gulped. "I can't go to an interview looking like this." I gestured to my bruised and swollen face. Although it wasn't as bad as it had been, it still made me look like the worst possible candidate for a job with oldies.

"They know about the assault. Alex has spoken to them."

I gasped and stood

She held up her hands and stuttered, "L-look, I know this

seems very underhanded of us, but... we were just looking out
for you."

"Since when have you and Alex been in cahoots?" My voice
squeaked. My shock very much evident.

"Since..." She covered her face briefly and peeped out
through her fingers. "Oh, God, don't hate me, Kel. He's been
taking me out for a few weeks. We met when you were in
hospital after the assault, and we just... hit it off." She shrugged
as if it were the most natural thing in the world. "I really like
him. I know there's an age gap, but..." She ended her half-
finished sentence with a simultaneous shrug and cringe.

Panic rushed through my veins at the thought of my past
misdemeanours with Cain being discussed over dinner. I opened
and closed my mouth like a goldfish out of its bowl.

As if she were reading my mind, she stood and came around
the table to me. "Under no circumstances would I ever tell him
anything about you and Cain, so you have nothing to worry
about. Nothing at all. Okay?"

My heart was racing and I suddenly felt lightheaded. "But
what if it slips out? By accident?" Or because Alex has a talent
for reading between the lines.

She placed her hands firmly on my shoulders. "You have
nothing to worry about. Just go for the interview and see about
that fresh start, okay?"

———

I met with Christian Sampson later that day. He was great. The
role with the elderly people sounded like a breath of fresh air
and very positive. For the first time in what felt like forever, I was
excited. This was something I could maybe get my teeth into. I
left the meeting with a smile on my face under the advisement
that I would receive a call at the end of the week.

That same evening, Esme had booked us a table at the

restaurant a couple of hundred metres away, and we sat munching on steak and chips. My appetite was back with a vengeance.

"So what was he like? Looks-wise I mean." The twinkle in Esme's eyes told me she was in matchmaking mode.

"Whoa... don't even go there. Even if I do get the job, there is no way on this earth I'll be mixing business with pleasure ever again. No thank you."

Esme laughed. "Okay, okay. Message received loud and clear."

"The only thing is... Cain won't know where I am."

She sighed and reached across the table. "I know. But... in all honesty, maybe that's a good thing. You won't be wondering if he's going to turn up one day. You can really move on."

She was right. He hadn't tried to contact me in all this time, and he wasn't going to. I needed to let it go. This fresh start would have to be a new beginning in every sense of the phrase.

CHAPTER THIRTY-FOUR

Cain

The ride north was a long one. But being back on my bike was astoundingly good. It was like coming home. I gripped the handlebars and grinned like an idiot as the cool wind whipped strands of my hair around my face. I glanced over at Six, who saluted me just before he dropped back and was replaced at my side by Colt, whose shoulders were jumping up and down as he shook his head.

Bastard's laughing at me!

I didn't care.

After hitting the road at the butt-crack of dawn, we were on our way to a small town in Idaho on the outskirts of Nampa, where my kid sister was holed up in some kind of safe house. The details I had been given were still sketchy, and I was being kept in the dark about her exact location until the last minute.

We all pulled up outside a coffee shop at around four in the afternoon. Once we all had parked up our bikes, we followed Colt as he made his way inside and to the counter. He got chatting to an old dude behind the cash register, who listened intently and glanced over to me every so often. He kept nodding and eventually shook Colt's hand. I wondered what the hell he had ordered that had gotten the guy so serious.

When Colt returned, I watched him expectantly as he rubbed his hand over his hair but said nothing.

Unable to stay quiet any longer, I had to break the silence. "Okay, so what's the plan of action? We eat first and then go get Rosa?"

He placed his hand on my shoulder and gripped me tightly. Come with me, buddy."

He turned and walked past the side of the counter, toward a door marked Private. He held the door open and allowed me to walk through. A staircase stood in front of me, and I turned to glance at Colt, wondering why he wasn't moving.

He gestured ahead of me. "Go on up and knock on the door at the top of the stairs."

I swallowed hard and turned to face the stairs. Did this mean what I hoped it meant?

I nervously made my way up the wooden staircase, and sure enough there was a white-painted door at the top. I knocked and waited. My heart hammered at the inside of my chest, and sweat beaded on my forehead. I trusted Colt, didn't I? What if I was wrong? What if I had proven to be too much of a liability to the Company?

The door opened, and a middle-aged woman stood before me. Okay, so I wasn't going to die today, but my heart sank and I scrunched my brow. "Oh... I was expecting—"

The grey haired woman smiled kindly at me and held up her hand to halt me. "It's okay. I've been expecting you. I'm Ellen, come on in."

She stepped aside so that I could enter what turned out to be a small apartment. I glanced around the tidy space and spotted a framed photo of the woman with the guy from the café downstairs and a dark-haired, blue-eyed girl I recognised immediately as my kid sister. A lump tightened my throat and my eyes misted over.

"She's a fine young woman. You should be very proud of the job you did bringing her up, Cain."

I sniffed and wiped my eyes on my sleeves before turning and offering a smile. Words evaded me. My heart ached. I wanted to hold Rosa just so that I could see for myself that she was okay.

"Come on and sit down." She gestured to the couch. "Can I get you a drink? Coffee perhaps?"

I walked over and sat, then I shook my head. "No, no thanks, I'm good. Where is—"

"Don't worry. She's at the local adult ed. centre. She's catching up on her high school diploma. She's a bright kid."

"Yeah, she always was. Even when she was a lot younger she wanted to know 'why' about every damn thing. Used to drive me crazy. In the best way though."

"Oh, I can imagine. It took her a little while to settle, but... she's doing well. Although she's restless. You can see it in her eyes. She's always looking to the horizon."

I chuckled. "Yeah. She must get that from me." I chewed at my lip for a moment and chose my words carefully. "Did she... did she cope okay after I was gone? You know, when they brought her here?"

"Honey, she is a tough cookie, but she'd been through such a lot. She hasn't been here that long really, but I feel she has made progress in the time she's been with Hank and me."

Something niggled at the back of my mind. "I thought she was being looked after by part of the Cosmic charter here in Idaho."

Ellen smiled warmly again. "Oh, she is, dear. Hank was president up until he hit sixty and started with heart trouble. I've spent many hours on the back of his bike. Too many. But we retired and bought the place downstairs. The house joined on is where Hank and I live and where Rosa has been staying. She comes up here to study. We usually have members of the club hanging out in the shop or in my kitchen, so she likes the quiet."

I smiled as I imagined her sitting with her nose in a book. "I'm proud of her for studying again. She hates school."

"Well... she's quite the artist, you know. I'm amazed no one has picked up on that before. And she's a whiz with a needle and thread."

"Yeah. I always tried to encourage that, but you know how kids are. You tell them one thing and they straight up go and do something different."

Ellen laughed as if she totally got what I meant. I was so happy that someone as kind as Ellen had been looking after Rosa. She had been missing a mother figure for many years. This was probably what she needed.

The front door opened, and I heard a familiar voice. "Hey, Ellen, I'm home! Are you here?"

My heart felt like it might swell right out of my chest. Rosa walked into the living room and stopped dead. Her eyes widened and she gasped and covered her mouth with her hands. She looked beautiful. Her long dark hair was now all shoulder length and choppy. She looked really grown up. She'd kept the blue streak in front, and that made me smile. I realised I was staring—but then again, she was staring too.

"You... you can't be here. You're... you're dead," she whispered through her fingers, and the colour drained from her cheeks. "You're not real. What the hell? I don't... Ellen!" she called as she dropped to her knees in the doorway. Both Ellen and I lunged for her, but I got there first.

I scooped her up in my arms and stroked her hair. "It's okay, sweetie. It's me and I'm not dead. I'm very much alive. And I'm not leaving you again."

She buried her face in my neck and clung to me as she sobbed my name over and over again. My own tears escaped once more and soaked into her hair. "Shhh... it's okay, Rosa. We're gonna be okay. You and me against the world, kiddo. Just like before." My voice cracked as I tried so damned hard to reassure her.

"But they killed you. They beat you and then when Colt got there, you were so badly injured that they couldn't save you. You can't be here!" she cried as she pulled away and hammered her fists into my chest. "You left me alone. I lost Mom and Dad then Melody and then I lost you. I was so alone. Where have you been? Why didn't you come home if you were okay? You fucking bastard! You were my only family. My only family and you left. Just like the rest of them." She stopped hitting me and crumpled into a heap in my lap, clutching onto my waist as if she thought I would float away on a breeze. Sobs racked her body and broke my heart as she let out all the anguish and pain she'd had pent up since I disappeared.

How the hell do I make this damn situation right?

I bent myself over her protectively and engulfed her in my arms as I spluttered out my words in an emotion-filled croak. "I know, sweetheart. And I am so, so sorry. I'll explain it all someday. I promise." How can I ever tell her I lost my mind in Scotland... and left my heart there when I came back? "But right now... from right now, I'm going nowhere. You hear me? You're stuck with me."

She pulled away and gazed up at me with clear blue eyes that matched mine. "You promise?"

I held her face in my palms and rested my forehead on hers, trying to focus on my sister and my life here with her, trying not to grieve for Kelly, though even now my body ached with missing her. Rosa was my family. And taking care of her had to be enough. "I swear on my life. And apart from you, that's the most precious thing I have."

CHAPTER THIRTY-FIVE

KELLY

Skye was fast becoming my favourite place in the world. The fact that I made a life-changing decision in the two weeks I was there told me it was fate. The job at the elderly people's centre had been meant for me. Alex and Esme had known it before I knew it myself. But they were so right. To be honest, the role really did appeal to me right from the start. And the meeting with Christian, the centre manager, had gone so well that I had butterflies fluttering around in my stomach whilst I waited for news to come in.

There I was in a stunning part of the world. Not too far away from my friends. With the possibility of a career change that would take me away from a job that was draining me emotionally and instead place me into something that could be wholly fulfilling. If I ignored the emptiness inside of me created when Cain left. Some of the time, I could.

Like I said... fate.

The eagerly awaited call came on the Friday of the second week on Skye. Esme and I were on the top of the world. Well, that's what it felt like, standing at the summit of one of the smaller mountains in the Quiraing when my cell rang. I stared at in disbelief for a while, wondering how the hell I had a signal all the way out there.

Esme nudged me and nodded at the thing. "It could be important, you nutter."

I hit the answer button and stuttered my greeting across the airwaves. "H-hello?"

"Kelly? It's Chris Sampson. Is this a good time? You sound a little windswept."

"Oh, hi, Chris. Yes I'm at the top of the Quiraing." I laughed at my explanation.

"Oh, I love it up there. Great views. Listen. You might get more opportunities to spend time up there from next month. We'd like to offer you the job. And we'd like you to start as soon as possible. Obviously we know you'll need time to think it through."

My heart skipped in my chest, and I began to hop from one foot to the other, waving my free hand and mouthing the words "I got it!" to my best friend, who stood a very short distance away.

She covered her mouth with her hands and also began to dance around silently. It's was a good thing we were the only people up there, or we may have been carted off to a secure unit.

"That's wonderful. I don't need time to think. I'd like to accept." My smile was wide and it felt good to be happy. Esme began to wipe errant tears from her cheeks.

"Well, I have to say that's wonderful news, Kelly. We can't wait to have you on board. Keep in touch and let us know when you have a start date in mind."

"I will, and thank you again for the opportunity, Christian."

"No, it's we here at the centre who are thankful. Speak soon, Kelly."

I hit the end call button and proceeded to continue jumping

around with Esme. Her blonde curls bounced around from under her woolly hat. We squealed and danced a jig on the top of the Quiraing like a pair of total fruit loops, but we didn't care.

Once back at the cottage Esme surprised me with a bottle of champagne. "Where the hell were you hiding that, you crafty bugger?" I laughed as the cork shot across the small kitchen, narrowly missing the light fitting.

"It's been in the wood shed. I knew you'd get the job. I just didn't expect it to be this week! I was going to surprise you with this tomorrow night for our last night here, but what the hell. Now we have a real reason to celebrate."

I held out the two wine glasses I had gotten out of the cupboard, and Esme filled them as far as the bubbles would allow. She made a toast and we both took a slurp of our delicious fizzy beverages. The log stove had been lit, and the amber glow in the living room matched the warm tingle I had inside.

It was going to be a fresh start. A completely blank slate.

And I couldn't wait.

If only Cain were going to be making the journey with me...

———

Back at home I began the task of working my notice at the hospital and searching for a place to rent near Portree on Skye until I sold my Inverness property. I also had to inform Dermott of my change of direction. I had arranged for him to come over with a Chinese takeaway, and I had bought a couple of bottles of wine in—mainly for my benefit, as my nerves were jangling.

We had arranged our meetup for the Friday that followed my Saturday arrival back in Inverness and I was sitting on the couch chewing on my thumb nail awaiting his arrival. The wine was already open and a half-drunk glass sat before me on the coffee table.

There was a knock at the door and I checked the clock. He

was bloody early. Typical. At least I can get this done and out of the way, I suppose. With a happy grin plastered on my face, I pulled the door open.

Dermott looked very handsome. His dirty-blonde hair was messy as if he had not long since been showered. His green eyes sparkled and his megawatt smile elicited an even bigger smile from me.

"Hey, you." I stepped aside so he could walk in.

"Hey, gorgeous. Get some plates out. I'm starving." He walked through to the kitchen like he owned the place and plonked the brown paper bag of food on the countertop.

The aroma of Szechuan chicken made my mouth water, and my stomach gave an appreciative gurgle. "So how are you? Apart from hungry that is?" I asked as I grabbed plates from the cupboard and then cutlery from the drawer.

He sighed. "Oh, you know... busy... horny... same old, same old."

I placed the utensils down, rolled my eyes, and turned to face him. "On *that* note, I have news." No time like the present. Rip off that Band-Aid, Kelly.

"Oh, yeah?" He stepped toward me and slipped his arms around my waist. "You horny too, eh?" He waggled his eyebrows.

Slapping his hands away and stepping back to create some much-needed distance, I fixed him with a steely stare. "No. You know very well that's not happening between us anymore."

He stuck out his bottom lip. "Spoilsport."

"Seriously, Dermott, I have something pretty major to tell you."

He folded his arms and leaned against the countertop. "Go on, then. What is it?"

"I'm... I'm moving."

He raised his eyebrows and grinned. "Oooh, that's exciting. This place *is* a bit small. You should look at those new apartments near me. Bigger. More contemporary. I could really see—"

"To Skye."

His brow furrowed and he opened his mouth but no sound came out.

I took a deep, calming breath. "I've been offered a job working at a residential centre for the elderly near Portree. It should be really great. I'm very excited about it."

He sniggered. "Are you joking? Is this a joke? You working with old folk?"

Strange reaction. I shook my head slowly. "No, Dermott. It's happening... for real."

I watched his Adam's apple as it bobbed and his jaw as it clenched. He snorted a ridiculous fake laugh. "I see. You know, if the sex was that bad, you could've just said so. And we did agree we weren't doing it again, so you didn't have to move that far away."

I watched as his cheeks turned a shade of pink that I had never witnessed on him before. I wondered why he was behaving that way. "Are you okay, Dermott?"

He nodded emphatically. "Oh, yeah... yeah, fine. So, long-distance fuck buddies, then, eh?" He forced another laugh and my concern grew.

Shit. He was taking it harder than I ever imagined. "Dermott, you just said we're not doing that anymore, remember?"

An uneasy silence fell over the room and neither of us made eye contact. The food was no doubt going cold and my hunger had turned into a knot of anxiety.

After what felt like hours, Dermott stepped toward me. "Don't go, Kelly. Please."

I pulled my brow in and met his panicked gaze. What the hell? "I'm sorry, but my mind is already made up. I've accepted the position. It's all sorted."

He stepped closer still and gripped my arms. "I love you, Kelly. I'm... I'm in love with you. Always have been. Please don't leave."

What!

Doing my best impersonation of a Venus fly trap awaiting its prey, I stood there, wide-eyed and open-mouthed, unable to find the words to respond to his shocking revelation.

"Say something, Kel. Please?"

"B-but Dermott... I don't feel that way about you, you know this. We talked about this a while ago when you stayed over and we agreed that we would just be friends. We tried a relationship at university—"

"We can make it work. The sex is amazing and... and I can protect you. No one will fucking hurt you again. Ever. Not bloody idiots who don't love you back and bugger off to God knows where. Not crazy bitches with staplers. No one, Kelly. I love you. Stay with me. Please?"

CHAPTER THIRTY-SIX

Kelly

I stood there before Dermott as he spilled his heart out to me, and all I could think about was Cain. How much I missed him. How much I wished it were him standing before me, expressing his innermost feelings. But Cain was thousands of miles away, moving on with his life.

Dermott and I had known each other for so long, and at one time I had thought we had a chance at making things work just like he had admitted not so long ago. But not anymore. Admittedly, since meeting Cain, I had been spoiled for any other man. I couldn't imagine any man making me feel the way Cain did. And I don't just mean sexually—though if anyone could even come close to that, it would be Dermott. But Cain had captured my heart, and in him I had found the other half of my soul. It was something that I couldn't really explain. But it was something that I knew. Suddenly things clicked into place as thoughts about Cain and Dermott rampaged around my head. The sex between Cain and me was so amazing because he was the yin to my yang. Because he was my other half. Because he had captured my heart. I gasped at the realisation and closed my eyes briefly, almost forgetting Dermott was standing before me.

I opened my eyes as guilt washed over me and Dermott pleaded at me with his vivid green gaze. Saltwater welled up, and my lip began to tremble. He caught an escaped droplet, and his own eyes began to glisten.

He smiled sadly. "I... I think maybe I should go."

"I'm so sorry, Dermott," I whispered as my heart squeezed in my chest.

He shrugged. "You can't help who you fall in love with. The heart wants what it wants. On paper we're a perfect match. But in real life... I guess in real life we're perfect as friends."

I nodded and pulled him into a hug. "I'm so sorry, Dermott. The last thing I want to do is hurt you. If I could change how I feel, believe me, I would. I don't want to feel this emptiness that I've been left with. And I wish I could love you the same way, I really do." I sniffled into his shoulder.

"Yeah... Maybe I should have said something a heck of a lot sooner, eh? Although I'm guessing it wouldn't have made much difference. Would it?"

I shook my head as more tears sprang forth. "No. I'm sorry, but no, it wouldn't."

"Well... sometimes these things have to be said out loud. I just wish the outcome had been different."

Panic suddenly knotted my stomach. Was I about to lose one of my best friends? "Will you still keep in touch with me?" I widened my eyes but feared for his response.

He kissed my forehead and then looked into my eyes. "I'll always be here for you, Kelly. I think I sold myself short where you're concerned. I acted all casual for so long when deep down, all I wanted was to admit how I really feel." He closed his eyes and shook his head. "There's no wonder you don't want me. I talked about us as fuck buddies, for God's sake."

"Hey, don't beat yourself up about it. Please. It's just not meant to be. But I do love you. Just not in that way."

He cupped my cheek. "If you ever change your mind... I'd move to Skye for you. I'd gladly leave everything here behind for you. Just so you know."

How many more revelations were coming? This was all too much. And all it did was compound the sense of loss inside of me. I began to sob, and Dermott enveloped me in his arms. A place where I had always felt safe—but now it just made me realise how much I missed being held... by Cain.

———

Cain

Living in the apartment above the café with Rosa wasn't ideal, but it was necessary until things had calmed down. Colt and Six kept contacting me and trying to convince me to move north of the border into Canadian territory. But as much as I loved the scenery up there, I didn't feel connected to the place in the slightest. It could never be home. Not for me or Rosa.

Rosa continued with her studies and was doing so well. She made me proud. And I was in awe of her determination. Staying out of sight was becoming impossible for me. I was going stir-crazy again. My love of the outdoors had returned and being stuck in a poky little two-bed apartment just didn't cut it. Plus I wasn't happy to be relying on two old folks to feed me. I needed to get the hell out and back to normal life.

But Colt was still reluctant for me to be seen out in public. I'd grown my hair and let a full beard grow in, but apparently it still wasn't enough. He kept in touch via text messages mostly but made the odd visit up too. Sometimes Six came along for the ride.

The final straw came when Rosa was late home from school

and I began to worry. It wasn't so far to walk from the school bus, but when we discovered that she hadn't even gotten on the bus, Ellen and Hank insisted that they go looking for her; and once again I was rendered fucking useless. The whole situation was at a point of no return.

They had been gone twenty minutes, and I could stand it no longer. I pulled my bike out of the yard around back and set off in the direction of the school. I passed Ellen and Hank as they were returning in an empty fucking car. My heart rate spiked and fear knotted my guts. Where the fuck was she? What had happened to her?

As soon as they realised it was me, they spun their car around and began to follow me. Hank was at the wheel, and he kept on flashing his lights to get my attention, but I forged ahead. No one was going to stop me from protecting Rosa now.

No one.

———

Later that day we all sat around the large gnarled oak kitchen table in Hank and Ellen's rustic home. The mood was sombre and the atmosphere thick with apprehension. In the heavy silence that hung over the room, I could almost hear the cogs turning in everyone's minds.

Rosa hadn't been found.

It was four hours on from when she hadn't returned from school, and everyone who could possibly know her whereabouts had been contacted several times. Colt was refusing to inform the police, saying it would only make matters worse. He was sure the Legion had her. And all I knew was that when I got my hands on whoever it was that had her, I would fucking rip them limb from limb.

The phone rang and Hank answered it in a hushed tone. With a worried expression, he handed the receiver to Colt, who listened with a frown. His knuckles became white where he gripped the handset. I stood, fists clenched, and walked to stand before him. I could see his jaw muscles ticking under his skin.

"Okay. We're on our way." He handed the phone back to Hank and rubbed his hands over his face.

"Where is she? Who the fuck has her, Colt?" My words came out in a rush.

"Up state. Old Legion warehouse. The bastards have gone too far this time."

His words sent the cold hand of fear trailing down my spine, leaving shivers in its wake. "W-why? What have they done?"

"You'd better sit down."

I shook my head. "Just fucking tell me. Please."

"She's been dating a guy in school. Some kid called Tyler. Turns out he was the son of one of the Legion. He's been getting close to her to find out about you. She must have told him you were back. Apparently she got on his bike after school. She told one of her friends that she would let you know where she was. Clearly that's not happening, and my guess is that's because they won't *let* her call you."

A wave of nausea washed over me and I felt the colour drain from my face. "Fuck. I have to find her, Colt. We have to go now!"

"I know, son." His expression was grim. "I know."

————

The warehouse was in darkness and I was glad Colt had returned my forty-five to me. Although I knew I had shot someone before, I couldn't piece together the memory of it. But if it's what was necessary to get my sister out of there, then I would do what I had to.

Colt, Six, and some of the other guys had the place surrounded, but I had told them it would be me who went in after her. They protested, saying I'd be a walking target, but she was my sister. She was my responsibility. My flesh and blood.

My reasoning prevailed. I would go in, and they'd wait for my signal if and when I needed them to back me up.

I tried a rotten old door and it creaked open. I cringed and hoped that the bastards hadn't heard me coming. But who was I kidding? They were lying in wait for me.

I crept through the minimal space I'd created and allowed my eyes to adjust to the darkness. The place stank of old diesel oil and there was a thick heaviness to the air—the kind of atmosphere that occurs when something really bad is on the verge of happening. The combination created a sensation and stench that made my gut churn. I held my gun aloft with the safety off. I wanted to be ready. I could hear raised voices coming from the office at the back of the warehouse and so I slowly crept toward it.

"You lied to me, Ty. I can't believe you'd do that. Not after everything you said." Rosa's emotion-filled voice rang out, and my heart clenched. I'll kill the bastard!

"I'm sorry, Rosie, really I am. They made me do it. I wanted to tell you but... well, you can imagine what would have happened if I'd done that."

"At this moment in time, Ty, you can fucking drop dead for all I care!" she screamed at her captor, and I found myself first cringing at her language and then feeling proud of her for standing up to him.

"Aww, come on, Rosie. Please. I meant it when I told you how much I like you. I'm sick of this fucking shit with the clubs sparring all the time. All's I want is to have you as my girl and the rest of them can go fuck themselves. But... it's like we're Romeo and Juliet, you know? It's not allowed and stuff."

I snorted from my hiding place. Oh yeah, very articulate, bro. You're putting Shakespeare to shame. Dumb fucking idiot.

"No, Ty. We are not Romeo and fucking Juliet. We are

nothing like them. Although there is one similarity. You could end up fucking dead if my brother finds me here."

I couldn't help chuckling to myself at her comeback. No doubting that she was my kid sister, that's for sure. I got the distinct feeling that this Tyler kid was under duress about the whole situation, and I calmed a little. He wasn't out to hurt her, and no one else seemed to be around.

"You... you think Cain would really kill me? I mean... I heard he was a badass, but I hoped he might go easy on me. I don't want to be doing this, Rosie." The kid sounded panicked. And I was glad.

"So let me go. Let me walk out of here, and I'll talk to Cain. Maybe I can make him go easy on you." Her voice had softened and I got what she was trying to do.

As for going easy on him? Huh! Not fucking likely.

"I... I can't. If the others come back, I'm dead if I let you go."

"You're dead either way then." She sounded defeated and I took that I my cue. With my gun held tight, I turned and kicked the door with a force that knocked it from its top hinge. The crash made Tyler spin around to face me, and when he saw me, he dropped to his knees, covering his head.

"Aww, fuck! I'm sorry, man. Please don't hurt me. I'm sorry! I didn't wanna do it. I like her!" he sobbed.

I walked over and pointed the gun at his head. Rosa gasped from the chair where she sat. Only when I got a closer look at her, I saw she was tied with her arms behind her back. I glanced over and shook my head slowly, hoping that she understood I wasn't going to hurt the asshole. Just scare him a little. Well... maybe rough him up a bit.

"Get up, you fucking little ass-wipe," I growled.

He made a little girly squeak. "I'm really sorry. Really sorry." He slowly got to his feet.

I glared at him, hoping I came off as menacing. "I suggest you untie my sister."

"Y-yes, sir." He walked behind her chair and began fumbling around. Just as he got the rope untied, I heard shouting outside. Then the crack of gunfire. My heart almost jumped out of my chest. Rosa screamed.

I turned to face my sister's kidnapper. "You, come with me. Do anything stupid, Romeo, and I will blow your fucking brains out. Understood?"

He nodded, wide-eyed, and a large wet patch appeared on the front of his jeans. I could smell the reek of piss.

I shook my head in disgust. "Rosa, follow close behind."

We made our way out of the little office and toward where the battle had broken out. I could see fists flying, and thankfully no more shots were fired. Sticking my thumb and forefinger in my mouth, I blew out a high-pitched, piercing whistle and everyone stopped dead.

I brandished my gun in the air. "I have your boy here. How does that saying go again? An eye for an eye? Well how about a teenager for a teenager? I'll be taking this little shit with me. Any of you try to follow, and he may just wind up dead in a fucking ditch. You reading me?"

One of the Legion stepped forward, hands held up in surrender. "Whoa, man! He's my son. Don't you fucking hurt him! Please, don't hurt him."

"I'll do you a deal, shall I? You keep away from our clubhouse and our members and we'll let him live."

The leather- and denim-clad middle-aged man sniggered at me. "You do know that you're dead when Deak hears about this, don't you?"

I grimaced at him. "I doubt that. He's getting old now. I reckon I could take him on." I was pretty damn sure that provoking the fucker wasn't the best way to go, but I couldn't resist. I shoved Ty away from me. "Weasel, get this asshole on the back of your bike." Well, come on, I didn't want my bike stinking of piss. "Rosa, you're coming with me. Let's get the fuck out of here."

The prick from the rival club laughed darkly and called after me, "He wasn't gonna harm your sister, dude. It was you Deak wanted. Can't say that will be the case anymore. I would think seriously about your next move, Somers. Reckon you're both gonna wind up dead now."

"I wouldn't go making threats if I were you, shithead," I told him as I pulled on my helmet and straddled my bike. The rest of the crew followed suit, and we peeled off down the long road. Rosa clung on to me and leaned into my back. Even over the rumble of the engine, I was sure I could feel the vibrations of her sobs through my cut. Poor kid. I bypassed the turnoff for Hank and Eleanor's home and headed straight for Rose Acres. There was no point going back into hiding now.

I was pretty sure I was done for.

It was just a matter of how long I had left.

CHAPTER THIRTY-SEVEN

KELLY

Four weeks after accepting the role on Skye, I was packed up and moving. I was following the removals van along the A87 and singing along to the MP3 player plugged into my car stereo. Images of Cain floated through my mind as I listened to the painful lyrics of "Simple Together" by Alanis Morissette, and tears began to fog my eyes. The rain beating down on the windscreen matched my solemn mood. I was supposed to be excited, but deep inside it felt like this new beginning was more of an ending.

Hearing Alanis sing about how she thought she was going to have this amazing life with the man she loved only to realise he didn't feel the same shattered my heart into pieces. Cain had said he loved me, but I still lost him. And now I was moving away and he could never find me even if he wanted to.

But I doubted that he'd even remember me by now.

And how the hell could he have loved me anyway?

We pulled over the Skye Bridge and along the main road

heading toward the little town of Portree. The quaint cottage I was renting was remote but beautiful and outside of the town, so I had the space and fresh air I wanted but also all the amenities like shops, doctors, and dentist only a short drive away. The best of both worlds. It was a complete contrast to North Kessock and Inverness, but it felt like the right move.

Several hours later, and the removal van pulled away, leaving me to begin my new life all alone. Esme was unable to help me on moving day due to work commitments, and even though Dermott had tried to insist, I had been strong and said no to his offer of help. I didn't want to lead him on following his recent profession of undying love. But as I sat there on my leather couch surrounded by boxes, I wondered if I had made a phenomenal mistake. In more ways than one.

It had been a long and tiring day. I had kept bursting into tears for no apparent reason and I'd had to switch off my background music, as not only was it not helping me feel settled, it was stirring up emotions in me that I really needed to be free from.

At six in the evening, it was very dark outside. My cottage was the end one of a row of four on a farm track off the main road into Portree, and during the daytime the scenery was stunning. At night, however, the place was eerily quiet.

I wrapped my furry couch throw blanket around my shoulders and stepped out the back door. Peering up at the sky took my breath away. The blackness overhead hadn't got the usual patches of light pollution I was used to. Instead the canopy was dotted with tiny white lights; some flickered and some just glowed. The sight was one I was sure I would never cease to be affected by, and a lump of emotion tightened my throat once more.

I turned to walk back into the house and inhaled a deep, cleansing breath of Skye's cool evening air. Before I entered the house I exhaled, hoping that all my worries would leave my body along with the contents of my lungs.

Deciding that more unpacking could wait until morning, I walked through to my cute little hand-built kitchen and tugged the cork out of a bottle of Cabernet Sauvignon. I reached for a large wine glass and filled it almost to the brim with the dark red liquid. With one hand holding my blanket and the other clutching my glass, I made my way back through to the living room and flopped onto the sofa, almost spilling the precious contents of my glass.

I thought back to the conversation I'd had with Dermott the day after his revelation. He had turned up on my doorstep with a huge bunch of flowers and a heartfelt apology for vomiting his emotions all over me. But his resolve was set firm. Although he was sorry for how he had presented me with the news, he was still offering me a new start with him. And I would have been crazy if I totally dismissed it. He was a decent guy. Handsome, sexy, and sweet. The sex between us had always been good, but in all honesty the feelings just were not there. I had tried to explain this to him.

"But Kelly, you could learn to love me. Maybe I'm not the man for you right now because you're still hung up on that arsehole—"

"Not helping, Dermott."

"Sorry... sorry, I'm just jealous and bitter. But think about it. We have so many of the important things in common. We understand each other's work life. We get on so well. We're great friends. I think you're fucking gorgeous, and I get the feeling you don't find me utterly repulsive. Can't we just give it a try? See how things go?"

I sighed deeply. "Dermott, I'll be living over on Skye and you'll be here. How the hell would it work?" And why was I sounding like I was actually considering this again?

He stepped toward me and cupped my face in his large hands. "We would make it work. I would do anything for you, Kelly. Anything." His voice had lowered to a lust-filled whisper as he peered into my eyes and moved his face closer to mine. His hot breath tickled my lips and I locked my eyes on his, desperately wanting to feel something that would mean I could move on. Forget Cain.

"Long distance is just so... hard," I croaked.

He brushed his lips against mine gently and ran his nose along my cheek. "We would make it work," he repeated hopefully. "Please say you'll think about it. About us."

I closed my eyes and nodded. "I'll think about us, Dermott, but I can't promise anything."

"I know and that's fine. Seeing as you won't let me help you move, I may just turn up on your doorstep with flowers."

I opened my eyes and smiled. "Maybe call first?"

He shrugged. "Maybe I will. Maybe I won't."

Back in the present, I took a gulp of my wine and stared out of the window into the diamond-speckled night sky. I wondered if Cain was safe—or had the rival bike gang found him? My heart stuttered in my chest at the thought of his not being alive, and my eyes began to sting. The probability was, however, that I wouldn't find out either way.

Later on I took myself off to bed with a heaviness in my heart that I desperately hoped would be gone by morning. Esme was due to come up, and I wanted to make the most of the visit from my best friend.

Snuggling under my duvet, I lay in silence in my new and unfamiliar surroundings, suddenly feeling wide awake. And the problem with being wide awake was that every noise freaked me out and every thought was of Cain and me together...

I opened my eyes and Cain was lying on top of me, kissing my neck as he glided his cock in and out of my slick, wet pussy. I gasped and darted my eyes around the room, suddenly completely disorientated. It was my new room... but what was Cain doing here?

"It's okay, baby. You're dreaming."

My heart sank at his words, but I could smell him and feel him deep inside of me, so I doubted my subconscious mind anyway. "Unh... Are you sure?" I gripped his body, relishing the rhythm of our bodies' movements and held onto him as tightly as I could—pulling him deeper still—as I began my climb toward the ecstasy only he could bring.

He groaned carnally but nodded. "I wanted to tell you... you should move on. Dermott is offering you a life that I can't give you. He loves you... I always knew it. You should be with him. He deserves you, Kelly. You should be with someone who can give you all the things you need. I'm not that man." The pain in his voice made my heart shatter.

I shook my head as I gazed up at him. I reached out to touch his cheek. His skin was cool and he closed his eyes for a moment, sighing deeply.

I bit my lip as he ground his pelvis into mine. "But I want you. It's you that I love." Pleasure and love coursed through my veins and I wanted to stay there forever.

He opened his eyes and shook his head as he suddenly pulled out of my body "It was just sex, Kelly. That's all. I could never be good enough for you."

The feeling of loss and emptiness was overwhelming, and I was pulled back from the precipice of my orgasm. I reached out for him. "No! No, please don't say that. It's not true, Cain. Take that back."

As if he wasn't listening, he pushed himself off of the bed and continued, "I could never be what you need. And it doesn't matter anymore. I'm not here... Dermott could be if you let him." He stood and walked toward the door, and I tried to shout out, but my voice became trapped in my throat. The bed sheets wrapped around my limbs and I was tied in place, unable to move. Unable to go to him. I tried in vain to shout once more as tears sprang from my eyes, leaving cold, wet trails down my face. My heart rate picked up. What did he mean, he wasn't here? Did he mean physically? Had something happened to him in America? Oh my God, I needed to get up, but regardless of how much I tried to flail, I couldn't move...

"Nooooo!" I woke myself up as I screamed into the cool morning air of my new bedroom. I must have been tossing and turning, as my legs were tangled in the bedding and I was covered in a sheen of sweat despite the low temperature in the room. Immediately I went against every single promise I had made to myself and clambered out of bed, grabbed my robe, and dashed down the stairs to where my laptop sat on the coffee table.

Firing it up, I was grateful that broadband worked out in the sticks, and I chewed on my nails whilst I waited for the search engine to appear before me. After three attempts of trying to type with my shaking fingers, I managed to search for Cain's name. Nothing at all relating to my Cain Somers was found, and my heart rate began to calm a little. "They say that no news is good news, right?" I asked the room full of boxes.

Taking a deep breath and mentally chastising myself for being ridiculous, I closed the lid on the laptop and went to the kitchen to make myself a coffee. Once I was holding the cup of Italian roast, I leaned against the countertop and surveyed the work needed to get the place looking and feeling like home. I decided that I wouldn't get it done by the time Esme arrived and instead went back to the living room to sit on the couch.

As I sat there, I replayed the dream I had about Cain. Maybe this was my subconscious telling me what I needed to hear. And maybe Cain being the one to tell me to move on was something that deep down I really needed. It was like he was giving me permission. Even though I didn't believe in premonitions, my state of mind was telling me that I needed to take heed. I didn't like it, admittedly, but if I really thought about it, moving on was all I could do. And this latest torturous dream had made me realise that I was doomed to a miserable life if I didn't at least try to let go.

CHAPTER THIRTY-EIGHT

CAIN

Being in lockdown at the clubhouse again was not my idea of a fucking good time. But thanks to the events of the past few days, I had little choice. Colt insisted that my actions had instigated a situation that had put the whole of the Company of Sinners MC in jeopardy. All's I knew was that Rosa was back with me and she was unharmed. So I didn't fucking care what Colt said.

The rest of the crew were giving me the cold shoulder. All except for Rosa, Six and Delilah. Although with the way Six was obsessing about the girl from the fucking library, I was beginning to wish he was snubbing me too. All he could talk about was her beautiful eyes and what she could do with the pole when she worked at the club. Man, he had it bad.

Everyone was downstairs playing pool, drinking beer, and generally partying, seeing as there was little else to do when we were on lockdown. But I was being my usual antisocial self. I had taken a bottle of Jack from the bar and gone up to my room. After drinking half of it, I lay on my bed in the dark in just my fitted boxers, staring at the ceiling.

In my drunken half-dozing stupor, I heard the door open and soft footsteps padding across the floor. A familiar fragrance infiltrated my senses, but I knew I was dreaming on account of the fact that it was Kelly's perfume I could smell. A wave of melancholy washed over me as I felt the bed dip. She smelled amazing as she usually did, and I wished so fucking much that it were real. Her feather-light fingertips traced circles up my calves, toward my thighs and up to my cock, which sprang to life at her touch. I inhaled deeply, taking her rose scent into my lungs and picturing her there with me. Loving me even though I didn't fucking deserve her.

She gripped my underwear and pulled them down my legs, allowing my cock to spring free, and I inhaled sharply as she gripped my shaft. Next thing I knew, her fragrance became stronger and I gripped the sheets beneath me as she sank her warm, wet mouth over the tip of my cock and laved at me with her tongue. It felt so good and I wanted the fantasy to last as long as possible. I squeezed my eyes closed tight, and she slid her mouth over me, taking me deep and cradling my balls gently as she did. I groaned as my entire body was filled with intense pleasure.

Pure, hedonistic pleasure.

My heart hammered at my ribs as she nibbled and licked at my sensitive, rigid flesh, moaning in the back of her throat and making vibrations travel down my shaft.

"Fuck... fuck that's so good." My ragged breathing and the sound of her taking me in and out was all that could be heard in the otherwise silent darkness. The wetness of her mouth on me had images flashing through my mind. Long auburn waves trailing across my stomach... Naked breasts pressed against my thighs... Cheeks hollowing as she drew me in... Her green eyes locking on mine as she pleasured me, watching my every reaction.

Fuck, that woman was everything to me. An overwhelming sense of love, adoration, and awe swept through me as my muscles tensed and the movement of her hands increased along with the speed of her sucking. The intensity built and I could hold back no longer. Electric shocks ripped through every nerve ending, and I sky-rocketed as my orgasm shot through me.

"Oh, fuck, Kelly... Kelly... I fucking love you, baby... fucking love you." Momentarily forgetting it was a dream, I reached out to grab her and my hand landed on her head, but as I ran my fingers down toward her chin, her hair stopped at jaw length. I sat bolt upright and scrambled for the lamp on my nightstand.

"What the fuck?"

Delilah sat there naked, straddling my left thigh and circling my navel with her fingertips, smiling up adoringly at me. Her blonde hair was now auburn.

"What the fuck are you doing in my fucking room?" I bellowed at her.

Tilting her head to one side, she licked her glistening lips. "I wanted to please you, and you wouldn't let me."

I ran my hands through my hair. "Are you fucking crazy? Are you fucking out of your mind, woman?" I yanked my leg free and clambered from the bed, knocking her back slightly. "What the fuck were you thinking? And why the fuck do you smell like Kelly?" My heart was trying to escape from my chest, and my fists were clenched as anger and bile bubbled up inside of me.

She dropped her gaze and fiddled with her newly coloured hair. "I heard you talking about her with Six and I found her perfume in your drawer. I figured if I smelled like her and had the same hair colour, you'd like me."

What the fuck? I grabbed my boxers and yanked them up my legs. "Delilah, this is not about a smell or a fucking hair colour, or a fucking blow job. I love her. Do you hear me? I. Fucking. Love. Her. You can't just fucking switch that shit off! And you certainly can't become her by dying your hair and wearing her perfume, you dumb bitch. Fuck! And what the hell are you doing snooping in my drawers anyway? Who the fuck does that shit?"

Every shred of sympathy I had for Delilah and her unrequited crush on me flew out the window. Even watching tears trail down her cheeks did nothing to soften my anger at her actions. I felt fucking violated. Okay, so I had enjoyed the experience when I had thought it was a dream, but fuck. This shit wasn't right.

"Get the fuck out of my room, Delilah. Now!"

She grabbed her pink robe from the floor and dashed for the door just as Six appeared in the doorway. "You lovers had a little tiff?" He sniggered as she shoved past him.

"This is not a fucking joke, man. I'm outta here, dude. This whole place is going crazy. I can't deal, Six." I pulled on my sweatpants and a T-shirt and I too shoved past my friend and stormed into the hallway.

"Whoa, Cain, what happened? Why are you so pissed?"

I stopped in my tracks and swung my body around to face him. Pointing in the direction Delilah left, I shouted, "Delilah broke into my room and stole the perfume I bought that reminded me of Kelly and wore it so that she could smell like her. She even dyed her fucking hair. And then she snuck into my room sucked me off in the dark. She's sick. And I can't be here anymore."

His eyes widened and he shook his head. "Oh, man. That's some fucked-up shit."

"Ya think?" I walked away and arrived at the back door that led outside into the fenced compound. The security lights came on and almost blinded me, so I rubbed my eyes and allowed them to adjust. I walked to the perimeter fence and hooked my fingers through the links, inhaling deeply and trying my best to shed the feeling of unfaithfulness that was twisting at my gut. It was crazy. Kelly was thousands of miles away in Scotland and I was here, and I had been blindsided. But what had just happened turned my stomach.

"Cain! You shouldn't be out here, man. It's not safe." I spun around in the direction of Six's voice but the security lights dazzled me again and all I could see was white spots.

A loud crack rent the silent night air, and a shooting pain sliced through my chest. I clutched my ribs and dropped to my knees as the white spots came again with a vengeance. Numbness seeped into my bones and in the distance I could hear an agonising scream.

"Cain! Noooooo!"

I could make out shapes coming toward me and I tried to lift my hand, but the energy I needed to do so just wasn't available.

I gave into the blackness as it overtook my senses and I fell into the abyss.

———

KELLY

Once again I awoke with a start. This time I was clutching my chest and calling out Cain's name. I couldn't remember the nightmare, but I was certain there had been one. I rubbed my hands over my face as the ache in my chest began to subside and my heart rate calmed. A strange numbness washed over me and I suddenly began to cry.

The stream of tears became a deluge, and sobs racked my body at the unexplainable emptiness I was experiencing. It must have been some nightmare to have such a negative residual effect on me. I allowed the tears to fall and a light in my peripheral vision made me jump. The screen of my cell had oddly lit up, showing me the screen saver. It was the one photo I had of Cain and me—a silly selfie from the day I took the Christmas tree around to his flat.

The phone didn't ring as I had expected it to—as it usually did when it lit up—and the screen became black once again as I let the tears flow...

CHAPTER THIRTY-NINE

KELLY

Half a year had passed since Cain had left for the USA. That equates to one hundred and eighty-two days or, if you want to be picky, four thousand three hundred and eighty-two hours. Not that I had been counting. No... I was trying hard to forget him and move on with my life.

Really I was.

My job was amazing, and I had settled in well to life on the Isle of Skye. So much so, in fact, that I couldn't remember how it felt to live in North Kessock. The old dears I worked with were fantastic and I knew I was making a positive difference to their lives. I had job fulfilment and very little stress, except occasionally when I happened to see a couple in their eighties or nineties holding hands and looking at each other with such love, the old emptiness came back and I couldn't help but mourn the fact that I never would grow old with the one person my heart loved above all others. But it was good enough. It had to be. My colleagues were a great bunch and they had quickly introduced me to the live music scene of the Isle.

Esme visited as often as she could, and Dermott was still trying to win my heart. He was giving me space and time, but he was as tenacious as ever. Although if I'm honest, I was still very shocked that he had feelings for me at all. That particular revelation wasn't one I would recover from in a hurry.

Flowers would often turn up from Dermott, delivered in the little white van from Big Bloomers in Portree. The old chap who carried out the deliveries—Errol—was the husband of Aileen the florist, and I had been getting deliveries so frequently that he and I were on first-name terms. He had even stopped in for tea and shortbread on a few occasions, and we had sat in my kitchen, chatting and putting the world to rights.

People around the place were so friendly, and it was good to be a part of something so positive. Even though I'd had reservations before moving, I knew there and then, sitting with Errol at my wee table, that I would never move back to the mainland.

It was a summer Saturday, and Errol had just been by to deliver yet another huge arrangement. He smiled knowingly as he handed the flowers over to me. With the bouquet was a little card that simply read:

I want to marry you someday Kelly.

Please say you'll think about it.

See you soon,

D

I smiled but rolled my eyes and placed the fragrant flowers in a glass vase that I'd had to buy especially for my frequent deliveries. He was persistent, that was for sure. And the more I thought about him, the more I decided that a life with Dermott wouldn't be so bad. He certainly loved me. But the fact remained that I didn't love him.

His visits, whilst infrequent, were purely platonic. He took me out for lovely dinners, and we took walks along the shores of Loch Portree. We talked and we laughed. He slept in my guest room and brought me breakfast in bed. Being with him felt...

comfortable, like an old pair of jeans that you've had forever and can't bear to throw out. And the more time I spent with him, the more I felt I would be silly to throw Dermott out.

The last time he had been to see me, he had brought a ring and I had cried at the gesture, unable to let go of the sinking feeling inside. It was a white gold band with a single diamond set into it. He had told me that it was a symbol of what he wanted for us in the future. He had asked me to think about it but demanded I didn't answer there and then. I couldn't have said yes, and I suspect he knew it.

He hadn't visited for a month or so since that, and I actually did miss him. Well, his friendship and company anyway. I took that as a good sign. The ring had been on my right hand a few times as I had tried to get my head around *us*. But I still couldn't bring myself to wear it on my left.

I felt sure he'd be surprising me fairly soon, because regardless of the fact that I had pleaded with him to call first, he insisted on turning up on my doorstep with more flowers. I had laughed when Errol commented that he got the impression Dermott was keen to help our local economy.

Once the latest delivery was in water and placed on the coffee table in the living room, I took my mug of steaming, fresh coffee into the back garden and breathed in the warm air that smelled of wild flowers and fresh pine. The small wooded area at the back of the cottages seemed to have a life of its own in the summer, and I had already seen rabbits and encountered a young deer prancing through the trees. The island was vibrant with colour as the June sun cast a warm glow over my surroundings and a feeling of serenity washed over me.

I was right where I was supposed to be.

And Dermott had said he wanted to be wherever I was.

Making a concerted effort to rid my mind of confusing thoughts of Dermott, I sat there thinking about the fun of the previous week when I had accompanied some of the residents I worked with on a walk around the local countryside. But as I was lost in an amusing memory of one of the staff stepping in some kind of animal dung, I heard the doorbell. I guessed it was the postman, as he hadn't been and I was expecting a delivery of books that I'd ordered online. I placed my coffee mug on the wooden garden table and made my way into the house. I opened the front door and was surprised to find Errol had returned.

"Sorry to bother you again, lass, but I must have missed this batch back at the shop. I got a wee telling off from Aileen when I got back." He chuckled as he handed me a hand-tied bouquet that was more modest than the last one but beautiful nonetheless.

"Good grief, he's on form today, isn't he?" I laughed.

"Aye, lass. That he is. Just marry the lad and put him out his misery, eh? Maybe then we'll be able to find some new customers!" Errol turned and walked back toward his van.

"Can I offer you some coffee for your trouble, Errol? I've just made a pot and I baked chocolate-chip shortbread this time," I called after him.

"Oh, I'd love to, but... no thank you, hen. I should get back before I create more trouble for myself." He laughed as he climbed into the driver's seat and switched on the engine. Pavarotti belted out "Nessun Dorma" from the van's CD player, and it floated through the open window as the van pulled away. Errol waved his hand and I watched him retreat back to the main road.

I closed my front door and carried the beautiful flowers through to the living room. Plonking myself down on the couch, I pulled off the card.

"Okay, Dermott, what do you have to say for yourself this time?"

I read the words aloud. "Meet me on the shore of Loch Portree at three. I'll be sitting by the boathouse near the jetty."

I smiled. "Ah, so you're here for your next not-so-subtle woo-

Kelly visit, are you?" My heart skipped anxiously as the thought that he may propose again flitted through my mind. What the hell would I say? How could I let him down and stop his persistent proposals? I wanted to return to just being friends. I needed friends.

There was no time to dwell on it. I only had an hour to get ready.

I placed my iPod into the docking station and hit random. "Set Fire to the Third Bar" filled my auditory senses and I quickly hit skip. I didn't need memories to cloud the good mood of the day. My dear friend was coming to see me, and he wouldn't want me to be all puffy faced after crying over someone from my past.

After showering, I shaggily dried my long wavy tresses and dressed in a floaty white cotton skirt and a turquoise vest top. My cheeks were flushed from the heat of the water, and so I needed no other make-up apart from a little berry lip gloss. I slipped on my beaded turquoise sandals and grabbed my car keys.

The drive to the shore wasn't too far, and I had the windows of the car open to allow the warm summer breeze to circulate around me. A smile played on my lips as I took in the vista. The vast open spaces made breathing feel so much easier than in the large town I had come from. The cloudless blue sky above acted as a stunning backdrop, highlighting the rugged mountains of the Quiraing.

After a short journey, I pulled off the main road into a gravel car park. I climbed out of the car and walked through the line of trees to the shingles at the edge of the loch. There was no sign of Dermott at first; but as I glanced around, I could see I could see a figure off in the distance skimming stones, and so I made my way toward him.

The sun was dazzling me, and as I tried to shield my eyes, I realised my mistake. Dammit! That's not bloody Dermott. I huffed and turned. There was another figure further back in the direction I had just come from, and I was just about to begin walking again when someone grabbed my arm from behind me. With a pounding heart, I swung around, ready to hit out—and was stunned by the most amazing pair of cerulean eyes.

"C... Cain?" I gasped with wide eyes and a racing heart as his mouth crashed into mine.

CHAPTER FORTY

KELLY

When the kiss ended, I stood there blinking, trying to figure out if I was dreaming. It certainly wouldn't have been the first time. But his lips were so familiar and warm and the contact had set my blood on fire. The masculine, cedar wood scent of his skin infiltrated my senses and my heart pounded with desire at the familiarity of it. His face was covered in a full but neat beard that had felt deliciously soft against my face, and his hair was swept back and tied in a knot at the back of his head. He looked very different than the last time I had seen him.

But there was no mistaking those eyes.

"I'm... I'm not Cain," he told me as he gazed down longingly at me.

Confusion washed over me and I shook my head. I was dreaming. Oh, no. Please don't let it be a dream. I swallowed and scrunched my brow. "I don't understand... You... you look like—" The mind was such a powerful yet cruel thing. I should have remembered that fact. I must have fallen asleep after my shower. That was the only explanation.

"Allow me to introduce myself, Kelly." He held out his hand and took mine. "I'm Cameron Iss. And you're still beautiful."

I dug my nails into the palm of my free hand, still unable to grasp what the hell was happening. Dizziness overcame me and the heat of the sun suddenly overwhelmed me. My knees began to buckle and I felt myself being scooped up into big, strong arms.

I opened my eyes and glanced up into a concerned blue gaze. Cain—Cameron?—smiled down at me. "You had me a little scared there for a minute. Are you okay?" He was still there and my heart skipped a beat.

"I'm... I'm fine... Just... a little confused."

He squeezed me to him in his arms. "I'd better explain, huh?"

"You better had, yes."

He carried me until we got to my car, and then he set me on my feet. Everything was so surreal, and I kept expecting to wake up at home, sobbing and alone in my bed.

"You kept your car." He smiled as he smoothed his hand over the bonnet. I couldn't reply. I had no words. Only confusion. He took the keys from my hand and opened the passenger-side door. "Get in."

He somehow knew the way to my house, and we drove along without speaking. When we stopped, he climbed out of the car and came around to open my door again. He held out his hand, and I slipped mine into it before we made our way to the front door.

I fumbled with the keys and dropped them, so he bent to pick them up and proceeded to open the lock for me, just as he had so long ago. Still without words, we walked through the house to the living room, and I sank down onto the couch before my legs gave way with the shock of the whole situation. He sat beside me.

"Am I dreaming? Am I going to wake up and find myself alone?" I whispered.

He shook his head. "You're not dreaming, Kelly. And I will explain. But my God, I've missed you so much, and all I can think about right now is making love to you."

Without needing any explanation and without any cognitive thought, I was drawn to him once again. I clambered into his lap and crushed my mouth to his, gripping his hair and yanking out the tie that bound it. I whimpered as I revelled in how good it felt to be held by him again. He slipped one hand around my back and pulled me hard into his chest. His other hand found its way into my hair and he breathed deeply through his nose—an urgent, ragged breath that spoke of desperation and lust.

Our tongues tangled and I couldn't get close enough to him. All the feelings I'd had before came rushing back tenfold, and my eyes overflowed with tears.

He stood with me in his arms and began to carry me toward the wooden staircase by the front door. Our mouths remained locked together, and the kiss gained fervour. How the hell we made it up the stairs, I'll never know.

We almost collapsed through the door into my room and he placed me down so that my feet touched the floor. He stood there just staring at me for a few moments. His chest heaving and his eyes sparkling. I couldn't take the barriers between us any longer, and so I stripped the clothes from my body as he watched me. When I was naked before him, I stepped closer and smoothed my hands up his sleeves to grip his biceps. His muscles tensed under my caress, but he still didn't speak. It was as if he were mesmerised by me.

Suddenly, he snapped out of his trance-like state, reached up and smoothed his hands down my neck, over my collar bone, and over my breasts, as he sighed deeply.

He rolled my nipples under his thumbs, shaking his head. "I'd forgotten how beautiful you are," he whispered. I watched his gaze move over my skin as if he were memorising my every curve. The urgency had gone, but the desire was still evident in his eyes.

I gripped the hem of his shirt and dragged it up his body and he stooped, allowing me to remove it completely. There was a new and rather alarming addition to his chest. But it wasn't a tattoo—it was a large newly healed scar that looked distinctly like a bullet wound. As I trailed my gaze over his pecs and down his muscular arms, I noticed that the tattooed word "Cosmic" on his forearm had been filled in so that it was now illegible. The woman draped over the lettering was still there but she looked more like me than she had before. I wanted to know why these things on his body had changed and why he was so brutally scarred, but he removed something from his pocket, drawing my attention away. He then unfastened the buttons at the front of his jeans and pushed them down his legs. Once he had kicked them aside, my gaze was travelled down his sculpted body to his thick arousal. My core clenched as my own need for him became more urgent.

He cupped my face and gazed at me with lust-clouded eyes. "I need to be inside you, Kelly. I need you right now. It's been so long, and I don't know how I got through the last six months without you." His voice cracked as he spoke. "But I don't want to go through another day alone. I can't be without you any longer."

The urgency in his words brought me back to earth, and I stepped back from him to sit on the bed. Keeping my gaze on his, I lay back and opened my thighs in wanton invitation to him. His chest was rising and falling fast again, and he knelt on the edge of the bed. Ripping open the packet he was holding, he deftly slipped the condom over his thick shaft and moved up my body. With his rigid cock poised at my entrance, he leaned down and suckled on my nipple. I gasped and allowed my head to roll back as I basked in the sensation of being close to him again.

"Later, after I've explained all the shit that's happened in my life, I'm going to make love to you and I'll take my time then, I promise you that. But right now... right now I just need to fuck you. I need to lose myself in you. I've missed you so much, and I don't think I'll be able to hold back." He smoothed a hand down my chest and gripped my breast roughly, eliciting another sharp gasp from me as he tweaked my nipple.

I couldn't seem to speak and so I reached down, gripped his firm arse, and pulled him into me. He released my breast and groaned in pleasure as he sunk himself into my body, holding his large frame up on his forearms. "Oh, fuck, I've missed you so much, baby, so fucking much," he mumbled as he covered my mouth with his and pulled my lower lip between his teeth.

He began to move slowly at first. Sliding in and out of my sex with such restraint that I wondered if he had changed his mind about needing to just fuck me. But no sooner had the thought entered my head than he picked up the pace as carnal growls left his body. Grinding his pubic bone into my clit and pounding his cock deep inside me, hitting every sensitive place and drawing moans from my throat. I could feel my breasts bounce as he thrust, and each time it happened, my nipples grazed his chest, building my need to climax to the point of sheer desperation.

Each rough, delicious movement knocked the air from my lungs in a pleasured grunt until I didn't care anymore how loud I was being. I completely let go. I dug my nails into his skin, and he suckled on my neck in between muttering things I couldn't make out.

———

CAMERON

Being totally enveloped and immersed in Kelly's pussy was just as amazing as I remembered. Every noise she made only fuelled the fire burning beneath my skin as I pounded into her. In the back of my mind, I hoped that I wasn't being too rough, but the way she moaned and dug her nails into me told me that she needed this kind of connection as much as I did.

In between deep thrusts, I kissed her neck and told her how fucking amazing she felt as her pussy pulled me deeper. And how wet she was for me. Fuck. She was so damn sexy and she didn't even fucking know how much she affected me.

I pulled away and locked my gaze on her as I clenched my jaw. "You feel amazing, Kelly, I can't believe how well you fit me. It's like we were made just for this. Just for each other."

She gripped my shoulders and wrapped her legs around me, and I couldn't hold back any longer. My hips mirrored her movements and her head fell back. Her lips parted and the most erotic noises left her body as I buried myself deep inside her over and over.

"Come for me, Kelly I want to feel you come around my cock." My words were her undoing and she pulsed around me, triggering my own climax. I let go of a string of emotion-filled expletives as I emptied myself and clung to her while she nuzzled her face into my neck.

When my breathing had calmed, I opened my eyes to find hers closed. Tears were leaving glistening trails down her cheeks, and her chin quivered.

Panicking that I'd hurt her, I wiped the tears away with my thumbs. "Hey... Kelly, baby, don't cry. Shhhh. I'm so sorry for not being here. Please forgive me. I never stopped thinking about you. And I never stopped loving you."

Her eyes opened, and a sob left her throat as she pulled me down and buried her face in the crook of my neck once more. We stayed there, just holding each other for what felt like hours, and I couldn't help the niggling sense in the back of my mind that instead of being a kind of reunion for us, this was actually goodbye.

CHAPTER FORTY-ONE

CAMERON

I must have dozed off because I when I opened my eyes, she was gone. Worrying that my fears had been realised, I grabbed my jeans and slipped them on, not bothering with my underwear or shirt, and I ran down the stairs and through to the living room; but she wasn't there either. With a pounding heart and twisted gut, I made my way through to the back of the house.

She had to be there.

"Hey," I whispered as I arrived behind her where she stood looking out the kitchen window. The sun was beginning to set, and it cast an orange glow above the trees out back. I slipped my arms around her waist and kissed her neck.

"Dermott wants to marry me."

I froze. The words stung like needles to my heart. Swallowing hard, I dropped my arms and stepped back. "What?"

She sniffed and lowered her head forward. "He's been visiting and sending flowers. We've done a lot of talking, and I know he's serious about me. He gave me a ring and says he wants to offer me a life with him... here on Skye."

It was like a blow to my solar plexus, and I gripped my chest where the bullet had passed through me. I was losing her all over again. "Oh... I see... H-have you accepted?" The question tasted like bile as it fell from my lips, and I was pretty sure I didn't want to hear the answer.

She shook her head no. I should've been relieved but her general demeanour told me I had nothing to feel good about. I nodded silently even though she wasn't looking at me, and I allowed the news to sink in. "Why are you telling me this now, Kelly?"

"Because I have a feeling he's going to turn up any day now, and I don't know what to do. He has a habit of turning up unannounced to surprise me."

The next question almost choked me as a knot formed in my throat making it hard for me to speak. "Do you... do you love him?"

She dropped her head forward and her shoulders slumped. "Yes."

I exhaled the contents of my lungs and slumped onto a chair beside the small wooden table just inside the room. "Fuck." What the hell had I done?

She turned to face me. "But I'm not in love with him, and that's the problem."

I was unsure how the hell to deal with this new information. My head began to pound and I pinched the bridge of my nose. My world was falling away and my stomach dropped with it.

She came and sat opposite me at the table. "He and I are perfect for each other. We're alike in so many ways. We understand each other, Cain."

I gritted my teeth. "My name is Cameron," I informed her, although what fucking difference it made I wasn't sure. Whatever the hell my name was, I could sense I was getting my heart handed to me.

Her brow furrowed as if it was finally dawning on her that I'd changed my name. "Why are you suddenly Cameron?"

"It's a long story." I closed my eyes. I couldn't look at her.

"Why do you have a scar on your chest?"

"It's part of the long story."

She sighed in what sounded like frustration. "Are you going to tell me?"

I opened my eyes and she was staring at me. Part of me wanted to ask why she cared enough to ask, since it was Dermott she loved and not me. Another part of me, the part that never existed until I met her, understood that my pain at losing her didn't justify lashing out at her. "I was shot."

She gasped and covered her mouth. "When? Why?"

"Rival gang. They didn't do a good enough job the first time." I laughed darkly. "Seems they fucked up yet again."

"Cain... Cameron... why are you here?"

Another humourless laugh left me. "I came back to be with you, Kelly. Rosa and I had to leave the US for our own safety. And all I've been able to think about since I left North Kessock is my Scottish girl. And so... stupidly I see now... I figured I'd come back to you."

A look of incredulity washed over her features. "It's been six months without a word. Did you expect me to just be waiting?"

I shook my head. She did have a point. With no contact, how the hell could she know what I was thinking? But then again, she had asked for me not to contact her. "No... but I suppose I hoped you would."

She didn't reply, but instead more tears began to leave her eyes, and all I wanted to do was hold her.

I stood, needing to create some space and needing time to gather my thoughts. The problem was, there was nowhere for me to go, and so I made my way back to the bedroom and got myself dressed. When I arrived back at the kitchen door, Kelly was still sitting at the kitchen table, looking dazed.

As I entered the room, she looked up at me with such sadness in her beautiful emerald eyes. "Cameron... before you left, you told me that you couldn't be what I needed. You said that and you meant it. What's changed?"

I smiled sadly. "Everything has changed, Kelly." I sat opposite her again, desperate to take her hand, but I fought the urge. I looked down at my fingers in the hope that I would be able to continue to fight it. "I guess I realised that although Utah has been where I live, I don't belong there anymore. It's not my home. Things went to shit. After I was shot, I was in hospital for a while, and I had a lot of time to think. I'd wanted out of the club for a while before all the fucking rival gang shit. But almost dying... again... just cemented that. Colt and the rest of the guys had a meeting while I was out of commission, and they decided it was best for me to leave Utah. But the only place I want to be is... wherever you are.

"So... I made contact with the hospital in North Kessock, and they said you'd left. I couldn't get anything else out of them, and I thought it was all over then. But we got on a plane and went to Inverness anyway. I had to just be there again. Where I'd known you." I dared to glance up at her and my heart cracked. Tears were streaming down her face and her eyes were closed. The urge to hold her rose up again and I clenched my fists. "Somehow... maybe it was fate, I don't know... I happened to bump into your friend Esme last week."

Her eyes sprang open and widened. "What? You saw Esme? But she didn't tell me she—"

It was clear that she was getting angry at her friend's apparent betrayal, and so I rushed to explain. "I took her for coffee and explained everything. But I made her swear not to say anything to you about seeing me. She reluctantly gave me your address even though she said we were wasting our time. She also said I broke your heart and that you still loved me. That filled me with hope, and we came here."

She closed her eyes again and covered her face with her hands.

I noticed a new addition to her finger. A white gold ring with diamonds. Fuck... Dermott is pretty serious, huh? I should've been happy that it wasn't on her wedding ring finger, but she was still wearing the damn thing. I pushed the hurt down... deep down, and tried to swallow past the lump that had begun to tighten my throat. "We have new names... new passports... new identities. Cameron and Rayna Iss." My voice broke as I explained, and my eyes remained locked on the stones glinting in the light. I laughed and lowered my gaze to my hands once more. "I think I got attached to that name because it reminds me of how you and I had met." I fell silent for a few moments, and when I lifted my head again, she was watching me intently and her eyes were still glistening with tears. Keeping my gaze locked on hers, I carried on. "I had my tats worked over. You would never know that I'd had any connection to Cosmic. Where my back piece used to say Company of Sinners, there's a whole new scene of ink. Roses to remind me of you. A broken heart to show what I felt when I left you."

She remained silent, just listening and watching me, and so I decided to keep going. "It was weird, you know... They held a funeral for Cain and Rosa. They spread the word that the gunshot had killed me and that Rosa had taken her own life through grief. And so from that point, we both ceased to exist. It was for the best. Well, that's what they kept telling us. I'm not so sure, to be honest with you. But anyways, when they heard about the funeral, I think the Legion realised that there had been too much death between the two clubs, and they called a kind of truce. This—coming here—was supposed to be a fresh start for us both." I sighed and the weight of my situation pushed me down. Kelly was marrying Dermott. I had no place in Utah, and now no place in Scotland either. "I guess I'll have to rethink things now."

She stared at me, still not speaking but with a trembling chin.

I stood again and walked around to stand before her. "Look, Kelly... I know I said some dumb shit, and I know that I'm not the best fit for you." My voice broke as I tried to get the rest of my words out, and the loss I was feeling twisted at my heart. "Fuck, you can do so much better, and no doubt Dermott is all the fucking man you'll ever really need. But the thing is... you fit me, Kelly. And regardless of what I said before about not wanting the marriage and commitment thing after Melody... I was stupid. And I would have made an exception for you. I want you to know that. You would be the only woman I could ever consider making that kind of commitment to. The only exception, Kelly." I bent and kissed her forehead and then with one last long look into her beautiful green eyes, I left.

As I closed the door behind me, I paused in the hope that she would come running after me.

She didn't.

I scraped my hair back and tied it up as I walked away from the woman I loved with all my heart, and as I did, a car pulled up and a guy with dirty-blonde hair climbed out. He was holding a huge bouquet of flowers in one hand, a small blue gift bag with white ribbon in the other, and he was grinning like an idiot.

It dawned on me who he was.

"Dermott," I growled to myself.

He heard me and stopped.

"Yeah?" The look of confusion told me that he was rifling through his mind trying to place who I was. But I knew we'd never actually met. Suddenly his eyes widened. "Oh... you're... it's..."

I nodded. "Cameron. I'm Cameron," I told him, and then I walked away without looking back.

CHAPTER FORTY-TWO

CAMERON

With a heavy and defeated heart, I opened the front door to the little cottage I was renting for me and Rayna. It was still fucking weird calling Rosa by a totally different name, but she was doing great with remembering to call me Cameron. She even called me Cam on occasion; she figured, she informed me, that she'd shorten it if it were my real name. Crazy kid.

There was a mouth-watering smell of baking emanating from the kitchen, and I made my way through to find Rayna putting the finishing touches to a chocolate cake with chocolate frosting. It smelled amazing, but I knew why she'd made it, and it hurt like hell that I was about to let her down. I walked over and ruffled her hair before placing a kiss on the top of her newly dyed red hair. And when I say red, I mean the colour they paint mailboxes in the UK. It suited her and somehow made her eyes even more vivid blue.

"Hey, big bro. How'd it go with Kelly? Did you propose on the shore of the loch? When do I get to meet her? Is she your wee lassie now?" Her barrage of questions and terrible attempt at a Scottish accent made me smile in spite of my heartache. She was nothing if not enthusiastic about love.

But my smile soon faded. "I'm sorry, sweetheart. She's..." I cleared my throat. "She's marrying someone else."

Rayna dropped the utensil she was using and flung herself into my arms. "Oh my gosh, no! That wasn't supposed to happen. I don't understand. You loved each other. It's only been six months or so."

"Yeah... but sometimes love just isn't enough."

She pulled away and glared at me. "You're wrong. Love is always enough. Take that back."

I shrugged as the weight of the realisation that I had lost Kelly forever pushed down on me and my lip trembled. I fought the emotion hard. The last thing I wanted to do was break down in front of my kid sister. "Not this time, Ray."

She scrunched her brow and shook her head defiantly. "But you'll make it work. She'll see sense."

I cupped her cheek and kissed her forehead. "I'm gonna go take a nap, kiddo." I turned and walked away as she began slamming the dishes into the sink.

As I made my way up the stairs, I stuck my fingers into my pocket and pulled out the silver ring I'd been keeping there. Holding it aloft, I watched as the tiny diamonds set into the infinity symbol glinted in the light coming through the glass in the front door. It wasn't an engagement ring. More of a promise of what I had wanted from our future. It was such a shame that Dermott had beaten me to it.

Clutching the silver band in my fist, I closed my eyes as sadness washed over me.

———

Kelly

Dermott turned around to blow a kiss in my direction as he left. Completely daft but such a sweet guy all the same.

I twisted the ring he gave me around my finger. I didn't deserve his love.

The day so far had been an exhausting period of discussions and difficult decisions, and I felt drained. As I stood there watching his retreating form, I spotted a young woman wearing post-box-red hair, skinny jeans, a white tank top, and bright white trainers, walking down toward my house. I glanced along at the other houses, but everyone appeared to be out, and I absently felt for the poor wee girl for having wasted a very long walk from the main road.

As I turned to go back inside, a voice stopped me in my tracks. "Kelly!"

Turning around again, I watched as the young woman jogged toward me, looking rather upset. "It is Kelly, right?"

"Yes... yes, I'm Kelly. And... who are you?" I didn't really need an answer, as the American accent gave her away.

"My name is... um... Rayna... Rayna Iss. I'm—"

"Cameron's sister. Yes, I figured that out, actually. What are you doing here?"

She stopped at the end of my front path and folded her arms defensively across her chest as she narrowed her eyes. "I need to talk with you."

I nodded. "Well, you'd better come in, then."

Surprise registered on her face as if she'd thought I would've sent her away. But when I stepped inside she followed me.

"Can I get you a cup of tea or coffee, Rayna?"

"Um... sure. Coffee, thanks. Your accent's cute."

I smiled. "Thanks. So is yours."

We walked through to the kitchen, and I gestured for her to sit. She glanced at the table for a moment, still appearing to have doubts about my reaction toward her. She sat and folded her arms once more. "He never stopped thinking about you." Blunt and to the point.

I kept my back to her and prepared the mugs before me. "Yeah. He said that when he came to see me."

"He thinks he's not worthy of you. He just gave up because he thinks that the other guy is more your type." With the way she said your type I could imagine her making little air quotes, and I smiled to myself. "But the truth is, Kelly your type is whomever you're in love with. And you're in love with my brother."

And crack went my heart. She was right.

She heaved a frustrated sigh and slapped her hands on her thighs. "When Melody got pregnant, he always said he'd never marry her. Did you know that? He loved her. Of course he did. He adored her and took care of her like she was some fragile little doll. But marriage? Nah... that wasn't something he could ever see working for him. Even she wasn't enough to make him want that kind of commitment. But you. Whole other story. You were the one exception to that rule. Marrying you is something he wanted even though he couldn't admit it to you. And the reason he couldn't admit it is because he still feels he's not good enough for you. The criminal biker and the shrink. It's not what happens in real life, you know?"

I slowly turned to face her as my stomach dropped. I'd had no idea about that particular fact. He hadn't told me that he hadn't wanted to marry Melody. As far as I was concerned, she was the love of his life and I was second fiddle to anything he had ever felt for her.

I carried the two mugs across to the table and with shaking hands I placed them down as carefully as I could. "He... he wasn't going to marry Melody?"

She snorted. "Nope. I was so damned angry with him over the whole thing. He'd been such a player before her. A different woman every night. Leaving 'em begging for more. It was disgusting. Truly. But you can't choose your family. And I do love the bastard. Then he met Mel and he seemed to change. Seeing him being monogamous was weird. And boy, did Mel come in for some shit from his other hos. But all that said... he wouldn't do the marriage thing. Insisted that no woman would convince him otherwise." She tentatively sipped at her steaming coffee and stared at my hands. I glanced down too and realised that the ring Dermott gave me looked out of place even on my right hand. As if she knew what I was thinking Rayna chimed in, "The idiot. Did Cam even give you the ring he got you?"

I snapped my gaze up to meet her vivid blue eyes straight on and opened my mouth as the words took root in my mind and echoed around my head like I was standing in the Grand Canyon. "W-what?"

"I'll take that as a no, huh?" She placed her mug down and held both hands up in a cease gesture. "Don't freak out, okay? He wasn't gonna propose or anything dumb like that. Not yet anyway. He knew he had a lot of making up to do. But he wanted to show you he was committed to you. He got you this gorgeous infinity symbol ring. Infinity, Kelly." She raised her eyebrows to punctuate her point before huffing out a long breath through puffed cheeks. "Fucking coward never even gave it to you. Shit, what an asshole my brother is, huh? How the hell are you gonna know he means business if he doesn't go the extra mile?"

Assuming the questions were rhetorical, I stared open-mouthed, still trying to process the fact that he had bought me a ring.

A ring with an infinity symbol on it.

A bloody ring, for goodness' sake!

"Tell me something, Kelly. Why would you marry someone else when it's clear you're crazy about my dumb-ass brother? I mean, if you didn't love him you'd have told me to leave by now."

Her words brought me back to earth with a bump. "Marry someone else?"

"Yeah. The guy who was leaving as I got here. I take it he's the 'perfect' guy for you?" *Yep...* she did the air quotes thing. "The one that my hulking, tattooed, jerk of a brother couldn't clean the boots of?"

What the hell did she mean that Cain... Cameron couldn't clean Dermott's boots? "I'm... I'm sorry Rayna I have no clue what you mean by that."

She rolled her eyes like an errant teenager and shook her head. "Fuck, seriously? Jeez, I'm only just an adult and I see things so much clearer than you douches." She heaved a disgruntled sigh. "Cam arrived home looking all broken-hearted. Said you were marrying some other guy. I get here and see Mr Perfect-Ass leaving and blowing you a kiss. In my head, that's a serious two-plus-two-making-four situation right there."

Ah. Okay, now I get it. I disappeared into my head once again, and my thoughts left my mouth before I could rein them in. "Dermott is just... so right for me." Obviously I was still trying to process this new batch of information that Rayna had dumped on me like a heavy snowfall.

Sadness washed over her pretty features, and for a moment I thought she was going to cry. But instead she leaned across the table and squeezed my arm gently. "Look... if you really do believe that... then I wish you all the happiness in the world. I really do. I'd... I'd better go. I'm sorry to have taken up your time. I had to try though. For Cain's sake. You understand right?"

Hearing her call him by his real name again snapped me from my daze. "Yes... of course you did. I totally understand. You're just looking out for your brother."

She stood and walked around the table to hug me, and my eyes suddenly began to sting as the sweet but feisty young woman held me tight.

Her voice wavered as she spoke. "It's a shame, you know. I was kinda looking forward to having a big sister. Be happy, Kelly. Whatever you do, make sure it's what makes you happy." She released me from her embrace and walked away; and as I heard the front door close behind her, I began to sob.

CHAPTER FORTY-THREE

CAMERON

I'd never had a doorbell before. And lying there in bed after my feeble attempt at trying to sleep, I was ready to rip the fucking thing from the wall.

"Rayna! Could you get the goddamn door?" I shouted at the top of my lungs, but she didn't answer. "Ray-na!" I shouted again. Still no fucking answer. She'd obviously gone out in a bad mood after our earlier conversation. I huffed and pulled my jeans up my legs and made my way down the stairs.

I almost yanked the door off its hinges in my frustration. An old guy stood there holding a bouquet of flowers. It obviously hadn't taken Rayna long to get an admirer. I frowned. "Sorry, sir. My sister's out. Can I sign for them?"

A look of confusion settled on his wrinkled features. "Oh... erm... these are for you, I think, young man. Are you... are you Cameron?"

For a split second in my sleep-fogged mind, I almost said no dude, my name's Cain. "Oh... um, yeah... yeah, that's me."

"Well, here you go, sonny." He handed me the small hand-tied bunch of roses, and I inhaled the sweet scent of them as I took them from him. I was immediately transported into Kelly's arms, and I had to shake my head to dislodge the disconcerting image in my mind.

The old guy brandished something at me. "Oh, and this goes with them." He handed me a CD. I furrowed my brow and took it from him. The envelope was blank.

"Thank you. Do you happen to know who sent them?"

The old guy shrugged and turned away without speaking, leaving me to wonder who the hell had sent a bearded ex-biker flowers. The one person who came to mind was Kelly, but I didn't want to be right, because what could they mean but goodbye?

I inhaled the intoxicating scent again before placing the flowers on the coffee table, and I pulled the CD out of the sleeve. A piece of paper dropped to the floor and I bent to grab it.

Hi.

I know we don't know each other, but it appears that this song means something to you that I could never understand. It turns out that what's right in theory isn't always right in practise.

Just listen, okay?

And whatever you do... don't let her go.

The note wasn't signed. Curiosity got the better of me, so I switched on my stereo, opened the CD, drawer and placed the disc in the tray.

I hesitated, hit play, and waited.

As the opening bars of the song began, a shiver travelled down my spine and I slumped onto the chair beside me. The song took me back to my plane journey home to Utah. The female voice of Paramore's lead vocalist sang the message that Kelly had sent to me the day I left. That I was her only exception. It was a phrase I'd said to her earlier in the day when I had left her house. It was a phrase that rang true in so many fucking ways when it came to Kelly that it hurt so bad to listen.

After the life she'd had growing up, she was still willing to give me a chance. Me. Someone who represented everything that was wrong in a man. And I had blown it by going back to America and not contacting her at all. It was what she'd asked me to do, but why the hell hadn't I fought harder for her?

I would have married her. No one else had made me feel that way. She was my only exception. But... the flowers were from someone telling me to not let her go.

Then it hit me.

Dermott had sent the flowers and the CD. Maybe he wasn't quite as much of a prick as I'd thought.

The realisation hit. She must have told him no. Fuck! Needing to see her, I ran to the front door and ripped it open, ready to run all the fucking way to her home barefoot if necessary. But what I found on my doorstep almost jolted my heart to a stop. There before me stood a beautiful, auburn-haired, green-eyed woman.

"Kelly?" Her name left my body as a quick exhale as shock stunned me to the spot.

She gasped. "Oh... I was just about to knock. I... I made a mistake, Cameron."

She didn't want me after all. The world crashed down around me.

Tears sprang from her eyes. "I can't be with Dermott."

My heart was trying to burst out of my chest as I stared at her. "You... you can't?"

"No..." Her voice wavered as she continued, "Because I'm head over heels in love with my only exception. I... I told Dermott no. I told him everything. He... he was shocked at first, but he said he understands because he loves me the same way I love you. He left and said he had something to do... somewhere to go, and I was worried he would turn up here and then... Rayna turned up on my doorstep, and she thought I was marrying him and—" Her words came out in a rush as if she thought she needed to say everything in one breath before I told her to get the hell out of my life.

But in one long stride I stepped over the threshold, scooped her up in my arms, and crushed my lips to hers. I clung to her like I was never letting her go again and carried her into the house, kicking the door closed behind me.

———

KELLY

When he opened the door he stood before me shirtless and sleep mussed. His shaggy hair falling over his forehead was begging for me to sweep it back. I trailed my gaze over his taut flesh and my body tingled as I remembered the feel of his skin on mine. He was the most gorgeous man I'd ever seen and my heart squeezed in my chest at the mere sight of him. Would he forgive me? Could he?

I had come here needing to explain. Needing to tell him exactly what had happened. But I was sure it was too late. What if Rayna had got here first? What if she had told him her version of things? But he hadn't given me a chance to finish explaining. When his arms encircled me and he lifted me from the doorstep, my heart soared. He crushed his lips to mine and carried me up the stairs to his room. I swiped the tears from my cheeks as the song that meant so much to me—to both of us, I now knew— floated through the air and enveloped us as we were locked in a passionate kiss.

Once inside his room, my feet reconnected with the floor. He cupped my face and shook his head. "You're really here? Or am I dreaming?" His voice was a hoarse, disbelieving whisper.

I couldn't speak and so I pulled myself up on my toes and

kissed him with every ounce of the love I had held for him since he lay sleeping in a hospital bed all those months ago. He returned my kiss with just as much fervour, like he couldn't get enough of my lips. And that was okay because I couldn't get enough of his.

Keeping our gazes on each other's body, we removed our clothing piece by piece—neither of us wanting anything between us but skin—and once we were naked, he dropped to his knees before me. He pressed his nose into the soft line of hairs covering my pussy and inhaled. "You always smell so fucking good." His actions and his words made my nipples peak and my core muscles clench with need. He gripped my behind with his hands, and I stroked his hair tenderly as he nuzzled me and slipped his tongue into my sex to taste me, circling my clit with precision. I groaned in ecstasy at the intimate contact, and he held me to him as he began to place kisses everywhere he could reach.

It was all too much.

Too good to be true.

He stood and with one swift, deft motion, he lifted me and laid me back on the bed. He stroked his hand down my chest, leaving it resting over my heart for a moment as his gaze penetrated my soul. Then, dipping his head, he sucked my nipple into his mouth as he caressed the other one with his fingertips, squeezing and rolling the sensitive bud around. The sensation of intense pleasure shot through my entire body like shafts of light and sparked at the junction of my thighs, making me close my eyes and bite down on my lip to stifle a desperate moan.

I was on the verge of begging him to fuck me.

To love me.

I needed to feel that connection again. To have him inside of my body, not just my heart and my soul—he had already left his permanent mark there.

I heard his breath hitch as he continued to touch me with

reverence. "My God, you're so fucking beautiful. How the hell did I think I'd live without you?" His voice cracked, filled with emotion.

I opened my eyes and they locked immediately on his vivid blue irises. I reached out to touch his face. "You don't have to think about that now." And then, purely out of selfishness, I added, "But you did promise you'd make love to me slowly."

He needed no further encouragement as he smiled and moved his body to cover mine. I parted my thighs, and my wet pussy pulsed in readiness for him. Keeping his eyes focused on mine, he buried his cock deep in my body once again, connecting with me not only physically but emotionally. He lowered his mouth to mine, stealing my breath in a kiss filled with his own love and need.

Our breath mingled as we explored each other's body, re-familiarising ourselves with every curve and indentation and remembering what elicited those erotic, pleasured moans and gasps.

In all the time we'd been apart and in all the time I had mentally beaten myself up over my feelings for him, never once had they subsided; and as he moved inside of me, driving me toward my delicious release, he muttered words of love and adoration and peppered my skin with feather-light kisses once more.

His movements were slower and more measured than they had been before. He reached down between us and circled his fingers over my clit, forcing me to tighten around him which in turn triggered a deep, throaty groan to be drawn from his chest. Pulling myself up onto my elbows, I watched in awe as his cock sank into me and withdrew... sank in and withdrew.

He was right. We fit together so well. We were made for each other; and when he pulled himself and me up to a sitting position, I gazed into his eyes as he held me close. Our glistening, sweaty bodies slipping and sliding together in perfect synchronisation as we found our release together. He swallowed my cries as he clung to me like he would never let me go. And at that moment I wanted more than anything for him to hold me and love me forever.

In our connection we found a soul-deep love that no amount of miles, bullets, or taboo situations could ruin. And hours later as the soundtrack to our passionate reconnection looped around, once more reminding us that we were indeed each other's only exception, we fell asleep in each other's arms.

This was it.

This was real.

This was forever.

EPILOGUE

Two years later...

CAMERON

She takes my breath away.

There's no other way to put it.

It's been the same right from the first moment I laid eyes on her as she hovered over me in the hospital bed all pert breasts, amazing smell, and sexy-as-all-get-out Scottish accent. And now here I am waiting for her to say she'll be mine forever. She's on the arm of Colt as he walks her down the aisle toward me like a proud fucking father. Whoever would have thought it, huh?

The pretty little church on the Isle of Skye is full of the weirdest crowd you could ever wish to see. But I love each and every one of them. From the middle-aged couple that lives two doors down from us to the sweet old folks who deliver flowers, to the hairy, bad-ass, Harley riding bikers who came all the way from fucking Utah.

Six stands beside me with a shit-eating grin on his face. He thinks it's funny that I'm standing here in a kilt and that I have tears leaving damp trails down my stubbled cheeks as I watch Kelly coming to me. But I don't give a fucking damn. I'm the luckiest bastard on the face of the earth right now, and I don't give a shit who knows what I feel for her.

She looks so incredibly hot. All womanly curves in her ivory lace dress with her long auburn waves cascading down to her breasts. Knowing that my baby is growing in her belly just makes her even fucking sexier, and I can't wait for the wedding night, if you know what I mean.

She arrives beside me and I lean in to kiss her. I tell her I love her more than anything in this whole world as I rest my hand on the curve of her bump—our bump—and she gazes up at me with such adoration, it makes me wonder what the hell I did to get to keep her.

Because come hell or high water, come Loki's Legion or Company of Sinners, this woman is mine.

And no man will ever put *that* shit asunder.

No fucking exceptions.

The End

ACKNOWLEDGMENTS

As always I should thank the two people who make every day incredibly special: Rich and Gee. Your continued support means the world and the fact that you drag me away from my computer every so often to replenish my energy makes me so incredibly grateful.

Lots of love to my awesome mum and dad. Even though this book was totally different to my others, I appreciate that you supported and encouraged me in this new venture.

A huge thank you to the lovely ladies who beta read the first draft of the book and gave me encouragement and fantastic feedback. Your belief in me was a massive boost.

A mahooooosive thank you to Tammy at The Graphics Shed for giving me covers that I absolutely adore. I was so worried about re-covering this trio but you really worked your magic as always!

And finally a huge hug and thank you to each and every blog who has supported me and helped spread the word for me and my team. You guys make the indie author world such a special place to work. I hope you know how much I and all my fellow authors appreciate what you do.

Lots and lots of love
Lisa xxx

ABOUT THE AUTHOR

Lisa is happily married to her best friend and together she and her husband have one child and two daft dogs. Writing has always been her passion although it has only been in recent years that she has taken the plunge to try her hand at novels. Back in 2014 her debut *Bridge Over the Atlantic* (later republished by *Aria Fiction* as *A Seaside Escape*) was published by an American company and was shortlisted in the Romantic Novelists Association RONAs for their prestigious Romance Novel of the Year.

Lisa is now the proud author of both self-published *and* traditionally published titles since being signed on a four book deal to *Aria Fiction*, an imprint of award winning *Head of Zeus Publishing*.

Originally from Yorkshire, Lisa now lives in bonny Scotland, a place that features in many of her titles. And when she's not writing, reading *or* editing she can be found being taken for a walk by her energetic dogs.

ALSO BY LISA J HOBMAN

(Please note these titles are not erotic novels)

A Seaside Escape

A Year of Finding Happiness

Christmas Presence

(*A Seaside Escape Christmas Novella*)

What Becomes of the Broken Hearted

Reasons to Leave

Reasons to Stay

Duplicity

Through the Glass

The Girl Before Eve

Last Christmas

(*A TGBE Christmas Novella*)

The Worst of Me

In His Place

And coming soon:

Zara Bailey's Summer of New Beginnings